DEC 2 2 2017

W9-BOB-169

DEC 0 8 2017

PLYMOUTH PUBLIC LIBRARY

PLYMOUTH PUBLIC LIBRARY
PLYMOUTH MA 02360

Nobody's Pawn

The Never Veil Series Book Three

Amy McNulty

PLYMOUTH PUBLIC LIBRARY
PLYMOUTH, MA 02360

www.patchwork-press.com

COPYRIGHT

Nobody's Pawn by Amy McNulty

© 2016 by Amy McNulty. All rights reserved.

First edition.

No part of this book may be reproduced or transmitted in any form, including written, electronic, recording, or photocopying, without written permission of the author. The exception would be in the case of brief quotations embodied in critical articles or reviews.

Published by Patchwork Press and Amy McNulty

Cover by Makeready Designs. Photography provided by Meet Cute Photography, featuring Sakinah Caradine.

The characters and events appearing in this work are fictitious. Existing brands and businesses are used in a fictitious manner, and the author claims no ownership of or affiliation with trademarked properties. Any resemblance to real persons, living or dead, is purely coincidental, and not intended by the author.

ISBN-13: 978-1-927940-70-9

To everyone who stuck with Noll, Ailill and everyone else in their world through this journey.

Chapter One

I CLUTCHED THE BOOK TO my chest, the open page crinkling as I moved. I was afraid to look at it, afraid to see that I'd just imagined the throne room exploding to life. My damp dress raised bumps on my skin, which the cool morning breeze of an autumn day did nothing to alleviate. Even as the sunlight trickled through the leaves overhead, there was no hope of warming. No hope of going back to how things were just a day before.

My first thought had been to run to my friends, to run to Jurij when I saw the movement on the pages—but then my breath caught. Jurij had *killed* him. He might have returned—at least, that was what I wanted to see, to confirm with my own eyes—but that wouldn't change the fact that Jurij had driven his sword clear through his back. No, I couldn't go to Jurij. I couldn't go to any of the men, to those fools who'd destroyed the tavern and my father along with it.

I'd considered telling Mother at least what I'd seen. In my hazy thoughts of the previous few hours, I didn't remember if I'd have to explain to her what the book was, and how I'd known what had happened. But she had Father's death to come to terms with, and as I'd flipped through the book to find her page—my hand keeping my place on that last page, I couldn't risk losing that page—I saw her standing in our home besides the wood, Elfriede at her side, their faces both contorted as the full awareness of what we'd lost sunk over them. I could see the tears even in the black ink, see the puzzlement on Arrow's face as he looked up at them, but my eyes weren't drawn to their tears for long. Jurij walked onto the page and flung his arms around my sister.

I slammed the book shut, losing my place. Panicked, I flung it back open to the last page, and it was still there. It still followed the drawing of the young man who was and was not Ailill.

"Ailill." I said his name to the dawn, to the empty path through the woods before me. "Ailill, you didn't die for the last time. You came back. I know it." I squeezed the book harder to my chest, afraid to check, afraid to see if the page would turn red with blood and fire, like it had with my father's. I tried not to think of how it was selfish of me to want that. How he'd practically said he was ready to die at last after this life, how I was the one who'd doomed him to all his many lives.

My boot squished into the soft dirt, and I felt the sash around my waist loosen. I was prepared to trod on it as it flitted to the ground, but the heavy weight that hit my foot drew my attention. I paused as a trickle of sunlight glinted off the ground and caught my eye. The golden copper. It had stayed in my sash through all that time in the cavern pool, through almost drowning.

Still clutching the book, I crouched to pick the copper up. I held it out above my head and it caught the light. Before I'd realized it, I'd arrived at the black castle that nestled against the eastern mountains. Fear spread throughout my body at the thought that the gate doors might not open for me. I clenched the coin in my fist, feeling the weight of carrying the book with one hand but refusing to let the coin go. *Let me in*, I thought, and the gates parted quietly.

They hadn't even finished opening before I squeezed through them and stepped inside. "Ailill?" I called out, not caring how hollow the echo of my voice sounded in the entryway. *The throne room*, I thought, heading toward the stairway and coming face-to-face with a specter.

"I..." The sentence caught in my throat. I wanted to embrace the specter, but it would be too strange. They were back. It was proof he was, too. I studied the specter, the weak light pouring into the room through the open door not enough to fully make out his face. "I need to see Ailill," I said at last.

The specter said nothing. He was joined by a wave of other specters descending the staircase. They fanned out on either side of me, ignoring me, some even bumping me aside.

"Where are you going?" I asked, fully aware that none of them would answer. I stepped back, letting the specter who had blocked my path join the group, and I found myself tracing my steps back toward the doorway to make room for the flurry of movement. The sunlight from the doorway wasn't enough to make the entryway light up entirely, and no torches were lit, making the already usually dark room difficult to navigate. Yet the group of specters knew exactly what they were doing as they lined up in two parallel lines between the exit and the doorway at the back. They stilled all at once, their hands behind their backs, their legs slightly parted.

Sunlight streamed in from the doorway to the garden at the center of the castle, the place that had been my sanctuary all those months before. The dueling sunbeams from that door and from the open doorway behind me lit up the line of specters just enough that I could make out their stern, unmoving faces. My eyes roved over them and came to a halt at the end of the line.

"Ailill...?" I asked, my throat parched. "Ailill?" I crossed the room, ignoring the line of specters to reach the one who'd caught my attention.

I knew they were all "Ailill" in one way or another, but this specter—this young face, this disheveled hair—was mine. I was sure of it. "Ailill," I said again, reaching out to touch the white hair that cascaded off his shoulder with two fingers, leaving the coin clutched in the remaining three. "You're a specter now." I shook my head, remembering he never called them that.

"You're one of them. A servant." The hair that ought to have been deep brown was brittle in my hand. The eyes that ought to have been dark brown were red, and they focused over my head, not looking at me even as I fondled him. I gripped the hair harder, and the book dropped from my other hand to the floor. It echoed loudly in the entryway as I grabbed hold of Ailill's shoulders.

"Talk to me!" I said, my cheeks burning. Tears I hadn't even noticed cascaded down my face. "Say something!" I pounded his chest, determined to get a reaction out of him, not caring when the coin fell to the ground beside the book with a clatter. I'd never outright assaulted one of them. Surely there came a point at which they reacted. "Ailill—"

I felt a tap on my shoulder, and I turned. One of the specters had broken the line, and he held his hand out to me, his palm open.

"What?" I snapped, rubbing a haze of tears out of my eyes. This specter seemed familiar—what a farce, they all seemed familiar, and since they were all shades of the same man, I knew why. I couldn't shake the feeling that I knew this one more personally than the others. He was older than my Ailill, but not too old, perhaps a couple of decades older. This specter was looking at me, his red eyes boring through me. I hesitated and took his hand, which was holding the golden copper I'd dropped. "Thanks," I muttered. I reached for the book tucked beneath the specter's arm, and he drew back. I stared at him in shock. "I need that."

He fell back in line, carrying the book with him.

"Ailill," I started, not knowing what else to call him, "give that back! I only dropped it a moment—"

"May I ask how many times you are going to call me before you come inside the garden? Surely it has not escaped your notice that these men are clearly leading you here."

I froze, my hand still extended toward the specter who had taken the book from me. My ears picked up the trickle of the water fountain from the garden. I *knew* that voice. It felt a little off, perhaps, too calm, too blithe, but he had spoken.

"Ailill!"

A young man—perhaps a year or two older or younger than me—leaned against the door frame to the garden, his arms crossed against his chest, one leg crossed in front of the other.

"As you have said. Many times now." He nodded at me. "Come join me. I believe you have a lot to tell me."

He turned, crossing past the rose bushes—the bushes no longer withering, no longer dying, even with the chill of winter soon upon us—and sitting at the nearest stone bench. My eyes flitted over the rest of the garden. The entire place looked so much more cared-for than it had the last time I'd seen it, months before when I'd first sought out Ailill after the curse had broken. The benches were upright, and there wasn't a speck of brush out of place to litter the walkway or the table. Even the fountain spurted clear water, and the broken statue of the boy crying was conspicuously missing.

"Come," repeated the young man, gesturing to the bench on the other side of him. On the table was a chess game, and I remembered the matches I'd had with Ailill, and the brother I'd mistaken for him. I clutched the coin harder.

"Do not bother to hide that," said the young man, nodding. "You bring gold into my castle, and you stand

5

there, your mouth agape, as if you do not know what it means."

"Gold?" I repeated, opening my hand to look at the coin I held there tightly. "The golden coin?" Some instinct compelled me not to betray my ignorance. *Ailill told me this token gave me the right to know...* I straightened my back and stepped in farther.

"Of course I know," I lied, trying to put that confidence into my shaky, soggy steps. I stopped suddenly, my eyes scanning the man's face. Of course. This was why he was shaded darker in the book; he came back, but he was no longer faded. He was born again, but younger—only slightly younger—but how? Why at this age? This was Ailill, as dark and as beautiful as any man in the village—no, even more so. I gasped. "Ailill!"

He shook his head, and the corner of his lips upturned into a smile that set my body on fire. "As you have said," he repeated. He gestured to the chess board. "Then come. Join me. I should enjoy a game with a lady in on the bet, my future bride."

Chapter Two

I NEARLY DROPPED THE COIN from my clammy fingers. "Your bride?" I sputtered, unable to stop myself. The look on Ailill's face was almost convincing enough to make me think he was genuinely surprised.

"I assumed you knew." He studied me. I saw something in his expression I could hardly remember ever seeing before: uncertainty.

I tucked a piece of hair behind my ear; it was nearly dry now, although I still felt soaked to the bone. *"A lady in on the bet."* I'd been so flustered by the "bride" part that I hadn't even stopped to think about the first thing he'd called me. I closed the distance between us and sat down on the bench, keeping the coin clutched tightly in my palm. I reached out and lifted one of the chess pieces, a pawn.

"You are soaked," he said, regarding me.

I put the piece down in entirely the wrong place. "Yes... The pool, in the cavern. That was merely an hour ago, even less. How long has it been for you?"

Ailill had his hand on the pawn piece I'd moved, but he froze as he lifted it off the board. "How long... has it been?"

"Since you..." I shook my head. "Ailill, what happened to you?"

Ailill frowned slightly, putting the pawn back where it had been to begin with. "You moved that piece incorrectly," he said. "I would have thought you would know how to play, if you were in on the bet."

I yanked the board to the side of the table, not caring that the pieces tumbled as a result. The white queen rolled off the board and to the dirt beside the nearest rose bush. "I *do* know how to play," I snapped. I stopped myself from reminding him *he* taught me. There was something off about him, something more than the fact that he was younger and altered. "I'm not in the mood for games."

Ailill's eyebrows arched as he regarded the mess I'd made of the game board. "I see that." He leaned back in his seat, supporting his back against the castle wall. "Then what *have* you come for?"

"Answers."

"Answers? To what questions?"

I took a deep breath and watched Ailill, thinking through what I was about to say. I wanted to ask him about the "they" he kept bringing up before everything got out of hand, the "always-watching" people he barely spoke of above a whispered hush. But I couldn't disavow my feeling that something more than just physical appearance had changed with him.

"What happened to you?" I repeated.

Ailill looked down at me over his nose. "You know me," he said after a moment's silence.

"Of course I—" The words caught in my throat. "You don't know me?"

"I do," Ailill said as he leaned forward and put his arms on the table. "I think. There's something about you... But no. It can't be."

"Can't be *what*?"

Ailill waved a hand in the air dismissively. "You remind me of someone I knew as a boy. But I have not *been* a boy in so many years, you are sure not to believe it. Unless...?" He stared at me again, and I looked away. "You might believe it. If you knew me in my last life. If you carry that gold with purpose."

I cocked my head slightly, staring at Ailill's black-gloved hands on the table, careful to avoid his eyes. "I know you die and are reborn," I said. "You died not very long ago." I gestured at myself. "So little time has passed, I haven't even bothered to throw on a fresh pair of clothes."

"Drowning?"

My eyes snapped back up to meet his. "Pardon?"

"Did I drown this time?" Ailill asked. He seemed drawn to the dampness of my clothing. "I cannot say I know how, unless I left the castle..."

"You *did* leave!" I decided not to correct his assumption that he'd drowned, not just yet, not just now. "Are you telling me you remember nothing from your past life?"

Ailill frowned and looked away. His gaze was drawn to the rose bush, and he plucked a withering bloom from the leaves and branches. "I do. I remember all of them. But none so clear as my first." He turned the dying rose in his hand, examining it closer. "I remember the pain, mostly. The never-ending pain. The always-enduring loneliness."

"Don't tell me your last life isn't *clear* to you! You seemed perfectly aware of your other lives before that..." I stopped, biting my lip. He hadn't said anything specific about any of those other lives beyond the first one. Nothing beyond watching the villagers in the book, sending servants out to get food and clothing. "You *have to* remember. You're sitting here right now without covering your face—"

Panicked, Ailill dropped the rose bud onto the table and put his hands toward his face, as if feeling for something. He laughed at my surprised reaction and dropped his hands, reaching for the rose bud again to twirl between his fingers. "That is no surprise," he said, and I had to wonder why he made a show of panicking. Ailill didn't joke. Did he? "They told me the curse was broken before they sent me back. I had to wonder why I *was* being sent back, then, but—say." He smiled awkwardly. "You haven't met them, have you?"

"No, I haven't." I took a deep breath, trying to bite back my annoyance. "Maybe you'll introduce me."

Ailill laughed and let the remnants of the petals fall from his gloved fingers. "How did you come across that gold then?"

"*They* sent it to me," I replied. It may not have been fact, but for all I knew, it wasn't a lie, either. Who else could get their hands on this color metal, if Ailill insisted it wasn't him?

Ailill shrugged. "Then you should know how to find them."

I cleared my throat. "I do. The hole behind the throne room."

Ailill frowned, but his attention was drawn to something behind me. "Ah. So that is where it was."

I flinched as a specter appeared from behind me and placed the book he'd stolen from me on the table. I reached out for it, but Ailill grabbed it first, raising an eyebrow as my hands landed on his.

"This belongs in the castle," he said. "How did you come to have it with you?"

"*You* brought it with us when we left yesterday evening. To deal with the tavern fight."

"Fight...?" Ailill's brow furrowed as he flipped through the pages. He gasped. "Dear goddess! How has this village come to this?"

I couldn't stop the blush that flitted across my cheeks at Ailill still invoking the deity we both knew—at least I *thought* we both knew—was just a foolish girl. Namely, me. "There was a fight at the tavern last night. And a fire, you told me."

"A fight? But how?" Ailill scowled and stopped leafing through the book to stare at one page in particular. "The game has changed," he said, and I didn't understand his meaning. He slapped the book shut and stood. He looked me over. "You had best put on warmer clothes."

"Why?" I asked, not taking his meaning. I needed him to explain to me what was going on, to take me to "them"—but I hadn't even been back to Mother and Elfriede, even if Jurij was with them. I hadn't seen who else might have been hurt in the fight and the fire, or how else my world had fallen apart since the night before.

Ailill passed by me and headed toward the door, the book tucked beneath his arm. He paused just for a second to favor me with an incredulous look. "You say they sent you that gold. Then you should know we have work to do."

Chapter Three

THERE WAS STILL A STASH of those dresses Ailill had had made for me in the room that used to be mine. I was hesitant to bother changing—there was so much I kept thinking about, so many questions I wanted answered. But before I could go after this new, forgetful Ailill, before I could even figure out where he went, two specters blocked me at the garden doorway. One was the one who'd stolen the book from me, and I was just about to let him have it for that, when I realized the other was *my* Ailill, the one who'd been stabbed through the back to save me. I clamped my mouth shut.

They led me to my room, where I rummaged through the chest of clothes until I found the least ostentatious dress in there. The drabber clothing that had been mine since before I became the lord's goddess, the kind of dresses most women in the village wore, had been sent back to my house shortly after the curse was broken. So I was stuck with silkier dresses covered with little flourishes that had no business being on something someone was going to wear to do anything more than sit there like an ornament. I chose a dark red one, as it seemed the closest color I could find to the browns and tans I usually wore. It also had a little pocket in the material behind a flower that was perfect for my coin.

I glanced at the two specters who'd followed me into the room and ducked behind the changing screen, peeking back out again to grab a lovely yellow dress, which I turned into a rag and used to dry myself off after I'd peeled off the soaked outfit. I cringed a little to use a dress as a rag that I was sure Siofra, and perhaps Nissa, had made after Ailill paid them, but I never would have worn it anyway.

By the time I stepped out, drier, a bit warmer, but still clammy, the specter who had stolen my book stepped up to greet me, a hair brush in hand.

"No, thank you. I remember a specter's skills with a hair brush quite well," I said, fluffing my hair with my fingers. It was wet and could probably use a good brushing. I ducked over to the mirror and saw it had grown longer since I last looked in a mirror—not as long as it once was, but longer than I thought it was—I didn't exactly have access to many mirrors. I cringed when I saw how lovely the dress looked, after I'd gone out of my way to find one that wouldn't make me stand out too much. I placed a hand atop the brush as the specter held it out toward me. "Let's not bother with that," I said, looking into his eyes, speaking to him as a person. Something unsettled me as I held his gaze, and I felt the tug of something familiar beyond his similar appearance to a somewhat-older Ailill.

"You—" I started, but I felt a brush run through my hair and jumped, ripping my head backward. "Ailill!" The most recently-created specter had snuck up behind me to brush my hair. I cradled my head in my hands. I couldn't keep thinking of them all as "Ailill," even if that's what Ailill—*my* Ailill and the new Ailill—called them. I snatched the brush from the most recently-created specter and began running it through my hair, gasping as it ripped through knots. "Fine. If it must be done, I'll do it." I turned to the mirror and cringed as the brush caught on another knot.

I flung the brush down on the small vanity after I finished and gripped the table, taking a deep breath. "You," I said, turning and facing the most recently-created specter.

"You're the one I knew. The one who hated me. The one I sort of disliked, too." A cloud of something flashed over that Ailill's face and I stopped, surprised to see anything resembling emotion on those pure-white features. "I didn't hate you, though. Not in the end." I straightened my shoulders and tugged at my dress, smoothing out the wrinkles. "You'll be 'Scorn' when I talk to you, all right?"

The cloud of emotion that had passed over "Scorn's" face dispelled, and I couldn't tell whether this hurt or pleased him or made no difference at all. I turned to the other specter. "And you. I'm sure I recognize you. You dropped the prison key for me, didn't you? And you were going to speak to me, I know it. You opened your mouth that one time..." I paused, waiting to see if my words had any effect on him. He just kept looking at me, though. That in and of itself was odd, as they usually looked over my head when they didn't want something from me. I threw my hands up in the air.

"Fine, don't speak. Keep pretending you can't, even though I've seen you all whisper to your lord from time to time." I pulled out a pair of new shoes from the chest, comfortable shoes but shoes not as practical as my soggy boots were. I slipped them on and swept past the specters, pointing to the one I was addressing as I passed. "You'll be 'Spurn.'" I stopped and looked from Scorn to Spurn and back and then nodded. "Well, gentlemen, let's get moving." I held out both arms apart from my torso, inviting them to slip in on either side. They stood there a moment and then the strangest thing happened. They exchanged a look with one another, just the slightest of nods, and moved forward as one to slide in on either side of me.

ŋ ŋ ŋ

"Ailill!" I called as I arrived outside the castle, dropping my escorts' arms and gathering my too-long skirt in my hands. I stepped up the black carriage steps and swept into the open door, ignoring the hands the other specters on either side offered up for assistance. "You waited for me!"

"Of course," replied the darker, younger lord of the village. The door of the carriage shut behind me and Ailill tapped on the roof of the carriage, signaling the specter driver to let us be off. "The Ailills had to go get the carriage anyway. They found it halfway along the path in the woods for some reason."

I grimaced and said nothing.

Ailill smiled. "There is no need to explain. I assume it has something to do with the state of your previous attire," he said. "And the fate of my last incarnation."

"Yes," I admitted, my eyes dropping to my hands, which I held together in my lap. I thought of the last time we shared a ride in this carriage, just the night before, and how close we'd come to... Well, how close we'd come to something. I eyed the book that Ailill kept on the seat beside him. "You should know at least, if you're going to investigate the tavern fight and the fire... Some of my friends were responsible."

"Your friends?" Ailill leaned back into his chair.

"Not directly," I said. "Although they were the ones who came up with the idea. They thought a fight might distract you, and things got..." I stopped, choking on my words, remembering the fate of my father. The thought was like a fresh knife, tearing apart a barely-scabbed wound. "Things got out of hand," I added quietly.

Ailill sighed. "Need I ask why your friends intended to 'distract' me?"

"I can tell you, but right now—"

"Right now we have other things that require our attention." Ailill smiled, although it seemed to require some effort. "You look lovely."

"What?" The comment was so off topic, so completely unexpected, that I momentarily lost my train of thought. I tucked my hair behind my ears, unable to take his comment in stride, not when my stomach was already a wave of so many other emotions. I could feel his eyes burning into me, so I looked away, out the window.

"Stop—" I started.

"I apologize. Now is hardly the time for that, either. I couldn't help myself. You—"

"No, stop! Stop the carriage!" I knocked on the roof, and the carriage ground to a halt. Ailill hardly had time to register his surprise before he had to fling his hands out, grabbing hold of the walls to stop himself from falling.

"Where are you—" Ailill began as I thrust open the carriage door.

But I was already down the steps and running toward the cottage at the end of the woods, the home of Gideon Woodcarver and his family—my family. The home of Gideon Woodcarver's widow. "Mother!" I shouted as I clutched my skirt higher; that insufferable dress was simply too long to be practical. "Mother," I called again, flinging open the cottage door. "Elfriede," I said, quieter. My gaze fell over the room, and I saw Mother sitting at the edge of her bed, clutching something to her chest, with Elfriede beside her, her arm around her.

"Noll?" Mother's voice croaked as she looked up to see me.

I glanced around. "Where's Jurij?" I asked, thinking of the scene out of the book.

Elfriede's water-filled eyes narrowed. "Not here." Her tone seemed too hostile, considering the tragedy that should have bound us.

"You just missed him," said Mother, oblivious. She paused to catch her breath between sobs. "He went to the site of the tavern after... After that. And he found this." She held out the cloth she'd been cradling.

I couldn't place it, but I knew it was a jerkin. Whether because it was covered in soot or because I hadn't seen him enough the past few months—the past year or more—to recognize it, I couldn't say for sure I knew whose it was. But I did. Just from the way Mother gazed at, I knew it was Father's.

I rushed over to her and put a hand on her knee, sitting on the other side of her. "So he's gone," I said, after a moment of silence.

"*Of course* he's gone!" Elfriede let go of Mother as I reached out to hug her myself. She stood and paced the room. "I thought... I thought maybe he got out. It was *burned down*, how would they know so quickly who survived?" Elfriede's eyes flitted accusingly toward me. "But Jurij—but *he* said he heard it from Vena herself. Father was the first to die before the fire even started. Stabbed through the back with a broken glass. Vena was so shocked, she was still clutching the clothes he'd left behind as she made her way out of there." She spat, an act so strange I found myself leaning back away from her instinctively. "What could he have been *thinking*?"

"Elfriede, please," said Mother quietly. "You'll just upset yourself—"

"I've reason to be upset!" Elfriede whirled on Mother and me, the tears in her eyes hardly hiding the anger. "Mother, Father participated in this plan of Jaron's. He *started* that commotion at the tavern—"

Mother squeezed the clothing tighter. "We don't know that!"

"We do! Even he—even Jurij admitted as much!" Elfriede pointed at me accusingly. "And you, Noll? What was your part in all of this?"

"My... part?"

Elfriede flung her hands in my direction. "Just look at yourself! Our father just died, and here you are, sitting there in a pretty dress like it's your wedding day!" She took a deep breath, gathering more energy for her tirade. "You have to know something!"

"No more than you. Not about that fight at the tavern, or the tavern fire—"

"You *lived with* Jurij. You spent time with these men, you have to know something!" She sat back down beside Mother, the volume of her voice lowering. "You have to know what to do."

What to do? My fingers clutched the fabric of my dress, so silky and fine, so out of place on me and in the middle of this grief.

"Elfriede, please. Settle down. Your father wasn't the only loss Noll has dealt with today." Mother scoffed at herself, her eyes drawn to her lap. "Today. It must be yesterday by now. But we haven't slept, and this day just keeps on going..." She stopped, suddenly choking on a sob. Elfriede rushed in to wrap her arms around her as Mother pressed the sooty jerkin to her lips. No one said anything for a while longer, and even Elfriede's sadness seemed to have won out against her anger, as her sobs joined Mother's. I froze, suddenly incapable of feeling. It was like I was dreaming, like my grief belonged to another person. I'd lost a parent before and she sat there now, right beside me. Could I go through that again? Could I convince myself it was real this time, that there would never come a day in which I'd see Father again?

"I feel terrible," came a voice after a moment. Mother, Elfriede and I all lifted our heads in tandem toward the open doorway.

Ailill stepped in, but he stopped when he saw the expressions on Mother's and Elfriede's faces. Elfriede's jaw dropped open.

"I overheard your exchange. I was curious to know why you suddenly leapt out of the carriage." Ailill clenched his hands into fists at his side. "I did not realize you had lost your father. And then, I realized... I do not even know your name."

Elfriede glanced at Mother and then me, the puzzlement clear on her features. *Does he mean me?* she seemed to be asking me. *Or Mother?* Why he'd care to ask either name right now was probably just as bizarre a question as why he was standing there breathing, a bit younger and far darker than he was the only time she'd really seen him before.

I stood and fixed the fabric of the dress that caught at my thighs, smoothing out the dark red material. I knew exactly what he meant, and, looking into his eyes, and seeing how they searched me, *really* searched me, I fully believed it finally. This was and was not the Ailill I knew. And he didn't remember me—well, he didn't remember anything that could tie the two of us together. Anything that would make us enemies. Anything that would make us friends.

Or more than that.

I extended my hand so he could take it. "I'm Noll," I said, as he took the hand and raised it toward his lips. "But you once knew me as Olivière."

Ailill's eyes widened and he dropped my hand before he managed to kiss it.

Chapter Four

THE NEXT FEW DAYS WERE a blur. Mother, Elfriede and I hardly slept and could barely eat, and I had more than just Father's passing and the mourning arrangements to fret about. There was work to be done in the village to get us all past this and to introduce Ailill to his people. Thinking back on it, so few people had actually seen him—and those few who had had seen him die in the cavern—that no one questioned his new appearance, not at first. No one even knew he'd been killed. My former friends and Elfriede's friends must have been so in shock, they didn't have the chance to spread the rumor before Ailill showed up in the middle of the village the next day to introduce himself.

I wasn't there, not then. I heard later from Alvilda how Ailill had exited the carriage, stunned an already-stunned crowd into silence, and walked over to Elweard and Vena, his arms extended. He'd embraced them both, but they didn't embrace him back. Their faces got more astonished, if anything. Even Alvilda was too tongue-tied to ask just who he was, and why he was claiming to be the lord, when she knew for a fact he was dead. Yet she saw the resemblance regardless.

I'd been so shocked about Ailill's return, so numb about Father's death, it hadn't occurred to me to consider how the fire had eventually stopped and kept from spreading too far. It had rained in the night, while we were in the cavern. That rain had saved most of the village, but there were already too many who were lost. There was something no one in the village would ever be able to get back: their sense of safety.

First men started realizing the freedom of their hearts, and that freedom lead most of them away from their goddesses—only there weren't any "goddesses," not really. No woman was worthy of worship anymore, not in men's eyes. And so went the safety and security of love, of family.

Then the men discovered there was more to life than love, and they wandered freely from their jobs, leaving behind the things that needed to be done. Too many wandered into the tavern, and too much drink and too much freedom led them to that day when they discovered violence. "Rediscovered" violence, I should say. I knew that long ago, the men who were their ancestors knew it all too well.

Violence led to destruction and death and astonishment. It died down in the dawn of the new day, as the smell of burnt wood floated away with the after-rain breeze. It was gone for now, as people mourned the twelve men and two women who'd perished in that fight or in the blaze thereafter. I didn't trust it to be gone forever. Not now that I knew what even the men I loved and trusted were capable of.

But those were thoughts for another day.

"What do you think about these?" asked Alvilda, for probably the second or third time. I spent far too long gazing at the wall and thinking about other things the past week. I counted on Alvilda to remind me I had a job to do. Apparently.

I pulled the drawing of small cottages closer to where I sat at Mother's table. Arrow lifted his head at the movement, no doubt hoping it was something to eat. I hadn't been back to my own cottage since this whole mess had begun. I wound up asking Nissa to go and fetch some of the clothes I'd left there. Elfriede seemed more subdued now that I wore less noticeable clothing. "It's fine," I said, quickly pushing the drawing back to Alvilda. Disappointed, Arrow let his head droop. "Whatever you want."

"Whatever *I* want?" Alvilda sighed and put the drawing back on the top of her stack of similar images. "Noll, the quarry workers can help with the stone foundations, but you're the only one I can count on to help me with the wood parts, now that..." She bit her lip as I met her eye. "I'm sorry. I wasn't thinking. I didn't even mean your father, although that's part of it. I just meant... The village is in even worse shape than it has been the past few months."

"I'm the only other skilled woodcarver left," I admitted. Not that we could have counted on my father to help out these past few years regardless. *That's not fair. Who's to say? Maybe he would have stepped up. If he wasn't one of the ones who caused this problem in the first place.* "You need my help, and I can't fully focus. I'm sorry."

"I didn't mean it like that." Alvilda shuffled her papers, looking for one in particular. "You have other responsibilities. I can't really expect you to be out there, rolling your sleeves back and building a new commune for the men displaced by the tavern fire, all things considered."

"Maybe not, but I should be. I'd *like* to be." It was true that I'd grown fond of carving animals—little wooden toys for the kids in the village—in the past few months. My woodcarving skills leaned more toward the little details than the practical, but I'd helped Alvilda fill orders before, and she'd even started building her own workshop on the outskirts of the abandoned commune with a little of my input. I could help her do something productive, something I knew would help the village, and there was a selfish reason I wanted to help, too. Working with the wood just might keep my mind off of everything else.

Alvilda stopped her flutter of movement and reached out to grab my hand. "Are you really going to be the 'lady' of the village?"

I swallowed. "That's what he seems to think. Although... I'm not sure that's what he wants."

"Who *is* he exactly? He resembles the lord we saw in the cavern, but—"

"It's him. Just... reborn."

"Reborn?" Alvilda pulled her hand from mine so she could lean back. "Are you telling me when he dies he's just... reborn? As a young, but grown, man?"

"I guess so." I grabbed the drawing sticking out from the rest of the pile and looked it over, bending a corner of the page. "Those servants you hate?" I said, hesitating. "They're his former lives."

"You *must* be joking!" Alvilda scoffed, but then she studied me, and the smile vanished from her face. "You're serious."

I nodded. "Don't ask me to explain how—or why—it happens to him."

"But—"

I glowered at her. "No, *don't*. Please."

She sighed and straightened her pile. "All right. *I'll* let it go. For now. But you know I'm not the only one who saw him before this—"

"But you're one of the only ones who might make a fuss about it right now." I stared at the drawing of the cottage on the page. It seemed comfortable, inviting. I ran my fingers over it subconsciously. "The men who were involved in that have been cowering, their tails between their legs—"

"I'd hardly count going back to their daily lives 'cowering.'" Alvilda sounded skeptical. "Actually, they're being more productive than they have in weeks. Months. All of a sudden, blacksmiths are actually smithing. Quarry workers are digging. Luuk and Jurij are actually interested in woodworking—"

The page fell out of my hands. "What about Jurij's job at the quarry?"

Alvilda tossed her head to flick her hair over her shoulders. "He moved back in with Siofra and me. I had to make sure he was doing *something*. Lo and behold, the woodwork he was so reluctant to help out with actually suits him."

I reached for my sash, gripping the coin through the soft material. Holding it calmed me, even if I still had so many questions about it. "I'm glad *someone's* with him."

"Noll—"

"No, I mean it. If he was alone, I just might track him down and—"

"*Noll!*"

I jammed my finger on the drawing. "This one," I said. I'd been staring at it for so long, maybe my mind was playing tricks on me, but it seemed so inviting. "Make them look like this."

Alvilda frowned, clearly not happy to let my comment slide, but she did so anyway, reaching for the drawing I'd taken. She nodded, studying it, and some of the tension in her forehead dissipated. "Hmm. Sturdy but small. We could build these quickly. They're not too complicated. I'll have to ask for help."

"Take what labor you need," I said, pushing back from the table. "Any able-bodied person not busy with work—man, woman, or older child. And there's plenty of other help for you." I stood and went to the door, opening it. "Spurn!" I called, ignoring Scorn on the other side of the door. It unnerved me to look at him for too long, and Spurn had shown more signs of life even before Scorn came to be. "Alvilda and her builders need plenty of wood for the commune project. Can you and some of the other specters handle it?" I didn't care that I called them "specters" when Ailill left them to attend to me as "servants." It was a hard habit for me to break.

Spurn met my eyes and nodded, and he was off, down the road that led through the woods to the castle. I stared at Scorn, who kept looking dully forward, ignoring me, not bothering to fulfill the task I'd asked of them. I shrugged and turned around.

"Olivière!" If the voice weren't so high pitched and friendly, hearing my full name right then might have made my heart ache terribly. Instead, I turned back around and did my best to smile as Roslyn came over the hill from the direction of the village. I returned her wave and took note of Mother's haggard appearance as she came into view, leaning into Elfriede on one side, Mistress Baker holding her arm on the other. I took a deep breath and turned back in, leaving the door open.

"Who is it?" asked Alvilda, a little leery.

"Just Mother and Elfriede returned. With Mistress Baker and Roslyn." I sat down again and straightened my shoulders, grabbing the chosen drawing from where it lay on top of the pile of other ideas. "I've asked the servants to get you ample wood for the project. Work with what labor you can on crafting the homes until then. When they've finished chopping, you can rely on their help for the building."

Out of the corner of my eye, I saw Alvilda smile smugly. "And here I thought if anything *you'd* request to chop down the wood."

"All by myself?" The thought actually comforted me for a bit. Just me, an axe, the woods and nothing but silence to accompany me. I laughed. "There's too much else to do. Vena and Elweard lost their tools for ale making in the fire—not that I'm sure that's a bad thing—so I have to see about getting the blacksmith to craft hoops for new kegs and all the other things they'll have to describe to me. And then we have to make sure enough of the men have gone back to farming so we can get the last of the autumn crop in before winter—"

"You know," interrupted Alvilda, "you don't have to do *that* by yourself, either."

I stiffened. "I don't mind." I nodded toward the door. "And I have them to help when you can spare them."

"Good day, Alvilda, Olivière." Although I hadn't meant that group at all, Roslyn entered the cottage just then, a basket on her arm, followed by Mother, Elfriede and Mistress Baker. "Olivière, you should have seen your mother this morning. She was so helpful in helping us fill our excess order..." Roslyn kept talking, but she turned to the women behind her, fussing with trying to cheer up my mother.

Alvilda leaned over and whispered to me. "I didn't mean the labor. You're not the only one leading the village."

"We've delegated the tasks," I answered quietly. "I'm... not sure he's ready to see me again just yet."

"*Olivi...*" *Ailill clutched his hands behind his back, leaving my own hand out and hanging. I lowered it to my side, awkwardly, as Ailill cleared his throat. "Olivière?" he repeated. "Like the—"*

"*Woman you knew as a child," I finished for him.*

His eyes darted to Mother and Elfriede behind me, but I didn't turn to look, though I could feel them staring at us. I wanted to see Ailill's reaction. It was like I'd stabbed him and robbed him of all that new vigor he seemed to have in this new life.

Ailill clicked his heels together and nodded, struggling to smile. "Yes, well. There is so much work to do." He turned, and I walked after him, but he stopped, looking back over his shoulder. "Stay," he said, softly. "You have your own mourning to arrange."

"*Yes, but I want to help—"*

"*You shall." Ailill snapped his fingers, and two specters entered my home. I blinked. They were clearly Scorn and Spurn, the two I'd named to keep them separate from the others in my mind. "I'll leave them with you," continued Ailill, as the two men filed quietly into the room. "No, they better wait outside." He nodded and they followed him out.*

26

I was too steps behind, ignoring Scorn and Spurn as they took their posts on either side of my family home's door. "I can help," I repeated. "If you'll wait for me."

Ailill paused with one foot on the first step leading to the carriage. "You shall," he repeated, and he turned around, lowering his foot back to the ground. He stared at me for a moment and seemed at war with himself. In the end, though, he reached out quickly, taking my hand in his. He didn't raise it to his lips but instead squeezed it lightly with both hands. "The people know you are to rule beside me, I assume?"

"No," I admitted. "That is... They knew I was your goddess, but now there are no—"

Ailill dropped my hand, cutting me off. "It matters not. I will make sure they are aware, so they can turn to you as well as me in the upcoming weeks." He climbed into the carriage and poked his head out as he reached for the carriage door. "Rest. Mourn. I will send word with my plans for settling this unrest as soon as I can."

He shut the door before I could say more, and the carriage moved down the road toward the heart of the village.

I hadn't seen him since. He was apologetic in his letters, always citing the work to be done in rebuilding and setting up temporary housing for those displaced, in settling the villagers' fears. But I'd seen his carriage drive back and forth between the castle and the village at least twice a day and he'd yet to do more than send a specter to look in on me. Even during the memorial we'd had for Father in our backyard. I couldn't bring myself to send word, but with Spurn and Scorn there, always watching, and with the book left behind, I knew he must have seen me in one of my darkest hours, and he hadn't come.

He barely knew me now, but he knew enough to detest me again.

"Well," said Alvilda, oblivious to the dark turn of my thoughts, "I suppose you're right. He seems to be efficiently running things. Men who can't stand to go back home have been staying with friends until the commune is ready. Vena and Elweard may not have ale, but they're cooking and serving what they can inside the Great Hall."

I stood with Alvilda to show her out the door. I smiled best I could in reaction to her news, but I felt like it was more like a grimace. "Give my best to Siofra and Nissa," I told her. "And to Luuk." I decided he was young enough to get a pass on his part in it all. His father and brother had practically forced him into it.

Roslyn and Mistress Baker added logs to the fire as Elfriede brought out the iron pot she'd cleaned the night before. *Stew again*, I thought. That meant she'd need some help peeling potatoes.

"You can tell them yourself," said Alvilda, distracting me. "If you're going to speak to Vena and Elweard, you're bound to run into us at the Great Hall one of these days. There's been so much work to be done, we haven't had time for cooking. We've been relying entirely on what Vena's been providing."

"I can eat here," I snapped, harsher than I meant to. "I don't need to go there, I mean." I rolled back my sleeves, prepping for Elfriede's rather disdainful call to potato-peeling duty, but Mother surprised me by getting up from her chair by the fire and offering to peel the vegetables instead.

"Farewell, Alvilda," Mother said, doing her best to smile. Her smile was beautiful, even if it didn't reach her eyes.

"Take care," said Mistress Baker, and Elfriede and Roslyn added their farewells as well, and Alvilda returned in kind.

I was left with nothing else to do other than to escort Alvilda outside for a bit, doing my best to ignore Scorn posted beside the doorway.

"You know, Noll," said Alvilda as she adjusted the piles of papers she'd tucked beneath her arms. "Rebuilding a village after this.... this *tragedy* is more than simply

28

constructing new cottages and figuring out how to make ale."

"I realize that," I said. "I'm just not sure I'm the one most suited to, well, to anything other than fixing the things that are broken."

Alvilda squeezed the pile of parchments tightly against her chest so she could take both my hands in hers. "The people *are* what's broken, Noll. The damage to them could last far longer than the damage to the buildings and the things."

"I know." I couldn't look into her eyes for long, but I made the mistake of looking away. My eyes caught Scorn's, if only for a second. He still seemed like he was looking past me. *He's not him,* I reminded myself. *Not anymore. That new Ailill, he's the one who's living. Even if he doesn't remember you. That's... probably for the best anyway.* "I'm not good at... fixing people."

"You don't have to be," said Alvilda, squeezing my hands. "You just have to show them how to fix themselves." She took a deep breath. "Well, I'd best be off." She turned to go but stopped to look at me one more time over her shoulder. "Drop by for dinner at the Great Hall one of these evenings," she added. "If you're afraid to go alone, then bring a friend."

I grunted, not in the mood for her to give me some lecture if I pointed out that all of the friends I'd gained in the past few months after losing them as a child were the ones I was sure were most broken of all.

I turned to go back inside, my chest strangely tightening as I heard the sound of laughter. *You should be glad they're laughing. We need some laughter in this household.* I found myself gazing at Scorn and I realized my twinge of jealousy at the sound was because I was outside the cottage when it happened. Because I was always outside, even when I thought I was in. If my "friends" had cared enough about me, they would have told me what they were planning. And I could have stopped them. Maybe. At the very least, I could have warned him.

"Olivière?" said Roslyn, tearing my eyes from the statue-still reminder of my failure to save him. "Care for a roll?"

I stepped inside, taking the roll she held out to me.

Chapter Five

THERE'S A PIN COMING OUT of your hair," said
Roslyn, and she reached over, making me stop. My
hair was growing longer, but I wasn't in the mood
to cut it. Roslyn had urged Elfriede to (reluctantly, and only
with Roslyn watching) teach me how to pin back the pieces
that would have otherwise kept whapping across my face.
Evidently, I still had a ways to go in my lessons.

Roslyn slipped her arm back through mine when she
finished adjusting my loose tendril. "It's sweet of you to ask
me to come," she said, not for the first time. "But wouldn't
you rather ask Elfriede?"

"She's eating at home. With Mother and Marden."
We had a string of visitors in the weeks since Father's
memorial, all kind and concerned for Mother and Elfriede.
But that wasn't the real reason I hadn't asked Elfriede. The
truth was, I'd be just as awkward with her at my side as I
would be going alone—or more awkward. We were on
speaking terms, but we only seemed united in making sure
Mother didn't slip too far beyond where we could reach her.
There was still something that hung in the air between us,
something that existed many years before for a very
different reason than it did now, but something that only
worsened over time and never went away. I thought after
what we'd seen, we could at least be united in our dislike of

Jurij, but his name never passed either of our lips. His visit that first day after the fire and the cavern, from what I could gather, was only half welcome.

"That's right. Marden did tell me she was going over there." Roslyn's skirt swished almost annoyingly close to mine, practically tangling the two together. So this was what it was like to have a female friend—friend?—other than the decidedly masculine Alvilda. Roslyn lowered her voice, bringing her head in toward mine. "Did you know she has a new man?"

I faltered, practically tripping over some empty baskets next to a marketplace stall. The stand was pretty bare. The influx of farmers after the fire roused some of the men back to work was still not enough to get us enough vegetables to eat for the present, considering we were more concerned about storing what we had for winter. "Marden?" I asked, suddenly feeling very stupid that my first instinct had been that she was referring to Elfriede.

"Yup," said Roslyn, pulling back and breaking into a smile. She winked. "You wouldn't have guessed it, right? Not after all those sour things she had to say about Sindri. But Mother and Father invited some of the displaced men over to stay at the Tannery, and one took to the work real fast." She jabbed me with her elbow, almost sending me toppling over. "And took to Marden even faster."

I smiled, not sure if I was supposed to laugh. "She didn't seem to want a new husband—"

Roslyn waved a hand. "Well, I wouldn't say she's grooming him to be a husband or anything. I don't think women are too eager to jump right back into that." She paused, thinking a moment. "But she likes him, and he makes her happy. And she's much nicer to be around when she's happy."

I just hoped she learned that this time she'd have to keep being "nicer" if she wanted him to keep making her happy. Still, it wasn't my business. I barely knew Roslyn's sister, and in any case, from what little I knew, I at least understood she wasn't thrilled to be around me. "That's good," I said, patting Roslyn's forearm awkwardly. "I'm happy for her." I felt the strain of the effort, but I knew it was the right thing to do. I'd asked her to join me for dinner at the Great Hall when she finished work at the bakery for the afternoon and I'd touched base both with Alvilda in the commune construction area and the farmers in the crop fields. The least I could do was try to *be* a friend to someone I hoped could be mine. Even if the last time I'd spent so much time with other girls my age, I was running at them and threatening to strike them with a wooden stick.

"And you?" I thought, wondering if that's what Elfriede or one of the other young women would do. Continue talking about men and love, wanting to know every detail of each other's feelings.

"Me?" asked Roslyn, incredulous. "I have no time for men with all the baking I have to do. Besides..." She grew quiet, her face a little grave. "I didn't really have the best of luck last time."

"No one did. Not really. None of us can hope to find that kind of love again." Still, I felt foolish for asking her, and bringing up the sore spot that was her former husband, Darwyn, my former friend. In the past few months, he somehow discovered a passion for another man, another former friend, Tayton. I supposed if Alvilda and Siofra could love one another with free hearts, it only made sense that some men would feel the same for others of their gender as soon as their hearts were set free. Roslyn and Darwyn got on well enough shortly before that night, but what she'd witnessed in the cavern might have changed that... Darwyn was no longer even living at home with his mother, instead staying at his older brother's family's house with Tayton, from what Roslyn told me.

"Yes, well..." Roslyn turned over her shoulder, and I knew exactly who she was staring at. "Some of us have a lot more hope than others, don't we?" She smiled and nudged me. I knew she was teasing, and she meant well, but I couldn't even begin to explain how wrong she was.

"What's it like?" asked Roslyn, not picking up on my discomfort. "Having them follow you all over? Do they ever leave you to run messages between you and his lordship?"

Without thinking, I gazed over my shoulder to find Scorn and Spurn a few steps behind me, silent, faithful pets always keeping an eye on me—to protect me (from what?) or to see what I was up to, I couldn't be sure. Spurn had done well in gathering more specters to supply Alvilda and the men and women helping her with the wood she'd need to finish the new commune. She hadn't been thrilled with the idea of them helping her build it, though, and she'd shooed them away, and now Spurn took his place beside Scorn always at my beck and call.

"Yes," I said, at last remembering Roslyn's question. "But just about getting the village back on its feet."

"Sure," said Roslyn, and she nudged me. She laughed. "Keep your secrets."

You have no idea.

"You know, Elfriede still thinks—watch it!" Roslyn pulled me back, just in time to keep me out of the way of three children who ran past us to get into the Great Hall. Laughing and screaming, they paid us no mind. Roslyn shook her head. "Someone ought to be watching them."

I smiled, taking a very different lesson from the children who'd nearly run us down. "I think it's good they're happy," I said, my eyes following them as we stepped into the crowded room. "These past few weeks, I wasn't sure any of us were going to be happy again. Even those not directly affected by the fire seemed to have..." I stopped as the murmur of voices died down only moments after we entered the echoing room. People nudged those beside them, and soon, nearly every set of eyes in the building was on us as we made our way toward the back of the hall. This was where mothers once performed Returnings, and it was now occupied with a makeshift fire pit and tables for all the meal fixings.

Roslyn nodded at the villagers who stared at us sheepishly, clutching my arm tighter like I might prove some protection from all of the glowering. That was a mistake, of course. If she wanted to escape the staring, she'd never be safe at my side. She should have stood farther apart, not closer.

We approached Elweard and Vena, and I took a deep breath as I remembered the reason for my visit and the things I hoped to accomplish while there. "Good evening, Elweard. Vena." I gently shrugged out of Roslyn's grasp to bend over the karge table and examine the roast the former tavern masters had made. "I came to see how you're getting on. It smells divine," I added, weaving my fingers together.

"Noll! Good of you to drop by and see us." Vena smiled and reached for a wooden plate. Hers had all burnt up in the fire, but she'd salvaged a new collection from donations from the villagers. The set hardly matched anymore, but it could be argued that the mismatched dinnerware was more appropriate for the awkward new tavern settings. The place couldn't be used for Returnings any more, after all, and there were no unmasked men and boys who needed the space for socializing away from women's eyes. Why not let it become the site of the new tavern, as large and oversized as it was? Vena could make a welcoming tavern out of a stump and tree clearing. "Can I get you and Roslyn something?" she asked, already scooping some mashed potatoes onto the plate. Elweard hummed a tune behind her as he spun a roast over the fire at the back of the hall.

"Yes, thank you," I said, reaching for my sash, only to fumble and reach again for the new pocket Elfriede had sewn into my dresses. Nissa had suggested it, after seeing me subconsciously reach for the golden coin I kept in the sash I tied around my waist, and suggesting a more secure way of keeping my things with me. Nissa started the project one afternoon she visited but encouraged Elfriede and me to work on the rest together, claiming she had far too much sewing to do for Siofra and Master Tailor. She was probably just trying to get Elfriede and me to bond over work, but I was no more skilled at that as I was with hair pins and hairdos. It didn't take long for Elfriede to snatch the dress I'd been working on and claim she'd finish the rest since I had enough to take care of. It sounded almost like she *blamed* me for that, but I wasn't about to argue with her.

"Oh, no, your copper's no good with us," said Vena, eyeing the small collection of coins I withdrew from my pocket. I caught just a glint of gold and quickly cupped my hand around the pile of coins, eyeing Vena to see if she'd noticed it. She didn't seem to have as she handed me a plate piled with sliced beef, potatoes, a sharp knife and a wooden fork and spoon. "We owe you thanks for getting us back into business and letting us use this Great Hall. And *you*, Roslyn, for giving us a hand when we were in over our heads with diners and drinkers."

I passed the plate to Roslyn behind me, and Roslyn thanked her former boss, and there seemed to be no ill will at all between them.

"Speaking of drinkers," I said, tucking the coins back into my pocket. "How is everything working out for making new ale?"

"Fine, thank you," said Vena, pointing to the back of the Great Hall. "It'll take us some time to get up and running, but your *friends* have been quite helpful." She peered over my shoulder as she handed me my plate. "Will they be needing anything?"

I followed her gaze to see Spurn and Scorn standing stock still behind Roslyn. They drew most of the stares now, which I found strange, considering how far and wide Ailill had sent the specters to help the people settle in. Still, many of the villagers had gone back to eating and talking amongst themselves, which helped relieve some of the tension in my shoulders.

"No," I answered Vena, not tearing my eyes from Spurn. He was the one who'd shown some signs of life previously. I kept hoping he'd start talking, but then I might stop accepting that Scorn, the Ailill I knew, was gone for good, this young stranger who couldn't stand to be near me left in his place. Not that Scorn could stand to be near me when he was the lord. It was different with the new Ailill, more like he found out something unflattering about a stranger he had business with, and he'd do his best to keep his distance without outright cursing her. Actually, that was exactly true. "They don't eat."

"Really? Well, I suppose so." Vena wiped her hands on her apron. "I guess I've never seen one eat in public. They used to ask for such large amounts of food in the castle..."

I grimaced.

Vena stopped wiping her brow with the back of her forearm, examining me curiously. "I mean, they *do* eat, don't they?" She frowned. "Although the lord has decreased the amount of food he has delivered. He did that even before the fire—"

"Watch it!" Roslyn raised her plate over her head as that same trio of children ran past us again, squealing. "Honestly, if I were their mother—"

"Let's sit," I said, putting a hand on Roslyn's back to guide her to the upturned crate that made up the nearest empty table back in the corner. "Thank you for the food!" I called to Vena as we retreated from her questioning, but she was back to being a flurry, taking an empty mug from a man and rushing to fill it with water from the barrel behind the table.

Roslyn followed my lead, pinching her lips and clutching her plate tightly with both hands, determined not to let any of the crowd jostle the food off of it. We arrived at the empty crate-table, the seats used for Great Hall functions towering well over the "table" surface, and I put my plate down on one end.

"Hey!" I turned and saw the three running children come to a sudden halt between Roslyn and me, almost causing her to drop her plate. She looked annoyed as she waited for them to move. But they didn't.

"Are you going to make the animals again?" asked a boy.

"Not anytime soon," I admitted, but I did my best to smile. Roslyn rolled her eyes and stepped around them, placing her plate beside mine and taking a seat.

"Aw," said one of the girls. She unclenched her fist to show me what was inside and I immediately recognized one of my carvings, a squirrel. "We wanted another one."

"I do have some I haven't sold yet," I said. "But I'll have to go back and get them." I studied the animal the girl held out in front of her. "Didn't you buy that when you were alone, sometime after your friend bought one?"

"Yup!" She smiled at her friend, who pulled a wooden cat out of the sash around her waist. They clicked them together, giggling.

I rummaged around in my pocket and found the golden coin. I hesitated, looking to see if Roslyn was watching me, but she seemed bored, and her gaze wandered around the room as she started eating potatoes.

"Did you use this to buy it?" I whispered as I placed the golden copper on my lap.

The girl bent over to inspect it and she grinned. "Yup!"

"Who gave it to you?" I asked, which I should have done immediately. I just assumed I'd known. But if he wasn't lying, it wasn't Ailill.

The girl shrugged and leaned back. "I just found it." She cocked her head and pointed behind me. "He might have dropped it." She scuffed her toe on the floor, sheepish. "Okay. It fell out of one of his pockets. Finders keepers and all..."

"His?" I turned around and saw her looking at Spurn and Scorn behind me. Scorn, of course, hadn't existed yet, so that left Spurn, but surely she couldn't tell one from the other. Still, it was definitely one of the specters. Did that mean Ailill had been lying to me?

The shrieks of the kids snapped my attention back to them.

"Show us the ones that are left!" called the boy, as the girls started running again.

"I'll bring them here," I promised. "And you won't have to pay for them. Every kid who wants one can get one. Until I run out anyway!"

"Really?" The boy seemed incredibly pleased. "Thank you!" He ran after the girls, shouting something about how he was "getting one of them."

Roslyn eyed me over a spoonful of potatoes. "That's nice of you," she said as I tucked the golden copper into my pocket, grateful she didn't seem to notice it.

I shrugged and picked up my own spoon. "I have other things to worry about just now. Besides, I guess I don't need the copper to live on my own. At least not until Elfriede tells me to get out of there."

Roslyn scoffed, shaking her head. "You really don't get along with your sister, do you?" I opened my mouth, but she put her spoon down and pointed at me. "Don't answer that." Her eyes flitted up as she watched Spurn and Scorn stand against the wall behind me. "I didn't want to say anything while those kids were nearby, but did you just tell Vena that the servants don't *eat*?"

I took a bite of my potatoes. "No. She must have misunderstood me."

Roslyn leaned forward, putting her elbows on her knees, not at all interested in her dinner. "Ah. So it's a secret, is it?" she asked, her voice a hushed whisper. "I understand." She leaned back in her chair and grinned. "Does that have something to do with why *someone else* seems so changed—"

"Scorn!" I said, perhaps a little too loudly. I felt my face flush as the man in white stepped beside me. "Get us

39

both a mug of water, would you?" He left to do my bidding, and I felt like merging into the wall and never resurfacing. I shouldn't have asked *him* of the two if I was going to ask either of them.

"Sorry," said Roslyn, her head sinking into her shoulders. "I know with everything going on, we haven't really had a chance to talk about... about that night. But you have to know, we're all curious—ah. Thank you." She grabbed the mug that Scorn extended out to her, and I did the same, only I downed half of it in one gulp. Roslyn took a dainty sip and cradled her mug. "I could get used to that."

I stabbed a piece of beef with my fork and raised an eyebrow. "Having someone follow your orders?"

Roslyn sighed and put her mug down next to mine. We were running out of room on the table. "No, of course not. You're right. I don't want normal men to act like that again. Not now that we know how they really felt about it." We ate in silence for a moment, the buzzing of tavern talk the only thing hanging in the air between us. "Still, that makes me wonder. Are *they* like the rest of the men? Do you think they resent being servants?"

"I don't know," I said, realizing until Scorn had come into existence, I hadn't really thought of them as former people. "If they're like people at all, I suppose they resent a lot of things." I paused. "Like the person who cursed them in the first place."

Roslyn gasped, but she kept the noise quiet, quickly covering her mouth. "Cursed? Olivière, I know you have your secrets, but you can't exactly expect me to let that pass without asking—"

"Noll. Roslyn." I'd been so ashamed of all the information that kept leaking past my lips, I hadn't even noticed someone approaching the table. "I'm surprised to see you."

Chapter Six

I LOOKED UP AND SAW Sindri, Darwyn's brother, and a friend I once had as a child. A friend I had as of late until he followed in his brother's footsteps to do something incredibly foolhardy and reckless. Sindri tried to smile, and I could almost see the sweat glistening on his brow in the dim light of the wall torches.

"Oh. Good evening, Sindri," said Roslyn, but her eyes dropped immediately to her lap, where her hands smoothed out the wrinkles in her skirt.

That's right. Not only is he her former husband's brother, but Sindri was married to her sister Marden. And Marden never unmasked him, never had their Returning.

"Does our presence bother you?" I asked, picking up my knife and fork and coolly avoiding looking at him.

"No." I could see out of the corner of my eye that Sindri ran a hand over the back of his head. "That is, it's a good surprise. I'm glad to see you, I mean."

I silently continued eating, determined to keep my strength up even if I'd suddenly lost my appetite. It wasn't like I didn't expect to run into any of them here—that was why I'd dragged Roslyn along, after all, so I wouldn't have to face them alone or tempt them to have too private a conversation—and I'd decided to come anyway. I might not be sure I was going to be Ailill's bride, despite what he'd said—and I wasn't sure that even mattered to me. He wasn't the same, and in fact, if he'd forgotten me, well... He was better off without me. Still, I was willing to try to undo this mess, as far as those who were innocent in the matter were concerned. I couldn't retreat back to my lonesome cottage and ignore it all, not after I'd seen what this village could become if men became too comfortable in their freedom and boredom.

Roslyn didn't have as personal a qualm with Sindri as her sister did, and maybe that dislike for extended periods of silence I'd observed in her drove her to speak. "Why don't you grab a chair and join us?" she asked.

I nearly choked on the last slice of meat on my plate, but it went unnoticed. Sindri grabbed a chair from the excess behind me and brought it to our tiny table. At least he didn't bring any food or drink because there wasn't room for it.

Sindri took no cue from my silence and skipped over the social graces that would have required him to thank Roslyn for the invite. He put the chair down, backwards, so he could lean his arms across the top of it. "I've wanted to speak with you for weeks," he said, staring at me uncomfortably, "but I know you've had a lot to deal with. I should have come to your father's memorial—"

"I'm glad you didn't. That none of you did." Actually, their absence had hurt a little, even though I didn't want to see them. But to see Alvilda, Siofra and Nissa come without the rest of their family, not even young Luuk, seemed awfully insensitive considering the role they played in Father's passing.

"We wanted to," said Sindri, undeterred. "We all did. We talked about it, though, and we thought it wasn't the best place to see you for the first time since that night. We wanted to talk, but it wasn't the right moment."

Our table fell into silence for a few moments, but Roslyn interrupted it. "You were missed," she said, laying her spoon down, the somber mood making her as done with her dinner as I was despite the half portion remaining on the plate.

The corner of Sindri's mouth twitched upward. "That's kind of you to say, Roslyn. I don't think everyone missed me, though." Whether he was talking about his former wife, who'd been there for Elfriede, or me or most of us, I didn't bother to ask.

"It would have been nice of Jurij to show," said Roslyn, surprising both Sindri and me at the mention of his name. Roslyn seemed to notice our distaste for the name, although why Sindri should feel the same, I had no idea. "For Elfriede," Roslyn added, as if that explained everything.

It might explain why I saw Jurij with his arms around Elfriede in a half embrace in the book mere moments after the cavern.

"Jurij misses you," said Sindri, turning to me. "*And* Elfriede. He's such a mess these days, easily the worst off of all of us—"

"Good," I said, interrupting him.

Sindri sighed. "Noll, we didn't mean for this to happen. It was never supposed to lead to all of this destruction, all of these deaths."

"What did you expect would happen?" I demanded. "Didn't you fully understand the consequences of fighting, of waving around swords like they were toys?"

"No, I don't think we did!" Sindri raised his voice and a nearby table of people stopped talking to stare at us curiously. Sindri glared back at them, and I wasn't comfortable seeing the flash of anger there. Men had never been so quick to anger before the curse was broken, not usually, and I worried that it was the first step in a process that might lead to men like those in the village from Ailill's childhood. Sindri turned back after the gaping people returned to their conversation and drummed his fingers atop the back of his chair in front of him. "Swords and fighting—that was just a game to us. Something we played with *you* as children."

43

"Don't blame *me* for this—"

"I *don't*. Of course I don't." Sindri paused as Roslyn stood, gathering her plate and mine, and bringing them back to Vena without a word. *So much for using her presence for protection from this sort of confrontation.* "I'm just trying to explain to you that we didn't have such bad intentions. When Jaron and Jurij came up with the idea—"

"*Jurij* was responsible for all of that?"

Sindri shook his head. "It was mostly Jaron. I mean, Jurij thought he could use a marriage to you as a means of distracting the lord, but—"

"Yeah. I remember that brilliant idea." I sighed and watched Roslyn deposit the plates on the table by Vena, hoping she'd wander back. Instead, she seemed to notice how busy Vena was and took our plates and the whole stack of them to a bin in the back filled with soap and water, earning Vena's overwhelming adoration.

You're on your own. Be thankful it's just Sindri and not one of the ones who came up with the idea or one of the muscle-bound brutes who kept you pinned and unable to move.

Sindri's gaze followed my own. "She's doing well, it seems," he said. "I don't remember her ever looking so rosy. She's far more beautiful than her sister, and kinder. I can't believe I didn't notice back then. That I was *incapable* of noticing."

I threw my hands up in the air, not in the mood to foster new romance. "So what *did* you hope would happen, Sindri, when you all concocted this elaborate plan?"

Sindri rubbed the back of his neck sheepishly. "We wanted answers, Noll. Answers you seemed to have but weren't up to sharing with us."

"I didn't realize they were that important to you," I admitted, thinking back to every time Jurij or anyone else had asked me to explain something I only half understood myself. It hadn't happened *that* often. They were all consumed with moping about their former wives and goddesses more than anything, and that was something I assumed they'd soon get over.

"They were. They *are*. Wouldn't you want to know? Why you were born one way, and then suddenly had everything you knew pulled out from under you?"

"Ha," I laughed, not hiding my sarcasm. "You don't even know how much everything changed for me. Much more than everything changed for you."

"I'd like to know," Sindri said, not really convincing me he cared that much about my own suffering. To be fair, we were only newly friends again over the summer, and even then, I spent less time interacting with him than I had the others. "That's why we agreed we wouldn't be idiots this time. We'd ask you—*beg* you—to just share what you know with us—"

"I can't." I shook my head. "Even if I wanted to—and I'm not exactly in the mood for it, I have to say—I really can't. I'm sorry." I stood and pushed my chair back, remembering what I came for, what I risked seeing any of my former friends for. I passed Sindri, intending to walk to the nearest table and talk to the people seated there to see how everything was affecting them and ask them if they needed anything to feel safe and comfortable, when Sindri grabbed me by the wrist, stopping me from moving forward.

"Is what Jurij told us true?" he asked, and I shuddered, thinking of how much I had told Jurij that night on the way to the castle, how Ailill had said that anyone who knew as much without a golden ring or coin was in danger.

I yanked my elbow out of Sindri's grip and tossed my head. "And what did Jurij tell you?"

Sindri's gaze darted from me to Scorn and Spurn, who had taken their places behind me. His hand lowered slowly. His voice was quiet, hushed. "That you're key to everything. That you know how this curse got started. That you're responsible for it ending."

I pinched my lips together. So he hadn't told them the details. I wondered if he knew telling them I was the first goddess—that the pool in the cavern had thrust me into the past—would endanger them, or if he had other reasons to keep what I'd told him secret. If he even believed me, despite all he had seen. And why, if knowing was putting oneself in danger, he hadn't been killed or taken away.

Sindri raised an eyebrow. "Noll, you can tell me. You have to admit that I at least know the lord's been replaced—"

Scorn stepped between us and wrapped his hands around Sindri's neck.

Chapter Seven

"WHAT ARE YOU DOING?" I shrieked. "Let him
go! Let him go, let him go, let him go!" I started
slapping Scorn's arms as hard as I could, trying
to grip those cold white gloves and pry them off of Sindri's
neck. Sindri slapped at Scorn's arms as well, pushing back
his chair and kicking his legs out as he thrashed around.

"Scorn, stop!" I screamed. "*Stop!*" I turned to Spurn
helplessly. "Stop him!" I commanded.

Spurn didn't move at all, his hands tucked behind
his back, his legs slightly apart like he was merely watching
over me. There might have been a quick flicker of his eyes,
but I didn't care. If he wasn't going to help me, he was
absolutely useless.

"STOP!" I started kicking at Scorn's legs. Sindri's face
was darkening, and there was foam spurting out from his
lips. "Someone help me!" I turned around to see the entire
Great Hall gawking, not a single person moving, not a single
person willing to help.

I lunged at Scorn, wrapping my hands around his
torso and throwing my entire body weight at him, trying to
drag him to the ground with me. "AILILL!" I screeched.
"AILILL, STOP THIS RIGHT NOW!"

Scorn barely flinched even despite all of my efforts. Sindri had stopped sputtering, and his limbs weren't moving. He was limp, and that could only mean...

"NO!" I looked up at Spurn, even as I still had my arms around Scorn, even as I tried and tried to get him off of Sindri. "Please," I begged. "*Please!*"

Spurn moved at once, stepping in behind Scorn and placing his hands on both of his arms. I tumbled backward to give him more room and fell to the floor, my eyes unable to tear themselves away from the struggle. They both strained, their arms twitching, their hair becoming untidy, their jackets undone. I'd never seen a specter so disheveled. What felt like ages later, Spurn won, pulling Scorn's hands from Sindri's throat and tackling him to the ground, the two rolling away from us.

In shock, I almost joined the crowd of useless villagers murmuring and staring at us. Then I regained my senses and crawled over toward Sindri, where he'd collapsed to the ground, knocking into the crate-table.

I grabbed him and pulled his head onto my lap, shaking him. There was blood from where his head had struck the table, and it smeared against my skirt and spilled onto the floor. "Sindri! Sindri!" He was bleeding, but more importantly, he wasn't breathing. That seemed more pressing, even as the blood soaked through to my legs. I turned back to the crowd. "Someone *help!*"

Roslyn dropped the plate she'd held in her hands, the clattering practically the only sound in the hall. She raised her skirt so it didn't trail on the floor and ran over, taking a longer route only to avoid the still-tumbling specters. She slid in beside me, her face ghastly, her hands cradling her head. "What do we do?" She seemed too panicked to do anything.

"We have to get him breathing!" I said. "And *fast!* How? How?"

Roslyn beat her head with her hands. "There's a way, there's a way." The words tumbled out of her. "You remember that girl who nearly drowned in the pond in the fields when we were kids?"

"What?" I said, confused and angry and panicked. Girls playing in the pond? When was this? Girls couldn't be bothered to get off of their butts to do anything when we were kids. "What? No."

"You weren't playing with us." Roslyn grabbed Sindri by the temples, gently moving his head so it rested on the ground. The squish of the blood almost made me vomit. "That old crone came out of nowhere, and she said—she said we have to breathe the life back into her!" She pinched Sindri's nose and bent down to give Sindri a kiss.

"What are you *doing*?" I demanded. How in the name of the goddess did she think *that* was an appropriate thing to do just now?

Roslyn came up from the kiss and grabbed me by the front of my dress. "I'm saving him!" She looked angry and determined, more serious than I'd ever seen her before. "You go the other side! Start pressing hard on his chest!"

"*What*?"

"Do it!"

I did as Roslyn asked, crawling through the pooling blood and pressing hard on his chest with my fists every time Roslyn came up from a kiss. It couldn't have been long, surely if time had passed, *someone* else would have come to help us, but it felt like forever. Kiss and pound. Kiss and pound. Until eventually...

"It worked!" Roslyn beamed.

Sindri's eyes popped open and he started sputtering and choking. She helped him up and I immediately rushed in behind him to steady him.

"Hold him still," Roslyn said, and she let go. She shifted to bring the fabric of the back of her skirt forward a little. It was less stained with blood. She brought the edge of the skirt to her mouth and ripped it, swooping in to wrap it around Sindri's head even as she kept talking.

"It's less serious than it looks." Roslyn tied the fabric tight. "It's a pretty small gash. There's a bump, but—did I hurt you?" she asked as Sindri winced.

Sindri stared at her as his coughs died down. He kept staring and staring and staring.

Roslyn didn't seem to notice. She looked at me, as she stood and wiped her cheek with the back of her wrist, not noticing the blood she smeared all over her lovely complexion. She looked around at the crowd. "We should get him out of here," she said under her breath. "Let's bring him to the Bakers'. His mother will want to know what happened—"

A shriek cut her short. It sounded like Vena.

"Watch him," I said, nodding at her to support his head as I had before. I scrambled to my feet, nearly slipping on the puddle of blood. *I hope she was right about the wound*, I thought. *There's so much blood.*

My entire mind went blank as I pushed aside the last of the useless villagers and approached the table where Vena had been serving.

Spurn staggered to his feet from where he crouched, nearly toppling over. I pushed aside a woman, leaving blood on her shoulder, not caring, diving in to catch him and stop him from falling.

"He *killed* him!" shrieked Vena from somewhere behind him.

Spurn wouldn't look at me, and white hair tumbled across his forehead to dangle over his eyes. If he could breathe—they didn't breathe, did they?—he would be panting, but he just appeared exhausted, and there was no air coming out of his mouth to blow the tresses away.

My gaze fell to his hand, which held the knife Vena had used to cut the beef. It was stained dark and dripping—with juice from the meat?—and my eyes moved past that to the ground, where a set of white rumpled clothing lay. There was no other specter. Scorn—the ghost of Ailill, *my*

Ailill—was gone. Vanished. They couldn't die a second time, could they?

"...must go..." The voice was so quiet, so soft, I didn't at first realize I was hearing it. Spurn spoke in my ear. He *spoke*. His lips parted again. *"Now."*

Chapter Eight

BUT I CAN'T... SINDRI..." THE words were hard to get past my lips, but the stares of everyone in the Great Hall quickly silenced me. I looked at Spurn, and I saw something like *life* in his eyes, which made what had just happened even more terrifying. *Ailill is gone. He's really gone. But he tried to kill Sindri!* I checked to be sure Roslyn was still with Sindri, and that he still seemed awake and moving.

Please let him be all right. I grabbed Spurn's arm. "Drop it," I hissed, and he let go of the knife. It fell to the floor with a thud, and I started dragging him out, happy to see the group of onlookers parting as we made our way past.

"Noll, what are we to do with th-the clothing?" I could hear Vena ask behind me.

"Burn it," I said, still dragging Spurn behind. We were almost to the door.

A man stepped in front of me, blocking our way. "There's been death in this village for weeks now," he said, scowling. "We thought *you* were going to help us get past that, and now your own servants act like *monsters*."

"I know. Please, step aside. I need to speak with the lord."

"He told us you were to be 'the lady'! To rule beside him, to guide us through all of these troubles—"

"I will," I sputtered, surprised at my own lie. "I'm trying. Please step aside."

Spurn escaped from my grip and stood between us, pushing me back with a hand on my chest.

"Spurn, don't!"

He didn't have to do anything. The man looked up into his red eyes and stood in our way for just a breath longer, stepping aside without any violence between them. As I passed him, though, I could see more of that anger on his face, and the thought of what condition I was leaving these villagers in scared me. Spurn had been so insistent we leave, and I really had no idea what to do, anyway. It was a relief to get out into the crisp, chilled air of the early evening, to leave the chaos of the Great Hall behind.

Spurn wasn't following me. He was leading, and I felt stranger and stranger seeing him act like he was human. Like he was a man, suddenly no longer cursed, suddenly given freedom.

I grabbed him by the arm again, and he spun around. "We have to talk!"

His face didn't have the same range of emotions as I'd expect from a man who'd just stabbed someone to death, but there was something a little more there than I was used to seeing in specters. His red eyes moved too much—they searched me. He didn't open his mouth, instead cocking his head behind him and turning around, as if to tell me to follow him.

"No," I said, grabbing his arm and dragging him down a dark alleyway. There was just enough moonlight to see where we were going, but not too much that we might be seen. At least I hoped not. Dressed all in white, he reflected what little light there was.

Even though he'd had the strength to resist me, he'd allowed me to drag him down here. "Talk," I said. "I *know* you can. Don't pretend you can't."

He said nothing and tucked his hands behind his back, standing with his feet slightly apart, in almost-perfect imitation of a specter at the ready. He hadn't fixed his white hair, which hung limply over one of his eyes, his nose and mouth.

"You've talked to Ailill," I said. "Or at least another few of you have—you whisper in his ear—and you just talked to *me* in there." I dug into my pocket and withdrew my handful of coins. Sorting through them in my palm, I quickly latched on to the golden one. "See?" I said, putting the copper coins back and holding the golden one between my thumb and forefinger. "Ailill said I have a right to know because of this."

Spurn's shoulders twitched just slightly. Holding onto the coin tightly, I tucked it out of sight. "But you made sure I got this, didn't you?"

"Yes," said Spurn, and I was struck again by the hollowness of his voice.

It's frightening.

"You wanted me to have this? To have the right to know about everything?"

Spurn didn't move, but his mouth opened up just enough to say, "No."

"It was Ailill, then, who asked you to make sure I got it?"

"No."

I bit my lip. "Not the current Ailill, the one before, I mean?"

"No."

I threw my hands in the air, my fingers still clenched around the coin. "Make no sense, then! Why not? You know, I didn't want to know more about this village. I was content to make a life of my own in a quiet place, away from everything. I could close my eyes and forget." I did close my eyes, and I didn't forget. The image of the violet pool, the sensation of traveling through water, was replaced with the suffocating pull of the red one. I opened my eyes. *You're asking the wrong questions.*

"Who wanted you to make sure I got this coin?"

Spurn opened his mouth slightly, hesitating, but then he spoke, every word causing him pain, like there were shards of glass on his tongue. "*They* did. They lost... strength in this village after... curse was broken. They are at war. They should not... have been able to compel me. But they did."

"Who are *they*?" I asked. He didn't answer.

I grabbed Spurn's arm and pulled it out from behind him, clutching his hand. "You're different from the rest of the servants, aren't you?"

"Yes."

"Can other servants speak to me?"

"Yes. But will not."

"Even though they speak to Ailill?"

"Different. He is lord first, and he is part of us all."

I sighed. "You dropped the key for me, didn't you? That night when the fight at the tavern started? So I could let my friends go."

"Yes."

"Why?"

"Two reasons."

I waited for him to elaborate. When he didn't, I spoke again. "Two?"

"I know... you."

"I know you know me. You all know me."

"No... I *know* you. I was the... first."

"First?" It was going to take me forever to get him to speak enough to start making sense. "You were the first to know me, so you were one of the specters who kept visiting my house after I met Ailill..." I trailed off, searching his eyes. I'd been about to ask why that made a difference, why that could possibly be important, but all of a sudden, it dawned on me. "You were the first Ailill! You're the grown-up shadow of the child I met, all those years ago."

Ever so slightly, Spurn nodded.

I threw myself at him and hugged him, and it was like hugging ice, both cold and unresponsive, as he didn't so much as twitch beneath my embrace. "I'm sorry," I whispered. He said nothing. "You look so much older. You spent all those years alone, not knowing what was going on, not understanding... You must have been so frightened."

After a moment, I pulled back, wiping the trail of tears that still stuck to my cheek. "I know it's little solace, but... I didn't mean to do that to you. I didn't mean to make you suffer like that."

Spurn's gaze slipped slightly above my head, like he was just remembering he wasn't supposed to look me in the eye, and I could have sworn I saw the lump at this throat move—but he didn't swallow. The specters had no need for such things.

I cleared my throat and clutched my skirt with both hands. "You said two reasons. What was the other?"

This alone enduced Spurn to speak again. "They... wanted."

I shook my head, not about to frustrate myself by demanding to know who "they" were. I changed topics. "Why did Scorn attack Sindri?"

Spurn looked pitiful, like a wayward dog on its last breaths. I took his hand again and squeezed it in encouragement.

"He knows."

"About the lord being reborn?" I fought to stop myself from losing patience. "But... Everyone there that night knows. And they've been left in peace until now."

"He... spoke of it. Others in danger, too."

I felt like someone had kicked me—not Spurn, not poor pitiful Spurn, but someone unseen. "But the others... How can no one else have spoken about it? Things have been hectic since, but you can't expect them all to remain silent. They might not have quite come right out and asked me, but I know they're all curious."

"Spoke... to you. In front of us." Spurn dropped his hand, and it fell limply to his side, not joining the other one behind his back. "Always watching. But cannot hear. We can."

I clenched my fist tightly around the coin. "So even if *they* observe someone talking, they can't say for certain what it is they're talking about. But if all the people in the cavern that night need to keep silent around the specters, with so many out and about these past few weeks..." I bit my lip, a horrifying thought entering my head. "It's only a matter of time before any of them are at risk again! I have to speak to Ailill!" I don't know why I hoped he'd be able to— he'd even *care* to—save the people I cared about. At the very least, he could take me to these annoyingly mysterious "they" so I could put an end to it all.

I started walking back to the village road, but I stopped, spinning around to face Spurn. "The specters—the servants—you can die?"

Spurn nodded, slowly.

"Aren't you already dead?"

"Yes."

I shook my head incredulously. That would have to be a secret for another time. "Let's go," I barked, leading the way to the castle.

ŋ ŋ ŋ

We made it as far as my family's cottage before we ran into anyone who might speak to us, considering news of what had happened at the Great Hall hadn't quite spread yet. Unfortunately, the sight of Alvilda, Siofra, Nissa, Luuk, and even Master Tailor outside of my family's door did little to assuage me. I couldn't rush past them, hoping to get my answers from Ailill.

"What's happened?" I asked as Spurn and I climbed the last hill to join them.

Siofra turned away from looking through my open door. I peered inside quickly to find Mother and Elfriede at the door talking to them, Marden behind them at the table, half-eaten dishes in front of her.

"Jurij is missing," said Siofra plainly. Her voice wavered, and I thought I might be about to see the stern woman cry.

My stomach jumped up into my throat as I studied each of the faces in front of me. Most were screwed up with worry, and I couldn't imagine any of them knew anything— I wondered if Jurij's family had mistakenly assumed he'd come to see Elfriede or me—until my gaze rested on Master Tailor. He never struck me as much of a thinker, but I knew he'd been involved with what had happened. He'd even risked his youngest son's safety by having him play a part.

"Coll," I said, remembering that at almost eighteen, I was a year past being a grown woman and I could dispense with giving my friends' parents the respect of addressing them by their titles. He hadn't really earned it anyway. "Do you have any idea where he could have gone?"

Coll shook his head banefully and stared at his feet. "I haven't seen him in a couple of days. Siofra and Alvilda said he'd been with them—"

"He *was* until yesterday evening," interrupted Alvilda. "He left after we'd had dinner at the Great Hall, and he told us he was going to spend the night with *you*."

"He didn't come over," snapped Coll. "I didn't see him at all."

That gnawing feeling in my stomach was growing worse and worse. "There's something you must know." As if everyone expected me to tell them I'd found Jurij's empty clothing, the color drained almost immediately out of every face. What I had to tell them might not be much different, but *no*. I refused to believe there'd been more deaths until I could confirm it. *What a fine time to go missing, though, Jurij.*

I told them what had happened with Sindri and Scorn in the Great Hall, leaving out the exact words Sindri had said to earn the death sentence.

"That's terrible!" Mother's voice warbled. "Why, then, he's still in danger. I have to tell Thea—"

I raised a hand to cut her off. "He's with Roslyn, and they're going back to Mistress Baker's." I paused, reminding myself to call the woman "Thea." "Actually, if you could go visit them," I said, looking to Elfriede, too, and hoping she'd join her, "and explain that they should stay away from the lord and his servants. At least until I've been able to talk with Ailill."

"What... do you mean?" asked Alvilda. I'd never heard her sound so uncertain. She was clearly eyeing Spurn over my shoulder, and I wondered if his haggard appearance fed into her alarm.

"This one's okay." I glanced at Spurn for confirmation, but he was doing his best to seem as immobile and unaffected as any other specter. "But I wouldn't expect you to spot him from any other, so best to steer clear of any of them for a bit. I hope not for long. Still, you must all be careful what you say around any of them." I looked over Mother's shoulder to see if Marden was listening. "This applies to you, too, Marden. Please come here."

Marden cocked an eyebrow but stood, probably biting her tongue to stand behind Elfriede.

"All right," I said, looking at each in turn. "Listen to me, and say nothing. Don't respond at all, no matter what you may want to know. You never know when a servant might be around the corner. They're so quiet, they might catch you unawares." I looked above Siofra's and Alvilda's heads to the path that cut through the woods. There was no sign of movement, other than the slight rusting of the bright orange and red leaves. "What you witnessed that night in the cavern has left you with a lot of questions, I know that." I glanced at Coll accusingly. "You may think I'm

59

hiding all of the answers from you, but I have a lot of questions, too.

"You may also have noticed that... not everyone looks the same since that night."

"I'll say," began Alvilda, "the lord—"

Siofra nudged her quiet as I lifted a hand. Raising my voice, I spoke over her. "It was Sindri commenting on that difference, specifically mentioning *the lord* that made one of the servants reach out and choke him."

Alvilda immediately clamped her mouth shut. I took a deep breath and continued. "It's incredible it hasn't happened to anyone who was there in the cavern so far, but speak of what you noticed that night within the earshot of a servant, and he will attack you."

Mother gasped as Alvilda threw her hands up in the air. "That's appalling! The lord talks about rebuilding the village, about rebuilding that feeling of safety lost after the fight and the fire, and then he orders that we're to be killed for asking questions?"

"It's not him. Please don't ask. Just don't blame him."

Siofra looked from Alvilda to me and back. "All right," she said. "We'll trust you." Alvilda scowled, but Siofra kept speaking. "We'll trust Noll to take care of it," she said, commandingly. It was almost like when she used to order Coll around. "But..." She stopped and put a hand on Luuk's shoulder, dragging him close to her. He looked awkward and uncomfortable, but he didn't escape from her grip.

"Are you saying Jurij was attacked by a servant?" asked Coll quietly.

"Maybe." My eyes darted guiltily to the ground. I was still so angry with Jurij, but I didn't want him to die. Still, the thought of his fate being unknown should have bothered me more. A dark part of me thought that maybe he deserved it. And that thought made me want to cry. *How far we've come since those days when I could think of little but him.* "I don't know," I added to mollify them. "He would have left clothing behind, surely."

"If we don't know where he went, how could we find them?" said Elfriede, speaking up for the first time since the conversation had begun. "Or what was to stop the servant from disposing of the clothes afterward to keep us from knowing?"

I frowned. She was right. Would Ailill know? I knew *they* would know, though, and Ailill could at least let me speak with them.

"What about Darwyn and Tayton?" asked Mother. She stepped out from the doorway and Siofra and Luuk moved aside to let her pass. She had her shawl on, and she seemed determined. The look suited her well.

Alvilda spoke. "I saw them not two hours ago. They're taking one of the new cottages in the commune, and they've been helping with the rebuilding."

Mother's eyes widened. "They're surrounded by servants; they could be in danger."

Alvilda shook her head. "The servants brought the firewood, but I said we could do without them for the construction. Looks like my instinct was right."

I nodded. "Still. Mother, perhaps you and Thea should warn them. Elfriede? Marden? If you set out with Mother and start looking, you'll find them sooner. I think they're staying with Malek."

Marden shrugged and stepped out, but Elfriede shook her head. "They're probably with Sindri. Thea would have sent for Malek at least, as he's her oldest—if not all of her sons. She gets really upset when one of them is ill or injured."

Marden's lips curled into a sneer. "I wonder if she'd even tell his father. *I* wouldn't, after he left her for some tavern drunkard. In fact, I'd hardly care about Sindri being injured if I weren't so done with fretting about him—"

"Willard's new love died," interrupted Coll. We all turned to look at him. "Willard, the former baker. Sindri and Darwyn's father. She was with him in the tavern during the fight."

"Hmph," mumbled Marden. She crossed her arms, almost as if to say "she deserved it."

"All right," I said, not about to let the conversation wander. "I have to speak with Ailill. I'll see if he knows anything about Jurij."

"What about Jaron?" Elfriede asked, turning back into the house. She reappeared at the door quickly, a shawl around her shoulders. "Someone has to warn him."

My gaze flit between Mother and Elfriede. Mother stared off at the village, refusing to acknowledge the man. I understood entirely. He was as much, if not more to blame, than Jurij. And he'd once meant something more to Mother. Something like Jurij had meant to me.

"Look for him, too," I said, raising my chin defiantly. "He's the most likely to talk of any of them." I hadn't asked where Jaron was staying now that his room in the tavern was gone. I hadn't wanted to think about him, but I should have. I should have told Ailill what he had done even if I hadn't wanted to.

"Noll, let us go with you," said Siofra. "You can't go alone to the castle."

"I'm afraid I must." I took her free hand, the one not bitterly clutching her son to her. I did my best to smile. *I'm going to reassure someone. I may not have been able to do anything in the Great Hall but make things worse, but I'm going to do this. I'm going to make this village safe again.* "I promise you. I'll find him."

"You'll find out what *happened* to him," said Luuk, almost too quiet. He looked devastated, like he knew more than he let on. Maybe he just assumed that Jurij was gone, that he'd spoken and a servant had heard him. I dropped his mother's hand, entirely unsure of myself again.

"Noll will *find* him," said Nissa, stepping forward. "The elf queen can always find her retainers."

I laughed, all doubt forgotten. *It'll be fine. Ailill has that book. With a flip of the page, I'll find him hiding somewhere they haven't thought to look.*

Spurn stepped closer, his elbow brushing mine. He still appeared docile, but I knew he was trying to tell me something without others noticing.

"Spread out!" I said, heading back toward the path. "Search the village for the rest of them! I know how to find them, but if you get to them sooner and speak to them, all the better. Be careful, though, how you explain things." I took my first steps into the woods that stood between me and the castle, Spurn close behind me.

The elf queen and her retainer are off to confront some monsters.

Chapter Nine

NO ONE WAS IN THE entryway to the castle when Spurn and I arrived. The door to the garden was shut, but I opened it anyway to make sure no one was hiding. "Ailill?" I called. "We need to talk. It's important!"

The chilly autumn wind rustled through the rose bushes, scattering leaves and grass.

I turned around and bumped into Spurn. He was following far too closely behind me. I backed up and rubbed my sore forehead. "Is he upstairs? Do you know?"

Spurn's lips twitched in what might be considered his version of a frown.

"Never mind," I said, too impatient for an answer. "Let's go."

I poked my head into the dining room as we passed, but there was no fire burning, and no sign of life—or whatever it was that could describe the specters. I took the stairs nearly two at a time, pausing at the second floor landing where Ailill's bedroom and the other rooms were, but something told me I wouldn't find him in any of them. I continued up the stairs to the third floor, heading for the throne room.

The moment I reached the landing, I knew my instinct had served me well. The third floor hallway was the only hallway lit up with torches, and both walls were lined with specters at attention, their hands clutched behind their back, their feet slightly apart. *I guess I never thought about where they rested when not doing their work*, I thought as I passed the first few in silence. *Ailill forbade me from coming to this floor when I stayed here because my mother was in that room by the prison. Perhaps they all stood here, silently, waiting for Ailill's call.*

I passed an open door I'd never bothered exploring before—there were a number of rooms on the third floor I'd never seen, including one of them that must have held a cache of weapons my former friends found during their escape—and I stopped suddenly, noticing the light pouring into the hallway. I looked up, the throne room forgotten.

"...does not need that much seasoning. What is it?" Ailill, addressing a specter, had his back to me. The specter, bent over a table near a roaring fire, had paused in his work over a pot to stare at me. Ailill followed suit. He quickly masked his surprise with a stilted smile.

"My... lady," he said, putting his hands behind his back like a specter and bowing his head slightly. "What brings you here?" He gestured behind him. "I had not instructed enough food to be prepared for us both, but if you have not yet eaten—"

I cut him off with a gesture. "I have." *Come to think of it, I never saw where the food for our meals was prepared, either. Why are so many important rooms on the third floor? The throne room, the prison, and even the kitchen—wasn't it a pain for the specters to bring it down two floors to the dining room for serving?*

"I see," said Ailill, looking around the room awkwardly. "Just as well. I have not yet used the dining hall this rebirth. I found it rather large and drafty for one person." He crossed the room and sat at a small table.

I followed him, not taking the sole other seat at the table, instead wringing my hands nervously. *Spit it out, for the love of the goddess! This is an emergency. And you're not leaving this time until you have answers.*

Ailill studied me, his face puzzled. "May I ask to what do I owe this visit?" The specter who'd been cooking stepped between us, laying down a cloth napkin, a bowl and a spoon in front of his master.

I watched the specter nervously as he went back to the table to grab the pot. He used no cloth to shield his hands from the heat, and I had to wonder again how a specter could feel no pain and didn't even breathe, and yet I'd seen one die. Or others had seen him die, anyway.

"There's been a problem," I said, fascinated by the way the specter poured the stew into the bowl silently. Truly silently, without producing even a clink.

Ailill picked up his spoon and eyed me curiously, his gaze shifting to somewhere up over my shoulder. I turned around and saw Spurn there, doing his best to seem immobile, but he couldn't hide the way his hair and clothes were disheveled. "Apparently," said Ailill, but he didn't seem concerned. Instead, he started eating, not bothering to look up again.

"One of the spec—the servants is dead." Ailill's hand froze with the spoon halfway to his mouth, but only for a moment. He went back to eating.

"A shame," he said at last, putting the spoon down and wiping his lips with the napkin. "Still, you know they are not truly living."

"I know that," I snapped. "Which makes me wonder how one can truly *die*."

"They can vanish, just like people." Ailill lifted his head and nodded at the specter who'd served him, and the specter came over with a glass full of wine. "Whether you choose to believe that means they are dead depends on your point of view."

That was about the last thing I expected him to say. My knees weakened, and despite the gravity of the situation at hand, I sat down in the seat across from Ailill. At least that way, he'd have no choice but to look at me.

"When people vanish," I said, "they die. They're no longer with us—what did *you* mean?"

"Yes, I know," said Ailill flippantly. "They are dead. I did not mean to imply otherwise for the villagers. They no longer appear in this village, so they are dead, gone, and vanished." Before I could ask him to elaborate, he put his glass down and picked up his spoon again. "As for the Ailills, I wouldn't consider one of them *dying* to be a problem. They're already dead." His eyes flickered just slightly to Spurn, who stood behind me.

I clutched the edge of the table. "It was Scorn—that is, it was the latest Ailill. The one before you. The one I knew."

Ailill shrugged and took some more stew. "He wouldn't remember you any more than I would. They have no more feelings left, these shades."

I studied Spurn at that, questioning that assessment of them. He may not have explicitly said so, but he had memories, whatever Ailill said. And while his reactions were muted, he certainly didn't seem devoid of feelings. Unless there was something special about Spurn that made him different from all the others... I actually had to believe he was different because I didn't want to think about the Ailill I knew, *my* Ailill, attempting murder like that. He *wasn't* capable of that. It was maddening to think about.

I switched tracks. "That servant tried to kill my fr— one of the villagers." I lifted my chin and studied Ailill's reaction haughtily. "And I know why."

Ailill put his spoon down and wiped his fingers. "You know why? May I ask then if you killed him?"

"Who? The specter?" I shook my head. "It wasn't me—"

"It was the other Ailill I left you with." He nodded his head at Spurn. "Him."

I waited to see if Spurn would react, but he hardly moved. "Yes, but I didn't ask him to. I wanted him to stop the other specter from killing Sindri, but—"

"He responded to your orders," interrupted Ailill. "He must have thought the only way to stop him was to kill him."

"They're not *that* loyal! If they were, Scorn would have responded to my orders to stop."

Ailill raised his eyebrows. "'Scorn'? No, do not bother to explain that." He sighed and gestured at the serving specter, who came over with the bottle of wine for a refill. Ailill held his full glass for a moment, swishing its contents and staring somewhere off at the wall behind me. "You say an Ailill—a servant—tried to kill your friend." *Sort of friend*, I thought to myself. "And that wasn't at your own order?"

"Of course not! Who in the name of the first goddess would ever order *that*?"

"The name of the first goddess?" repeated Ailill, his brow furrowed. "You mean your own name?" So he knew. I suspected as much. He could remember his childhood, but the rest of his lives still were unclear? Then it shouldn't have bothered the last Ailill so much that he'd been reborn over and over, if he didn't *feel* the length of all those lives.

"Never mind that. A slip of the tongue, a careless expression."

"So," said Ailill, taking a sip and ignoring me. "you are certain. You did not even *think* you wanted that man dead."

"*No*, I certainly did not!" If specters acted even at my thoughts, then Jurij wouldn't have lasted more than a day.

"Then whose orders would supersede your own?" The glass almost tumbled from his fingers. He stood, slamming the glass down and staring at me accusingly. "What was he talking about when the servant attacked him?"

I pulled the gold coin out of my pocket and clutched it tightly. "*You.* He wanted to know why you were back, younger, darker—how you could be back after he saw you die."

Ailill swallowed uncomfortably and rapped his knuckles against the table. "He does not have the sign of a ruler," he said, quietly, rubbing his arm. He was wearing one of the golden bangles. "He is not supposed to know."

I nodded, thinking about how this wouldn't have been a problem before. No one bothered about the lord, not when they had their own affairs to attend to. When I'd spoken about my theories with Alvilda after Elfriede and Jurij's wedding, nothing ill had happened to us. Maybe speculation was different than actually *witnessing* it, and then speaking of it.

"You say he witnessed my last death," said Ailill, and he let go of his bangle to raise his hand to silence me. "Do not bother to relay the details at this moment. He was not the only witness, I gather?"

"No. But I spoke with most of them right before I came here and told them to watch what they said, and to warn the others."

"Good." Ailill ran a hand over his chin in thought. "Yet... Will it be enough? Never before have so many been privy to even a *hint* at what lies beyond the mountains, I am sure of it."

"All right," I said, standing. "We shall ask your mysterious *them*. I need you to take me 'beyond the mountains.'"

"You have never been to see them before?"

"No." I wasn't sure if I should admit I didn't even know who "they" were. Other than some people who lived beyond the mountains, always watching us. A version of the lord himself, only farther away. "I have never had the pleasure."

Ailill cocked his head. "I would hardly call it a pleasure." He looked up at the ceiling. "You have to grant me at least that much honesty," he said, almost as if speaking to someone.

But I thought "they" couldn't hear us. Just like Ailill can't hear through the pages of his book.

The book. "Even so, I must see them, but I need to check on Jurij's welfare first."

"Jurij?" asked Ailill, curious.

If I weren't so certain he was telling the truth about not remembering his last life in detail, I would roll my eyes at his display of ignorance.

"He was... a friend. Married to my sister, before the end of the curse."

"I admit I am still curious as to how the curse ended," said Ailill. "They told me little this time, but I could tell something was different. They were not pleased."

Again. "They."

I brushed past Spurn to exit to the hallway. "Is the book on its stand in the throne room?" I asked Ailill over my shoulder.

Ailill caught up in a few strides, joining me as I walked toward the throne room a few doors over. "You certainly know your way around." He seemed amused.

"I do," I quipped tersely. "Perhaps too well."

"Wait!" Ailill grabbed hold of my hand just before I took my first step into the throne room. "If it is a friend you inquire after, one who claims responsibility for the events of that evening, then I may already know where you will find him."

I felt the weight of Ailill's hand on mine, the coldness of his black leather gloves. Before I lost him last time, we'd held each other's hands without the leather between us. It felt different then. There was heat even despite the cold. "Where?" I asked, not willing to let his hand go.

But Ailill dropped it first and pointed down the hallway. "In my prison."

Chapter Ten

"STEP ASIDE!" I WAVED MY hand at the specter standing outside of the door leading to the prison, and he actually did what I asked of him. I looked over my shoulder to find both Ailill and Spurn behind me, and I wondered if they gave some signal that I was to be obeyed, or if the coin I clutched in my fist was really enough to get the specter to bother with me.

Since Ailill was initially convinced Scorn acted on my orders, I'll choose to believe the latter.

I grabbed hold of the door handle with the hand not clinging to the golden piece and pulled, but it didn't budge. I had no choice but to put the coin back into my pocket and use both hands, but I still struggled with the effort.

"Let me," said Ailill, stepping behind me. "It is probably a poor design for a prison, but it is much easier to push open from the other side than pull open from this one."

I looked over my shoulder to glare at him, but I immediately dropped my head, my cheeks burning. He was *right* behind me, and he put one arm on either side of me to put his hands above and below mine on the door. I could feel his chest behind my shoulders, his arms against mine.

"Pull," he said, and it took me a moment to reconsider the task at hand. I faltered, but I went back to pulling, and the door gave way much easier.

Ailill stepped back to make room, and I examined him, biting my lip. Should I thank him? When he imprisoned Jurij?

It's not like Jurij didn't deserve it.

I settled for grunting at him, and I brushed my hands on my skirt. They were wet with sweat from the effort. I refused to believe it was from nervousness.

"Jurij!" I called, walking into the hallway lining the prison cells. When Ailill had kept my mother in his castle, he'd put her in the room next to these. Unconscious, she wasn't at risk for escape, I supposed. But I hadn't even known these actual cells existed until he'd thrown my friends and me into them that evening the mess of the fight and the fire all started. "Jurij!" I called again, passing the second empty cell. "Your parents are looking for you—"

"Good evening, Noll," came the casual voice from the third cell. It sounded bored and a touch depressed—and extremely familiar.

"Jaron." I peered into his cell and found no one else, so I kept walking to check the last cell, but I didn't see anyone else in that, either.

"He's not here," said Jaron. "Not unless his lordship brought in a second prisoner while I slumbered."

I chose to ignore Jaron for the moment and confronted Ailill. "You told me you had Jurij in your prison."

"I told you I had a *friend*," responded Ailill. "He claimed to be a friend of yours, anyway. Can you blame me for forgetting the name he gave me?"

If it didn't also mean a clean slate for all of those problems between us, I'd blame you for forgetting a lot of things.

"He didn't seem much interested in my name," interjected Jaron. "Just took me at my word that I was responsible for the fight that started the fire."

"I'm looking for someone else," I said, raising my voice to be heard over Jaron.

"What's this?" asked Jaron, clearly hurt. "No shred of forgiveness for a man who's owned up to his stupidity but still desperately seeking a man who hurt you more than I did?"

"I didn't say anything about forgiveness," I snapped at Jaron, forgetting my attempts to ignore him. I tapped my foot. "His parents are worried."

"Have they cause to be?" Jaron looked from me to Ailill and back. His eyes rested curiously on the untidy appearance of Spurn behind Ailill.

"Yes," I said, watching for Ailill's reaction. "Everyone who witnessed what happened in the cavern that evening is in danger."

"You mean everyone who has a clue that the lord standing there isn't—"

I strode over to the cell and kicked through the space between bars, slamming the toe of my boot into Jaron's shin as hard as I could.

"Ow! Damn it!" Jaron cradled his shin and bounced a little, losing his balance and leaning against the cell bars. "What in the name of the first goddess is wrong with you?" He put his foot down again, tentatively. "That's you, though, right? That's what Jurij said."

I chose to ignore the comment and focused on telling the man to shut up before he put himself at risk any further.

"You have no proof of that," I said, swiftly realizing that the difference between Sindri talking about the lord being replaced by a younger, darker version and Jaron or Alvilda or anyone conjecturing about the strange things that were part of this village was that Sindri had witnessed what he saw. Still, I'd rather Jaron refrain from speaking of such things. "And I'll have you know I did you a favor. Sindri was attacked not long ago, for speaking in front of a lord's servant about what he saw that evening."

73

Jaron turned around and stuck one arm back through the cell bars, gripping the bars with his other. "I talked about that night in front of plenty of servants when I walked in here."

"What exactly *are* you doing in here?"

Jaron shrugged and looked at the ground. "Where else would I be? I couldn't stop thinking about how my plan had failed."

"So you decided to exile yourself to the prison?"

"It was only a matter of time."

I shook my head. "No one was going to come and arrest you. I hadn't even thought about it, and Ailill didn't remember—" I cut myself short, biting my lip.

"You knew this man was responsible for the fight?" asked Ailill, curiously. "And you did not think fit to tell me?"

"I've barely *seen* you since that night," I answered. "And it was hard for me to think about what happened then. I just didn't consider that the men responsible should be locked up."

"The *men*? How many men came up with this idea?" demanded Ailill.

"I was the leader," said Jaron. "It was my idea, really. That's all that's important."

Ailill didn't seem convinced. I was wondering why Jaron was still breathing. "What exactly did you tell Ailill then? When you turned yourself in?"

Jaron leaned back from the cells and crossed his arms, resting his back against the wall. "That I told your father—'a man,' I said, that is, didn't want to sully his name—to cause trouble that night at the tavern."

I waited for him to continue, but he didn't. "That's it?" I looked from Jaron to Ailill and back. "Well, that explains why you're still breathing. The details put you in danger. The details about..." I stopped, studying Ailill.

Jaron seemed to catch on. "Ah." He nodded. "All right, then, I won't talk about it."

"He would not give his reasons," interjected Ailill. "For causing a fight. I gathered that he and others were 'at the cavern,' as you so often say, but he would not tell me more."

I watched Jaron, taking note of his placid reaction. I started wondering if more than just a sense of guilt had led Jaron to the castle. "Did he return the sword he took from your castle?"

"No," said Ailill, rubbing his chin with his hand and studying Jaron carefully. "Are there more of those missing?"

"There are," I said, before Jaron could come up with some lie. "They weren't used in the fight in the tavern, but Jaron and a number of others took swords with them that night."

"Noll—" started Jaron, but I ignored him.

"And you know who else has them?" asked Ailill, also turning away from Jaron. His mouth turned into a frown and he reached out to grab me by the elbow. "Perhaps we can finish this conversation elsewhere."

"Aw, come on," said Jaron, exasperated. "What are you so afraid of? I'm not going anywhere. I won't tell anybody."

I let Ailill guide me past the other empty cells and out of the prison. He and Spurn shut the door tight behind us, and Ailill didn't grab my arm again.

"Is he actually locked up?" I asked. "I have to wonder if the only reason he brought himself here willingly was to snoop around for answers."

"Yes, he is confined." Ailill nodded at the specter standing watch at the door as we passed him. "I was not sure I ought to confine him based on his confession alone. But he was so insistent, and I was sure that isolating the instigator of the violence might prove beneficial for the village, at least for a short while."

I stopped. "You plan to let him go?"

Ailill paused, realizing I was no longer walking with him. "Should I not?"

75

"No. I... I don't know." I looked over my shoulder, as if expecting Jaron to be there, but all I found was Spurn. I gritted my teeth. "He can stay for now. I need to use the book to look for Jurij."

We arrived at the throne room before Ailill began speaking. "This Jurij? Is he one of the friends who took the swords I had sequestered?"

"Yes," I admitted, although I was reluctant to explain just what he'd done with the one he'd stolen. "I should have asked for them back immediately. I'm sorry, I..." I shook my head. "I haven't been thinking clearly."

I stopped in the middle of the room, uncomfortable moving farther into the pitch black. There was a scratch of flint and Spurn appeared in the darkness, lighting one of the torches. He took it off the wall, shook the dying embers off of the flint and immediately set to lighting the next torch.

As the room came into better view, I found Ailill already at the book on the stand, poring over the pages. I approached him, eyeing the throne warily as I did. *This is how we'll find "them,"* I thought. *Through the hole behind that throne.*

"How many years ago was he born?" asked Ailill. "Around your birth?"

"Jurij's a year younger." I tucked some hair behind my ear and watched as Ailill flipped the pages. Something hit me suddenly. "The pages are organized by when we're born?"

"Yes." Ailill stopped, studying me. "I would have thought you would know. Was the book not in your possession until recently?"

"Briefly," I said, ignoring the implied accusations. I flipped through the pages, recognizing some of my contemporaries. Roslyn sat in a chair beside Sindri on a bed, Thea nearby. Their faces were serious, their frowns evident, as they spoke to people whose backs were to the page. They were my mother and Marden, likely come to warn them as I requested. I hoped Sindri was recuperating.

I kept flipping. "Jurij should be somewhere around here." I frowned. "He has to be. One of these." I froze. I'd come to an entirely blank page. I thought there was some mistake, so I flipped it again and I saw a moving drawing. My heart racing, I realized the image was of Darwyn. Tayton was walking somewhere with him, and they looked concerned. They stopped in front of the bakery door, and Alvilda, Siofra and the half figure of someone—probably Coll—came into view as the door opened and the former Master Baker appeared. *So they tracked them down and warned them, and they were off to visit Sindri.*

I flipped the page back to the blank one, but it hadn't changed.

Ailill slammed the book shut, nearly smashing my hands in with it.

"Hey!" I said, but the look on Ailill's face stopped me cold.

Ailill stared at the throne. "Does he know about this entryway?" he asked quietly. "Your friend?"

I stared at the throne, too. The longer I looked, the more I swore I could feel the chilly air and hear subtle whispers. "He does, but... What are you saying?"

Ailill pursed his lips. "The *only* way the page turns blank is if the person is on the other side of the mountains."

The other side... Why had no one else considered a world beyond the mountains? Unless they couldn't?

"If the person dies," continued Ailill, "the page burns and—"

"—vanishes," I finished for him. I frowned. "But that doesn't explain how Jurij would be allowed to cross over." I reached into my pocket and clutched my golden coin tightly. "If someone who's witnessed peculiarities so much as mentions it, they're attacked, so then how can someone without a piece of gold..." I felt like someone had kicked me in the stomach. "He has a golden bangle!" The memory hit me like a gale. "I saw him take one that night, when they were lying on the dining room floor."

"I thought they were rather ill-placed when I found the excess of them there." Ailill scowled and moved closer to the throne, studying it. He raised a hand and Spurn hung his torch back on the wall to join him. Together they pushed it aside. Ailill took a deep breath and wiped his brow after they'd finished.

I stepped up the dais and joined them, staring into the void.

"*Olivière,*" spoke the whispers. When Ailill reacted, I knew I wasn't imagining it.

"You're saying Jurij went in there?" I asked. "But how? Wouldn't he need help to push the throne? And how did he push it back into place after he passed through it?"

"Not through here exactly." Ailill bit his lip. It was strangely alluring, and I shook myself, focusing on what was important. "There is another way, if they desire to open it to someone."

"The cavern pool," I said, and I could feel Ailill's curiosity burn beside me. "Which Jurij also knows about. He's the only one of the group of witnesses whom I told about the magic of the pool."

"Then he has gone to see them," said Ailill. "Although why they should let him pass, I cannot say."

I clutched Ailill's arm nervously and he gave me a strange look, an almost embarrassed look, but I was too nervous to think on it. "Then he's in danger! And you and I are the only ones who even know how to find him."

The lump at Ailill's throat bobbed perceptively. He gently removed himself from my grip. "Then we shall have to step through the mountains and confront them."

Chapter Eleven

"YOU WILL NOT NEED THAT. It will not show you what he is up to, even if you bring it with you."

I hesitated, my hand on the book on the stand. It wasn't just Jurij I hoped the book would show me, but if we were going there, wherever *there* might be, I felt like I needed to keep an eye on the village we would be leaving behind. Especially considering what I'd just seen Scorn do.

Still, it was awfully bulky, and I had no idea how long we'd be gone. "What should we take with us?" I placed my hand back in my pocket to clutch the coin.

"Nothing but the proof of your status." Ailill tapped the bangle around his wrist. He hesitated. "But keep it out of sight."

Spurn approached the dais again, a torch in hand. Ailill took it and looked at me, his face awash in the ember light. "Since it is your first time through, we shall bring a torch to light the way." He reached back to take my hand in his. His touch through the leather was cold and formal. "You need not be afraid. It is but a short trip, and once we pass the veil, we will be at our destination."

"The veil?" I asked, as he took the first step into the cavern.

"Yes," he replied, and with one last look over my shoulder at Spurn—who stood still and at attention, but whose frown was hard to miss—I stepped through.

I expected the shadows and the chill. The dark, hollow space of the cavern prepared me for the emptiness of these harsh, stone places. Subconsciously, I'd come to associate them with an echo and the trickle of water, quiet small noises in an otherwise near-empty void.

Instead, I was treated to the loudest sound that had ever passed through my ears. "Argh!" I screamed, dropping Ailill's hand to cover my ears with both hands. "What is that?"

Ailill didn't respond, and I could see the puzzlement clear on his face in the flicker of his torch light.

The echoing boom—far worse than any cave-in at the quarry, almost like the mountains themselves were tumbling down—continued, and a wash of red glowing light appeared from deep within the darkness, like it was approaching us on a gust of wind.

Ailill dropped the torch, which I could hardly hear clatter, and grabbed my hand again in his, urgently, squeezing hard. "RUN!" he shouted, pulling me.

I ran, clutching my skirt with my other hand to keep from tripping. The light was growing larger, that sense of coldness drawing closer, but Ailill kept us running, faster than I had in months, harder than I had in years. I wanted to ask why we were running toward the light and not away from it, but there was no time. I had no breath.

"WE ARE ALMOST THERE!" encouraged Ailill, his own breaths short and staggered.

I wanted to shield my ears from the boom that pierced my head—the sound I swore I could feel in my bones—but I couldn't. I just had to keep running and running toward the red light.

We dashed through it before I even realized it was before us: a long, thin sheet of dark material. Gauze-like, the material let the red light through but filtered it, and it was only once we were entangled in the material that I noticed it: the material was a veil much like the one Ailill once wore, and the one he hung in his dining room to keep my eyes from him.

There was no end to it, but Ailill kept pulling me through. I felt the veil wrap around me and I tried to scream, but no sound came out over the sound of the booming, and I felt the wispy material caress my lips. I tried tugging his arm to make him slow, but he kept pulling and I got more and more entwined in it until we broke through, and the booming sound ended without fading, just like someone had reached out and silenced the mountain with a hand. We fell.

Ailill grabbed me at once, slamming my body against his, putting a hand on my back and the other on the back of my head to clutch me to him tightly. We both rolled down, and I felt the unevenness of the surface with every sharp jab, every aching poke to my body.

We couldn't have fallen long, but it felt like such a long time, I was almost becoming numb to it. When we stopped rolling at last, Ailill didn't immediately let me go, and I knew he must be feeling the same aches and bruises and the same swimming headache I did.

Ailill breathed hard above my ear, and I felt the race of his heartbeat against my chin. We stayed like that, silently, for some time until he finally relaxed his grip and shifted apart from me.

"Are you... hurt?" he asked between deep breaths.

I slammed my palms against the ground and noticed the dry dust that flew into the air with the movement. I ignored it and pushed myself up, groaning involuntarily as I adjusted myself to sit beside Ailill. The light was dull but blinding after having been inside the dark castle and mountainside. It was sunlight—at dusk. We were outside.

"What is it?" asked Ailill at once, all of his fatigue wiped away by worry.

"My foot." I winced as I readjusted myself and ripped my boot off, annoyed by the layers of skirt in my way.

"It is not bruised." Ailill lifted my foot before I could even drop the boot to the ground, stunning me into silence. "At least not yet." He raised one hand to his mouth, ripping off his leather glove with his teeth and spitting the glove onto the ground beside him. He switched hands and repeated the process before proceeding to touch my foot lightly, pushing and prodding. "Can you put weight on it?" he asked.

I finally got my wits about me and blushed, pulling my leg back to get my foot out of his hands. I put it down and felt no discomfort, but all the movement caused a rattling in the boot in my hands. I turned it over and a large, dark rock fell out, with a pointy edge that had probably stabbed my sole. "I'm fine." I scrambled to put the boot back on, not looking at him.

Ailill sighed. "That is good news. We both seem to have survived intact, albeit a little worse for wear." He stood, and I studied him, noting the dirt all over his clothing that matched my own, the occasional tears to the material and the disarray of his hair.

"We did not fall far," he said. "But it is too far of a climb to go back, I am afraid to say. Not with that incline."

I stood, almost losing my balance and accepting Ailill's help reluctantly as I steadied myself on two feet. He let me go and I followed his gaze upward, where a large hole, the size of the hole behind the throne, appeared on the side of a—mountain?

I studied the brown, small flat mountain and felt unnerved. I twirled around, taking note of more smaller mountains, even some far in the distance, each with a flat peak. The ground was dry and brown and barren but for a few small strange green plants with needles protruding from them. The only thing that looked at all familiar was the sky above it, all awash in the great orange glow of a sunset. It wasn't the red light we'd seen in the tunnel. No, that was too much like the light that had replaced the violet glow in the cavern.

"Those are called cliffs," said Ailill, perhaps thinking my thoughts dwelled on the flat, small mountains. He looked around. "We appear to be in the canyon, outside the castle."

"This... is on the other side of the castle? This is what lies beyond the mountains?" I stepped forward, my body trembling. I didn't want to be afraid. I hadn't come here to turn back.

"Yes." Ailill let out a deep breath and put his hands on his hips, turning back to look up at the hole in the cliff. "In a way. But I was not referring to our castle, but the castle we came to visit. The Never Veil usually takes me directly to them, right out through their own hole behind their middle throne."

"That was the 'Never Veil'? That hanging veil we passed through to get here?"

"Like the pool in the cavern, as you seem to be familiar with, the hole behind my throne can lead to various places. It is not until you pass through the veil that you know just where you will go. The Never Veil lies between us and them, a curtain to shield us from the truth as it shields them from the *intrusion* of us." He bit his lip. "Still, they have never found cause to send me anywhere but right to them."

So I wasn't to see "them" right away or find out what any of these cryptic messages meant. Ailill took a few steps one way and then another, shading his eyes with a hand as he looked off into the horizon.

I bent down to grab the black leather gloves where he'd left them and clutched them tightly between both palms. *Should I ask him? Should I admit just how entirely unknowledgeable I am, that I'm no "lady in on the bet"? Clearly he knows something is already off about me, but to what extent? If he only remembered his last life, he'd already know all of that, but he also would never have taken me here.*

I swallowed back the questions I wanted to ask. He knew I'd never been here, but he couldn't know I'd never even spoken to any of them. He couldn't know I didn't fully realize who "they" are. "So what do we do next?" I asked. I was here to meet them, and I would. I needed his help, not his scorn. The less he knew about our history, the better. What he knew was already damaging enough.

Ailill nodded at me. "Well, I know we are in the right place, but the question is how far we are from the castle." He grabbed the gloves from me and tucked one under his arm while he pulled the other over his right hand. "If the queens were responsible for sending that red light to stop us, they would have resorted to sending us the farthest possible distance once they realized we had already breached the veil."

The queens? My heart fluttered. Here was the answer already, and I didn't even ask for it.

"But if the kings intervened," continued Ailill, tugging the second glove over his left hand. "They would have tried to stop them, bringing us much closer to the castle than the queens would like."

The kings? Kings and queens? Which are "they," or are they both the ones who watch over us?

"In any case, we have no choice but to walk there." He pointed one way, opposite of the setting sun. "The castles are always in the east," he said, as if that made any sense to me. "So east we must go."

He set off before I could say anything more.

Chapter Twelve

$\mathcal{J}$'D HARDLY HAD TIME TO notice the temperature before, but as the sunlight grew dimmer, I couldn't help but shiver. I wondered if it was already winter here, but I didn't remember it being abnormally cold when we first broke through the veil.

Probably noticing my distress, Ailill stopped, removed his black jacket, and swung it behind me.

I put a hand out to stop him. "You don't have to—"

"Nonsense. You are clearly cold." He let the jacket rest on my shoulders as I crossed my arms tightly against my chest.

I grabbed hold of the jacket and frowned, staring at Ailill's dark, exposed arms. His shirt seemed to be missing sleeves. "But what about you?"

He shrugged. "What do I have to fear? Freezing to death? Clearly, there is no end to the number of times I am able come back to life."

I hesitated, but then I slid my arms through the jacket, wrapping myself in his warmth, in his scent. I remembered vividly the first time he wrapped his jacket around me, when I first met him, my eyes closed.

Ailill continued walking onward, and I jogged a few paces to catch up. "But you won't be the same person if you die and come back," I said. *He's not the same person at all. There's no rage, no bitterness.*

"Does that matter?" Ailill kicked a rock with his foot. He glanced at the twilight sky and sighed before leading me to the edge of one of the cliffs. "We had better build a fire. It gets cold in a canyon after the sun sets."

"I think it does matter," I said, trying not to dwell on my disappointment in not meeting these kings and queens immediately. *Who knows what Jurij is up to. Or if all of the people back home have managed to stay out of danger.* "You're leaving the castle this life. You're leading the village in person. Maybe this life will be worth living."

Ailill paused mid-movement as he picked up a dusty ball of twigs and weeds that got caught against the cliff side and a rock. "Were my previous lives not worth living then?"

I watched as he broke the ball up into a flatter pile of brush and wiped his hands on his jerkin. He smiled awkwardly and took a few steps closer. "Pardon me," he said, reaching toward my chest. "May I? I left my flint in my inner lining."

I flushed and dug inside the jacket flaps, too nervous to let him reach inside himself. I withdrew the flint and handed it to him. He picked up a rock and struck the flint against it. "You cannot completely not remember," I said, trying to make sense of the new Ailill before me. It was true that it was only his first life he told me in detail, but he did mention subsequent lives. Getting food for himself from "sources"—these kings and queens?—and watching as every last person he knew died and faded away.

Ailill kept striking his flint with no success. He crouched beside the pile of brush and looked up before striking it again, smiling slightly. "I remember my first life clearly, but if you are wondering why my previous incarnation knew of his previous lives, the answer is quite simple: The other Ailills told him." He blew on the rock, and small bits of flint went flying. "And the one who knew the most about my previous life is gone, you told me." He struck again, this time causing the flint to set fire. "Ah!" He touched it to the brush over and over again until the little spark went out. "This is so much easier when they are here to help us, is it not?" He started pacing around the small campfire, picking up any twig he found and tossing it in to keep the fire burning. But there were few twigs and sticks in this barren place.

I helped him, searching for what little scraps I could find. I wished I'd brought some of the spare chunks of wood I used to carve with me. The fire wasn't going to last all evening.

Ailill settled down facing the fire, his back against the cliff side. I hesitated with my twigs over the small fire, observing as his eyes flickered with the reflection of the firelight. Why did the men ever have fire in their eyes? There were so many things I hoped to ask these kings and queens, not least of which was why they'd allowed Jurij to find them but had tried to stop me from coming.

I threw the small pile into the burning brush and sat down beside Ailill. "Your previous incarnation talked of infinite pain," I said, watching Ailill's reaction carefully. "He seemed to *feel* the torment of being alone for every one of his lives. You'd have me believe he'd been alone for just a few years, reborn as a young man like you, grown and faded no more than a decade before his life ended?"

I thought I noticed Ailill's lips twitch just slightly, but he masked any reaction by gathering his legs together in front of him and hugging them close to his chest. I didn't know what to believe. Part of me felt like he was lying, that he could remember everything, but I really knew nothing about this process, and there was no way this younger man, this happier, kinder man sitting so casually beside me, was the same man who hated me with every breath he took not so very long ago.

"Being alone for any period of time can be a torment," said Ailill at last, not meeting my eyes. "Especially if I could not walk among the people I looked after."

"Looked after" was a generous way of describing it. Did he even give his blessing to the Returnings, like so many people thought he was doing? Did he even care if we invited everyone in the village to attend? What was the meaning of all those stale traditions?

Nothing more than the curse you weaved with your very own mouth, I reminded myself.

"And what of you?" asked Ailill, breaking into my thoughts. "Why do you not tell me more about my previous life, if you are so eager that I know it?"

"You don't have to know about your previous life." I ran my fingers nervously over one of the arms of the jacket. The embroidery on this jacket was different than the previous one's. Instead of roses and thorns, the flowers were clearly lilies. "I just can't believe... I can't believe how much you've changed."

Ailill shifted beside me and lowered his legs to the ground. "Change is a good thing, is it not?"

"It can be," I admitted. "But not always."

"What about now?" Ailill gestured to himself. "Have I changed for the better?"

"I suppose so. You're more..." I struggled to find a word that wouldn't offend him, or make him think I hated him previously. "You're more relaxed," I said at last.

"Relaxed?" Ailill cocked his head. "How so?"

I looked over to find him practically lying against the cliff side, so relaxed he was practically asleep. I stifled a laugh. "In almost every way! Although I have to ask... Why do you speak so formally?"

"Formally?" Ailill frowned slightly. The flickering fire made shadows dance across his jaw and neckline, shadows that drew my gaze to his tight jerkin and the tight form beneath it.

I tore my eyes away. "You spoke that way in the previous life, too. Still, I'm surprised if you're so much more *relaxed* now that you still speak like no other."

Ailill nodded, and I peeked over to see realization wash over his face. "You speak of words like 'I'm' and 'you're.' Taking less time to speak."

I screamed giddily, making him flinch, and grabbed his arm lightly. "You said them! You can actually say them!" Ailill's cheeks darkened slightly and he rolled his eyes and looked away, but I didn't miss the smile playing on his lips. "Of course I can say them. I understand you, do I not?"

I let go of his arm and pointed at him. "Uh huh. Right there! Right there, anyone but *you* would have said 'don't I'!"

Ailill removed one of his gloves, making a point of being consumed by the task. I noticed his jaw twitch just slightly. "It is a habit passed down from lord to lord, or from lady to lady, an imitation of those who rule over all of us. I knew immediately you were only a new lady, one who must have been allowed to be such through marriage, when you spoke to me like a common villager."

I frowned, not entirely sure what he meant. From "lady to lady"? "Allowed to be"? Were there other lady rulers of the village, and who allowed a marriage? The kings and queens? Had they *allowed* Ailill's father to force himself on that poor woman in the commune who was Ailill's mother? Or did she not count as a lady because she had no gold of her own?

"Here." Ailill took my hand in his and slipped his glove over it. "When you touched my arm, your hand was like ice." He took off his second glove.

"Don't," I said, only just understanding I'd let him dress me like one of the dolls Elfriede had had as a child. I started peeling the other glove off. "You'll freeze for certain at this rate. You can't just strip everything off and—" I choked on my words, a startling image appearing in my head. *Strip everything off.* Like a goddess and her man did. *Elfriede and Jurij. There are no goddesses anymore.* Like a husband and wife, then. *But what of Alvilda and Siofra? Or a* wife and a wife. *And Darwyn and Tayton.* Or just two people who chose each other... I was so flustered, I couldn't keep my thoughts straight.

"I see your point," said Ailill, grinning slightly. He slid his glove back on and put his bare hand on my gloved one, stopping me from removing it. "Keep that one. We shall share." He turned his attention to the fire and picked up a small handful of twigs to throw into it. It was dwindling, and I feared there wasn't enough material to keep the fire going.

I tried to suppress a shiver as I looked at my hands, one gloved and one not, and remembered my first meeting with Ailill. I was so scared and taken aback, so unprepared to become his goddess, I never realized how nice his concern for me had been. True, it was a bit excessive—what man's wasn't for his goddess?—but I wondered if he hadn't been so cold and dismissive the next time I'd seen him, if I could have learned to be happy. Would he have been so maddening the following time if I'd been able to accept that I was no longer nobody's goddess much sooner? If I'd given up on my feelings for Jurij?

I laughed spitefully to myself. My feelings for Jurij. How much things had changed.

"Does something amuse you?" asked Ailill, tearing me from my thoughts.

I tucked my hands beneath my arms and hugged them tight. I looked at Ailill, prepared to talk, and the words caught in my throat. When had I come to feel this way about him? Because I *did* feel something for him, something different, but somehow better than what I'd ever felt for Jurij. There had been so much hate between us—and while I certainly wouldn't count him blameless, despite everything I now knew—and I regretted clinging so desperately to my stubbornness. I hadn't known Jurij, not really, not like I came to know Ailill. And now Ailill barely knew me.

Maybe that was for the best. Maybe... I could teach him to love me this time. Actually *love* me.

I want him to choose *to love me.*

I pushed that too-long strand of hair out of my face. "It's nothing. What do you think the..." I hesitated, but then I decided to throw myself into everything that puzzled me. "The kings and queens want with Jurij?" Part of me wanted not to care, but I did. I wasn't yet ready to forgive him for his act of violence, intentional or unintentional, but I felt bad for the way he'd wound up in that position. I felt bad that he thought he loved me when he didn't, not really. We were best friends once, whether he'd chosen that or not.

"I cannot say." Ailill frowned as our tiny fire died out, leaving us drenched in nothing but night and starlight. "Stolen golden token or not, no other man from our village should have the right to meet them."

"No other *man*?" I asked, noticing the emphasis.

"Well, yes," said Ailill, standing. He stomped the life out of the last few embers. "Each village has either one man or one woman in charge of it—or on occasion, one of both."

"*Each* village?" I practically screamed it into the darkness.

Even in the dim light, I could see Ailill pause and study me. "Are you certain you were given the token from the queens, and that you haven't stolen—" His question was interrupted by the sound of something strange and hollow, like a dog crooning at the moonlight. Only it was higher pitched than that. More soulless.

"A coyote," said Ailill, sitting back on the ground. "They are relatively harmless."

Relatively?

Ailill stretched his bare arms above his head and lay down. "We should rest," he said. "We will continue walking at first light. It cannot be much farther."

My stomach growled, releasing some of the tension I felt at the echoing howl. I was thirsty and my feet ached, and I felt the throbbing of bruises forming all over my body from the tumble.

"There will be food there," said Ailill, reading my thoughts. "And once we are inside, they will not be able to help but welcome us. They have kept me fed in the past." I could hear his leather clothing rustling as he tried to make himself comfortable. "During that first life," he added. *Because he can't remember the other ones?*

So these kings and queens were his original sources of food. Even so, after what little he'd told me of them, I couldn't see why he trusted them.

I was too tired to think. If I stayed up much longer, I was sure to dwell on my thirst and hunger. I moved to lie down, my head at Ailill's feet.

Ailill stirred in the darkness. "Lie up here. Beside me." He gestured out toward the small space he'd left between himself and the cliff side. "It will be warmer. And we will be better able to react together should a coyote come wandering over."

I scrambled over to the space he indicated, a jolt of energy at his words giving me the strength to make the movement. I lay down on the painfully hard ground, using one of my hands as a bony, uncomfortable pillow.

I stared at Ailill's back in front of me. Blinking, letting my eyes adjust to the darkness, I saw the gentle rhythm of his shoulders move just slightly with each breath.

I've never seen him sleeping, I thought. *It makes him feel more... amenable.*

I ran the soothing softness of the glove he'd lent me against my cheek.

"We shall share," he'd said. Only that wasn't what we were doing at all.

I sat up slowly, doing my best not to disturb him. Removing my arms from the jacket he'd given me, I draped half of it over my side and lay down again, gently laying the other half across his side like a blanket. My bare hand lingered on his bicep as I let go of the jacket, and I had to stop myself from leaving it there and feeling the cold of his skin transform into warmth.

His hand shot out to grab mine. Bare skin on bare skin, he squeezed it, and the iciness of his touch gave way to heat that made my heart pound faster. I was so tired, I couldn't say for sure whether or not that last part was just me dreaming. I think I tried to squeeze it back, but I soon lost touch with everything but the enveloping darkness of sleep.

Chapter Thirteen

LIGHT HAD JUST BROKEN OVER the horizon when I next opened my eyes, but that wasn't even the first thing I noticed.

Ailill had turned over to face me, the jacket we shared as a blanket pushed down off his shoulder. He held a finger over his lips.

I was still fatigued, and it took me a moment more to sense what was bothering him. There was a rustle of movement from somewhere above our heads.

"What is—" I whispered, but Ailill covered my mouth with his palm until I quieted. He let go, craning his head over his shoulder and pushing himself up.

A coyote? I wondered, thinking of the wild animals back home. There was nothing so frightening-sounding in the woods by my home, nothing that sent chills down my spine in the darkness.

Ailill shifted his feet beneath him, carefully and quietly, and rose slowly. He took a few steps eastward, and I sat up, scrambling to pick up the jacket as it fell, my hands trembling.

"I don't mean any harm, I just—oh, you."

I flinched at the sound of the familiar voice and stood quickly, clutching the jacket to my chest. *"Jurij!"*

Jurij stood in front of Ailill, the two young men about even in height. Jurij looked exhausted, and there were puffy circles under his eyes. I noticed his clothes were dusty but intact, and as the aches in my thighs, arm, and head began pounding, I couldn't help but wonder if he was spared Ailill's and my rather dramatic entrance into this dusty, forsaken land.

Ailill kept a wary eye on Jurij but shifted his head just slightly to address me. "This is the man you sought, then?"

"Yes." I stepped up to stand beside Ailill, watching Jurij warily. "How in the name of the first goddess did you come here? *Why* did you come here?"

"The first goddess?" said Jurij, a sad smile playing on his lips. "Do you mean—"

"Me, yes, thank you. It's a force of habit. You're avoiding my questions."

"I don't know." Jurij shrugged. "I felt compelled to go back to the cavern and I fell in and..." He put a hand to his waist as if lost in thought, calling attention to the sword in a scabbard at his side, and the golden bangle around the wrist of the hand that patted it.

"You still have that sword? And you stole that golden bangle, too! Give them back!" I dropped Ailill's jacket and lashed out to grab the sword's hilt. Jurij leaned back out of my reach.

"They weren't *yours*, though, were they?" Jurij's face soured.

I bent over to grab Ailill's jacket, huffing. "They're not *yours*, either! And you clearly have no right to them."

I folded the jacket over my arm as Jurij and Ailill stared each other down, the tension palatable.

"You never formally introduced me to the lord," said Jurij, smirking. "If this is even the same lord."

"I could use a proper introduction to this man myself," added Ailill, and I felt like there was more than just an introduction at stake.

I sighed. "Ailill, this is Jurij, the fri—the man everyone was looking for. Jurij, this is the lord, albeit altered, and his name is Ailill."

"Altered?" snorted Jurij. "I'll say."

Ailill broke the eye contact at last and turned to me, puzzled. "Does this man bear some ill will toward me?"

"If anything," I said, before Jurij could answer himself, "you ought to bear ill will toward *him*."

Jurij scoffed. "I'd say the feeling was mutual, considering how he treated his villagers like play things."

"He didn't treat us all like *play things!*" I protested. "And who put *that* nonsense in your head? I don't think what you *did* to him is equal to that."

"I *told* you it was an accident, and I was *trying* to save you, no matter how ungrateful you've been about it—"

"You also *told* me that you'd pictured yourself doing something like that regardless—"

Ailill raised a hand. "I see there is clearly something I am missing that happened between you two, but if I might ask that we put any further discussion on hold? The sun has risen, and we best make haste. The castle cannot be much farther, but we cannot afford to spend another night out here without arriving at our destination."

Jurij looked like he had plenty more to say, but he settled for scratching his arm. The bangle jostled against his wrist as he did. *It's because I led him to the dining room that he got his hands on that. It's because of that that he's here.*

"All right," I said. "I'll wait to discuss that. But I want to know why he's here to begin with."

"I told you," started Jurij, "I went to the cavern and fell in—"

"I guessed that." I turned to Ailill, ignoring Jurij. "Yet he shouldn't be here, right? What use could *they* have for him?" It was nice being on the other side of the mystery for once, even though I was no more sure who the "kings and queens" were than I'd been just the day before.

96

"We shall have to ask them." Ailill took the coat from my arms and draped it over his forearm. It was hotter now that the sun had risen, and I didn't think either of us would need it. I removed the one glove from my hand sheepishly as I noticed Jurij watching us, and Ailill took it from me silently, slipping it back over his own hand. "Shall we be off then?" He didn't await either of our answers and strode forward past Jurij to lead the way.

Jurij and I exchanged a wary glance before we both picked up our feet and followed him.

ᶯ ᶯ ᶯ

I opened my dry lips, desperate to fill what must have now been an hour or two of silence with something. "I hear you've taken to woodworking."

Jurij's shoulders shook perceptively from what must have been surprise at my willingness to talk.

"I suppose I owe Alvilda for that compliment." He peered down at me from beneath his hand, which he used to shield his eyes from the sun overhead. "I couldn't tell you, not really. After the cav—well, after that night, I felt too numb to work. I didn't go back to the quarry. I didn't go back to your cottage. So at some point my aunt must have been tired of me sitting there like a lump of wood and sought to correct that by putting a lump of wood in my idle hands."

Ailill was a few paces ahead of us, leading the way without stopping for a rest. He'd claimed it couldn't be much farther, but all I saw were a maze of cliff sides blocking out the skyline.

It was strange to hear Jurij so jovial, like the night in the cavern was just a dream. "You said the cavern called to you, like it did to me once," I said.

97

"Yes," said Jurij after a moment. "It was in that instant that everything made sense. It's not that I didn't believe you, but I fully believed you when I went into the cavern and saw the violet glow. It was red before, wasn't it?"

"Yeah," I admitted. "It has been since I traveled through it."

"I should have realized that." Jurij took a deep breath. "I should have realized it'd changed colors. I'd seen it before, after all, the day of Elfriede's and my Returning." He frowned.

That day used to be a painful day for me because it was then I'd realized that Jurij was only compelled to be my friend through an accidental command of Elfriede's. I didn't think the day had any painful significance for Jurij, but maybe now that he was free to think for himself, he finally saw the injustice in it. I'd gotten over that pain already. The night I thought I'd lost Ailill in the cavern was far fresher for me.

"Your family is worried about you," I said, switching topics. "We were all... Well, it was a fine time to go missing, as I'd just realized everyone who was in the cavern that night was in danger."

Jurij stopped in his tracks, but Ailill didn't, and I kept moving. Jurij jogged a few paces to catch up to me. "What do you mean?"

I lowered my voice. Ailill already knew this, but I didn't want to invite any discussion between the two of them. "One of the servants attacked Sindri because he mentioned the lord's altered appearance."

Jurij grabbed my arm, stopping me. I noticed he used the hand with the golden bangle. "Is he all right?"

"Yes," I said. Ailill seemed to have noticed our absence and stopped just ahead, right as the cliff side began curving outward. "Everyone's all right. I warned them not to discuss what they saw in the cavern within earshot of any servants."

"But why?" Jurij's grip tightened on my arm.

"I don't know. Ailill said these people called the kings and queens know. They live here, watching over us."

Jurij ran his head across his sweat-caked forehead. "If I weren't already astounded by jumping into a pool and coming out through a curtain on the side of one of these flat mountains, I would hardly believe you. Kings and queens. Like the rulers in stories..."

"You didn't come out in water?" I asked, confused. When I'd swum through the pool, I'd come right back up through the top of it, albeit in a different time.

"No," said Jurij, turning his attention back to me. "Or maybe I just dreamt it all. I don't know. I remember the violet glow, the cavern pond, my name being called by whispering voices... I jumped in, but instead of water, all I can remember is breaking through a gauze black curtain, and then I was here."

"It's a veil," I said. I doubted it would have the same significance to him, considering he never stared at the veiled lord for as long as I had. "Still, I don't understand. How? Could you go back through it?"

Jurij shook his head. "No. I tried, but when I walked back into the small cave opening, there was only stone wall, no 'veil' as you called it."

"But if the kings and queens wanted you here, and they didn't want me here, why not at least bring you directly to the castle?"

"You keep mentioning a castle."

I ignored him. "Unless... Ailill said the queens don't want me here, but the kings would be fighting back? Are the two in some sort of conflict?" My surmises didn't matter. As Ailill said, the answers awaited ahead of us. "Where were you going, Jurij, with that sword on your hip last night? I assume you hadn't planned on jumping through the cavern pool to find yourself lost in a land unfamiliar to you."

"No," admitted Jurij. His eyes darted nervously over to where Ailill stood, his back to the cliff and one of his feet resting flat against it. "I was on my way to see him."

"Why?"

"Jaron and I... came to an agreement." He put his hands out in front of him. "It was nothing nefarious, I swear to you! We decided to turn ourselves in."

I bit my lip. Jaron *had* turned himself in, but he hadn't mentioned Jurij supposedly coming to join him, even though he knew I'd been looking for him. My eyes darted to the sword at Jurij's side, which he touched nervously as he watched Ailill.

"You wanted to be put in prison?" I asked. *And you prepared to go with a sword?* I wanted to add, but I wanted Jurij to tell me about that himself.

Jurij looked at his feet. "No, not really, of course. But we felt the pain of what we'd done every day. Those men and women gone. The tavern fire. Even if he was back, I knew it wasn't the same man, and I knew, deep down, I'd killed someone with my own two hands." He sighed. "And for what? We had more questions than ever—and very few answers."

"But *you* had some answers. Jaron hinted he knew more than he should have. How much did you tell him—tell anyone? About me being the first goddess, about the power of the cavern?"

"I didn't say anything. I told you I didn't believe you entirely myself until I traveled through the Never Veil."

My blood ran cold. Out of the corner of my eye, I kept checking to see if Ailill was watching, but to my horror, he'd vanished. Had he gone around the corner to scout ahead? I picked up my skirt and darted after him.

"Noll, wait—"

"I have to find him!" I called, not bothering to look back over my shoulder. "He's the only one who knows where he's going." And to tell the truth, I felt uncomfortable at the prospect of being left alone with Jurij.

"Noll! Slow down! I haven't finished talking to you!"

I was almost there, and I was sure to find Ailill just around the corner. *Keep going. Keep going!*

"Noll!"

I'm almost there. "Ailill! Where did you go? AILILL!"

Jurij seized me by the shoulders, spinning me back to face him. I nearly collapsed, I was so out of breath, but I was determined to get away from him. "Relax!" Jurij said, and he smiled awkwardly. "He's just around the corner. I saw him peek ahead while we were talking."

"Let go of me!" I said, and I gripped both of his arms tightly. I tried to tear them away, but I didn't have the strength.

"Noll, what's wrong with you? I know we've had our issues, but you're acting like I want to kill you—"

I gave up trying to get his arms off of me, but I stood my ground defensively. "How did you know it was called the Never Veil?"

Jurij frowned. "You told me. You said it wasn't a curtain—"

"—it was a veil. But I didn't tell you the name of it."

Jurij sighed and he looked over my head. "That was stupid of me. I wanted this to go another way." He shifted his grip to one of my arms and tugged me back down the path behind him.

Even though I dug my heels into the ground, I couldn't stop him from pulling me. "AILILL!" *Help me!*

Jurij tugged harder. "Noll, please don't make this any harder. Come with me, or I'll have to—"

"You'll have to what?" I demanded. "Use that sword on me?"

Jurij frowned and gripped the hilt with his free hand. "If I must." He drew it out from the scabbard slowly and raised it above his head. "I'm sorry."

I turned and started to run. Everything went black.

Chapter Fourteen

BEFORE I EVEN OPENED MY eyes, I could feel his arms under my knees and around my back, and my face pressed against his chest. The back of my head throbbed.

I was still for half a moment longer before I screamed, not caring that it made my head hurt so much worse. "Let me go!"

I pushed against his chest and tried to get my eyes all the way open. The light was blinding.

"Olivi—Noll! Noll, wait, please! It is I."

I stilled instantly. The sound of my name was foreign with that voice's timbre, but there was no way Jurij could imitate Ailill down to the stilted speech. I blinked away tears until I could see.

Ailill's deep brown eyes looked straight into mine, and even without the flames, I found them mesmerizing. We didn't stay that way long, though, before he broke away and slowly crouched, so he could set me down on the coarse and barren ground.

I ran a hand to the back of my head and winced. Instead of my hair, I found a strip of cloth there. "What happened?" I asked groggily. "Where's Jurij?"

Ailill scoffed and gently grabbed my forearm, pulling it away from my head. His other hand still supported my back. "Your *friend* hit you on the back of the head with the hilt of that sword."

How had it come to this? How was Jurij so lost to me? Was it my fault? Should I never have loved him, never have stopped loving him? What was it like to finally return the affections of someone you thought loved you, only to find that person no longer in your reach?

I stared at Ailill as I considered those questions. My eyes darted to his abdomen, which was bare, the shirt he wore beneath his open jacket torn hastily above the navel. I felt heat rush to my face as I took note of the edge of his hip bones, so sharp and defined around the top of his thighs before they vanished out of sight beneath his trousers.

"Where were you?" I asked, the question surprising me, as well as the shaky voice with which I delivered it. "I searched for you, and you were gone."

"I had just gone around the corner," said Ailill, his face clearly pained. "I had a feeling we were near, and I wanted to be certain. I... I apologize. I should never have left you alone with him."

I frowned, considering everything. Never have left me alone with Jurij? That was once all I had longed for. And now... Now I didn't even know who he was anymore.

"What happened?" I repeated. "Where is he now?"

A slight breeze stroked Ailill's face, dancing through the hair that framed his sharp cheekbones. Every sharp bone in his body called out to be touched. "I do not know where he is. Only that I heard you screaming, and I ran back. I saw you coming toward me, your *friend* with that sword you say he stole raised above your head, both hands on the hilt, and he hit you with the bottom of it."

"He could have *killed* me!" I'd been determined not to be so angry with him, to remember what was once between us, but it seemed all he did was make things worse.

"Yes," said Ailill. "I cannot say for certain whether he realized that, but despite it all, I will grant him the benefit of the doubt. When you fell to the ground, he looked like death. He was afraid he had killed you."

I scoffed and winced at the movement. My head throbbed, and my side was still sore. "What did he expect?"

"He was incoherent," said Ailill flatly. "By the time I got to you both, he had flung the sword to the ground and was cradling you, repeating your name over and over." He pinched his lips. "He said he only wanted you to 'go with' him."

"I got that part." I took a deep breath, doing my best to ignore the pain. "What I don't get is why he would hurt me to get me to go with him."

"I do not think he understands what he does."

I thought of Jurij's sword through Ailill's chest and how cruel he seemed at my anger over it. "He understands enough."

"He let you go as soon as I got there. I worked quickly to staunch your wound." He bit his lip. "If only I still had my power..."

"Don't blame yourself," I said. "You used the last of it to save my mother. I couldn't be more grateful." I wished the words had flown so easily after he did it, that I could go back and thank him properly when he truly understood.

"Well, they will be able to treat you, if they prove welcoming." Again with the *they*, but it no longer felt as ominous now that I had an inkling of who they were. Although considering how little I truly knew, perhaps it still should be.

"So where is he?"

"Gone." The tips of Ailill's gloves brushed my cheek and he gestured in the air as if he was letting a bug he caught go. "I could hardly question him or accuse him before he ran, leaving that sword behind in the dust beside you. I could not carry it without its sheath as well as you, so I left it behind."

"I can't believe this." I started to shake my head but had to stop when I felt the pain reverberate in my skull. "I know he's changed, but I never imagined Jurij capable of hurting *anyone*, let alone me."

Ailill swallowed visibly. "Freedom can be a difficult burden. One most men would ask for nonetheless, but one not suited for everyone." Even after a night spent out here, the faint tumble of the weeds through the empty landscape between beats in our conversations was a strange sound to get used to, like we were lying in the midst of a dance of wool. "In any case, your friend's panic set us on the right path."

I slowly turned my head to get a look.

"He retreated down a path between cliffs I had hardly noticed, and I picked you up and followed soon after to confront him. He was out of sight once I turned the corner, but he led us straight here."

I blinked, sure the pain in my head was causing me to see falsely. Because off in the distance, less than an hour's walk away, were two castles that looked just like Ailill's. Joined in the middle with a single doorway, it was almost like Ailill's castle was reflected in a mirror. Instead of mountains, they were surrounded by cliffs. Instead of being dark and black and ominous, they glowed softly in violet.

And I could almost hear my name spoken on that desolate wind.

η η η

Ailill quickly relented when I protested at the idea of him bringing me to these queens and kings in his arms like an infant. It was more than just the fact that the memory of waking up in his arms like that made my face hot and my head dizzy. I didn't understand most of this, but I did remember that feeling of being dragged beneath the water in the cavern. These people may have tried to kill me, and I knew I wasn't about to like what I found in their castle, but

I had to go. I had to know. And I needed to start off with as much strength in my corner as I could get.

Unfortunately, the pain in my head and the aches all over wouldn't let me walk upright with my shoulders thrown back. When Ailill suggested I at least let him wrap his arm around my shoulders to settle me against him as we walked, I had to oblige. We only took a few steps before I slipped my arm around his back.

"For better balance," I said. He didn't say anything.

There was no outer wall in front of these twin castles, no outer door to swing open at our approach. The land was so barren, it was little wonder. These people surely expected no visitors—at least none who would walk through their front doors. Ailill had made it clear the Never Veil usually brought him straight inside this place when he stepped through.

Still, I thought we might be expected. Especially if this was where Jurij was headed—and where else could he have gone?

The doors to the joined castles swung open slowly at our approach.

The lovely coolness of Ailill's jacket—returned to me after I insisted on walking myself—caressed my cheek as I lifted my head back slightly. "Is that a good thing?"

The lump at his throat moved subtly. "It is rarely the fate of pawns to encounter a 'good thing' at the hand of more powerful pieces."

And to think, I thought. *I used to believe he was one of the more powerful pieces.*

We stepped inside together, our feet crossing the threshold at the same time. It was like coming home.

The entryway looked exactly like Ailill's castle, only brighter, as the sunlight filtered in from every open doorway. Some part of me felt like it was more than the light, though, it was the fact that I was walking through here, leaning on Ailill, feeling his supportive hand on my shoulder. The open door straight across from us led to a garden, and I could hear the trickle of a water fountain. Through another doorway I spotted a long dining table. And there was the stairway at our right, and to the left—

A second stairway. A mirror image of the first.

Of course. You're not home. You saw two castles. There have to be two stairways.

Ailill paused halfway inside. His lips were pursed, his brow furrowed, as his eyes darted back and forth between the stairway, but his gaze landed on the garden ahead of us.

I blinked, trying to adjust to the light. The flowers on the bushes—the roses?—weren't just white as they were in Ailill's garden. They weren't hibernating for the upcoming winter, either. The bushes were verdant and lively, the blooms bright and colorful. Each seemed to be a different shape, every bloom was a different color.

"Should we go in?" I asked, already letting my hand fall from Ailill's back and stepping away, toward the open garden.

"Halt! Olivière Woodcarver."

It wasn't Ailill's voice, although the stilted, affected delivery reminded me of him. It wasn't even a single voice. It was a multitude of them, both male and female.

I turned slowly. Ailill was already turned around and backing toward me, his hands out behind his back as if to stop me from pushing past him.

Three men descended from my left, which I supposed was the south castle, in perfect tandem with three women from my right and the northern castle. They were spaced evenly apart and moved almost as one, the one side a mirror image of the other in movement.

They wore clothing, but they may as well not have, as it clung so tightly to their skin, they could have been naked. I saw every curve, every bulge of their bodies, and although they differed in height and weight—even among their own gender—they were all an example of the form of the body at its finest. The golden material of the tight suits shined and glimmered in the rays of the sunlight as they filed into a half circle, as did the identical golden crowns they each wore upon their heads.

I don't know how long they stood there before speaking. I was too entranced by their appearances. I noticed they each had rounded ears—even the men—and my hands moved subconsciously to caress my own. But that was practically where what was similar about their appearances stopped.

The tallest man was the most familiar to my eyes, not that he reminded me of anyone in particular, but because his appearance was the least surprising, as he resembled the men in my village. His face, neck, and hands were as dark as wet soil, as was the short but voluminous hair that peeked out from beneath the crown. His shoulders were broad, and he carried himself with an air of power and beauty.

The shortest woman, still taller than I and quite imposing, shared the look somewhat of Ailill's paler form, that creamy rose complexion almost but not quite as pale as a specter. Her hips were wide, her chest buxom, and her gorgeous long hair was almost the color of copper—red— and curly as it tumbled over her shoulders.

The man of middle height looked like no one I'd ever seen before. Slim, but still with greater muscle than Ailill, his skin was almost golden in tone to match his golden outfit. His dark, black hair reached his shoulders in almost perfectly straight lines, and his eyes, dark and powerful even from where I was standing, were slightly smaller than I'd expect, more blended into his lovely features.

The woman of middle height was as light in skin as Elfriede, but the richness of her long, wavy brown hair made her beauty something else entirely. Her nose was straighter, thinner than I expected, her dark eyes penetrating. She was the only one of them who stood with a hand on her hip, the others content to let their arms hang beside them.

The shortest man shared the light oak skin tone of this woman and of Elfriede, and his handsome, sharply defined features looked bold against the long black braid that rested over his shoulders. His eyes were wide, his nose sharp and pointed, and his lips came together in a long, thin line.

The tallest woman—the one who stood at the middle beside the tallest man—commanded my gaze as soon as I laid eyes on her. She wore her hair short, but I saw it was shiny and black and straight from where it peeked out beneath her crown. Her skin tone was about as fair as the man with startlingly different eyes. Her eyes were even similar to his but wider, more distinctive than his. Her face was fuller than his too, the tip of her nose rounder. She was thin, almost one straight line, the curves where I expected them just slightly prominent. She studied me across the top of her nose, her chin jutted just a bit forward.

"You have done wrong, Ailill, and you forget yourself." It was the tall, dark man who spoke, and it was only by his speaking that I could tear myself from the tallest woman's gaze.

Ailill grabbed my hand in his and I let him, but he still wouldn't move from where he stood in front of me. Ailill spoke, loudly, his voice cracking. "I am surprised you lecture me so, Your Majesty Adeyemi. Was it not you and the other kings who stopped the queens from sending us even farther from the castles?"

The tall woman laughed, glancing at the women beside her. "You are mistaken. It was we who stopped *them*."

"You, Your Majesty Jangmi?" asked Ailill. He frowned. "You have never helped me—"

"We had no intention of helping *you*, foolish child." It was the middle woman who spoke. "It was her." Her eyes fell immediately on me.

The quiet, calm room exploded as the men started shouting, the women turning to them and shouting back in response. I couldn't make sense of the argument, but I heard my name, my full name, over and over, spoken with both distaste and triumph, but spoken coldly regardless.

"Enough!" called Adeyemi, and everyone fell calmly back into lines. They stared at us.

I opened my mouth to speak, but Ailill dropped my hand and crossed his hand over his chest, bending forward. "I apologize if I have done wrongly," he said. He straightened from his bow. "She has a token, though."

"A token?" sneered the middle man. "What token? I see no token on her arm."

I rubbed my wrist absently, knowing there would be no golden bangle there. The pressure of the eyes on me made me reach into my pocket and bring out my golden coin. "This," I said, my voice catching in my throat.

The shortest man stepped forward and studied my open palm. He asked me to turn it over and I did, grateful he didn't just snatch it out of my hands. He turned back to his companion. "How does she come by this—this mockery of a token?"

"That is no mockery!" said the shortest woman, and she stepped up to examine it. She nodded. "It is made of gold, and so it belongs here. That is what we agreed to."

"It is not a bangle," said the man.

"What does the shape of it matter?" said the middle woman. "Nowhere in the rules does it say it has to be a bangle!"

"You seem remarkably familiar with this object," said the middle man, stepping forward. "If you are found to have sent it—"

"It will be no different than you letting that boy through the veil with the stolen bangle!" shouted the middle woman.

"The two incidents are not even comparable," said the shortest man. "You know who this girl is—"

"Silence!" said Jangmi, holding a hand up, and the others fell mute, walking back into place. "Ailill," she said more calmly. "Let us at least start with introductions."

"She has no right to be here!" called the middle man.

"Kin, be still," spoke Adeyemi.

Ailill put an arm behind my back and guided me slightly forward. "These are the kings and queens of the realm," he said, as if "the realm" would make any sense to me. "They watch over us and all of our villages, ever playing games to win their bet."

I was speechless. I wanted to say something—*anything*—but nothing could make it past my lips. *A fine show of strength you're giving them.*

"I am Jangmi," spoke the tallest woman. She cupped her hands in front of her waist.

"I am, as you may have observed, Adeyemi," said the tallest man.

"Chrysilla," said the middle woman.

"Kin," echoed the middle man.

"Marigold," spoke the shortest woman.

"And Estavan," finished the shortest man.

Their names were as strange as their faces to me. It took all of my effort to keep each of them straight.

"You must have many questions," said Jangmi, "but I am afraid we cannot answer them as of yet. We must consult on how you came into possession of that coin."

"We know *full well* it was you who sent it," interrupted Estavan. "You have thought of her as your champion pawn piece ever since she altered the purpose of that pathway."

"And we know *full well* it was you who attempted to bar her entrance from the castles," said Marigold, "even though we let that boy with the stolen bangle through without interference. And that pawn was simply a cheat."

The argument moved so fast, I could hardly keep up with which of the shorter kings and queens were speaking.

"It is not a cheat if we were not the ones who sent him the bangle!" said a king.

"There should not have *been* excess bangles in that village!" said a queen.

"Do not blame *us* for that!" said a king. "It was *her* who made that village so strange!"

"It worked out very well for you with your never-dying lord there, has it not?" said a queen. "Why are you then complaining?"

"I will tell you why," said one of the kings. "Because we did not attempt to stop her. If it was not *you*, it had to be the girl herself! Every time she passes through an entryway, things do not go as expected. She did not even cross paths with the Never Veil the first time. Instead she somehow *turned back time* without our consent."

"*We* did not give her consent," snapped a queen. "Restarting a village without permission from both sides is such an affront to the rules—"

"Be careful what you say to them," whispered Ailill beside me, startling me. "They do not take kindly to lack of respect."

Jangmi's eyes were strangely on Ailill as he pulled away from me. She turned back to Adeyemi. "Might we settle this argument more peacefully?"

The rest of the kings and queens fell silent. Adeyemi cradled his chin with his hand. "Yes, perhaps we better. Let us retreat to the gardens to discuss their punishment. Ailill and Olivière's both."

They moved as one, circling around us to head to the open doorway.

"Wait," I said, and they actually paused. I tried to ignore Ailill's panicked face, and I clenched my fists, feeling the coin press into my palm. "You can't just..." I grimaced. "Whatever you decide, I'd like some answers first." I thought of Ailill's whispered warning. "Please."

Their faces went aghast, except for Jangmi's. She smiled coolly. "Then come with us to the garden, child." And they all went through the door.

Ailill spun on me as the last king stepped through, grabbing my shoulders and quietly shouting in a strained whisper, "What did I just tell you?"

"What are we here for then?"

Ailill ran a hand through his hair, his voice dropping. "We will get answers for you. I promise. But please, follow my lead. You have to be careful."

"Children!" called Adeyemi from the garden door. He gestured behind him. "Come and join us. We have agreed. We will heal you, refresh you—and then discuss your punishment."

Ailill held his palm out to me and gave me a weak smile. I took his hand in mine and squeezed it, and we stepped forward into the sunlight, our footsteps in tandem.

Chapter Fifteen

THE GREEN LIGHT COMING FROM Jangmi's fingers felt warm and comforting. I closed my eyes, and I could picture a little boy healing my wounds in the stocks, running that warmth over a bruise on my face. I opened one eye carefully, reminding myself that the "little boy" was sitting right next to me on a garden bench, getting his bumps and scratches healed by Adeyemi.

It was hard to remember Ailill as a little boy. It hadn't been anywhere near as long for me as it had been for him, but for the little time I knew him, I never imagined he would grow up to be the man who would find the goddess in me. I never imagined I would set that into motion.

In any case, though, it wouldn't have felt that long ago to Ailill, either, if he only remembered his first life. Every time I thought about the paler Ailill whom I'd fought with, pleaded with, even loved... I couldn't believe he hadn't remembered his previous lives. He seemed to live the pain of a hundred or more lives in isolation. It couldn't have all been the specters telling him about their own lifetimes.

"There," said Jangmi, drawing me out of my reverie. She crossed one leg over the other and folded her hands upon her lap. "I have restored your health completely."

"Thank you," I said, quieter than I meant to. I rubbed the back of my head absently, searching for evidence of the bump. There was none, other than the matting of my hair. I looked down at the strip of black cloth Ailill had used to wrap my head wound. It was soaked with a dark stain.

"We have finished here as well," spoke Adeyemi. "And just in time."

Marigold and Kin brought two trays of charred meat with roasted potatoes and carrots and set them in front of Ailill and me. I watched him tentatively and only picked up my fork to start eating once he did.

"Thank you." Ailill kept his head down. He was strangely meek beyond measure around these kings and queens, even if it was true that I'd yet to see him overly stubborn this rebirth at all.

"Thank you," I echoed, but I didn't put my head down. Instead, I let my gaze wander over the garden. I'd been right about the bushes. They weren't just different colored roses; they were different colored flowers. Flowers that had no business being on what I thought of as rose bushes to begin with—like the violet lily-covered bush a short distance in front of me.

"Now that that is settled," said Adeyemi, standing. "We must discuss what is to be done."

I laid down my spoon—golden, as was so much in this place—and opened my mouth to speak. I stopped when I felt Ailill's hand on my knee. He squeezed it but didn't tear his eyes from his plate. *Wait*, he seemed to be saying. *Listen.* His eyes weren't focused on his food. Instead, he was actually paying close attention to the kings' and queens' movements. I took a drink of unnaturally clear water from the golden goblet on my plate.

"Very well," said Jangmi. She stood as well, joining Chrysilla and Marigold in facing the kings. She looked at both of the women in turn, took note of their slight nods, and proceeded. "We think we should keep Olivière here, for study."

I choked on my sip, but the kings and queens paid me no mind. Ailill's hand squeezed harder.

"What is there to study?" demanded Estavan. "She is an anomaly. She should be removed from the game immediately!"

"Keeping her here for study *would* remove her from the game," said Chrysilla. She tossed her head back and clutched her hands together in front of her abdomen, the image of elegance.

"So would eliminating her," said Kin. He was the first to tear his eyes from the other rulers in order to look at me, and I felt a chilling menace in his gaze. I put my goblet down overly carefully.

"That is poor sport!" scoffed Marigold, whipping her hands to her hips. "After what we allowed for you, this man who never fully dies—"

Estavan stepped forward to meet her. "You *allowed* it because it was a woman who made it happen!"

Jangmi moved between them. "It is only fair, then. If Olivière is to die, then Ailill must too."

"Hold on!" I said, ignoring Ailill's pleading glance. "You can't heal us and feed us, just to kill us!" I pushed the tray forward, most of it untouched. My appetite was gone.

Adeyemi raised an eyebrow in my direction but soon turned back to Jangmi, my outburst unremarked upon. "Ailill cannot die. He has not fathered a child. We have yet to see if a lord or lady will replace him as that village's guardian."

"Oh?" said Jangmi, as if humoring him. "I thought you planned to anoint a new lord of that village. Is that not what you promised the interloper who stumbled upon a golden bangle and found his way here?"

Jurij. He wanted to be lord of the village? What in the name of the goddess for? What kinds of aspirations could he possibly have to lead the village, to live in the castle—

To get rid of Ailill.

"Where is Jurij?" I stood, ignoring Ailill's tug on my arm to sit down. "What have you promised him?"

Kin shook his head. "You see what I mean about her? She must be eliminated."

"She must be *studied*," said Marigold fiercely. "You really want to eliminate this anomaly, this pawn who has been able to affect the rules of the game, before we even know why or how she does it?"

"She puts us all in danger," insisted Estavan.

"Danger?" Chrysilla snorted. "Maybe if you are so weak that a pawn might pose a threat."

Estavan pointed a finger at her. "You only say that because she's a woman and her advantages are an advantage for you!"

"Enough!" I said, raising my voice. I ignored Ailill's whispers of my name—"Noll" again; I cringed—and pounded my palms against the table. "Where is Jurij?"

I finally had all of their attention. Jangmi exchanged a look with Adeyemi, and then nodded at Chrysilla. "Perhaps you best fetch the Lily Book," she told her, and Chrysilla left the garden.

Jangmi turned back to Adeyemi. "Your Majesty," she began, strangely addressing another ruler with the same title she might earn herself. "Perhaps we can agree at least that the village that produced these two is a win for both genders."

"*Your Majesty!*" said Marigold, appalled.

Jangmi lifted a finger in the air to stop her. "No. It is. Freewill led to gender equality in that village."

"But—" began Marigold.

Adeyemi jutted his chin outward. "You would dispense with the idea that it was a woman's power that caused the most impact in that village?"

Jangmi nodded. "If you will give up any conviction that it is your man who never dies who allows you sovereignty over that village."

I felt Ailill's hand grab mine. At some point he'd removed his gloves when Adeyemi had healed him, and his palm was cold and clammy. I tore my eyes from the bickering kings and queens to look at his face, and he looked paler than I'd seen him since this rebirth, almost like some of the life was draining right out of him. I didn't want to sit, but seeing him like that scared me, so I did.

"What is it?" I whispered.

Ailill simply shook his head and kept watching the scene unfolding, all pretense of eating his meal forgotten.

Then I realized. It was these kings and queens who allowed him to rebirth, somehow, even if it was me who'd ordered it. They held Ailill's fate in their hands even now. *"I grow weary of this life."* He hadn't wanted to come back, but he had. How did I reconcile that with this kinder, younger man who held my hand now?

"Your Majesty," said Estavan. "We have never had such an advantage in any village. If we concede defeat here..."

Adeyemi shook his head. "We will still have other villages. It has been so long since we have found one where there is equality—where a lord and lady both have a golden token. It is just one battle."

"It only takes one battle to turn the tide of the game," said Kin. "To allow *them* this advantage."

"They are sacrificing their very obvious advantage in this woman at the same time." Adeyemi's eyes fell on me. "It will be worth it."

"Good," said Jangmi, just as Chrysilla appeared through the doorway, a large book in hand. I knew immediately it was like the book we left back home on Ailill's stand, the book that showed what every villager was up to. Marigold and Estavan broke rank to sweep away the trays as Chrysilla laid the book down on the table in front of us. She flipped it open silently, pushing past pages of moving pictures until she reached one. She pushed the book closer to Ailill and me.

We both peered at the page. Jurij, back home in the village. Jurij... with Jaron in the castle, each with enough sheathed swords trundled under their arms to give half the village a weapon to fight with. To fight *who* with? What were those two up to?

I gasped, covering my mouth with my free hand. "What's he *doing*?"

"You asked where that pawn was," said Adeyemi. "We sent him back through the Never Veil, back to your village."

"Why does he have so many swords?" I demanded. I looked at Ailill. "You didn't dispose of them, even after what happened that night in the cavern?" I shook my head, exasperated at myself. "No, I should have done it. I should have told you. You didn't even remember the danger the men put us in, grabbing those relics from the village's past, swinging them around wildly—"

"Does not remember?" It was Kin who spoke, and he said it so condescendingly, I looked up immediately to glare at him. "Who does not remember?"

"Ailill," I said. "He doesn't remember his last life, and the specter of that life vanished before he told him about it."

Kin laughed, and it was the first time I saw a smile on his lips. It wasn't convivial. "He suffers no loss of memory at rebirth. I suppose it is not possible for a mere pawn's mind to recall everything in a lifetime, let alone over a hundred, but his last life would certainly be prominent in his mind. Especially one so eventful as that one."

My hand dropped Ailill's as a chill ran through my body. I looked at his face, ready for him to dispute what the smug king had told me. He said nothing, and he wouldn't even look at me. He stared ahead at the open book, watching the village. Always watching. Never forgetting.

And always lying to me.

Chapter Sixteen

EVERYTHING I THOUGHT TO BE true over the past few weeks was a lie. Everything I thought I could count on, everything that seemed to give me some semblance of hope, was stolen from me. Jurij had turned into someone else entirely, someone far beyond what his newfound freedom justified. And Ailill—this kinder, gentler Ailill, the one who seemed to forgive me for what I'd done to him as a child, the one who wasn't tainted by all that time we spent together in his castle... didn't exist.

He was *playing* with me.

I didn't know if my discomfort gave Kin or any of the others any more pleasure. I couldn't look up at them. I was too busy trying to bite back the tears that were forming in my eyes as I stared down at my hands, which I clutched together in my lap.

"If we are agreed," said Jangmi, "that this village is a tie, there is still the issue of what is to be done with them."

"I move we adjourn to the dining room," said Adeyemi. "We could use some food, and in any case, we shall not be able to discuss this in front of them without interruption."

I was too hurt just then to interrupt or to care what they did with me. What a stupid thing to think when my life could very well be in jeopardy, when the lives of the people I left behind were in danger in so many ways.

Ailill finally found it fit to break his silence. "Your Majesties," he said, rising, "if you would but permit us to go home..."

I shook my head. A tear fell and I used the back of my hand to wipe it away. "I haven't asked—"

Ailill held a hand out in front of my face to quiet me. "I did not realize our presence would be so unwelcome. Please."

The kings and queens moved to the garden door and filed through it without comment. Adeyemi was the last to exit, and he turned to Ailill. "You two will stay here. I will do what I can to save you."

"Save *her*," Ailill said, startling me. He walked over toward Adeyemi. "I know I do service to the kings, but please, consider her life. She has yet to live one, and I have had so many—"

"Stay put," said Adeyemi, and he shut the door. I heard what may have been a bolt closing on the other side of it—I didn't notice any lock beforehand, but the door had been open. It didn't matter. I wasn't foolish enough to think we could sneak out of the castles and get home. There was no way to get back there unless these people allowed it.

Ailill and I were left alone, the only sound the trickling of the water fountain, the only real movement Jurij and Jaron on the page in front of me. Ailill didn't join me again at the table, instead deciding it was the perfect time to stroll through the garden. I watched through blurry tears. My head ached with the effort of hiding them.

"Why," I started, feeling the word croak in my throat. "Why did you lie to me?"

Ailill acted as if he hadn't heard me. I might have believed him if it weren't so quiet.

The longer I stared at him, the more I saw the Ailill I knew. How could I have ever doubted it? How could I have not seen?

Ailill stopped beside a bush covered with violet lilies. He put his hands behind his back. "Come here, would you?"

As if he deserved to order me about. As if I was going to stand beside him and patiently wait for him to say whatever it was he had to say, what little he felt fit to tell me. I was so tired of these games between us.

"I hope you're not going to ignore my question." I stood and crossed the garden. "Although I doubt there's anything you could say that would make me..." Ailill pushed aside a few branches on the bush covered in lilies to reveal a smaller bush inside of it. It was almost like the impossible bush with the lilies was just the outer wrappings to a regular rose bush with white roses beneath it. I gritted my teeth. There was plenty about this place I didn't understand, but what I didn't understand the most was why Ailill had lied to me. After all we'd been through.

I grabbed his wrist and tugged it away from the bush, letting the lilies fall back into place. "Tell me!" I said, dropping his arm.

Ailill pushed aside the branches again and plucked a single white rose petal from a bloom. He held it out in his palm carefully and walked back to the table and benches, flipping through the pages.

I could feel the anger boiling over inside me. "What are you *doing*?" I demanded, approaching him. My eyes flitted to the open page, and I felt my breath hitch in my throat. My anger toward Ailill forgotten—at least for that moment—I pushed in beside him, my arm brushing against his, to get a better look.

It was Elfriede's page. And she wasn't with Mother or any of her friends, as I'd asked her to be. *She wanted to look for Jaron*, I remembered. Although now I had to wonder if she'd really wanted to look for Jurij. No matter. She'd found them both.

Elfriede was waiting in front of the cavern pool. I could see the ripples in the outlines of the water. She had her back to the pool, and she sat on a rock, her hands folded across her lap. She stared up at the two men, a tangle of swords on the ground beside her. I stared at the scene, trying to make sense of it. Had she seen Jurij go through the pool or come back from it? Had she helped Jaron and Jurij this whole time? Was she helping them now, or had she simply come across the scene, her intention of looking for one or either more innocently motivated? Oh, why couldn't we *hear* what they were saying?

"That is... actually not what I meant to show you," said Ailill, snapping me out of my reverie. "Not just yet. We have problems of our own here."

He thrust his hand, palm up, over the page. Then he grabbed the petal from his palm with the other hand and crushed it.

I didn't know what he meant to show me at first, but soon my attention was caught by the flutter of movement on the page below. Elfriede, her face frozen in horror, fell off the rock on which she was sitting, and Jurij dove forward to catch her. She landed on his torso. Jaron's knees buckled as he attempted to stay standing, his hands reaching out for the nearest stalagmite to steady him. The swords began spreading out on the ground, as if someone was tilting the entire book, and the village along with it. The ripples on the water became splashes, like someone had jumped into the surface, even though no one had.

Then it stopped. The three figures stared at each other, each more perplexed than the next. Jurij, frozen in place, lingered with his arms around Elfriede's shoulders for a moment before she pushed him away and stood, slapping her skirt, and sending little specks of dust flying.

I pulled the book closer and began flipping the pages. Every page showed a mess: pots and pans on the ground; spilled bowls of stew; tables and chairs turned over. Every face had the same expression of shock and wonder.

"Did you do this?" I demanded, glaring at Ailill.

He recoiled at my stare. "Ye-Yes," he said, regaining composure. He tossed the crumpled petal on the table beside the book. "That is how the earthquakes were created," he added. "Whenever I left the castle."

"You could have hurt somebody!" I flipped through the pages quickly, but I saw none that were burning up like my father's had. None that showed anyone with any alarming injuries. I frowned as I reached my mother's page and saw the group around Sindri. Darwyn and Tayton were no longer among them.

"You are right. I did not think—"

"No, you didn't. After all our village has been through, the last thing it needs is more grief and danger." I kept flipping toward the back, looking for Darwyn or Tayton.

"You would make a better lady than I do a lord, despite the best of my efforts in the past few weeks," said Ailill. He spoke quietly. "Noll," he said with more authority, and the name seemed especially strange on his tongue, knowing that there was no need for him to pretend anymore that he'd known me better by my other name. He grabbed me by both shoulders and spun me around to face him, making me drop my search through the pages. "Please. I apologize. But you need to listen to me right now."

Looking into his eyes was a mistake, I knew that the moment I found myself staring into his dark gaze. I faltered under those pleading eyes, only remembering to grab his hands and pry them off of me a moment too late. "Are you going to tell me why you lied to me?" I said, looking at his shoulder instead of his face. "Because that's the only thing I want to hear right now."

"You are wrong about that." He took a deep breath and ran a hand over his hair. "I will tell you all I know about the kings and queens." He paused, waiting for me to try to stop him, but I found myself meeting his eyes again. "And the risk we took in coming to this place."

Chapter Seventeen

ILILL CHOSE THE *PERFECT* TIME for another stroll through the gardens. He had me eagerly awaiting his words, but instead he broke away from me, choosing that moment to run his hand over the strange-flowered bushes around the edges of the garden.

I stood my ground, my arms crossed, refusing to move.

"Each of these bushes," said Ailill at last, his hand lingering on a bright yellow flower. "Represents a village." He paused, letting go of the colorful bloom.

I bit my lip, surveying the garden. There had to be at least two dozen bushes, each with a strange-looking flower. "The lilies," I said, lingering on the bush with the bloom I recognized from home. "Violet lilies dot our fields in the warmer months, so that one represents us."

"Yes!" said Ailill, like he was a tutor with a very smart student. I felt a little condescended to, but I didn't remark on it. He pushed aside the branches of the bush he stood by, revealing black roses. I winced, thinking of what even damaging one petal had done back home. "The roses you find beneath the outer layer of flowers match the rose bushes in each village's castle. Black for queens," he said, letting the branches fall back into place. He stepped back over to the violet lily bush and pushed those branches aside.

"White for kings." He frowned, staring at our village's bush before letting go of the greenery. "They have fought a long time over our village," he said. "It remains white for the kings because I am lord of it, but the power has clearly shifted from men to women a thousand years before."

"When I visited the village of the past." I swallowed hard. "When you first met me."

"Yes," said Ailill, and a flush spread over his face. He seemed paler than I remembered him since the rebirth. Nowhere near as pale as he was when I first knew him, but did he grow paler over time until he turned as white as a specter?

Ailill tossed his head back, ignoring the issue of what I had done in the past. "The point at which you met me, as the kings later told me, was precisely a thousand years into their game. And precisely a thousand years ago."

"*How* did I do that?" I asked. "Did the kings and queens send me there?"

Ailill shook his head. "They have no idea—or at least, they both claim to have no idea. I doubt the kings had anything to do with it. I am not as familiar with the queens, but I believe they had nothing to do with it, either."

I reached my fingers into my pocket and rubbed them across the coin. "I don't understand."

Ailill waved a hand and began to pace again through the garden. Instead of following the path in a circle, he merely walked a few steps back and forth. "Let us put that issue aside for now. As essential as it is to our fate and all that has happened to us, you must fully understand what I know first." He stopped walking and tucked his hands behind his back. "These people who live here in this barren place, they call themselves kings and queens."

I knew as much already. But there was a reason Ailill was reminding me of that now. "Like the made up stories," I said. "The ones that inspired me to think of myself as the 'little elf queen.'" I felt hot with embarrassment.

The corner of Ailill's lips twitched into a smile, like he genuinely was amused I'd said it aloud. "That is news to me," he said, and I realized I'd never fully explained my childhood delusion to him.

"Did you ever watch me as a child?" I asked. "Through the pages of the book?"

Ailill shook his head. "Not that I remember. I was in a bad place at that point. I hardly ever observed the villagers."

"Not that you *remember*?" I said, not willing to let that issue go. He frowned, realizing his choice of words, but I decided to save that conversation until this one was over. I sighed. "In any case. I used to pretend I was a queen who led retainers out on quests to slay monsters. We used sticks as swords—it never occurred to any of us that these things called 'swords' actually existed, let alone that they were holed up inside the castle."

"There was no need for them in our village anymore," said Ailill. "With the men's freedom of thought limited, there was no call for any tools that had no use."

I cocked my head. "Why is that, anyway? Why were women incapable of wielding swords? Why didn't they boss men around with swords at their sides, like the men did with them when you were a child?"

"I never said women were incapable of wielding swords. I thought you of all people would remember that, and the dagger my sister plunged through my brother's back." He winced.

I'd never spoken to Ailill about Elric. I wondered if even after all of these years, the pain of what the man had inflicted on him was still fresh.

"In any case, once those women died out, no even before that..." Ailill seemed lost in thought. "Women seem to find less use for them. Most women. If life is especially peaceful, their minds do not wander to violence."

"But men's do?" I thought of Jaron and Jurij, and whatever mischief they were up to now. I wondered if Elfriede was truly part of it.

"More often than women's. There are exceptions on both sides, but that is the general case. Something to do, I believe, with the natural state of man and woman, some piece inside men that women do not share."

I thought about that, but I was a terrible example. I'd spent my childhood whacking animals and stones with a stick, imagining the edge of a sword breaking through monstrous flesh. I'd goaded my friends, my *boy* friends, into the violence. They may not have had their complete freedom, but they had not yet found their goddesses, so they still had some minds of their own. Some were eager to take part in the pretend carnage, but others almost had to be forced into it. Jurij was one of them. Jurij, who'd hit me on the head with his sword's hilt...

"What about *these* men and women," I asked, deciding not to dwell on my own past just yet. "Are they prone to violence?"

Ailill laughed, and it wasn't out of joviality. He put a hand on his hip. "No, they will not take up a sword and stab each other, although they seem to desire it every waking moment of their existences. They agreed never to resort to violence in their war. No violence to each other, anyway. They leave that to the villages." He nodded at me. "Those stories you told each other as children, the ones that inspired you to playact as a violent queen? They are all the knowledge that remains of the kings and queens in the villages to all but the lords and ladies who rule over them. They are the history of a war between kings and queens that began long before the game ever started. Before the game, they were legion, and they took swords to one another's armies of subjects, thousands, maybe millions of people who once lived in places ruled by a king or queen. Now three of each such ruler remains, and they made a pact to fight through other methods."

"But *why*?" I asked, bewildered. "And what do you mean 'subjects'? What of these 'armies'?"

The corner of Ailill's lips turned up in a hesitant smile. "I cannot tell you for certain. It was long before my time. Over the years, between rebirths, the kings told me some of their history. There were many people in this land once. Many more than we know in our village."

I had to sit down. I went back to the table, reaching out behind me for balance as I lowered myself onto the bench. I couldn't keep everything straight. I didn't know what was important to know. "You come here between each rebirth?"

Ailill nodded, putting his hand behind his back and taking up his slow, deliberate pacing again. "We all come here when we pass." He paused. "This may be hard for you to grasp—I could not myself at first—but people are not meant to vanish at death. When they died here, long ago, in the age of the wars of kings and queens, they simply lay there, gone in spirit but not in body."

"What?" I cradled my forehead. "What do you mean?"

"Like livestock," said Ailill. He started pacing again. "No, that sounds terrible. But you know how the animals are still *there* after death."

"They have to be!" I grimaced at the thought of the farmers and butchers at work.

"They leave behind their flesh so we can eat it," Ailill added. "And so people, too, are meant to leave behind their flesh."

"So someone can eat it?" I nearly choked.

"No!" Ailill laughed softly. "No. No one eats them. They are just meant... to return to the land."

I let my eyes flit to the table behind me, to the open book. It showed a young woman I didn't fully recognize cleaning up the things that had tumbled over in her home. I let my fingers caress the pages, hesitating to flip through the book and pick up my search for Darwyn and Tayton, to check in with Jaron, Jurij and Elfriede. "They come here," I said. "And meet the kings and queens?"

"Yes," said Ailill. "The lords and ladies of the villages are given a golden token. A bangle from our village, perhaps something different from elsewhere. I have not met any others. I do know they are all allowed to go through the Never Veil and meet the kings and queens while still living when summoned—*if* they are summoned. For most, vanishing after death is their first time meeting them. And they do not remember them after."

I spun my head around. "What do you mean 'after'? Are you saying..." I stood, my heart thundering in my chest. "My father is alive?"

Ailill put a hand out and approached me. "No! No, you must not get your hopes up... *He* is not alive, you must understand."

I threw my hands up in the air. "I *don't* understand! You're telling me he—everyone who's ever died and vanished, Ingrith, Nissa's parents, your own family, your *brother*—came here at death and met the kings and queens. But they are not alive and do not remember. How can they 'not remember' if they are not alive?"

Ailill sighed and ran a hand through his hair. "They are reborn in their own ways. Not like how I was. There are a limited number of spirits, souls of the people who were once the subjects of the kings and queens when the games began, and the kings and queens reuse them for their game."

"'*Reuse*' them?" I could feel my face curling into a sneer at the repugnant way he described what was going on here.

Ailill gestured around him at the many bushes. "They are reborn—as infants, not as a newly-grown man as I am—in other villages, out of the reach of those who knew them before. They remember nothing of who they once were. Nothing. They cannot be considered who they were."

I didn't even feel my knees weaken before I was halfway to the ground. Ailill rushed in to steady me, but my knees clashed painfully against the stone beneath my feet before he could.

Chapter Eighteen

AILILL HAD GUIDED ME GENTLY to the bench at the table after my wave of dizziness, and we sat there now side by side in near silence. The kings and queens had yet to return, and Ailill seemed to think I was too overwhelmed to hear more of this bizarre fantasy—that I was too overwhelmed to handle my entire view of life and the village and everything torn down stone by stone. Perhaps he was right. I hadn't meant to fall, but my body clearly was less eager to learn than my mind was.

Still. Things made sense at last. The pain we experienced wasn't entirely my fault. And Father... was out there somewhere. No matter what Ailill thought, I considered him to be alive. That made me feel warm all over.

"Do you think your knees are bleeding?" Ailill looked down at my lap. "Or did you just bruise them? Is it all right if I..." He hesitated, his hands in the air above my knees.

We didn't have time to inspect for cuts and bruises. I grabbed his hands and laid them on my lap to draw his attention back to me. "Tell me more," I said, as hard and steady as I could.

"Do you think we should?" Ailill's gaze flicked to the garden door, but my eyes didn't follow. "You are not at full strength, and they could be back at any moment—"

"All the more reason." The touch of his hands on my thigh, where I'd placed them myself, was light and awkward, almost as if he feared his hands lingering there. I decided not to press him on the subject of rebirths any further, at least not yet. "So the villages are a game for the kings and queens?"

"Yes," said Ailill with a sigh. "That chess game we played together... It is an analogy for the war of the kings and queens."

I raised an eyebrow. "Even though the queen pieces had all the power?"

Ailill smirked. "True. Yet the game marches on even if she falls. The whole thing revolves around the king. You stumbled upon one of the arguments between the kings and queens already."

"Okay," I said, feeling the clamminess in my grip on the back of Ailill's hand. I wouldn't let it go just yet. "It still seems a strange imbalance of power if the game is to establish whose rule is superior."

Ailill tilted his head slightly, his gaze fixed on the bushes a short distance in front of us. "Perhaps the rules are different in the villages where a lady rules instead of a lord. That is just how I know the game, and there have only ever been lords of our village, back to the start of creation."

"The lord—you—hardly played a role in the village for a thousand years. I'm not sure if that counts." I grimaced as I said the words, waiting for the rebuke.

"You are correct," said Ailill instead, attempting a smile. "Our village is a mystery to the kings and queens. They have argued for a thousand years which gender truly has the upper hand there."

"With men devoting their entire lives to women, and women having the power to kill unloved men with a glance?

I'd have to say women ruled that one." I wiped the sweat on my palm off on my skirt.

"You sound like a queen." Ailill's hands lingered a moment longer on my lap, and he pulled them slowly away, twisting his torso away from me. "The kings argued that since no true lady presented herself to rule, that since I ruled and was immortal, the balance of power tipped in their favor."

I winced as my palm clutched at one of my sore knees. "And now women certainly don't have an advantage over men regardless."

"You know," said Ailill quietly. "That has happened before. The kings and queens created an even number of villages, half ruled by lords and half by ladies. They sometimes tweak a village based on the outcome of a small skirmish or an idea to prove superiority. Over time, sometimes a lord and lady will rule side by side."

I met his eyes then and felt my face flushing, so I focused on my knees, which stung even beneath the skirt. "And what do these kings and queens think of those villages? Which gender is superior then?"

Ailill shrugged and clutched his hands to his own knees. "They never decide that. A lifetime for the pawn in their games is but a small time for them. Eventually, when free will reigns, chaos descends. Eventually one gender or the other takes power in a village, almost like a violent reflection of these kings and queens who silently rule over them."

"So what happened in our village during your childhood... Wasn't such an anomaly."

"There you are wrong." Ailill patted his hands on his knees a few times. "*You* made it different. No king or queen gave you permission to travel to the past. I do not even think either group can *do* that."

That was unsettling news. He was being so good at explaining the bizarre nature of everything that I was hoping he'd have some explanation for what was most bizarre about me. "I don't understand." I brushed that too-long piece of hair behind my ear, but it flopped back forward immediately.

"Neither do they." Ailill lifted a hand to my head and I flinched back instinctively. "I am sorry," he said, his hand faltering. "I only meant to..." Steeling himself, he reached forward and tucked that same strand of hair behind my ear. "This," he said, and I felt his soft fingertips dance across the top of my ear.

I almost died right then and there. It was like he was doing what I imagined doing to Jurij, to him—to the men of the village—whenever I stared too long at their pointed ears.

Ailill's touch was brief, and I felt both relief and disappointment as he pulled his hands back. I clenched my knees hard, using the soreness to snap myself back awake.

"You have ears like they do," he said.

I wasn't sure I was following. I resisted the urge to caress my own ears. "Like all women do?" I asked. "I noticed the kings here have ears without points as well as the queens, but surely that doesn't mean much."

Ailill stood up from the bench quickly, making me jump in place. "It means *quite* a lot." He gestured around him at the garden. "Every one of these villages is filled with pointy-eared pawns. Only the kings and queens have no edges atop their ears. They are quite proud of the difference, I must tell you, as if that small thing is enough to prove they are a superior race. They consider our people, these people they created out of their former subjects, 'elves,' although they call us 'pawns' or 'children' more than anything. Which is why you insisting you were a 'little elf queen' amused me." His voice drifted off. "I wonder how you even knew that term..."

I scrunched my nose up. "What are you talking about? Every woman in our village has rounded ears—"

"Because of *you*." Ailill bent over the table, reaching over my shoulder to grab something behind me. His gloves, which he'd removed for Adeyemi's healing. "The women in our village when I was a child had pointed ears. Do you not remember?"

He was right. I'd noticed it immediately, but it was soon forgotten when there was so much else to consider, especially when women often wore their hair covering their ears anyway. "But... What has that to do with me?"

Ailill slipped on one of his gloves. "That is something the kings and queens would like to know. When you made those proclamations about the rules of the village, they decided to go along with it and see what would happen." He tugged on the bottom of his glove and began pulling on the second. "They chose to send me back to our village each time I died. They caused the earthquakes when I left the castle or when a woman looked at it."

I frowned. "I'm surprised they would allow that, if I went back in time without their permission."

He tugged hard on the second glove. "They fought about that. As they fight about everything. But they thought it different enough—*interesting* enough—to see what would happen."

"Even though I gave the women such an advantage?"

"In *every* village, one gender or the other has an advantage or two to see if it makes a difference in the overall war. They decide who gets to pick which advantage via games of chess, and then let free will of the pawns decide whether those advantages prove useful or not. In one village, the women are physically stronger than the men. In another, the kings tell me, the men can sing songs that lull those around them to sleep..."

I raised an eyebrow. *That* sounded terrifying.

Ailill noticed my expression and laughed a little. "Our village was initially meant to start the men off at an advantage. Each man was to be born incredibly beautiful, and with the power to heal—both of which you neutralized, by covering the men's faces and by ending their healing power."

So I wasn't just imagining those lovely faces... I blushed when Ailill caught me staring at him.

"I didn't mean to end the healing," I said, ignoring the distracting trail of my thoughts. "That would have come in handy. Wait—*I* neutralized? If *they* enforced my words, what does that have to do with me and the women of our village having rounded ears?"

"You made each woman a goddess. That word, another word you should not have known, was from the world as it was before the games began."

"I knew it because *everyone* knew it."

"Yes, but you created a paradox of sorts. No one would know what to call someone who is to be worshipped if not for you traveling back through the ages."

I frowned. "So are these kings and queens... goddesses?"

"*Gods* and goddesses, in a fashion. It's what they consider their race, but they prefer their titles of 'kings and queens.'" He sighed. "In any case, the women born after your decree all had rounded ears, and the kings and queens have not been happy with that."

"Don't they determine things like that? Didn't *they* enforce my decrees and make unloved men vanish whenever a woman caught sight of their faces?"

"No," said Ailill, quietly. He tucked his hands beneath his back and looked down. "They have no way of telling who loves whom. I do not think them capable of such a thing as love."

"But then what—" I cut myself off, my throat constricting. So I couldn't just blame them for what I'd done—it was me after all. Me who sent those men to their doom. "Tell me those men got reborn into other villages at least!"

"They did." Ailill frowned. "Still, the flames in men's eyes, those are not something the kings or queens gave them. They have no idea where that came from or how something was able to measure love and make these decisions for them. In fact, the queens hardly know whether or not to champion you, as they can hardly influence you themselves, and that might prove dangerous to them. But they have put their hopes in you so far, acquiescing to my frequent—frequent in terms of their life spans, that is—trips back here for rebirth because you yourself willed it. Otherwise, that is clearly a kings' advantage."

I laughed pitifully. "The kings hate me, don't they?"

"The kings and queens are no friend to anyone but themselves. But yes. The kings have argued that you have broken the rules of the games for a millennium now, and they wanted to take you out of the games entirely—but they couldn't until recently, until you were born. I do not think they recognized your spirit in any other form. I wonder even if your spirit existed in any other life before this one. They have not shared that information with me."

That was a strange thought. It was all strange. Was time a straight line to these unseen rulers? Did they see me appear in the past version of my village with no knowledge of who I was, or were they here with me in the present and there in the past simultaneously? It had to be a line, though, otherwise they would have been unable to account for my presence for a thousand years. I would never understand it. Maybe I didn't need to understand that much. Maybe I didn't want to.

And "recently," he'd said. I supposed almost eighteen years prior was recently enough for these immortals. "Yet the queens want to keep me alive?"

Ailill's brow scrunched together. "I would not trust them, either. I think they fear your power but are loath to admit it to the kings."

"And they clearly are not *your* supporters."

"No, they are not. Noll, you are bleeding." He sat back down beside me and lifted my skirt without hesitation. I was too surprised to stop him, and if it weren't for the fact that he found my knees to be a bloody, bruised mess, I would have been embarrassed to think of him seeing so much of my legs.

Ailill reached for the bottom of his torn shirt again, but I put a hand out to stop him. "No. At my rate of injury this journey, you'll be half naked before sunset." I ripped the hem of my skirt and used it to dab the knees gently. The caked blood made the wounds look far worse than they were, but even so, I winced.

"Allow me." Ailill removed his gloves again and set them beside him on the bench. He gently cupped his hands around my hand clutching the bloodied scrap and my hand went limp, allowing him to swoop in and take over.

I watched him dab for a time, and then he stood up, dunked the scrap in the fountain and wrung it out before returning. Instead of sitting back beside me, he got on his own knees in front of me on the ground and proceeded to wipe the wounds carefully. His face was at a height just above my knees and I found myself pushing my hands between my thighs, desperate to make sure the fabric of the skirt kept everything from his view.

"It is not bad," Ailill said, his voice a bit shaky and his eyes carefully not lifting from where they looked down at my knees. "After wiping away the blood, I can see that most of it is already healed. I am sure the queens will heal you if we ask—"

I grabbed his wrist, keeping my other hand carefully plunged between my legs. "What am I?" I asked, not caring whether or not they healed my scratches, especially considering they might not let me go home or even live. "What am I, then?" I had to know.

Ailill's face twisted like I'd slapped him, as if it caused him pain to deliver the news to me. "You are Noll. Olivière, Gideon the Woodcarver's daughter—a Woodcarver herself. The woman who was once my goddess." He took the scrap of fabric from the hand I clutched and tossed it on the ground, grabbing my own wrist in his hand. "Beyond that, beyond all of that that makes you even more extraordinary, I do not know."

I blinked and felt tears dotting my eyes. I couldn't even explain why I was crying if he'd asked. "And what are *you*?"

Ailill dropped my wrist, and I dropped his. He stood and looked away. "Nothing special."

"That's a lie!" I spoke so loud, I startled myself. "You said yourself you're the only one who's reborn into the same life—"

"I am a pet of sorts of the kings', I must admit." Ailill put his hands on his hips. "I have seen them so many times, and I remember them—they're not used to that. I even spent a month here after you looked at my face before you loved me."

I nearly jumped in my seat. "That month when the village was so altered! It wasn't a dream! How—where were my parents then? Where was the castle?"

Ailill cocked his head and smiled. "They were all here. The castle was even here, out there in the canyon. Everything came here to this limbo between rebirths. No one was sent on their way because the kings and queens were waiting to see if you were going to do what they already knew you *had* done, and go back and finish what you'd started in the past. Just don't expect any of those lost during that time to remember. No one from the village but you or I seems to remember that month clearly, no matter where they were."

I felt sick and strange. There was so much to absorb. So much to finally understand. I fretted with my skirt anxiously, covering my knees again with the torn material.

Ailill sat back down beside me, taking my hand in his, running his fingers lightly over my open palm. "Olivière, whatever specialness there is about me, *you* gave it to me. I was a pawn. I was nothing. I was lost and in pain, and *you* made me special."

I met his eyes, smiling slightly. "You called me 'Olivière' again."

"Would you prefer I called you 'Noll'?"

I shook my head. "No. No... At first I didn't like that you called me that, but every time you've called me 'Noll' since, I missed it. My name sounds so lovely on your tongue. Like it belongs to this special woman who isn't me, but whom you believe to be me."

Ailill laughed softly. "There is no argument that you are a special woman, Olivière, or that you deserve your own name. I just worried my reliance on it when so many others call you by your name of choice would make you suspect..." He stopped, biting his lip.

It'd finally come back to this.

"Why," I said, taking my hand out of his, "if you remembered everything the whole time, did you wait to tell me any of this here? I know you said I'd have to have a golden token to know, but I've had one for weeks."

"I thought it best that you *see*. That you understand what we are up against."

"'Up against'? Are *we* at war with *them*—"

Ailill reached out to cover my mouth, his eyes darting to the garden door. "No. Not now. Not *here*."

"You waited until we got here to tell me everything else..." My sentence cut short. Ailill's eyes widened and I heard the creak of the garden door behind me.

I turned around to face whatever was coming for me.

Chapter Nineteen

"WE HAVE COME TO A decision," said Jangmi. She entered at the same time as Adeyemi through the open garden door, the other kings and queens following in perfectly matched lines behind them. Marigold and Estavan shut the door behind them.

Why were there clearly leaders even among them?

Adeyemi clasped his hands together as he and Jangmi came to a stop in front of the bench where we sat. "We shall return you both to your village."

I felt a tension in my muscles that I hadn't even realized I'd had release. Even Ailill relaxed somewhat beside me, although his back was still stiff.

I felt I should thank them—but for what? I hadn't done anything *knowingly* against them. I hadn't known who *they* were. I couldn't help it if I'd broken rules I didn't know existed. I reached into my pocket to clutch my coin. "Thank you," I said stiffly. "But before—"

"However," said Jangmi, not acknowledging my gratitude. "There is one condition: Olivière is never to return here and never to travel through the Never Veil to anywhere, to any place—or time—ever again." She reached a palm out. "We could not agree whether or not what you possessed qualified as a token, but you are to leave that piece of gold here."

"Wait a minute!" I stood, ignoring Ailill's hand as it shot out to tug at my elbow. "Look, I have no *intention* of leaving the village. I never did. I don't know how I did so to begin with. Still, there may be reasons I should keep this token, problems that occur in my village—"

"There will be no *reasons*," snapped Estavan, taking a step forward. "You are not to assume the position of 'lady' in your village. You are not even to wed Ailill, nor bear him future lords." His snarling face was like a kick to the gut. Not that I'd been *thinking* of that. Not that I was ready for that, or sure how things stood between Ailill and me, but... My eyes traveled down to Ailill, who sat behind me, his hand letting go of my elbow, his eyes downcast. Estavan continued unabated. "You may live a life alone in your cottage or wed one of the other pawns, if you so choose, but you are to live within the confines of the rules of this game."

Adeyemi raised a hand and stopped him from speaking further. "She does not need to know anything more about the rules of this game. She will do her part as nothing more than a pawn or there will be greater consequences. Now please. The gold."

My eyes flit to the queens one by one, and I saw little evidence of emotion. They were confident, smug even. Not at all upset that I was to give over all semblance of power. Perhaps they'd decided that I was too unpredictable to have even on the side of women.

I brought my fist out of my pocket, but I didn't reach it out to Jangmi's waiting hand just yet. "My friends," I said.

"Olivi—" started Ailill quietly, but I continued.

"My family. The reason I was so eager to see you was because they are in danger at the hands of Ailill's servants for discussing Ailill's rebirth."

"As they should be," said Marigold, her nose wrinkling. "The last thing we need is pawns who know too much spreading rumors."

I clutched my coin tightly at my side. "It's not their fault they noticed his changes after his rebirth! It would be the same in any time in our village, if only Ailill had made himself known to the people there. They would have noticed he changed, especially if he died of natural causes as an old, pale man before reappearing as a dark, young one."

My plea for reason made no impression on them. "They know now, I trust, there are consequences to their actions?" asked Kin. I nodded. "Then they shall watch themselves and all shall be fine. You should be grateful we allow them to live even without them uttering a word."

"And yet Jurij—you let him know everything!" I shrieked. "You let him *come* here! What did you *say* to him?"

"I still do not like the idea of a new lord, either," said Chrysilla, ignoring the crux of my question.

"It is better than letting *that one* continue as he has been," interrupted Marigold. "Why was he allowed to come back, even after Olivière's curse was lifted?"

My curse. My chest tightened at the sound of that.

"We have already gone over this." Kin extended an accusing finger toward Marigold. "Ailill's resurrection was something *we all* agreed to. It was not connected to whatever it is that *this one* did. It was *we* who sent him back each time!"

"Why Jurij?" I demanded, not willing to give up until I had answers. "What do you have planned for him?"

"Will you look at her!" Estavan gestured toward me. "She keeps acting as if she were a player in this game!"

Jangmi, her palm still out toward me, raised her other hand toward the others to hush them. "She is not. She knows she is not," she said quietly. "Now give me the token."

"'Token'?" repeated Adeyemi. He watched Jangmi curiously. "I thought we agreed it would not count as a token."

"I misspoke," replied Jangmi, coolly. "I apologize."

Kin sneered. "Misspoke? I *told* you it was they who sent that coin, against the rules—"

"We did no such thing!" shouted Chrysilla. "And I will thank you not to lie like that again!"

"We have had this discussion," said Jangmi sternly. "The piece of gold, please."

I reached my fist out toward her slowly, still afraid to let this chance pass me by.

A rattling, shaking noise caught my attention, and I turned, looking at the garden door. Without even opening, the door went black, and the edges of a long black veil seemed to flow through it, fluttering like in a breeze. A woman stepped through the door, collapsing to the ground. I jumped in place and felt Ailill swoop in behind me, grabbing my shoulders. "Stand back," he whispered in my ears.

The kings and queens pushed past me, the coin still clutched in my fist forgotten. They gathered around the crumpled figure on the ground. She was young, *naked*, and she looked not at all like someone from my village. She had long, golden hair, and pointed ears. Her skin was as pale as Ailill's had been, or as Marigold's. She looked up at the kings and queens gathered around her, her eyes wide and frightened.

"Where... am I?" she croaked. "Dreaming...?"

"You are not dreaming," said Jangmi, and she bent down to wrap an arm around the woman's shoulders. "Your life has come to an end."

"What?" The woman allowed Jangmi to pull her up until she was standing, and her face flittered between all of the kings and queens around her, even stopping at Ailill and me. She seemed to be pleading with me to explain everything to her. Jangmi guided her to the bench and sat her down. The woman cradled her head. Noticing her nudity, she tried to cover her breasts with her arms and clutched her thighs tightly together, but there was no hiding her vulnerability.

"My child!" she said. "What happened to my child?"

Adeyemi turned to Kin and Chrysilla. "The tulip book. Quickly. To offer her some solace."

The king and queen grabbed hold of the door—now a plain garden door and no longer a dark veil—and stepped outside of it.

The woman was trembling. I turned around to face Ailill. "Your jacket," I whispered, removing it from my arms. "Please."

Ailill gripped my hands, stopping me. "No. You cannot," he said urgently. "Do not interfere, they will not be happy with you—"

"I'm not *interfering*," I said. I removed my hands from his grip and continued peeling away his jacket. "I just can't let her sit there like that with no comfort." This time he let me take it off, although he was frowning.

I stepped around Marigold to offer the woman Ailill's jacket, draping it around her shoulders. I didn't dare slip her arms into it for her, but just having the material over her exposed torso seemed to lift her spirits slightly.

"There." I smiled. "It's not much, but I hope it'll make you more comfortable." I couldn't imagine sitting on that cold stone bench without clothing. I had half a mind to tear my dress off and offer her the whole thing, the men present be damned.

"Thank you," the woman said, the pain evident even through her smile. "Who are you? I feel like I've met you before."

"*No one*," said Marigold curtly, pushing me aside and behind her. Ailill quickly grabbed my arm and pulled me farther out of the way, but I hadn't missed the anger on Marigold's features. "*We* are your rulers, child. We six." She pointed to Jangmi and the remaining kings, to the open garden doorway as Chrysilla and Kin stepped back through it. Kin held a book, while Chrysilla had her hands positioned awkwardly behind her back.

"We found it," said Kin, flipping through the pages of his book. He held the open book out to the woman.

146

The woman looked at Kin curiously before her gaze fell to the book. She gasped, putting a hand to her mouth, the jacket tumbling open, exposing her chest again, but her shame was forgotten. There were tears in her eyes. "Helewise... Oh, Helewise—"

"Your child," said Jangmi calmly. She stood with her hands behind her back, displaying no emotion. She glanced at the page and nodded. "She survived the fall, even if you did not."

"Good," said the woman, and she reached out to touch the page. I wished I could see it. I imagined a child beside a cliff or mountain, the clothing the woman had left behind all that remained of her mother. "Good," repeated the woman. She sounded tired. "There's Bradyn," she whispered. "He wasn't far behind. You must be strong. Raise our girl well."

Jangmi nodded at Chrysilla, who stepped forward. I still didn't understand why she clutched her hands so high behind her back—and then I saw the sword she'd kept hidden there. She raised it above her head, holding it downward like a gigantic dagger over the seated woman.

"No!" I shrieked, and Ailill grabbed me tightly around the waist, pulling me back.

Chrysilla brought the sword down, piercing the woman through the base of her throat.

Chapter Twenty

*T*HE JACKET SLUMPED TO THE bench, its wearer gone. Marigold glared at me for a moment, but I didn't care. My eyes were watering, and the strength in my legs was giving out.

"Watch," whispered Ailill. "Do not despair."

It was a strange thing to tell me. I was in such shock from the sight, but I blinked away the tears as Ailill's hands released me, his supporting grip shifting to my shoulders. I felt almost naked without his touch lately. When had it come to that? Chrysilla gently placed the sword down on the table beside the book that showed my village, just as Kin placed the woman's village's book on the table's surface. There was a violet light—a mist almost—in the air around the jacket, and Adeyemi and Jangmi stepped forward, their hands extended.

"Return, spirit, to your rulers," said Adeyemi and Jangmi in unison. The other kings and queens stepped back and Jangmi and Adeyemi stepped in tandem toward the fountain, their hands still clutching the light somehow between them. They paused before the fountain. "Return now, to the game. Find your way to your new home." They both extended their arms toward the trickling stream and the light vanished, almost like it was sucked into the movement of the water.

"The orchids!" called Chrysilla, and she stepped back so they could all stare at one of the bushes. It glowed bright with a violet light and rustled as if someone were shaking it. Then it stilled. Jangmi and Adeyemi turned to Chrysilla and Kin respectively and nodded, and both the shorter queen and king left through the garden door, taking the sword and book with them.

"She has been born again," said Ailill quietly. "As a different person in a different village."

I stepped away from Ailill, and he let me go this time. I wasn't at all comforted by the news, or what I'd seen. The woman had seen the sword coming for her. Her mouth had opened, her terror evident. She'd died violently *twice* within moments. I sat down numbly on the bench where she'd sat, noting the new rip at the neck of Ailill's jacket.

"It is a boy this time!" I heard Kin before I saw him coming back, a book in his hands. Chrysilla followed, frowning.

Adeyemi and Estavan exchanged a look of triumph. The disappointment on Marigold's face was evident, but Jangmi did little but nod her head toward the men. "Congratulations," she said. "May he bring you some advantage."

"Not likely in the orchid village," muttered Marigold, and she actually caused Jangmi to raise an eyebrow at her. "What?" she demanded, putting her hands on her hips. "It is a lady's village."

"And that could change at any moment," said Estavan.

I grew tired of all their bickering. I had no idea how Ailill had ever put up with them for his "frequent" visits. I had enough of them to last my entire life and then some.

All this time, even when I laid the jacket around the woman's shoulders, I hadn't let the golden coin out of my fist. Even now I clutched Ailill's jacket to my chest with two fingers.

"Back to the matter at hand," said Adeyemi, and all six of them shuffled back into place around me, Kin dropping the second book off on the table. Ailill hovered nervously behind the queens, now kept from me thanks to their semicircle.

I felt the coolness of the gold in my hand. "I'll give it to you," I said, taking note of Jangmi's extended hand. "And I'll stay away from the pool in the cavern and the hole behind the throne." My eyes darted nervously to Ailill's, and I could see he was pleading. Probably pleading for me to say no more, but was he going to accept what they demanded of me? Of him? Wasn't he worried about their plans with Jurij? I held my hand out toward Jangmi's palm, but I didn't drop the coin just yet. "But I refuse to allow you to dictate my life. I refuse to allow you to do whatever it is you have planned with Jurij."

Jangmi's usually calm and collected features twisted into a sneer. "You foolish child."

The other kings and queens broke out into chaos, each louder than the other, each repeating the same arguments I'd heard before. None were pleased with me, though. Even Chrysilla and Marigold implored Jangmi to do something "about me."

"She has outstayed her welcome, and she has overstepped her bounds for the last time!" Adeyemi walked to the bush covered in lilies. He reached inside of it with both hands and returned holding an entire white rose blossom. The other kings and queens went silent. Adeyemi stepped next to Jangmi and locked eyes with her, holding out the bloom for her to take.

My heart beat so quickly, I thought it was jumping up through my throat.

"Please," said Ailill, and he came around to the other side of the table. "She does not fully understand. This is *my* village more than it is hers, and if you punish it for her actions—"

"Quiet, Ailill," snapped Adeyemi, "lest you make more trouble for yourself. The kings are in agreement with the queens in this matter." He turned back to Jangmi. "Are we not?"

Jangmi took the bloom from him in the hand that had been held out for my coin and crushed it so hard I could see the muscles in her biceps bulging through her tight clothing. She slowly opened her palm, the dead, flattened petals dropping one by one to the ground, vanishing into a small burst of violet light before they reached it.

The harried turning of pages from behind me drew my attention. Ailill pored over one of the books on the table. His brow furrowed, his lips pinched thin, he stopped at one page and gasped.

I took a slow, careful step forward.

"Olivière, I should warn you..." Whatever else Ailill said, I couldn't hear him. I turned the book toward me to get a better look. Elfriede lay collapsed on the path through the woods, a panicked Jurij and Jaron beside her. They shouted something to one another, Jaron with one foot on the page, one off, Jurij with his arms wrapped around Elfriede's shoulders. I noticed there wasn't a single sword between them, and I wondered if they'd left them all in the cavern. Elfriede's eyes were closed, and Jurij shook her, but she didn't respond at all.

"What's wrong with her?" I asked, almost breathless. "She can't be dead, or this page wouldn't still be here."

"She is not dead yet," said Jangmi from behind me, "but she will be. And she is not the only one."

I flipped through the pages quickly, seeing woman after woman on the ground. Some were still standing—Roslyn, I noticed, and Mistress Baker—but too many had their eyes closed, their bodies splayed strangely. Alvilda was among them, Siofra and Nissa on the floor beside her, aghast. I couldn't find my mother—no, she was safe. She was there, distraught and holding Marden in her arms on the floor of the bakery, Roslyn and Mistress Baker rushing to join them at her side. What had *they* done? How had they decided this? I noticed no man in such distress. I finally found Darwyn and Tayton. They came out from the path through the woods that led to the cavern and joined Jurij and Jaron in their panic around the collapsed Elfriede.

"What have you done?" I asked, my throat constricting.

"This is the second time in your lifetime we have sent an illness to your village," said Adeyemi. He looked cool and composed through my forming veil of tears. "We did so the first time, after you first met Ailill in your lifetime."

The sickness that had taken some women's lives, and because they loved them, some men's with it. The sickness that had almost killed my mother, but for Ailill's long-fought efforts to stop it. Even so, there were so many *more* women collapsing this time! And for what? Because I dared to speak against the kings and queens?

"Why?" The coin practically burned into my palm. "Why?"

"It was then when we realized who you were," said Kin, referring to the earlier sickness. "And we had agreed long before, that once we found you, you would be made to suffer."

I fought the urge to scream. "Why not *me* then? Why the other people? And not just those I love—"

"Your village, your gender, your punishment." Estavan lifted his chin haughtily. "It was a shame that an equal number of men went with the women last time because of their devotion to them. This time, there will be no such collateral damage."

"But I didn't know what I was doing!" I pounded my fists against my thighs. "I hadn't even *done* anything then!"

"You knew at least that going to the castle as a woman was forbidden. Not that *we* made those rules, mind you." Marigold huffed. "However, we agreed you were

152

somewhat ignorant then, and so we decided to keep the punishment minimal. However, now you know better. Now you go too far."

"No! No, I don't know better!" I walked forward on trembling legs and grabbed Jangmi's hand from where it hung beside her, shoving the coin into her palm. She arched an eyebrow and took the coin, taking a step back. I collapsed to my knees. "Please! I'm sorry! I'll do whatever you want, just please undo this."

Jangmi looked down at me over the tip of her nose. "What is done is done. Be grateful we shall still allow you to go back."

I don't know whether the kings or queens spared me another glance. I couldn't look up. I don't know how much longer it was before I felt Ailill's hands on my shoulders, and his strength attempting to lift me up. "We must go," he whispered. "They have opened the door. We can step through the Never Veil."

I wanted to fight back, but I was too in shock. I couldn't risk angering the kings and queens any further. I let him guide me toward where the garden door had been, where a black gauzy piece of fabric was fluttering out from a dark hole, as it had been when that woman had stepped through.

"Ailill," said Adeyemi at our backs. "Remember our decree. Do not get too attached to that one."

"Of course." Ailill let go of my shoulders and shoved me through. "I never was," I heard him say, as I collapsed into the Never Veil and silent darkness.

Chapter Twenty-One

I SHOULD HAVE TAKEN A deep breath before I passed through, but I had no idea we were coming back this way. I snapped to life at the bottom of a pool of water, kicking violently to make it to the top through the blinding violet glow.

I felt Ailill's arm around my waist and with a few powerful kicks of his legs, we broke through the surface of the water. It took me only a moment of breathing to recognize the inside of the cavern, with Ailill swimming at my side, his arm still wrapped around me.

I wanted to shove him away, but I was too weak. Instead, I helped him kick us to the shore and then we climbed up onto the sediment. The water glowed red now, as if to remind me I was never to attempt to go back through it.

"That was rather nice of them to send us back through that passageway," said Ailill, and I wondered how he had become so acquainted with sarcasm. He went to run a sopping black glove through his hair and instead stared at it, shaking his head. "Considering we could have walked through the entryway behind the throne in the castle." He peeled it and the other glove off, tossing them on the sediment beside him. He must have left his jacket behind. His biceps glittered with the red light of the pool.

I had a feeling the inconvenience was intentional. And the least of our problems. I wasn't in the mood to discuss it. Not just for that last parting comment, but for all of his lies. I stood on shaky feet and tried to get my bearings.

"Olivière," said Ailill from behind me. "Do your best not to get angry with me. I have no doubt they will be watching us quite closely for quite some time."

I froze mid-step toward what I realized was the stash of swords I'd seen the men gathering through the book. I turned my head around slowly. "It didn't occur to me to get angry," I said. "We have more important things to worry about."

"Yes." Ailill stood. "But I wanted you to know that last thing I said before I pushed you through the Never Veil... It was not true."

"Sure." I nodded, barely interested. He wanted casual, he wanted to put on a show for those who might be watching, so he could have it. I was done with him. "It's clear you do what they tell you. They wanted you not to care about me, so you had to make that clear."

"Yes," said Ailill, but he looked worried. I examined the pile of swords, grabbing my torn skirt and wringing what water I could out of it. "You cannot blame me for—"

"I can blame you for a lot of things," I snapped, facing him. He'd closed the distance between us and I jumped back. "You lied to me. Maybe you lied to them. Maybe this is you lying to me again. How can I trust anything you say?"

A muscle in Ailill's jaw twitched. "It seems to me that I am not the only man in your life capable of hiding secrets."

I let out a breath, exasperated. "That has nothing to do with this. You can't absolve yourself by comparing your behavior to others."

Ailill ground his teeth. "You are willing to forgive whatever he does, but not me?"

"I don't *forgive* anything. Do you think I've forgotten the clonk on my head? Or how his actions led to my father's death? Or how he stabbed..." I couldn't say the rest.

"Olivière, I had *reasons*, I *have* reasons for everything."

I pointed a finger toward his chest. "Reasons? All right then. I'll just accept that without question because this is *your* village and I'm just a nobody."

"That is not true! Olivière—"

I threw my hands out. "No. I don't need to know. If it won't help us make things right in the village, fine, I don't need to know." I cradled my head. "It doesn't matter. I'm not supposed to do anything but fade into the background. If I do anything else, they'll hurt the people more."

"They are *already* hurting the people. Hurting people you love."

Tears filled my eyes, making it hard to focus on Ailill through the water. "What can I *do*? You said they're watching right now. Maybe they weren't always watching before, but they're sure to be always watching now."

"I can help..."

I wiped the moisture from my cheeks—not that it mattered, considering I was soaked from the pool. "You shouldn't have let me go there. You knew what might happen. You *remembered everything* and yet you took me there."

"I did not think *this* would happen. Regardless, you were so insistent..."

I laughed pitifully. "Fine. Blame me. Everyone does. *They* even do."

Ailill pinched his lips. "I am not *blaming* you." He grabbed my hand in his. "Olivière, what I did, I did..." He pitched forward, releasing my hand and I caught him, digging my feet into the ground as much as I could. The ground beneath us was shaking. It took all my strength, strength I barely knew I had left, but I shoved him away so he wouldn't cause us both to tumble over. He fell back. I

156

hadn't meant to shove him *that* hard. The ground stopped shaking.

"It doesn't matter. Ailill, it doesn't *matter*. I can't even... Apparently, we can't even touch each other..." I had to catch my breath. I hadn't expected to find the thought of not being able to touch him so painful. "I don't care anymore," I lied. "We have to go our separate ways."

"We can be smart about this." Ailill scrambled to his feet. "We will not touch each other, but I *must* see you. We can be discrete."

"*No.*" I started backing up into the darkness, not caring if I tripped over a rock. "There is no 'discrete.' It's over." I gestured to the pile of swords. "Please do what you can to make things better. Get rid of those. I'll try to talk some sense into them, if I can. But please... try to stay away from me if you see me."

"Olivière!" His voice echoed pitifully as I stepped into the shadows.

ŋ ŋ ŋ

Maybe Ailill finally understood. Perhaps he stayed behind to throw the swords into the cavern pool. Maybe he went back to his castle to meet the specters and ask for their assistance. He didn't follow me, and I broke through the woods to the path where I'd witnessed Elfriede collapse. There was no sign of her, nor of any of the men I'd seen with her.

Our cottage is somewhat near. They must have taken her there.

The walk through the woods toward the village went incredibly slowly. I was shivering—the air was so much colder here, I'd nearly forgotten, and my clothes were soaked through. I was sick with worry, and my mind wouldn't stop thinking about what had happened, what I'd done. What *they'd* done. What they blamed me for.

My fingers dipped uselessly into my pocket. It was gone. I'd given it to them. Too late, but I'd done what they'd asked, and they still punished my village for it.

My heart was pounding when I approached the clearing, but it quickly sank when I noticed there were no signs of a fire or even candlelight in my family's cottage. Perhaps they were too panicked about Elfriede. I gripped my skirt and ran.

"Friede!" I said, pushing the door open. "Jurij, Jaron!" I stopped cold. There was no one there. No one. Where could they have gone?

I gripped on to the headboard of Elfriede's and my bed—of *Jurij's* and Elfriede's bed, I remembered, as I stared at it in the moonlight—to support me. *Calm down,* I thought. *Perhaps they saw no one was home and decided to take her into the village. But they could have fetched help and had someone stay with her. Why would they carry her limp body into the village?*

Forget it. I was trying to make sense of *Jaron and Jurij.* They made little sense these days. *The bakers. Mother is there. I'll start there.*

As scared as I was, I knew I'd do little good rushing into the village dripping wet and cold. I rushed to the chest at the foot of the bed and pulled out the dresses. Spurn and Scorn had brought me more of the ones I'd left behind and had barely worn at the castle, but the feel of their soft, refined material in my hands made me sick to my stomach. There were so many bad memories I'd rather not think about just then—and most of all, there was that commandment that I just become a "pawn" again, that I stop thinking I was anyone important. I used a familiar violet dress to wipe my wet body and grabbed a plainer brown dress at the bottom. I slipped it on—it was slightly tight at the waist, too large at the bust—*Elfriede's*—but I was long past caring. It wasn't so ill-fitting as to be uncomfortable. *It will have to do*, I thought, looking at the dark stains on my knees. I let Elfriede's skirt fall down over them. She'd taken the time to sew the outline of lilies into this skirt, her idle hands always wanting work even where there was none of import.

I shifted the material at the shoulders to tighten the bagginess at my chest and before resting a shaking hand over my nerve-wracked stomach. *There has to be a way through this*, I thought. *There has to be. I'll be a good pawn, and then they'll fix things. And if they don't...*

...I'll offer my life instead. I'll make them understand.

I took one of Elfriede's shawls, too, and wrapped it around my shoulders. It did a better job at hiding the bagginess. I thought about grabbing a lantern, but I wasn't in the mood to carry it. The moonlight was bright enough— I hadn't even known it was night yet until I stepped out of the cavern—and I knew my way around the village. I pulled open the door to leave, coming face to face with a specter.

Chapter Twenty-Two

E WAS SO FAR FROM my mind that it took me a moment to realize I knew this specter. Even if he had somehow cleaned up his clothes—were there extras lying around?—and fixed his hair back into place.

"Spurn." I shut the door behind me. I clutched at the shawl at my throat and peered around him. There was no sign of any others. "I'm not... I'm not the lady of the village anymore."

Spurn nodded—that itself was a sign that he didn't fully understand that I wasn't the bearer of a golden token anymore. There should have been no sign of movement, no sign of acknowledgement in those hollow red eyes.

"Well, you can attend to Ailill," I said. "I'm sure he has things for you to do."

He didn't move. I decided to ignore him. I started down the path to the village, walking so quickly my legs burned. I was most of the way there when I thought to look behind me. Spurn was several paces behind, ever my attendant. I stopped, panicked.

"Stay away from me!" I said. "They won't like it if you treat me differently."

He paused but didn't leave. I sighed, cradling my head. "If you're following my orders then, I order you to go back to Ailill." He didn't budge. "Or go on ahead to the Great Hall. Find some way to be useful."

He still didn't move, and I gave up. I didn't have time for this. Surely the kings and queens realized I hadn't asked this man to follow me. I trudged ahead and jumped when the door to the Tailors opened and a figure tumbled out.

He wasn't looking at all where he was going. Or more likely, he wasn't expecting me. Luuk slammed into me, almost knocking me over. Panic colored his face. "Noll!"

I placed my hands on his shoulders and pushed him gently back. He was already my height somehow. "Luuk, where are they? Where're my sister and Alvilda?"

"You've heard." Luuk took my hand in his. "Come on," he said. I let him guide me.

We weren't the only ones on the roads despite the hour, but of those we encountered, no one was simply going about his or her business. When we turned one corner, a man carrying a sloshing bucket of water nearly barreled us over, and he didn't even slow down, just entreated us to get out of his way. A few paces past him, a small girl cried on a doorstep in her nightshirt. My heart went out to her—and I noticed the wooden squirrel she clutched tightly against her chest. When we reached the heart of the village, there was a crowd of harried figures around the well, buckets dangling from their arms.

"Does water help them?" I asked Luuk, daring to hope. There was such urgency to their movements, such impatience to get their buckets filled, I thought they may have stumbled on an answer.

"Nothing has worked," said Luuk, dashing all of my hopes. He clutched something folded up in his other hand, something he must have raced home to get. He stopped in front of the Great Hall and let go of my hand. "But no one is willing to give up. No one knows what to do." He laughed harshly and unfolded the fabric in his hands. It was just a kerchief, a little worn and ragged. "Mother sent me to

Father's to grab this. She said it was the first thing she made for Alvilda when they were girls—when Auntie was actually the one helping the Tailor, my grandfather. Alvilda taught Mother how to sew, although she herself never had much love for it. This was the first thing Mother made on her own, and Auntie gave it back to her the day she got married to Father." Luuk stared at the fabric in his hand, as if it might tell him something. "I suppose Auntie was angry with her, and Mother thought it too full of bad memories to take with her when she moved in with Auntie. But now... Now she's desperate. She seems to think that this *thing*, this piece of cloth, shoved in Auntie's hand might wake her."

"Luuk..." I wanted to reach out and wipe the tears forming in his eyes, but I saw anger there, too, and I didn't dare interrupt him.

Luuk clenched the handkerchief in his hands. "You have to do something." I followed his gaze to the open doors of the Great Hall, unable to make sense of the flurry of movement therein. There seemed to be collapsed bodies on the ground, with people flitting about, some shouting at one another while others sat on the ground beside those who had fallen. Had every fallen woman in town been taken here?

I took a deep breath and hitched my skirt up slightly, taking those first few steps toward the open doorway.

"I'll tell your mother you're here," said Luuk from behind me. I faced him, confused. "She's at the Baker's, with my mother and Nissa. Both Alvilda and Marden have fallen."

"What about Elfriede?" I asked, but Luuk had already turned and run.

I'd asked him to take me to them. Was Elfriede inside the Great Hall? Why wouldn't Jurij take her to Mother, if they hadn't left her in our cottage?

My eyes caught Spurn's. Of course, he was still a few steps behind me.

"Where are the others?" I asked, looking for a sign of white coats and white hair amid the village's hectic activity. Spurn didn't reply. As infuriatingly expected.

"Never mind." I headed inside.

No one seemed to be notice me at first. Men and women alike were barking orders to one another. People pushed past me with buckets in hand, sitting on the ground next to a sprawled-out woman, dipping a cloth inside the bucket and rubbing their foreheads. I could see even in the dying light the sheen of perspiration on the skin of all the collapsed women—even on the skin of those eager to help them, although theirs was probably from all the movement. The sick women must have been battling a fast-acting illness to be sweating so badly.

Mother and the women who perished after the first illness were still conscious for weeks, even months—Mother had lasted four months even before Ailill treated her. They were weakened, but not so visibly close to death's door so quickly. My eyes darted over the fallen women. I saw Vena among them, Elweard in tears at her side—almost as if this was before the curse was broken, and losing her might actually kill him too. I recognized a number of the fallen— perhaps not so much by name, as by occupation. I kept getting pushed aside. It wasn't until I was halfway into the room that the activity around me stilled, people nudging those still conscious around them until I drew almost every eye in the room.

I froze in place, realizing what Luuk had wanted of me. What any of these people expected of me. To lead. That was what I'd said I would be doing, after all. I hadn't yet told them otherwise, and I still had a servant dressed in white who wouldn't leave my side.

"What's happened?" demanded one man. I had no idea what explanation I could give him.

A woman with a young girl resting her head in her lap pointed at me accusingly. "Where were you? What have you done?"

I couldn't get my mouth to open. What had *I* done? She had no idea that it was my fault. But it was, in a way. They could blame me for everything.

I took a nervous step back, about to run away. I bumped into Spurn.

"Noll!" It wasn't Spurn who spoke, but I could tell that from the volume of the voice alone. Jaron shoved through the crowd from the place where Vena and Elweard had prepared the food.

My mouth fell open. I peered over his shoulder for signs of Jurij or Elfriede, but there were none.

Jaron smiled smugly. "I reckon you're surprised to see me here."

I latched on to his shoulders, shaking him. "Where's Elfriede? And Jurij?"

Jaron raised his eyebrows and gently pried my fingers off of him, taking a step back. "So you know. She fell, too."

"Yes, I know. I know the two of you—maybe even Darwyn and Tayton—have been rather busy since I last saw you. Now where are they?"

Jaron seemed fixated on Spurn behind me. "Jurij is with her. Darwyn and Tayton, too. They sent me to the Great Hall to see if we could find someone to help us." He gestured around the room. "And I come here to find... this. So many women have fallen ill. What's to be done to save them?"

I felt more than just the pressure of his question on me. I felt the pressure of every gaze in the room.

"I don't know," I responded quietly.

"What?" asked someone from behind me. He probably hadn't heard me.

I clenched my fists together at my side. "I don't know!" I said, louder. "I have no idea what the village needs, and I'm not even someone you should look to—I'm not going to be the lady of the village." My voice dropped. "I can't lead you."

The hall broke into shouts and whispers, curses and screams.

"I told you she couldn't help us—"

"I never cared for her anyway!"

"Trouble with the lord again?" said Jaron quietly beneath the uproar. When I didn't respond, he added, "The two of you sure like to keep your secrets."

"Why do we expect her or him to help us? We've never even seen the lord until recently, what good could he possibly do us?"

"You don't think... As soon as we see the lord, *this* happens!"

"No!" I said, spinning around to face the source of the accusation. I couldn't pinpoint who had spoken, so my eyes darted crazily between a large group of them. "It's not the lord's fault! I promise you that!"

Jaron surprised me by taking a step in front of me, gesturing behind him to shove me back. "On the contrary," he said loudly, commandingly, "I think the lord is responsible for a lot of the madness." The Great Hall quieted, the last echoes of the whispers fading into silence.

I was so stunned, it took me a moment to gather my wits about me. I stepped beside Jaron, shoving him back as he shoved me. "You're wrong! You don't know what you're talking about!"

Jaron shrugged. "That's right. None of us know what we're talking about. Only you and the lord seem to know anything."

My gaze darted between Jaron and the people watching anxiously around us. "There are things you have no need to know—"

"Do you or do you not know the reason for this illness?" demanded Jaron.

Lie, I told myself. *Just pretend you don't know.* I had a thought, then, that he would lay the blame at Ailill's feet if I refused to own up to it. Isn't this what the kings and queens wanted? Me to be nothing again, nobody's goddess, nobody's lady, nobody's anything? "I know," I said, biting my bottom lip. "It wasn't Ailill's fault. It was mine."

That brought the room back to a flutter, and I could hardly make out the screams and accusations hurled my way. A man jumped up from the ground and hurled himself toward me, his arms flailing. Spurn stepped in and held him back by the upper arms before I even flinched.

"Then *do* something!" the man said, and I realized the swollen and tear-stained face belonged to Elweard. Loyal Elweard, who loved Vena even when given the freedom to love freely, even though she took so long to love him back herself.

"I-I can't." My own tears were forming. "I want to— don't you know how much I want to? But I can't. I have to go. That's all I can do. I have to go." I bent my head down and hitched up my skirt, pushing past Spurn and Elweard, making my way to the door through the stunned crowd.

"Don't let her get away!" Jaron's voice was so halting, so angry, I froze.

I expected the people around me to block my path or shove me back toward Jaron to face their wrath, to face some sort of justice.

I felt two strong hands around my arms and looked down. They were hands as pale as snow—the white hands of a specter. "Spurn!" I said, shocked. He didn't even look at me.

"This is what I've been trying to tell you," said Jaron, making his way through the crowd and to my side. When he reached me, he wasn't speaking to me, though. He looked out at the crowd, and the people nearest stepped back to give him space. "Our village suffers under this lord. Under his choice of lady." He gestured his hands above him. "He is not the only one meant to be lord. Jurij, Tailor's Son, Quarry Worker and Woodcarver, has been given the chance to lead us."

"What?" I said, although the kings and queens had told me as much. But to think that Jurij had actually went along with it, that he was—oh, goddess. He was probably in the castle right now, right where I'd sent Ailill. No wonder no other specters had come out to the village yet.

"It's true," said Jaron, and this time he looked at me. He clasped his hands together. "And Jurij promises us there will be no more secrets. There will be no more suffering."

I fought hard against Spurn's grip, but I had no luck. "Impossible!" I shook my head. "If he were to tell you what he knows, he would *cause* suffering—"

Jaron ignored me. "Jurij will get us through this!" he said. "He'll help us treat our loved ones. And if they should die..." He faced me. "It will be the last terrible affair at a terrible reign's end."

He looked above me, nodding at Spurn. "You know what your new lord has asked of you."

Spurn dragged me out the door, ignoring my attempts to dig my heels into the ground, dodging the kicks I sent back into his shins. A black carriage awaited.

A specter opened the carriage door.

"Noll?" The timid voice called out from within the carriage. Mother poked her head out. Her eyes were red, her face puffed.

"Mother!" I stopped fighting. Spurn used the chance to lift me and shove me inside. He slammed the door behind me.

I brushed the hair out of my face and scrambled to my feet, almost falling over as the carriage started moving, only avoiding injury because my mother stood up to catch me and guided me to the bench beside her.

"Your sister is ill," said a familiar voice across from me. I also heard the familiar crinkle of leather as he crossed his black-clothed legs. "Come back with me to the castle, and we'll do what we can to treat her."

I looked up and stared into the dark eyes of Jurij.

Chapter Twenty-Three

"YOU." I LAUNCHED MYSELF OVER to Jurij, not sure what I was doing—was I going to slap him or choke him? All I remembered was wanting to just squeeze him—but it didn't matter. The carriage was moving faster than usual, and I took a tumble, falling not-so-gracefully into the seat beside Jurij.

Jurij patted my arm, and the golden bangle at his wrist slipped down toward his elbow like it was never intended to fit him. "Are you all right?" At least he hadn't donned Ailill's gloves, but the rest of his clothing... Oh, goddess, was this why Jurij had quit the quarry and taken a sudden interest in woodworking and sewing again? His outfit resembled Ailill's, but it wasn't quite the same. Instead of roses, Jurij had embroidered *swords* on his clothes. I could make the designs out at this close distance, through the bits of moonlight that filtered through the small carriage windows.

"Don't touch me," I snapped, recoiling backward.

Jurij let go. Something tugged at his face, something probably like pain, and he frowned. "Noll, I'm sorry about what I did back there—"

"You're sorry you hit my head until it bled and I lost consciousness, you mean."

Mother made a noise like a sheep being run down by Bow. The thought of happier times with this man who'd inspired more anger in me than anyone—was it because I had once loved and trusted him? Is that why I felt my blood boil more intensely than it had with Ailill or even Elric?— made my face hot.

"I'm fine now, Mother," I said, looking at the wall. "No thanks to this man here."

"I panicked," said Jurij after a short while. "I really didn't want to hurt you. I just needed to get you away from him."

That was enough to make me face him once more. "Praise the goddess he got me away from *you* instead."

Jurij sighed and cradled his head in his hand. "This is hardly the time for this. I came to get you and your mother because something has happened to your sister."

"She's ill." Mother's voice cracked. "Jurij found me at the Bakers' and told me she was one of the ones who'd fallen." She lifted her apron to her eyes and started sobbing.

"I know." I crossed back across the carriage to sit with Mother. I wrapped my arm around her and folded her into an embrace. I glared at Jurij over Mother's shoulder. "I've been looking for her."

Jurij's lips puckered, his brow drawn suspiciously. "Did Jaron tell you?"

"You're not the only one who can look at a book," I said as Mother shifted back from me. She leaned into the seat, her lips quivering.

"When Marden fell, I just knew it wasn't something ordinary," said Mother, almost oblivious to the people in the carriage with her. "And then Nissa came in, distraught, letting us know Alvilda had collapsed in the streets, that she'd left her back with Siofra. Thea and Roslyn went to help carry her inside. When they came back..." Mother lifted her apron to her face again, her eyes welling. "They told us there were so many people fallen. So many *women*. I just knew then and there that one or both of my girls was among them. That it wasn't enough that I'd grown apart from Gideon, that I'd lost him before we could figure out what it was to love again, that I'd be alone completely soon."

She sobbed, and I rubbed her back, not sure what to say. Not sure what I *could* say. In a fit of terrible selfishness, I wanted her out of the carriage and at Elfriede's side already so I could talk with Jurij freely. Surely, even if they were watching, the kings and queens wouldn't punish me for that. He had a golden bangle, and he'd been where I'd been. They'd forbidden me to spend much time with Ailill, or did they mean with this "lord" as well? I didn't know if my anger was worth taking the risk, but I felt so helpless, and Jurij owed me an explanation at least.

"I'm here," I said, my conscience winning out over that darker part of me. I squeezed Mother's hand and this time she took me into her arms. No one else might need me. No one else might want me. But Mother would need me. Especially if... No. *If they'd wanted them dead, they could have killed them instantly.*

I just didn't know if this was enough to make them happy. I hadn't done anything they'd asked me yet— anything but push Ailill away—but surely they would allow me to see my sister? Or understand that it was this imposter lord who'd forced me into this carriage, away from the small shack at the north end of the village where I might end out my days?

I couldn't picture my days there anymore. Quietly carving, hardly speaking to anyone but to sell my wares. Even though now I should *want* to stay away from people. Even though now I could blame myself more than ever.

That's not true. I felt a pressure in my throat as I tried to bite back the heat rising throughout my body. *Now "they" have faces. You can blame them, too.*

"We're here," said Jurij, and the carriage ground to a sudden halt.

It didn't feel like we'd been in the carriage long enough to have reached the castle, so I was a little taken aback. It seemed nothing good came of what Jurij might have to show me, and there were only so many places between the Great Hall and the castle that might interest this imposter lord. Mother let me go as the door to the carriage opened.

"Mother, wait!" I didn't want her walking into whatever Jurij might have waiting.

Jurij stood, crouched over to avoid hitting his head on the roof. He might be a little taller than Ailill, I realized. So far from the little boy trailing behind me in his kitten mask in so many ways. He paused, looking back at me over his shoulder. "Come along."

I squatted to get a better look at the sight beyond the doorway. It was the castle gates, after all. I just must not have had a good sense of time, so enraged was I during the drive over. Mother followed two specters—the traitors, how could *they* possibly serve a lord who wasn't Ailill?—inside the castle doors. Jurij made to leave the carriage.

"Hold on," I said, and I grabbed his arm with both hands, wrenching it backward. Jurij stared at me, puzzled. "We have things to discuss!"

"Inside." Jurij shook himself free and jumped out of the carriage. "Don't you want to see your sister?"

I wanted to tell him it wouldn't do any good to see Elfriede. Not if she were unconscious anyway. And if she were conscious, she probably wouldn't get much comfort from me regardless. But Jurij was gone inside after Mother, and I was left alone in the carriage. Were it not for the fact that two specters remained standing at either side of the open carriage door, I might be free to leave. Yet I was unlikely to do any good anywhere else. And I'd promised Mother I'd be with her.

I jumped out of the carriage, ignoring the specter's proffered hand, particularly when I realized it was Spurn doing the offering. I swiped swaying hair out of my mouth. "Traitor!" I said, wincing, as the hypocrisy of me calling that former young boy a traitor wasn't lost on me. "You know this man isn't your lord. I doubt he even knows who any of you are." I kept having to brush hair out of my eyes as a cold wind whipped toward the castle. At one point, I thought I saw Spurn's mouth part, but by the time the wind died down, he was as still and silent as ever.

I marched into the castle, determined to stop Jurij and talk to him privately before he joined up with my mother and Elfriede. Maybe we could save her—save all the women—if we called a truce and put our heads together. He clearly had the kings' favor at the moment.

"Jurij!" There was no sign of him. The dining hall seemed as dark as ever, so I was about to ascend the stairs where they'd surely taken Elfriede to a bedroom. I'd just grabbed hold of the banister when a creaking sound commanded my attention.

The garden door flew open and a gust of chilling wind slammed across the entryway and over to me. *The garden. He's gone to our garden.*

"Jurij!" I called again, stomping over to the open door. "Jurij, we need to talk, and I can see Friede after..."

It wasn't Jurij who sat at the stone table in the garden. I thought it was a specter for a moment. It was Ailill, slouched over, his arm across a game board. Chess pieces were strewn across the table, the bench and the ground around him.

"Ailill!" I shrieked, scattering fallen white petals from the rose bushes as I ran to his side. I bent over him— he was pale again, almost as pale as he had been the first time I'd seen him—and latched on to both of his shoulders. "Ai—"

The ground shook beneath my feet and I screamed, falling backward, a couple of rose bushes cushioning my fall. My arms were scratched, and a thorn wedged itself into one of my palms.

I can't touch him even now? When I just want to make sure he's still breathing? I could barely see through the haze of tears as I ripped the thorn out. *I never asked for this.*

172

I never asked to upset you, unseen kings and queens—why are you doing this to me?

"Olivi... ère..." His voice was quiet and slow, but there nonetheless. A cascade of breath I didn't realize I was holding flew out through my lungs.

I jumped back to my feet, the soreness from the scratches be damned. "What happened to you?" I asked, at once both demanding and pleading. "Who did this to you?"

Ailill seemed to strain with the effort of moving his head slightly. His hair had grown paler, too—a light brown instead of black. "Watch... out..."

"Jurij's wondering where you've gone," said someone from behind me. I spun around to find Darwyn running a hand over the back of his head. Tayton stood behind him, a grimace on his lips and his arms over his chest.

"You two!" I tried my best to stand between them and Ailill. "Did you do this to him?"

"No!" said Tayton, and his puckering lips looked especially sour and rounded. "He just sort of... collapsed." He lifted an eyebrow as he peered over my shoulder, my height not enough to shield Ailill from him. "He and Jurij played some odd game on that board and it only went on for half a minute, I swear, before Jurij won and this lord got as pale as one of the servants."

He wasn't *that* pale. Not yet, anyway. But I wasn't about to debate the smallest details. I spread my hands out to either side, like it might do some good and protect Ailill. "I don't believe you," I said, remembering my own chess matches. Even if Jurij knew how to play—and really, had the kings managed to teach him that? Was that as important to an imposter lord as it seemed to be to the real one?—there was no way he'd beat Ailill. There was no way the game would be over in a handful of moves.

Unless the kings *had* taught him something. Some way to win quickly. And yet that would be cheating, wouldn't it? Would the queens allow that?

I thought they already agreed they both won this village! Why are they so involved in everything still?

Darwyn shrugged. "Believe it or not, I don't care." He nodded his head behind me. "I bet he could tell you what happened, but he doesn't seem to be moving."

I spun back to check on Ailill. His eyes were still open, but his eyelids were drooping. His back moved just slightly with the rhythm of breaths, but I wouldn't expect Darwyn to be able to see that—not if he didn't care for Ailill like I did.

Ailill nodded ever so slightly. I had to wipe tears that had trickled down my cheeks, tears I didn't want any of them to see. "Then I just don't understand," I said. *Defeating a lord in chess made you lord and practically killed the last one?* I faced Darwyn and Tayton, who both had scabbards in full display at their waists.

"Why, you little bastards!" I tried to grab Darwyn's hilt to get the blade away from him—I'd already seen what "good" blades did in the hands of my *friends*. He stepped back to avoid my movement easily.

He rolled his eyes. "Come on," he said, gripping my bicep not too lightly. "Jurij is waiting for you upstairs. He thought you might have had something to do with that earthquake we just experienced."

I ripped my arm away from him. "I'm not going anywhere until someone helps Ailill."

"Who?" asked Tayton.

I grit my teeth and gestured behind me. "Your *lord*. The only person in this garden who's currently halfway to unconsciousness."

Tayton puckered his fishy lips. "Jurij's lord now. And he said to leave him until we've done all we can for the ill women. Their health is priority."

"There's nothing you can do for them!" I spat. "Only *they* can decide." I bit my lip, hard. "You can at least take Ailill to a bed. Keep him warmer."

Tayton and Darwyn exchanged a glance. "If you care so much, why don't *you* take him?"

"I... I can't," I said, remembering what had happened both times I'd touched him since returning to the village.

Tayton sighed and stepped around me. I instinctively went to block him and he jumped back, both hands in front of him. "Whoa! I'm just offering to help." I stepped back and kept a careful eye on him as he stared down at Ailill. He wrapped an arm around Ailill, picking him up halfway. Tayton stared at me. "Grab his other side already!"

"I can't!" I took a step back. My gaze caught Ailill's and I could feel the hot tears running down my cheeks.

"Well, *I'm* not helping out," said Darwyn from behind me, and I spun around, about ready to launch myself at him. He must have read that in my face because he held his own hands out in front of him like Tayton had. "Don't get so mad at me. *You're* the one who told us never to help a fallen comrade if it means you can't hold your sword. Or your stick."

"I was a child!" I clenched my fists. What a benevolent leader I'd made. "That was a game! Get over here and help him!"

Darwyn cupped his chin. "Hmm," he said. "Adamant enough that we ought to help him, but not adamant enough to help yourself?" He lunged forward and I jumped back, but it did no good as he grabbed hold of my wrist and twisted it.

I screamed in pain, and Darwyn looked taken aback. "I'm sorry, I just want to test something," he said. He didn't let go, instead dragging me over to Ailill. I dug my feet into the ground, determined not to let him bring me toward him, but there was no way I could stop Darwyn. Even though I clenched my fist, he managed to touch my knuckles to the top of Ailill's head. My heart beat thunderously as Ailill looked up at me in pity.

The ground beneath us shook and Darwyn dropped my hand. Tayton growled and tipped sideways a few steps, almost, but not quite, dropping Ailill. Darwyn stepped back, his eyes darting everywhere, and his hand on his sword's hilt, like that would help him in an earthquake. It was over before it'd hardly begun—stopping almost the instant Darwyn let go of my hand and I'd pulled it back from Ailill.

Darwyn kept his gaze locked on the sky. "Well, I'll be. Jurij will be glad to learn about that, I'm sure." He nodded at Tayton. "Leave him. We'll have Jurij send some of the servants to take him."

Tayton shrugged one shoulder and bent down to put Ailill back on the bench. At least he was as gentle as his tall, bulking frame would allow. I couldn't fully reconcile these men with my friends or with the menacing men I'd met in the past. They were somewhere in between, and I didn't understand how to feel about them anymore.

Darwyn gestured toward the door. "After you," he said, half bowing, "my elf queen. The lord awaits."

I spit at his feet and hitched my skirt up, striding toward the open door.

Chapter Twenty-Four

I STOPPED AT THE FIRST specter I saw, who was standing on the staircase, and folded my arms. "Your lord needs you. Take him to a bedroom." It wasn't Spurn. I didn't know how I'd come to tell him apart from the others even when he was being a traitorous, lifeless servant, but I did know this specter wasn't him.

When the specter didn't move, Darwyn stepped in front of me and put a hand on the specter's shoulder. "She means the former lord. Yeah, go ahead and take him to a bed. I don't think Jurij would mind."

The specter started moving, and he was joined soon after by another specter at the bottom of the stairs. They headed off toward the garden together. When I looked at Darwyn in disbelief, he shrugged. "Jurij told them to follow our orders."

I grabbed the banister and brushed past him, my nose in the air. "Yours, Tayton's and Jaron's, I take it? Or is Sindri back among you?"

Darwyn took two steps at a time to catch up to me, while Tayton lagged behind. "He's still recovering," he said, a hint of sourness in his voice. "We barely got to check on him before all of this happened."

"Alvilda and Siofra told us about being careful with what we say," Tayton said from behind us. Darwyn eyed the line of specters as we came to the second floor. They let us walk past without so much as blinking. Tayton took his place at my other side, so I was trapped between the two of them. "We wanted to see if Jaron knew anything more about it."

I stopped, causing the two of them stop with me. "Didn't they tell you I was going to discuss it with the lord?"

Tayton scratched his elbow and exchanged a glance with Darwyn. "Well, yeah. But..."

"We don't exactly trust that lord," said Darwyn. He glanced over my shoulder at the specters behind me. "For obvious reasons."

"But you trust this one."

"Well, yeah." Darwyn's nose twitched. "We grew up with him. Or you and I did, anyway."

Tayton, a little older than us, hadn't joined the group until recently. And he'd moved quite quickly from friend to Darwyn's love. Men and their freedom. It certainly resulted in interesting reactions—both of love and of violence.

I almost didn't bring it up. It might serve them right if they attracted *their* attention. Even after how angry they'd made me, we'd had enough of death and violence. "You know, though, not to discuss what you know about the previous lord. No matter if you 'trust' this new lord or not."

Tayton scratched his cheek. He was growing a patchy beard. "We figured. Just to be safe."

"All right. Where is he?"

Darwyn cocked his head. "Your mother and Elfriede are in a bedroom at the end of the hall."

"No," I said. "Not yet. Where is Jurij? Is he with them?" There was movement at the foot of the stairs. A specter climbed up the landing backward. After he took a few more steps, another specter made an appearance, with a dark figure—Ailill—prone between them. I started walking toward them before I even realized what I was doing.

A gentle pressure on my arm stopped me. "He's upstairs," said Darwyn, tugging me backward. "In the throne room."

Of course. Somehow I should have known I'd find him there.

ŋ ŋ ŋ

Darwyn and Tayton escorted me to the throne room door—what was I going to do? Poke around in the prison cells?—saying nothing. I stopped in front of the open kitchen doors, startled when something soared through the air. It was Arrow, who had jumped up to catch a flank of meat a specter had thrown. He munched on it beside his mother, who stretched out luxuriously in front of the fire. A specter chopping meat on the table beside the fire looked up briefly. He'd fed Arrow—or had at least let him steal a snack. Leave it to Jurij to be concerned about the animals' welfare, even with so much else going on around us.

"You know the rest of the way." Darwyn wove an arm through Tayton's to stop him.

I nodded, and the two left. I straightened my shoulders and clenched my fists. I had to do this. A couple of specters flanked the door as I approached, but I found none of them inside the room. *Good. He won't have anyone to help him if he gets out of hand.* That was a lie, I knew. With just a snap of his fingers, the specters—the *Ailills*—would come running if needed.

"Why aren't you with your mother and sister?" Jurij was sitting on the throne, the stand on which the book usually sat moved so he could easily look at it from his seat. The room was well lit with torches, and I saw at once that he'd actually forgotten about one sword. Elgar still hung over the throne, although it'd lost its violet glow.

"Why aren't *you?*" I asked, coming closer. "Why aren't you out there in the village pacifying people if you're so eager to play at being lord?"

Jurij jerked up from looking at the book. "I'm not *playing* anything."

I was at the dais now, and I took the step up slowly. "It seems like it to me."

Jurij sighed and bounced his leg, looking away. "I sent Jaron out to check on the people. I'll watch them from here."

"A lot of good that will do."

"It's more than the last lord did the last time women fell ill in the village."

"That's not true," I said. "You know it was he who healed my mother."

Jurij scoffed. "If only there were healing magic now, I could do the same."

I looked over my shoulder, but there were no signs that Darwyn and Tayton had returned. "You could talk to *them* about it."

It was like I'd slapped him. "Don't you think I've tried? The veil behind here doesn't lead to anywhere. The tunnel ends in a red light."

They didn't want to see Jurij even? After all that talk about how he might be the new lord? "How did you know to beat Ailill in a game of chess? I didn't even realize you knew what chess was."

"I didn't." Jurij ran a hand over his face. "The kings told me how to win. Quickly."

I frowned. "But I've beaten Ailill before," I said, but then I stopped, a pain in my chest. No, I hadn't actually. Both Ailill and Elric had stopped the game before I could actually win. I'd attributed it to stubbornness, but maybe it was more than that.

"You need one of these when you play," said Jurij, rubbing the ill-fitting bangle at his wrist.

So maybe those two actually were just stubborn.

It didn't matter. I was letting myself get distracted. I gripped my palms on my skirt, feeling the sweat soak through the material. "Why are you doing this?" My voice was quieter than I intended it to be. I cleared my throat and spoke louder. "Why are you trying to be the lord?"

"I *am* lord now," said Jurij harshly, although his brow soon softened. He sighed and stood up, gesturing behind him. "Maybe you better have a seat. This might take a while."

Cautiously, I slipped past him and took the proffered seat—the throne. I felt my blood run cold as I gripped the uncomfortably hard armrests. Would this upset the kings and queens? Did they think I was pretending to be the lady by sitting here?

There was no earthquake, so I had to assume they'd let this go for now. To be safe, though, I unclenched my hands from the armrests and folded them in my lap. Jurij paced back and forth in front of me on the dais, preparing himself to say whatever it was he felt he had to—and then he suddenly stopped.

"Those are Elfriede's clothes," he said. "I recognize the..." He gestured at me and turned away.

I looked down and found the material at my chest poorly sagging, my shawl not quite covering things up as I'd have liked it to. "I was in a hurry." I adjusted the material and ignored the flush at my cheeks. "You know Elfriede's things by sight? I wasn't aware you had any good memories of your time with Friede."

Jurij laid a hand on the book stand. The book was open to a page showing his mother, father, Luuk and Nissa crowded around a bed on which Alvilda rested. "On the contrary. I remember feeling happy. Ecstatic. I don't think I've ever felt anything like it since."

I stared at my hands in my lap. "The freedom to feel comes with the freedom to feel unhappiness, too. To feel anger."

"I know. I understand that now." He dropped his hand off the stand and began pacing again. "I especially understand resentment."

"I'm sorry," I said, although I still felt he had a lot to apologize for. "I never meant for any of this to happen."

"Do you mean the way life was in the village before? The way it is now?" He swallowed. "Or do you mean how things are between you and me?"

"All of it," I answered. I finally felt brave enough to look up and meet his eye. "You have to understand. I didn't know what I was doing when I cursed the village. And I thought I was doing the right thing when I gave Ailill the right to un-curse it."

"So it was him who undid it." Jurij broke away, resuming his pacing. "But how?"

"Since you've obviously been given more of their blessing than I have, I'll assume it's safe to tell you. But you have to understand that you put anyone else in danger if you discuss this with them."

I waited for Jurij to stop pacing, and he did. I took a deep breath and spoke. "When I went back to the distant history of this village, the men treated women like animals. Worse than animals. They were led by a lord whom I thought—whom I *mistook* for Ailill."

"Because you hadn't yet seen his face? Even so, why did you assume the man you knew was alive then?"

"He *was* alive then. I didn't fully realize I was in the past at that time anyway. It seemed like the village, but not the village. And I had seen his face by then. I got so angry after you were hurt after your wedding that I... I asked him to show me."

Jurij put his fingers to his temple. "The kings and queens sent you to the past?"

I shook my head. "No. No, in fact, they don't know how I went through the entryway without crossing through the Never Veil. They don't know how I got to the past."

"Then how did you?"

"I don't know! The first time, I didn't mean for anything to happen. I just wanted to get away from Ailill because he'd frustrated me. I heard voices calling my name. The second time, I wanted to go back. I thought I could visit Ailill in the past and help the women whom I'd met there and who needed some guidance."

Jurij lifted a hand to stop me. "All right. You don't know how. *They* don't even know how. Tell me about the men then, the ones who led you to... do what you did."

I wrung my hands together. "They were violent. Wicked. Worse than the monsters we used to pretend were our foes. They looked like us, but they acted so terribly. They made women do all the work in the village. They hurt women. They forced their grotesque version of love on them. They tore babies from their mothers, raised boys to treat women like lesser things—" I stopped and jumped as Jurij sat on the armrest beside me. There was pain on his features, his injured eye the punctuation to that misery.

"So the story was true. I always thought it was just a story. I... I actually never thought about it at all. Women as nothing but laborers, as bearers of children." He ran a finger over the figure of Alvilda on the page, over his mother. "Why?"

"I don't know. It was all our village knew for a thousand years. The kings used our village as part of their game, showing how things could be when men had the advantage over women."

"And they thought this showed men *favorably*?"

"I can't say. I suppose it showed men having more power."

Jurij rested against the tiny portion of the throne behind the armrest. "They told me that men once had power in this village. They encouraged me to take it back."

I leaned back in the throne with him. "The queens would probably like to know that. Seeing as how the two groups decided to call our village a draw between the genders. But that was after they last spoke to you, I suppose."

Jurij shifted his head to face me, and for a moment I felt like we were just spending time together like we once had. That no one's lives were in danger. That no ill will had ever passed between us. "You said Ailill undid the curse?"

"Yes, well..." I took a deep breath. "The lord I thought was him was his brother. They had similar features, and I was so eager to hate Ailill. To hate the 'lord' who took me away from my life. But it wasn't really him I was angry at. I was angry about the whole village."

"And yet you said yourself you became the first goddess, and started the village on its path of goddesses and their men."

"Yes." I squeezed my hands together tighter, trying to slow my rapid heartbeat. "The men were so terrible, I thought they deserved it. *They* did deserve it."

"What changed your mind?"

"When the other lord died right in front of me, I realized he wasn't the lord I knew. And somehow, at once, I knew it was Ailill, who was only a boy then. Yet at that point, I'd already cursed the lord of that time to a thousand years of suffering—only the lord, when I uttered my curse, was the innocent boy."

Jurij frowned. "I'm confused."

I straightened back into the seat. "So am I. Just know that I regretted dooming Ailill to this, and I tried to give him the power to undo it one day. If... If he forgave me for what I'd done."

"That was quite a risk you took," said Jurij, and there was a sharp stab in my stomach.

He was right. "Yes, but I didn't really know if it'd work. I didn't understand anything. That was part of why I shut everyone out after the curse broke."

"So the lor—*he* forgave you?"

"I guess he did." I clenched my fists until my knuckles turned pale. The paleness reminded me of Ailill's skin, and how losing the darkness in his skin seemed to signal his path toward vanishing. "But then he didn't. He sent me away when I came to him—that made my choice to live alone clear. I knew I had myself to blame, and I was tired of being responsible for everyone's pain."

Jurij nudged my arm. "You're being too harsh. You weren't responsible for everyone's pain. You tried undoing what you did, and it worked. Besides, giving men back their freedom—something they claim they wanted now—might not have worked out for the better." He leaned forward and flipped through the book again.

"The sickness wasn't you," I said. "It was me. The kings and queens were angry with me."

Jurij froze. "It was me who made your Ailill sick." He surprised me by taking my hand in his, and I surprised myself by not immediately ripping it away. "I'm sorry. I didn't realize winning would hurt him."

Tears started forming in my eyes, and I fought hard to ignore the pressure that built up in my head. "You left him lying there in the garden."

"I was more worried about the women." Jurij grimaced. "And I was angry at him, Noll. I've been nothing but upset about your love for him since I realized I loved you, too."

I pulled my hand away, but slowly and gently, without malice. I didn't know what to say.

Jurij did. "So this is how you felt. When you loved me as more than a friend, as more than a brother, and I kept turning away."

"You had no choice," I said, after a moment's silence.

"Maybe," he said. "But I wouldn't wish *this* choice on anyone. This choice to love where love isn't wanted—"

I grabbed his chin. His mouth fell open in the shock. "I will never not want your love." I leaned forward, blinking back tears, pushing away my thoughts of anger. I bent his head lower and kissed him on the forehead. "I just want you to love someone else more, to be happy with someone who will love you like I once did." I put my forehead to his, shaking my head slightly. "No. More than I ever did. More selflessly than I ever did."

"I doubt I'll find that." Jurij took both of my hands in his, not leaning back. "You rewrote the world for me."

I clenched my teeth together. It had started out that way. I had gone to meet Ailill, breaking one of the cardinal rules of the village, because I wanted to free Jurij. In the end, though, it was more than that. I'd done it out of anger. I'd done it out of hate. I hadn't even been thinking of Jurij because by then all of my thoughts were consumed by—

By Ailill. And now, even after so many of the world's mysteries had opened up to me, after I came to know so much, I'd lost the ability to be with him, to even touch him. Him and his stupid lies be damned, I wanted to hold him again. I started sobbing.

Jurij dropped one of his hands from mine to rub my back. "Noll..." he said, soothingly. "Oh, Noll. I'm sorry. Why did I ever listen to Jaron, to any of them? What have I done?"

He clenched the back of my dress hard, and my sobs choked to a stop.

Chapter Twenty-five

JWRESTLED MY HANDS FREE and pushed Jurij back. "What do you mean? What else have you done? Tell me!"

Jurij blew out a deep breath. "Where do I start?"

I thought about Elfriede in a room somewhere in the castle, about Alvilda, and all the women out there, ill. And Ailill, too. Was there anything I could do for any of them? Was demanding the truth from Jurij bound to make it all worse?

So far they hadn't done anything terrible to punish me for talking to Jurij, even though I knew they were watching from when I'd touched Ailill. I'm sure they didn't know what we were saying. I made a decision; I had to know. I couldn't go back to the cottage, forget about everyone else, until I was certain Jurij wasn't about to ruin everything worth sacrificing everything for. "From the beginning," I said. "From the night in the cavern."

Jurij stood, stepping back from the throne. "There isn't much to tell about that time. Not for a few days at least."

"Really?" I fought the urge to roll my eyes. "A whole few days?"

Jurij held a finger out. "No, listen. I was upset for weeks. I barely did anything."

"Alvilda told me you'd taken to sewing and woodwork."

"Only because I certainly didn't feel like going back to the quarry. And you know her, she wouldn't let me sit idle for more than a few days, no matter if I'd stabbed someone and inadvertently caused the tavern fire along with the rest of the group. *Especially* since there was so much work to be done." He ran a hand over his face. "Look at me, complaining about my aunt when she's lying there, dying..."

"So you never saw Jaron?" I said, getting him back on track. The truth was, I felt uncomfortable spending too long thinking about those women. "Or Darwyn, Sindri and Tayton?"

"I saw Darwyn and Tayton. I guess I saw Sindri, too." Jurij started pacing again. "I don't remember."

"What about Luuk? Your father?"

Jurij stopped, shaking his head. "They're not involved with any of this this time. Please don't think ill of them. They shouldn't have ever been involved. Father was just so angry with Mother and Alvilda..." He sat down on the step of the dais, his back to me. "Yes, I saw them. They were pretty shaken up, too. And they'd hardly played a role in what we'd done."

I got up from the throne and slid onto the floor, sitting on the dais beside Jurij. I could never picture Ailill treating the throne room so casually. "I imagine Siofra and Alvilda wouldn't have let Luuk out of their sights after that."

"Or me, neither," said Jurij, wrapping his arms around his knees. "They forgave Father, though. We spent the first few days all under one roof, with Nissa, too, like a strange, wedged-together family."

I nudged Jurij with my arm. "Not *like* a family. That is your family."

"Yeah." A small smile flittered onto his face. "I wasn't in good shape those first few days. I just sat there, carving.

Sewing. Doing whatever Mother and Alvilda tossed in front of me."

I gestured at his clothing with my elbow. "Did you sew that while you were at it?"

Jurij ran a hand over his sleeve, over the bangle that got caught halfway up his forearm. "It was a purchase," he said. "The lor—*he* asked for more clothing when he... came back."

Oh. So it was him who wanted a new design, to go along with his new life.

"That doesn't look like it would quite fit him."

"No." Jurij touched his cheek, fingering the slight scar that remained across his eye. "I adjusted it myself. Without realizing, I think."

You "think"? I decided to let that one go. "You must have met with Jaron at some point. What was he doing, 'turning himself in'?"

Jurij hugged his knees. "He dropped by Mother and Alvilda's one day, along with Darwyn and Tayton. They'd all three been displaced by the tavern fire—"

I blew air through my lips to show how little sympathy I felt for that, but Jurij kept going.

"—and Darwyn and Tayton, who'd been staying with Darwyn's brother, went one day to your cottage—Ingrith's old cottage, that is. They felt bad about the roles they played that night. But instead of you, they found Jaron."

I laughed, and not kindly. "Really? He indirectly killed my father and Ailill, then he decides to move into my house?"

"He'll move into one of the new commune homes eventually."

"Good. Back where he belongs." I felt a tightness in my stomach even as I said it, and I hugged my own knees to my chest in a reflection of Jurij. "It's not going to be a bad place anymore, anyway," I added, quietly.

"Yeah," said Jurij. "And besides, you don't need the cottage anymore. You have your family." His lips pinched almost as soon as he said it, probably thinking of Elfriede. My own heart clenched. Just because I hadn't visited her yet didn't mean I could deny the fact that she was ill, and it was my fault. "Sorry," said Jurij after a moment. "I wasn't thinking."

I tucked my knees under my cheek, resting on them. "Was Jaron the one with the plan again?"

"There wasn't a *plan*, not right away." Jurij tapped his hands together in front of his legs. "They just all felt so... lost. They thought I might, too."

"How many men were in on the first plan? You talk about men being unsatisfied not knowing why they were ever cursed or how the curse was broken, like it was all or at least most of the men who were on your side."

"Jaron tried to rouse them. For weeks. Months even." Jurij leaned back, putting his hands out on the dais behind him to support himself. "Maybe some were on the verge of paying attention, but too many of them were lost in the joys of drink. Of women—women they weren't forced to love. Women they could just have fun with—multiple women."

My eyes widened as I sat back up, and Jurij laughed. "Sorry. That's not what you asked. I think they would have gotten there. If Jaron had waited just a bit longer—but he felt sure you were keeping something from us."

"And now you know I was. Now you understand better *why*."

"I'm not sure I do."

"But—"

"No, I understand why you kept quiet." Jurij stood back up, grabbing the book from the stand, and sat back down on the dais beside me. "I just don't understand why *they* make us stay ignorant of them." He flipped through the pages. "Don't they want to be worshipped?"

I checked the door for signs of any of the specters, but there were none. A couple had to be posted outside the door at least, but we seemed to be far enough back that they weren't hearing this. Either that, or they gave Jurij a freedom I never had. "I guess not," I admitted. "I think they care more about what they think of each other, and think very little of us." My voice was quiet, but I couldn't stop my heart from hammering, my eyes from watching for a listening specter. I stopped Jurij from flipping through the book. "But don't let them suspect you're thinking too hard about their reasons. I dared to ask a few questions—I just wanted them not to hurt anyone who might talk about what they knew—and they did this." I looked down at the book, at a woman in bed I didn't recognize. "They punished all of them because of me."

Jurij let the book fall to his lap and took my hand in his. "It's not your fault."

I tore my hand away and went back to hugging my knees. "So this time. You said Jaron didn't have a plan. What did he want from you?"

Jurij laughed sourly. "To know what I knew. They figured out you'd told me some things I hadn't told them." He paused. "Why was I allowed to know, anyway?"

"Maybe the kings had you groomed for a replacement lord even then." I shrugged. "Or more likely, they couldn't hear me speak to you when I told you some of what I knew in the woods. They didn't know to punish either of us yet, and then you pocketed one of the golden bangles you found in the dining room, and that made it okay for you to know." I frowned. "There were a lot of those bangles there. Ailill got one every time he was reborn, and he started using them to hang the curtain that used to be there."

Jurij shut the book. "I remembered that. I—well, you have to go back. You have to understand how desperate Jaron still was to know, to make the sacrifices worth something."

"None of this was worth my father's death! Or the others'. Or the sense of uneasiness that permeates the village now."

"Since none of that can be changed, it's better for it to be worth something than nothing at all, right?" Jurij smiled haltingly, hesitatingly. "At least that's what we thought."

"So," I said, putting on my own false smile to help disperse some of the anger I was feeling, "Jaron wanted to get back into the castle, and he figured the only way to do that was to 'turn himself in.'"

"Yes," said Jurij. "And I was supposed to come along later to free him. Darwyn and Tayton were to follow if I didn't come back."

"Free him and what?" I threw my hands out to the side. "Explore the secrets of the castle? Enter the hole behind the throne? Gather more swords to cause more trouble?" The scabbard Jurij wore around his waist was empty. Like he was ready to take up a sword if he needed to but confident enough to walk around without one until that moment.

Jurij seemed to realize where I was looking and patted his empty scabbard. "I left it in the cavern. After I got back, after I realized what I'd done to you... Did they heal you?"

"Yes," I snapped, rubbing the back of my head. There was no evidence of Jurij's betrayal, besides what I would always know in my heart. "I wonder if you tossed it in the cavern pool to wash the blood off."

Jurij grimaced. "Most of the swords are in the pool now. I watched you and Ailill return from here, and I saw him throw our pile into the water after you parted."

"Good. Maybe at least if you jump in to get them, you'll fall through the Never Veil and leave our village in peace."

Jurij sighed and traced the cover of the book with his finger. "I didn't want to hurt you."

"Funny. Because when I asked the same thing about Ailill that night in the cavern, you seemed to imply that accident or not, you wouldn't have minded hurting Ailill."

Jurij clenched his jaw. "That was different."

"Not to me."

"I really did not mean to hurt him then, okay?" Jurij sounded exasperated. "I wasn't thinking straight. I thought maybe Jaron had you again and I... All I was thinking about was saving *you*."

I couldn't look into his eyes for long. "You left him at the garden table."

"And you had him brought to a bed." Jurij's face twisted. "I don't know what else to do for him, Noll. I thought it was some sort of lord ritual. I had other things to worry about." I could see the slight twitch of his jawline.

"Like Elfriede," I said for him.

Jurij didn't comment on that. "I didn't know what I know now about Ailill, after what you just told me." The name sounded strange and foreign on his tongue, and he made a face like he had a distaste for it. "I thought he'd treated you poorly. I thought he was keeping the truth from us all for no reason." He was half right with both ideas. "Jaron whipped us all up into a frenzy! If anything—if I shouldn't forgive someone, it should be Jaron, for using you like that. Or even me—I shouldn't forgive myself."

We'd gotten off track again, and I needed to know if there was anything left that I ought to add to my pile of worries. "And what was your plan with Jaron this time?"

"It was less involved than a 'plan,'" said Jurij, shifting uncomfortably. "We did want to get to the hole behind the throne. We did want to remove all those swords from the castle—Jaron worried the servants would take them up and use them against us, now that we knew they were there."

"And you believed him?" I snorted. "After he convinced you all to wear them at your hips like a king and his retainers?"

"Jaron is *not* interested in leading. He just wanted peace. He wanted the truth—he needs that for peace."

"Sure." I sighed. I took the book from Jurij's lap. He didn't protest, and I hesitated for a moment, wondering if looking at its pages—if being the one to turn the pages—without my golden token was a sign of defiance to the kings and queens. Yet they'd let Ailill send out those pages before, let a group of us discover the secret of the moving reflection of life in black and yellow.

"We thought at some point there might be fewer servants," said Jurij, letting my sarcasm slide. "And that the lord himself might be out, thanks to the rebuilding efforts. But he didn't leave the castle as much as he originally seemed to indicate he would."

Because he was staying away from me. Although now that I knew he was only pretending to be shocked to discover his "lady" was the woman from his childhood who'd doomed him to this existence, I had to wonder why he still hated me enough to stay away.

"The agreed-upon night came, the last night we were willing to wait." Jurij paused. "I was supposed to volunteer to turn myself in, maybe wrestle the keys away from a specter—"

"That doesn't sound very smart."

"—but instead, I heard my name coming from the cavern." Jurij grabbed his knees again and stared blankly in front of him. "It was almost like I had no choice. I had to go."

"And then you wound up there." I still hadn't opened the book. My pocket felt dangerously bare without the coin, and I wondered how I was allowed to speak about any of this without making them angry. Was the specters' distance my only salvation? "You don't have to tell me what happened there," I said quickly. "In fact, perhaps you better not." I stood up and placed the book back on the stand without flipping it open. I stood there a moment, thinking. "But I need to know: Why are you doing this? Why are you trying to become the lord?"

Jurij grimaced and stood, closing the distance between us with a few short steps. "I *am* lord now, Noll." He got uncomfortably close, and I tried backing up, but the stand dug into my back. "But I may not always be." He took a deep breath and put his hands on his hips. "Jaron was right. They have a right to know. So I let him take them."

There was something I didn't like dancing behind Jurij's eyes. "Take what?"

Jurij gripped the bangle at his wrist. "The rest of the golden bangles. If you have one, you can know... And you can rule this village." He turned to face the door. "Come in!" he shouted.

Two specters appeared before us, their arms extended toward me.

Chapter Twenty-Six

𝕵 TOOK A STEP BACK, shoving the bookstand between me and the approaching specters before crouching behind it.

"Noll, what are you doing?" Jurij looked between the specters and me. He waved a hand at the specters and they both stood still, lowering their arms.

I straightened up a little. "Weren't you going to make them take me somewhere?"

"I thought it was high time you visited your sister," said Jurij. One of the specters broke away and whispered something in Jurij's ear. In *Jurij's* ear. I still had to remind myself that he had stolen Ailill's place.

A faltering smile flickered on my face. "So you know they talk now—to the lord of the village."

There was a flash of embarrassment in Jurij's expression as the specter pulled away. "That was a strange revelation. In any case, your mother has been asking for you." He shoved aside the bookstand and put a hand on my elbow while he grabbed the book and tucked it under his other arm. "I'll escort you there."

The sword hanging over the throne caught my eye as he dragged me down from the dais. I swore I saw the slightest violet glow for a moment, but it was gone as soon as I blinked. Jurij took us past the specters, and I checked to see if either was Spurn, but I didn't think he was among them.

I pulled my arm from his grasp and walked a few steps away from Jurij. He looked slightly affronted, but I couldn't care less. "Why was Elfriede with you?" I asked, eyeing the book under his arm. There was no way all the specter told him was that my mother was looking for me. "After you came back from that place, when you met up with Jaron in the cavern?"

Jurij stopped abruptly in front of the kitchen. "You saw that? How?"

The specters were at work in the kitchen, and I practically felt their non-existent breath behind me. "Don't ask me that," I whispered.

Jurij looked over my shoulders and quickly took my meaning. "Of course. Well, she... She said she was looking for him."

She was acting strange when we last parted, and I didn't understand why she was so concerned with Jaron, even if they'd briefly courted one another. "Here?"

Jurij put a hand behind my back, pushing us both forward. "No, the cavern. She said she was also looking for me."

Naturally. Even after all they'd been through, her looking for Jurij made more sense. "But she found Jaron first?" I asked as we descended the staircase.

"He got out with the help of a servant, believe it or not."

I stopped, two steps from the second floor. "What?"

Jurij kept us moving down the hallway. "Maybe the kings let them know I'd want him free."

"But you weren't even lord yet," I said, realizing it was the first time I was admitting it, even if my heart still didn't believe it.

We stopped a few yards from a room where Darwyn and Tayton were chatting. Jurij lowered his voice. "I don't know, Noll, but that's what he told me. After he talked to you, one of the servants came back and let him go. A strangely disheveled servant at that."

Spurn. What *was* that specter up to? The queens and kings alike insisted they hadn't sent me that coin, but Spurn had claimed they had. *Is he capable of deceit? Who am I kidding? He's the shade of Ailill, of course he is.*

"How's it going, your lordship?" Darwyn placed one hand over his shoulder and bowed slightly. The devious smile on his lips made it clear he thought this was a game. And here I thought he'd evolved past childhood into someone a bit less exasperating.

Tayton watched Darwyn and echoed his posture, bowing more deeply, the subtle subversion of the gesture clearly lost on him. "Lordship," he said brusquely.

Jurij let go of my back, adjusting the book under his arm. "We must go," he said. "We're needed in the village."

"Why?" I searched for some telltale sign among the three of them. Darwyn's jaw twitched slightly. I grabbed Jurij's arm. "What's going on in the village?"

"Illness and unrest, of course. You know that." Jurij glanced over my shoulder and I turned around to see the two specters standing there. "You stay here with your mother and sister. Stay in this room."

Darwyn and Tayton headed for the stairs that would take them down to the entryway. Just before they turned the corner, a glistening at their waists caught my attention. Golden bangles were woven through their belts, and they shone as they passed the torchlight. I hadn't noticed them before because they were at their backs. Jurij moved to follow them.

"Jurij!" I squeezed his elbow tighter. Our eyes met, and for a moment I saw the flicker of firelight within those dark irises. But it was just the reflection of a nearby torch. "You aren't meant for this."

Jurij took my hand in his tenderly and moved it away. "Maybe not. But I can try. If being lord allows me to protect you from them, then I must." He followed Darwyn and Tayton. "She stays here," he said, over my head.

Protect me from them? What had the kings and queens promised him? "Wait!" Intending to follow, I took one step toward him, but the two specters' hands were soon around my arms, dragging me inside the room.

η η η

It couldn't have been that long since Jurij, Darwyn and Tayton left to do only-they-knew-what in the village with Jaron. It felt like ages. I paced in front of the fire lit in the room given to Elfriede—the same room I'd lived in over the course of a few months when I felt like a prisoner in these walls, but Jurij had no way of knowing that. It didn't feel real to be here again under such different circumstances.

"I wish you would stop doing that," said Mother, quietly. "Elfriede... Elfriede needs her peace and quiet." Mother lifted Elfriede's still hand to her lips for what must have been the hundredth time since I'd entered the room and started crying again.

"Peace and quiet won't help her now." I leaned against the mantle, staring at the flickering of the flames. My heart was still racing, my foot still tapping.

"Don't say that. You don't know that. You don't even know what's wrong with them."

I bit my tongue, letting Mother's sobs fall into murmurs, eager not to agitate her further. Even if Elfriede was beyond my help, Mother's fragile state of being actually was affected by my movements.

The crackling of the fire was the liveliest sight in the room, and it drew my gaze like it was a goddess and I was her man. I couldn't get Elfriede's quiet, restful face out of my head, but I didn't want to keep looking at it. *I did that to her. She'll die because of me, and we'll never have forgiven each other for Jurij and how we let that man come between us.*

There was also the fact that on the other side of the wall, I knew Ailill was lying in a bed much like Elfriede's—at least that was where I'd seen the two specters carry him. It wasn't his room when I lived here—that was upstairs, I assumed, in one of the rooms I'd yet to explore. I could imagine how agitated I'd have felt if I was sleeping just a wall's width away from him back when I hated him, and when I uttered the curse that brought us together. His illness was something of a different kind than the women's—he'd been conscious, if just barely. I could do more good at his side. I could say my farewells...

No. Don't think about farewells. He isn't going to die.

The most good I could do would be to round up all one hundred and some—how many specters had Ailill said there were?—golden bangles, and throw them all into the cavern pond because I thought I now knew what Jurij and Jaron were up to. I hit my forehead against the mantle, not even caring about the pain. *What were they thinking? Giving men bangles gives them the right to know—but there couldn't be over a hundred lords of this village. They'll kill each other. By playing that stupid chess game or just outright stabbing each other.*

If I did anything—if I *could* do anything considering Jurij demanded I stay here—the kings and queens were sure to be more than displeased. What else did they expect of me? Was I supposed to suffer quietly in a room away from it all, just watching my sister die? Was I supposed to sit by and let Ailill die, while Jurij and the other men tore each other apart?

Did they even care about our village now that they'd agreed it was a "draw" in their game? Were they just toying with us? Were they hoping we'd all die, so they could send us off to populate the villages that were calmer?

The door opened, and a specter stepped inside with a tray full of food. He set it down at a small table beside the bed. Mother, her head on the bed beside Elfriede's, didn't even seem to notice him.

"Wait." I crossed the room and put a hand on his arm. It was so cold, I nearly ripped my fingers away like they'd been burnt. "I need to see Ailill."

The specter gave little sign of acknowledging me. He moved his arm out of my reach and stepped outside the room, his hand gripping the handle behind him.

I shoved my body through the open door before he could fully close it. The two specters posted at my door joined the one who'd dropped off the food in staring at me.

I took a deep breath and tossed back my shoulders. "Jurij said I was supposed to stay 'here.' Everywhere in the castle is 'here,' isn't it?" Without waiting for the reply I knew would come in the form of hands on my arms, dragging me back into the room, I strode to the room next door. I put my hands on the handle, waiting for the specters standing there to challenge me, but they didn't. I pulled.

I'd gotten the door halfway open and seen the darkness of the room before I felt the cold hands on my arms.

"I'm allowed to be here!" I snapped, looking from one specter to the other.

They both let go of me at once. I didn't wait to see why they'd changed their minds, and I scrambled inside the room. I saw a prone form on the bed, felt the chill of the air, and spun on my heels, pointing at the fireplace behind me. "This should be lit! Do you have no concern for your own self?"

My rant died on my lips when I saw the specter who'd followed me inside the room.

"Spurn?"

He turned his head and nodded at the specters behind him, and they went to work, piling wood from the corner of the room into the fireplace. A fourth specter stepped inside with a torch and lit the pile.

I met Spurn's eyes and saw them burst to life in the flicker of fire, but I had other pressing matters on my mind. Ailill's almost lifeless body was on the bed, lying on his stomach. The specters had basically thrown him there without tucking him in for adequate warmth.

"Ailill?" I quickly pulled my hand back after I found myself reaching toward him. I turned to Spurn. "Help me get him under the blankets," I snapped. "It's the least you could do after all the trouble you caused me." As soon as I spoke, the irony of that statement wasn't lost on me, but I had other things to worry about just then.

Spurn moved into motion, shifting Ailill so I could pull the blanket out from under him before rolling him on his back to the center of the bed. I threw the blanket over him, careful not to let my fingers brush him as I did—dying to let my fingers brush him as I did.

Ailill breathed in and out, his eyelashes fluttering. That was more movement than I noticed in Elfriede, who might be completely gone if her body wasn't still there.

Bodies used to not vanish when we died. Spirits used to not get reborn.

But she'd been breathing. Just barely. I sat down at the edge of Ailill's bed, careful not to even let my backside brush against his leg beneath the covers. Perhaps they'd let me get away with that level of touching, but I didn't want to risk it. Not after everything. Ailill deserved some peace and quiet at least.

I gave it to him for quite a while, Spurn the only specter who remained in the room with us. Ailill did nothing but breathe as I cleared my mind, thinking of what could be going on in the village at that very moment. I didn't even notice that Spurn must have left the room at some point or at the very least met another specter at the door because eventually he held a mug out toward me, steam from the open cup looking like mist in front of his red eyes.

Taking the mug from him, I let out a single laugh despite myself. It was a brownish liquid, a little bitter on my tongue. I shuddered but drank again. It was better than eating and drinking nothing. When was the last time I had had any appetite? I hadn't eaten much when the kings and queens offered.

"Is this, my goddess, a dream?"

The mug almost slipped out of my hands. "Ailill!" I moved to touch him but quickly patted the bed beside his prone form instead. I gave him half a smile. "You're not dreaming, but if you still think of me as your goddess, I wonder if you're still half asleep."

Ailill took his arm out from under the covers and reached toward me. I recoiled, bringing my hand out of his reach.

"Not a dream," said Ailill. He grinned slightly. "In my dreams, you never shy away from me."

I cradled the mug with both hands, letting the warmth of the liquid bring life to my numb fingers. "You're not fully awake. You'd remember."

Ailill shifted up, sitting with his back against the headboard. He frowned. "They said you could not be with me."

"I can't even touch you, remember? The last few times I tried, they made the ground shake."

"They do not want you with me," said Ailill, his voice a little hoarse. "Yet they do not seem to want me as lord anymore, either. If I am to be a nobody, what difference does it make if we are nobodies together?" There was a slight upturn to his lips. "Not that I think you could ever be a nobody, as much as they want you to be."

I tucked my hair behind my ears. "Maybe they just don't want me to be happy."

"Would that make you happy? Being with me?"

I opened my mouth and then shut it the moment I looked into his eyes. The firelight continued to play tricks on me, dancing an echo of the magic that once shone across his irises. When I spoke again, it wasn't with the affirmation he seemed eager to get from me. I had to know first. "Why did you lie? About not being able to remember?"

It was as if I'd kicked him in the stomach; his face looked so twisted with pain. "My intentions were never to hurt you."

I wondered if my own face was similarly marred with pain. "Well, you did. At least once I realized you were lying. Once it struck me how much you wanted to forget."

"I never wanted to forget!" Ailill slammed his fist against the headboard behind him and I almost dropped my mug. He ran a hand through his hair and struggled to smile. "I apologize. There I go again. That is exactly why I wanted to start anew—and if I could not actually start over, at least pretend I could."

I set the mug on my lap. "You wanted to start anew?"

"Yes." Ailill bit his lip. "I wanted you to see me as someone you could love."

I do love you. I loved you months ago. I tried telling you. It was right there on the tip of my tongue again, but I couldn't say it. I couldn't just let his mistakes go. "You thought I could love someone who lied to me?"

Ailill got lost staring at the fire. "Better than someone who frightened you. Or was cruel to you."

I tapped my fingers against the mug, listening to the clank of my nails on the metal. "You didn't frighten me— especially not since I realized my trip to the past wasn't a figment of my imagination. When I realized you'd started as a good person, that it was my curse that twisted you—"

"Do not blame yourself. It took me a long time to realize it. I cursed my fate, rallied against my feelings for you even when I knew you were the one who had cursed me to it. Maybe I needed to see you again, to sit with my freedom at last. Eventually I did realize it. You never meant me harm. You meant harm to the man who had hurt me more than anyone, who deserved it more than anyone. You meant to save me, and to save others from him."

"I did," I said, after a moment. "But it's still my fault for not thinking things through."

"It is not." Ailill laughed softly. "Despite the loneliness, despite the long years of living without hope, I am grateful you cursed me. I would have never seen you again otherwise. I would have never realized the love I felt for you was something of my own choosing."

"I don't know why." The words practically caught in my throat. "I've rarely been kind to you, either."

"That is not true." Ailill shifted in the bed beside me, taking a deep breath and wincing as he did.

"You're in pain—"

He held a hand out. "No. I am fine. I just need time."

"Why is your skin lightening again? Are you so weak because Jurij beat you?"

He laughed sardonically. "I do not know. I have never had a successor, and I became lord only when my brother died. There was no need to fight for the title over a game of chess while wearing a golden bangle."

I gripped the mug tighter to stop myself from touching his leg. "Will you die?"

"Because of this?" Ailill gestured in the air. "I think they would have killed me immediately if they cared enough to see my death to its conclusion."

Unless they wanted you to suffer first—or me to suffer. To feel the full impact of their edict that I can never even touch you, nor comfort you as you're dying.

"Olivière. You were unkind only when I was unkind to you. I deserved it."

"Not always," I said. "You were kind to me—the kindest anyone has ever been to me—the first time I met you. Then, I didn't come to see you until I wanted something from you."

"That is all right," said Ailill. "You were not unkind to me, just afraid to accept I had found the goddess in you.

You did not feel as strongly for me as I felt for you—you did not feel anything for me. You could not have. With the freedom of my own heart, I understand that now."

My nose twitched. "I kissed Jurij on his wedding day."

"You were not happy with me then. I had kept you against your will here, when I knew, even then I knew, you had the right to send me the commune."

"'One does not send the lord of the village to the commune.'"

Ailill scoffed. "So I said. Would you expect any different of someone eager to save his own skin?"

"I wonder how that would have worked anyway," I said. "Seeing as how I banished you to the castle regardless."

Ailill shrugged. "I would have caused an earthquake when I set out, but it would have stopped shortly after. It is not as if the ground would not stop shaking the entire time I left the castle."

Not like what happens now whenever I touch you. I shook my head. "I guess I didn't think that command through."

"We have already established you did not realize the kind of power you were playing with." He smiled. "But see, I could have come out to join you all after a brief earthquake. I was just too bitter to."

"And after your rebirth? You were out and about among the people, like a real leader."

"I told you I wanted to start anew."

I sighed. "Then you pretended to realize I was the woman who had cursed you and pulled away from me. Away from everyone again."

"I still went to the village. But yes. I was surprised to find out how awkward being out among so many people made me feel, and well, then I had an excuse to spend more time back in the castle. I was still helping and sending out the Ailills." He bit his lip. "That was not the only reason. I thought pretending I was surprised to discover who you

206

were was going to work out in my favor. When you saw how kind I could still be to you, that I could forgive you far easier than I had before, I thought..."

"Ailill, do you remember when you were a child, and I covered you with a shawl, telling you to protect your face from women?"

"Of course. How could I forget?"

"Perhaps things were too chaotic for you to fully realize, but men were vanishing when women looked at them. I—a woman not related to you—looked at your uncovered face, and you went nowhere."

"Because the magic..." Ailill sat up straight abruptly. "Because you loved me! Even then? Why? How?"

I couldn't look at Ailill's pleading eyes for long. I stared instead at the mug in my lap. "I don't know. I didn't even realize it then. I guess when I found out you were the same as that boy—when somehow I could start thinking over all that had happened in that light—I felt something for you I couldn't even acknowledge yet." I brushed a tendril of hair out of my face. "I think I loved you even when you kept me here, but I was too angry with you to realize it."

Ailill kicked off the sheets and scrambled over toward me, surprising me so that I barely had time to jump off the bed and out of his reach. The rest of the liquid, long gone cold, spilled onto the ground and over my feet as the mug cluttered to the stone floor with a clang. "I do not care." He reached toward me. "Let the ground shake. Let me hold you just this once."

"No!" It came out sharper than I meant it to. Spurn crouched in front of me—I'd almost forgotten he was still there—and produced a cloth from his inner jacket pocket, which he used to mop up the fallen liquid.

Ailill collapsed back onto the bed, moaning, staring at the ceiling. "And then you came back to me, despite my stubbornness, and I pushed you away. I was too blind to realize my own feelings, too foolish to understand my own role in the terrible blood between us."

Ailill's skin shined with the flicker of the firelight, and I worried he was soaking in sweat. I clutched my skirt with my clammy palms even as Spurn patted my boots gently with his cloth. "I don't want to fight with you anymore, Ailill."

He rolled his head slightly to look at me. "I do not wish to ever fight with you again, either."

I let out a deep breath. "Whatever your intentions when you lied to me, I want you to know, it hurt me. I... I don't know if I can ever fully trust you again."

Ailill held his hand out toward me, but I wouldn't stand close enough to let him touch me. "I was wrong," he said. "Please forgive me. I did so much that was wrong, and I wished so badly for a new start. I should have just asked... I should never have deceived you."

"We were already almost there." I stopped as Spurn stood and blocked the sight of Ailill from me. He bent over one last time to grab the mug and stepped away. "I thought I felt something more honest between us, that day you died."

"You were right. I felt it, too." Ailill rolled slightly, cradling his head in his hand as he pushed himself to sit upright on the bed. "I was a fool to doubt it. After all I had done, I never believed you could forgive me. That you could feel even a tiny flicker of the passion I felt for you."

I could feel the heat rising on my cheeks. "I forgive you, Ailill. If you can forgive me."

Ailill leaned his head against the post of the bed, wrapping his arms around it as if embracing it gave him strength. "Do you not remember? My forgiving you was necessary for the curse to end."

"That's right." I practically wrung the fabric of my skirt in my sweaty palms. "Thank you."

"Thank you," echoed Ailill, his eyes fluttering shut. He struggled to keep them open. "Thank you."

"It doesn't matter now, does it?" I said, my voice a whisper. "It's too late."

"Not too late." Ailill slunk back down to the bed, his voice nearly exhausted. "Never too late. Help me stand... against them..."

He spoke about fighting against the kings and queens back in their garden. How? Why would he even think that was possible?

I stepped forward, about to touch him.

A hand clamped on my arm to stop me. I looked up to meet the eyes of Spurn, and he wasn't looking past me. He looked at me, and then he tugged me after him.

Chapter Twenty-Seven

SPURN DROPPED MY ARM AS soon as we left the room, and I peered through the door as he shut it closed behind us.

"See that he's made comfortable again," I pleaded.

Spurn nodded. He grabbed my hand in his and dragged me to Elfriede's opened door.

"Where are we..." I stopped. The peaceful breaths from Mother at the chair beside Elfriede's bedside were what drew my eyes at first. But that was forgotten by the slight movement under the blanket draped over Elfriede's feet.

"Friede!" The name was hoarse in my throat. I didn't even recall crossing the distance between us or lifting her hand and grabbing it in mine. It was ice cold to the touch, but I kept squeezing.

Elfriede's eyelashes fluttered open. "Noll?" Her voice was barely a whisper.

The smile I found on my lips was so rare, so out of place as of late, it felt like it was tearing through my skin. I didn't care; I could hardly stop myself if I wanted to.

"Mother!" I coughed, choking on the well of tears that leapt to my face. "Moth—"

Spurn's hand clamped down on my shoulder and I jumped in place. He shook his head, nodding back toward Elfriede.

I knew without being told that this was an anomaly, something meant for just me—which meant it couldn't last. Which meant they were playing with me.

"How do you feel?" I asked quietly, now determined not to wake Mother, to keep Elfriede awake and speaking with me for as long as possible. Elfriede's forehead was as cold as her hand, which was worrying. Heat would have at least meant she was alive, that she was fighting something.

"Is this a dream?" Elfriede's head rolled toward me. "Are you a dream?"

"No." It was strange to be asked that twice in one night. "No, this isn't a dream."

"I feel like... I've been dreaming. Where's Jurij?"

The smile on my lips was nothing but a memory now; the dread in my chest was all that pervaded. "He's... fine." I brushed a bit of hair out of Elfriede's face, remembering how I once envied its bright and cheery color. It would have looked out of place on me. It was better framing the face of a delicate little bird. "You've had us worried."

"What happened?" Elfriede's eyes seemed to flicker in and out of awareness, but it may have been the reflection of the firelight. "Where's Arrow?"

I laughed. I'd forgotten the dogs. "He's in the kitchen," I said, remembering the eager way he chomped into the flank of meat one of the specters had tossed him. "Jurij wouldn't forget them."

"Where are we?"

"The castle."

"Why?"

"Friede, I know you're confused and probably scared, but I need to know what happened between you and Jurij and Jaron. What you last remember—what you were doing in the cavern."

Elfriede found the strength to wrinkle her nose. "Not in the cavern. Not with Jurij. Swords and red water. Water and..."

She wasn't making sense, and I desperately needed her to. I glanced at Mother, making sure she was still asleep. I took Elfriede's hand in mine. "You said you were going to look for Jaron. You found both him and Jurij in the cavern, remember? They were standing with a pile of swords in front of the pool."

"Yes," croaked Elfriede. "I didn't like that. I told Jurij, but he was already upset with Jaron. I didn't know Jurij would be there. I hoped he would be... He was wet."

"You argued with them? Was Jurij trying to stop Jaron or—"

"Do you know what I think?" Elfriede's eyes grew slightly wider, but there was no masking the haze that plagued them. "I think you still love him. Jurij."

I took a deep breath. "Friede, I don't know how long we have before you fall back asleep—"

"You love him."

"I don't." It was true enough. "Not like that. Not now. I used to, but now I..." I searched Elfriede's face, determined to see if I could convince her to talk about more important things. The way she stared at me, the way she seemed barely with me, even though I held her hand in mine, made me realize this was all she'd woken for. The kings and queens may have woken her to tease me, to show me how little control I had over what they did, but this was all Elfriede would stay awake for. This was all she cared to discuss, and the only reason why she could finally speak it was because she was so weak—too weak for pride to halt her tongue.

"Friede. I know you'll find this hard to believe, but I tried to stay out of your and Jurij's way. I did."

"No." Elfriede tugged feebly on her hand and I let it fall to her side on the bed. "You were always there between us. Always."

"Always? I was always between you? What about when I was kept here, like a prisoner, for most of a year? What about..." I clamped my mouth shut. This wasn't the time.

"Before then. Before the Returning."

I cradled my head in my hands. Were we really doing this right now? "I seem to remember he was always eager to spend more time with you. I don't know if he told you, but you accidentally commanded him to be my friend, so there was no need to be jealous."

"It wasn't an accident." Elfriede coughed so delicately, there was no danger of her waking Mother up. "It was at first, maybe, but... I figured it out."

"And you were too upset about accepting Jurij as your man to do anything about it. You liked having him out of your hair."

"No, I didn't. I was nervous." Elfriede squeezed the blanket hard.

I understood her nervousness now. I understood not wanting to accept that someone you hadn't wanted to find the goddess in you was eager for your love.

Elfriede opened her cracked lips. "Also... I just didn't want you to be alone."

The way her eyes flicked quickly to mine, she seemed so earnest. I reached out to grab her hand again and she let me take it. "You probably expected my man to find me with a year or two. You must have expected I wouldn't be alone for long."

"Maybe." Elfriede smiled slightly.

"But I wasn't alone. I wouldn't have been, even if you'd rescinded your order to Jurij." I pulled her hand closer to me. "I had you."

"I couldn't offer you the kind of friendship Jurij could. I know that."

Mother drew a sharp intake of breath and I tensed, unsure if my hunch would prove right—that Elfriede would drift back to nothingness the moment we had a witness to

213

her waking. But Mother's head rolled back in her chair and she kept sleeping.

"Friede, I'm sorry." I took a deep breath. "It was never my intention to hurt you. Ever. I know I did, but I was a different person then."

"I don't know," Elfriede croaked. "You still push me away."

I didn't say anything for a moment, feeling the pain of the fleeting seconds of our time together slipping through my fingers. "I thought you wanted me away."

"I wanted..." Elfriede sighed. "I wanted you with me, but I was too blinded by envy and too upset to accept Jurij for who he became after he was free to love who he wanted." I didn't interrupt to explain how different Jurij was now and how little he had in common with the man who'd once been her husband. Elfriede's lax grip on my hand grew tighter. "You're my only sister."

"And you're mine." I gently put Elfriede's too-cold hand beside her and tucked her entirely beneath the blanket, hoping it'd keep her warmer. "If we were closer, if we could coexist in peace like we did back when you watched me play among the lilies on the hill, I'd have told you so much. I'd have convinced you I was in love with Ailill."

"It's still so strange to hear the lord addressed by a name." Elfriede's eyes fluttered shut, and I didn't dare correct her when it came to calling Ailill "the lord." "But I knew. I knew since the cavern you loved him. I just thought... Maybe you loved two... Maybe Jurij had to apologize to you for hurting Ailill, and you'd forgive him, and the three of you would leave me behind."

I would have laughed if there wasn't so much that was unbearable about the situation right then. Elfriede had been imagining I'd wind up with two men—how either of them would feel about sharing me with one another, I couldn't even fathom—as if I could hurt them both by never choosing one over the other, as if such a thing were even possible, even acceptable. I did laugh then, just slightly, as the idea that it *was* possible, it *could* be acceptable, entered my mind. It wasn't with those two partners. And it wasn't what I wanted.

"I'd never leave you behind," I said. "Not if I knew you were alone. I wouldn't hurt you like that. I won't let anyone else hurt you."

Elfriede's eyes fluttered shut as her head rolled back further into her pillow, and I jumped with a start as Mother snorted and sat straighter. "Noll? Did Elfriede wake?"

My gaze caught Spurn's. "No."

Mother bent over and patted the back of her hand against Elfriede's forehead. "I must have been dreaming. I thought I heard her voice."

Spurn headed out the door, and I paused, allowing myself one last look at what remained of my family, knowing Mother would stay with Elfriede no matter what happened, that she would never be alone again, before I left them behind.

η η η

I had to run to catch up to Spurn, struggling to keep up with his furious pace as we climbed to the third floor, passing the kitchen. I spared a glance inside, but there was no activity, no movement but the slight breathing of the two furry lumps curled up in front of the fire.

"Spurn! Where are you leading me? I can't..." My gaze fell on the throne—at the hole behind it. "I can't go through there."

Spurn ignored me, going by himself to the throne and climbing on top of it to grab Elgar. He held it out to me with both hands.

I shook my head vehemently. "They're watching," I said in a hushed whisper—like the volume of my voice made any difference. "They taunted me with Elfriede just now. If I do something foolish..."

Spurn shoved the sword against me until I felt like I had no choice but to accept it. He walked back toward the throne as soon as I did. The blade glowed faintly in the dim light; I hadn't been imagining it. I wanted to drop it, to show whoever might be watching that I'd have no part in this, that it was the fault of this strange, rogue specter and no other.

Spurn pushed the throne aside, the heavy metal grating across the stone floor.

"What are you doing?" I hissed, crossing the room to join him. "I can't go there! I—certainly not *alone*."

Spurn produced a parchment from his pocket. I tucked the sword under my arm awkwardly and took it from him:

Go now, read the note. *We hope you enjoyed speaking with your sister. We thought it wise to show you she can still be saved—they can all be saved. We have instructed this shade of a spirit to allow you passage. We have the kings distracted.*

I had no idea who could have written the note— other than the queens—but it had to be a lie, right? They hated me as much as the kings—or maybe not. Maybe a little less, since I was of their gender, but Ailill said never to trust them.

We sent the golden coin to you.

Those liars, I thought. They either lied to the kings then or lied to me now. What were they plotting?

I hesitated in front of the dark hole, not sure I wanted to play any part in it.

The light glowed violet deep in the back of the cavern.

I was startled as a pair of hands wrapped around my waist. Blushing at the absurdity of this older shade of Ailill, especially one I knew as a child, caressing me so, I jumped back, but it was Spurn tying a belt around my waist. A belt that included Elgar's scabbard.

Did they send that back, too? The sword and the scabbard should have disappeared into nothingness, having served its purpose in a loop of impossible visits through time.

I slid Elgar into its sheath.

I didn't trust them. I didn't think what lay on the other side of the Never Veil would be inviting. But it was my one chance to get back there. It was my one chance to save the women of this village—to save the men.

I stepped through the dark, feeling nothing but cold air until the caress of the black veil.

When I finally untangled from the fabric, I couldn't breathe. I was in water. I kicked hard, trying to get my bearings. I blinked and through the violet haze, I thought I saw a pile of glistening iron from beneath my feet.

The light faded from violet to silver. I pushed hard until I broke through the surface of the water, gasping for air.

Once I reoriented myself, I recognized the cavern. The cavern, not the land beyond the mountains. Not a castle, not a barren canyon. They'd tricked me again, forced me through the Never Veil into another spot in my village. But I'd been fooled before. Was I even still in the same time in my village?

I swam to the sediment and climbed out, bending over and spitting out some of the water I'd swallowed. Elgar still hung around my hips, clanging against my leg with each heave.

I wrung out my skirt and shawl with shaking hands before abandoning that annoyingly-frequent task and setting out for the mouth of the cavern. I stopped almost the moment I set off. There were still a small number of swords beside the rock where Jaron and Jurij had left them, which made me think I'd traveled a distance, but not to the past. I turned around to gaze into the water, trying to ignore the red glow. There were swords at the bottom of the pool, I could tell, but not enough for the pile to have near fully depleted. The sediment around the pool was too upset, and the image of many feet trudging around here, each to grab his own sword, came vividly to my mind. Perhaps Jurij had caught up with Ailill long before he was able to toss the entire pile into the water. Maybe the men had dived for the rest. Whatever the reason, I felt sure I was in my own village, and that once I stepped out there, I'd find more than a hundred men with golden bangles and swords.

I squeezed the water out of the long parts of my hair and threw my shoulders back. The queens or Spurn or both had simply given me passage past the other specters. It was ridiculous, thinking of what any of them might plan by this. How long could the queens keep the kings from watching me? Why would they feel any need to?

Because over a hundred men will be competing to lead the village, and not a single woman will be among them. Not just because of the illness that attacked only women, but because Jurij and Jaron wanted the *men* to hold the gold, so they'd have the right to know—and what they'd do with that knowledge hardly bore thinking.

I pushed aside the idea of why the queens should even care as I made my way through the cavern and onto the path. This village was supposed to be a draw between the genders. Besides, even if the men rose to power, they had always been the ones to rule because of the lords in this village—and there were other villages for the kings and queens to worry about. Maybe it was me. Maybe I'd so altered their plans that neither the kings nor the queens were really willing to let our village be. Maybe they thought this village played a role in declaring a victor for the games they played with our lives.

I didn't even pause as I passed my dark and empty house, even if I was sure to find another change of clothing inside. Streams of sunlight were making their way over the horizon behind me; they would have to do for drying me. I had no idea how much time I had.

The thing that worried me most as I approached the village was the silence of it. It was dawn, and most people rose at that time to begin the day's tasks. The illness of the women had distracted everyone, to be sure, but there were no longer people running around in a panic, grabbing buckets of water or handkerchiefs or other things that would do nothing to help them.

If I can't get back to the kings and queens, I can do nothing to help them, either. I'd gone through the Never Veil without a golden token. But if the queens had wanted me to have one, surely they would have tasked Spurn with it since they seemed to have him at their beck and call. Unless, they wanted me to take one for myself. They'd had my sword sent to me—they must have wanted me to take it through violence.

The thought made me queasy as I remembered the blade through Elric's chest. I was little comforted by the idea that he should be out there, alive, perhaps a hundred times over by now, in another village.

Although... who said he'd be in another village? There were far fewer than a hundred flower bushes in that garden. Even if he cycled through all of them, perhaps he'd been given a new life here in this one again and again. I shuddered. Even if he didn't remember his past villainy, surely a spirit that tainted didn't just start anew.

"Noll!"

Without realizing it, my feet had taken me past the bakery. If this were any other situation, I would have headed there first, eager to check on Alvilda and all the rest of them. Nevertheless, this wasn't any other situation and I could feel the ever-advancing threat of passing time.

"Noll!" the quiet voice repeated again. A hand rested on my elbow.

"Nissa." I crouched down and embraced her, unable to bear the sight of her trembling lips. I grabbed her by the shoulders, pushing her back. "Alvilda?"

"Still asleep," replied Nissa, and I realized at once that was a more accurate description of what had happened to the women. They were fading like Mother had during her illness, but they didn't cough or get sick. They were simply with us one moment and gone the next, asleep in their own little worlds. Nissa frowned. "Marden, too. Roslyn is beside herself, between that and the men leaving—"

"Leaving?" I almost asked for more details, but I figured they were all headed to see Jurij—and where were they likely to go? They weren't back at the castle. The Great Hall afforded the most room, if the men were willing to trample over all the fallen women's bodies. "Even Sindri?"

Nissa nodded. "He was doing better. Luuk almost stayed behind, but Master Tailor urged him to go with him." Nissa ran a trembling hand over her cheek. "Darwyn and Tayton stopped by. They told us Jurij was the new lord, and he called for all the men to gather in the village square. That only a hundred could enter the Great Hall at once, but that they should all be there. They would all get their turn." She grimaced. "What are they talking about?"

I patted Nissa's shoulder and stood, noticing her gaze locked on Elgar at my hip. "Go back inside," I said. "I'll try to send Luuk and Coll back to you. I don't want them caught up in this."

"Caught up in what?" Nissa's eyes widened. "Are you going to fight them, like you fought the unseen monsters? By yourself?"

I shook my head. "I won't fight them." *I won't.*

"You can't go alone."

"I must." I stood back. "Please go back inside. *Please.*"

Nissa hesitated, but she did as I asked. I waited until the door to the bakery shut and waited a moment more to make sure she didn't peek her head back out. Satisfied, I headed toward the heart of the village and the Great Hall.

Nissa was right. There were men as far as the eye could see packed in all corners of the center of the village, spilled into the connecting pathways. I had to slink against the wall and push past them to make any progress toward the Great Hall, and I didn't like the look many of the men gave me as I made my way past.

I could feel the tension in the air. Like the men were just one moment away from violence, and I didn't even know why. I didn't know if they knew why. *I don't know if they know who their foes are, or if they care.*

At the very least, none of them held weapons or wore swords at their hips. None of them until Darwyn and Tayton. They stood in front of the doors to the Great Halls, their hands on their sword hilts—who were they threatening to use them on?—their eyes poring over the crowd gathered before them. I crouched as soon as I realized they were there, hiding behind taller men, and drawing a few strange stares as I started crawling between their legs. I didn't want Darwyn and Tayton to see me coming just yet.

"What's taking so long?" a man from the front of the crowd shouted.

"There's a lot to explain." Darwyn held a hand out to stop the man from advancing. "You'll all get your turn, but we have to do it in groups. No more than a hundred can fit inside."

"My wife is in there!" said another man. I was surprised to find a man talk about a wife, considering so few had remarried—although it was entirely possible his wife wasn't originally his goddess.

"The women are safe," said Tayton. "Part of the reason everything is taking so long is Jaron asked those invited to help move the fallen women to the back of the Great Hall, out of the way of the meeting."

I froze. Elgar poked obnoxiously into my sopping thigh. Would the women be in danger if they were present for Jurij's reveal of the truth, even if they were unconscious? *Jurij, you fool.*

A man raised his foot and stared down at me to let me pass. He startled me as he crouched down beside me and whispered, "Noll? What are you doing?"

It was Luuk. A "man" indeed. He was certainly tall enough to be one. "I thought you'd be inside," I answered.

Luuk furrowed his brow. "Father went inside. He was worried about Jurij. He told me to go back to the bakery, but I..."

"You're worried about them." I tucked my legs underneath me and sat down, my progress halted. My eyes danced over the Great Hall, which never had a single window built into it, seeing as how it used to be a safe place for men and boys to gather without their masks when the danger of women looking at them loomed. There was just that one door Darwyn and Tayton were guarding.

"You need to get inside." Luuk studied Darwyn and Tayton at the door through the legs of the men in front of us.

"I have to try to stop them." I noticed the immediate effect my words had on Luuk, the way his shoulders tensed, as if I were confirming his fear about the situation. "And you must stay out of there. It's not safe. Promise me."

"I promise." Luuk met my eyes and looked away, sheepishly. I could see the features he shared with his brother, ones that had somehow evolved in the past few years from boyish to breathtakingly handsome. "But I'll help you get in there."

"How?"

Luuk screwed up his features into an echo of his brother's recent determination. He stood and adjusted his jerkin. "Leave it to me."

He pushed forward through the men in front of us and made his way to the Great Hall door.

Chapter Twenty-Eight

"JURIJ CLAIMS TO BE OUR new lord." A hush fell over the crowd as Luuk walked toward Darwyn and Tayton. I crouched slightly as I continued to push my way past a few more men who stood between me and that door. "Why should we believe him?" Luuk said loudly.

I was close enough now to see Darwyn's stunned features. He spoke with a softer voice than Luuk had, but I was just one row away and I could hear him. "Luuk, what are you doing?"

Luuk gestured to the crowd of men, like a leader before an audience. "Where is our *real* lord? He came down to visit us after our tragedy; he helped us get this village built again. Were we dissatisfied with him? I don't think so! Why is Jurij presuming to take his place?"

A number of men began murmuring to one another, and Tayton stepped forward to lay a hand on Luuk's shoulder. "Why are you acting like this?" He seemed worried, afraid even. "He's your own brother!"

Luuk spun on him. "Yes. He's my *brother*, not my *lord!*"

"Yeah!" said a man from the crowd. "Who made *him* lord?"

"What happened to the old lord? If he wanted Jurij to take his place, why isn't he out here telling us that?"

"I thought he was marrying the Woodcarver woman!"

Darwyn stepped in front of Luuk. "Calm down now. You'll all get a turn to ask your questions."

"Why are we waiting out here anyway?" said one man. "Why did they get to go in first?"

Tayton rolled his eyes and blew out a breath. "They weren't singled out. We let in as many as would fit, as many as could wear the bangles—"

Darwyn cut him off with a hand to his chest. "Be patient. You will be allowed in soon."

"Why should I be patient? My wife is in there!" It was the man who'd spoken about his wife before. "I dared to go back home for a blanket for just a short time, and now you won't let me back in!"

Darwyn stepped down the step toward the man. "You'll be able to go back in again—"

"No!" The man shoved Darwyn, and he fell on his backside, wincing as the scabbard twisted uncomfortably between his thighs.

"Darwyn!" Tayton let go of Luuk and ran after his love, tugging at his sword as he did. It got stuck and his hand fumbled, but eventually he pulled it all the way out.

"What is *that*?" asked a man standing near Tayton. He took a step back, his eyes transfixed.

"Tayton, put that back." Darwyn rolled over onto his knees, about to stand up. "They said not to brandish those about like toys."

"It's worse than the tavern!" screamed a burly man. "I was there!" His eyes went wide and he cradled his head with his hands. "That's like a huge knife! Men stabbed other men with their knives, the knives they'd used to cut the meat on their tables!"

"This isn't like the tavern," said Darwyn quickly, using Tayton's arm to scramble to his feet. He held his hands out toward the man. "Now I just need you to calm down."

"Noll," hissed Luuk in my ear. At some point he'd crossed back toward me, the men in front of me pushing him aside to get closer to the conflict. Luuk grabbed my wrist. "Come on!"

"But..." We used the shifting crowd for cover and managed to get up the stairs and to the door behind the line of men advancing on Darwyn and Tayton. I ripped my hand out from Luuk's as he reached for the door. "No! Luuk, these men could hurt each other. They could hurt Darwyn and Tayton. I didn't want this—"

I was cut short as Luuk stared pointedly at the sword I carried at my waist.

"We need it," said Luuk grimly. "We need this distraction. I'll try my best to calm them," he said, "but you must get inside."

"That's a sword!" shouted a man from somewhere behind us. "Like in those tales—do you remember? The tales of kings and queens and battling monsters?"

"Do they think we're monsters?"

"They both have one!"

"I saw Jurij with one, too. And Jaron!"

"Get those away from them!"

"Ow! It cut me!"

"Tayton!"

Luuk had already opened the door, and he put a hand on my back. "Inside!" he said, and before I could protest, I fell forward and the door shut behind me.

A room of a hundred men went silent and turned around to face me.

My eyes roved over all of them, over the shapes of the fallen women strewn out far in the back of the Great Hall, over Jurij, Jaron and Sindri, who stood before them.

"Noll?" Jurij's voice echoed loudly in the silence of the Great Hall.

As the echo faded, I could make out some of the grunting from outside.

I pointed to the door behind me and gritted my teeth. "There's trouble out there! It may lead to more violence!"

Jurij's face went ashen, but Jaron was hardly bothered by the news. He turned and whispered to Jurij, who turned to two specters standing behind him. "See to it," he said. "Summon as many of the others as you need. Keep everyone calm and stop them from harming one another."

I moved as far from the door as the crowd would allow to let the two specters past, afraid one or both of them might grab me and take me back to the castle while they were at it.

Why had he left so many specters behind at the castle? I hadn't noticed a single one outside. And if he was trying to keep what he said secret, why have the two with him? Did Jurij really want them to overhear what he was telling these men and report back to the kings and queens?

I strode forward, pushing into the gap the crowd had made to let the specters pass. "Jurij! You've put all these men at risk!" My eyes fell on the women behind him as I came to a stop in front of the crowd. "All these *people* at risk!"

"It's not our intention to harm anyone." Sindri rubbed his bruised neck. I wondered if that was intentional or a subconscious reminder of the harm he'd experienced himself. I noticed a golden bangle dangle from his wrist.

"Intentional or not, you haven't thought this through." I eyed Jurij and Jaron, waiting for either to dare to contradict me. I faced the crowd of men. "Whatever they've told you, did they also tell you that wearing those golden bangles is the only thing keeping you from harm?" I pointed behind me at Sindri. "Some of you might have seen what happened to Sindri here the other night. A lord's servant attacked him because he discussed something he shouldn't have when he wasn't wearing that golden bangle."

"We know that now," said Jaron smugly. "We've told them once they remove the bangles, they can't talk about what we've told them."

"And you expect them to be able to keep quiet?" I stared at Sindri, thinking of hundreds of men with specters' hands around their necks.

"I don't really get why we have to keep quiet!" shouted a man from the front of the crowd. I watched him rub a hand over the bangle at his wrist. "Or why we have to give these back."

"We went over this," said Jurij, stepping forward. "You pass them on to the next wave of men to come inside, so they can hear what you've heard—"

"Sounds pretty ridiculous and complex to me," spat one man. He nodded toward Jurij. "And why just the men? What if I want the woman I love to know all this?"

Jaron joined Jurij closer at the edge of the crowd, pushing him back with a hand to his chest. "Because women didn't really have to suffer through all those years of the curse, did they?"

The man raised both eyebrows. "I don't agree! My Mariah suffered plenty, forced to be with some dolt she didn't care about—"

"Hey!" snapped a man several rows over. "I *was* that dolt. I mean, that man! Although I should thank you for taking that bitch out of my life."

"Watch your mouth!" The first man shoved through several others to get toward his lover's former man. He slowed down as he got nearer, the men between the two attempting to stop the man from advancing.

"We aren't here to discuss women!" shouted Jaron over the noise of the crowd.

"*I* am!" said a man from beside Jaron. "I don't care about any of this—I want to know what you're doing to save my daughters!"

Jaron looked as if the man had slapped him. "You don't care? You don't care that we were cursed to be women's slaves because of the whims of the first goddess?"

My eyes caught Sindri's warily, eager to see how he reacted. He noticed and bent toward me, whispering slightly. "We haven't said anything about you in particular. Although Jaron objected—he's quite adamant we share all we now know. But Jurij insisted we keep your name out of it."

I let out a breath I didn't even realize had caught in my throat. I studied Jurij and Jaron as they moved around the front of the crowd. Jaron burnt with so much more anger than Jurij. So much more righteousness. Jurij was practically his helpless, quiet childhood self beside the bossy leader. The leader Jurij was convinced had no interest in leading.

Sindri nudged me and I looked up to see him studying me like I was a brand new species of cow. "I *still* can't believe that about you, by the way—"

I lay a hand on his arm to stop him. The man upset about his daughters shook the bangle off his arm with a flourish and slammed it to the ground. It echoed so loudly, the crowd went silent. "No, I don't care! I don't care about what happened—I care about my daughters! I care about my former wife!" He gestured at the fallen women behind us. "I care that there are women in our village who can't wake up!"

"Speak for yourself!" said one man. "I want to know what happened!"

"Now isn't the time," said another. "We have to work together."

"What can we do?" Jaron clenched his fists. "For the women? Nothing. Except accept this as a sign that maybe it's time for the men to take charge of this village again."

"Take charge?" Jurij put a hand on Jaron's elbow. "What are you talking about? This is just about sharing the truth."

Jaron spun on his heel, shaking Jurij's hand away. "Yeah, well, the truth ain't pretty. And I've had enough—"

Jurij raised a finger and Jaron went quiet. They both strained their heads slightly, and it took me a moment, but soon I heard it, too: roaring from outside the Great Hall, like a crowd in anger. A sound I hadn't heard since my time spent in the past, only this crowd was filled with deeper voices. I felt sick.

Coll stepped out from the crowd. I hadn't even noticed him in the front row. "Luuk!" he said, pushing through the crowd to get back to the Great Hall door.

"Father!" Jurij ran after him.

Master Tailor threw the door open. I heard the gasps of men in the crowd before I saw it. I couldn't make it out well from where I was standing, but the village center was a flurry of movement. A flurry of white movement, dotting the masses. The specters were in the middle of the crowd, *fighting*.

I didn't care who started it, or if the specters were only trying to quell rising violence. Luuk and I had given way to that violence, and I'd never forgive myself if anyone else got hurt. Or worse. I ran forward, hitting the back of the crowd as it spilled out into the village center. Before I was even halfway there, though, an arm flew down over my head, grabbing me across my shoulders.

"This is familiar." I recognized Jaron's voice at once, along with the stance. Sure enough, he drew his blade and held it out in front of me.

"These are rather inconvenient. They ought to be designed to be shorter." He sighed and started pulling me back, away from the merging crowds. Jurij and Coll had passed through and were beyond my sight. "Come on, first goddess. We have a few things to discuss."

"JURIJ!" I screamed, but I didn't know if he heard me.

Chapter Twenty-Nine

"WHAT ARE YOU DOING? ARE you mad?" Sindri stormed up to us as Jaron dragged me back toward the fallen women.

"Relax," said Jaron as he shoved me to the ground near a woman I didn't recognize. "I kept quiet about her to the crowd, didn't I?" He pointed the tip of his sword at me. "That doesn't mean I think she shouldn't be willing to talk to me."

Sindri looked about ready to rip his hair out. His eyes darted toward the door, as the last of the men interested in leaving made their way out to see what was going on. A few of the men had rushed to the back of the hall and now held the hands or stroked the foreheads of some of the women lying near me. None of them seemed to pay us much mind, but I noticed the man who had removed his bangle among them. And then I checked—there was a golden bangle unclaimed where he'd tossed it to the floor.

Either my eyes gave me away or Jaron thought much the same as I did at the same time. He stomped over toward the bangle and picked it up, sliding it on the hand without one. "Does this make me twice as worthy?" he asked to the sky. He knew about those who were watching, then.

Were the kings still distracted? Had they made the specters fight with the men? Or was it simply the specters defending themselves and the other men from the anxious crowd? Or were the specters on the side of the queens, or was it just Spurn? I couldn't keep my mind from racing.

I did find strength of mind enough to scramble to my feet, pulling out Elgar as I did.

Sindri stepped back as if I'd slapped him. "Goddess save us, that thing is glowing!"

Jaron stomped over, his own sword held clumsily with both hands. "The Goddess won't save us. *She's* the one threatening us with a sword."

I looked between Jaron and Sindri, unhappy to find Sindri's own hand clutching the hilt of his sword. "I'm not threatening anyone," I pointed out. "I'm defending myself against you."

With the doors open, the noise of the crowd outside was even more uproarious. I couldn't spare a moment to glance at it with Jaron and even Sindri staring me down. I backed up, my backside hitting against something— probably the table on which Vena and Elweard had prepared meals not so very long ago.

Jaron moved closer, and Sindri stepped between us, one hand on the top of his hilt, the other against Jaron's chest. "Now's not the time for this." He gazed over Jaron's shoulder. "We've got to calm them down—and get those bangles back!"

"No." Jaron shoved Sindri's hand aside. "Now's the perfect time for this. Jurij would never let me question her—" A high-pitched scream from the Great Hall door cut Jaron off. Sindri's face paled. Leaving me to face my would-be attacker alone, Sindri sprinted for the door.

Roslyn tumbled inside the Great Hall, clutching her arm. Sindri crouched down beside her, gathering her in his embrace.

The clack of Jaron's sword on mine snapped my attention back to my predicament. Even though I'd encouraged women to arm themselves with farm tools, even though I'd had stick-blade battles, I had never really heard the sound of sword on sword. It wasn't at all the elegant cling of metal on metal that I expected—more like the hollow whack of an axe on a tree.

I gripped my sword harder and Jaron failed to knock it out of my grasp as he'd intended. At least, I hoped that was what he intended. "Do you want to kill me?" I spoke loudly so my voice could be heard over the roar.

"Kill you?" Jaron lowered his sword just slightly, but it was no longer at level with my own. "Kill Aubree's daughter? She'd never forgive me. I don't *want* that."

"I'd like to think you wouldn't want to kill me, no matter whose daughter I was. Besides, my mother is in no mood for forgiveness since you indirectly caused my father's death."

"She never loved him."

"Yes, she did!" It was strange how despite everything that was going on, such a comment could still cause my knees to tremble.

Jaron let go of his sword with one hand to point at his chest. "She loved me!"

I opened my mouth before quickly snapping it shut. Mother had said as much. "That doesn't mean she didn't love Father, too."

Jaron shrugged. "I don't care. If things had been different, she wouldn't have. I could have returned the feelings of a woman who actually cared about me."

I scoffed. "How do you even remember my mother's childhood affections for you? Weren't decades of your life since consumed with thoughts of Alvilda?"

It was the wrong thing to say. Jaron's handsome face twisted, and a dark cloud passed over his features as he went back to gripping his sword with two hands. "Exactly. And whose fault was that? Yours, I discovered."

"I didn't mean for anyone to suffer." I wanted to stand my ground, but I found myself leaning even further back into the table. I had to drop a hand from Elgar to put it on the table behind me to steady myself. "Not anyone who didn't deserve it, anyway."

Jaron rolled his eyes. "So an entire gender? Every man deserved it?"

"No." A flurry of movement from far behind Jaron drew my eyes over his shoulder. "But the way you've been acting since you got your freedom, *you* might."

He roared and raised his sword again toward mine, jabbing at me like a boy poking a sheep with a stick. I wasn't much more skilled, but I managed to move sideways and roll my sword around his. I started making my way along the edge of the table, eager to put it between us. But it was a long, long table. "What is wrong with you?" I demanded. "I thought you were happy courting all the women in town!"

Jaron advanced on me, one slow step at a time. "Yes, a few months of fun makes up for a lifetime of torment." He thumped at his chest. "I want to experience the kind of love promised to me as a man who worshipped a goddess. The perfect love. A lifetime of happiness. I did nothing wrong! I should have been judged worthy."

"You can't blame Alvilda for that." I reached back to see how much more of the table I had left. "She loved someone else."

"Then I can blame the one who cursed me to be that way."

I finally reached the corner of the table. "That wasn't real love anyway." I slipped slowly around the edge, hoping he wouldn't notice. "Real love isn't all happy. It's full of pain and disagreements and it *hurts*." I clenched the damp shawl at my chest and finally succeeded in putting the table between us. "It hurts, but it's worth the fight. It's worth coming to a true understanding of yourself and what you're willing to give up." Hot tears burned my cheek and I blinked hard so I wouldn't lose sight of the man across from me. "You're wrong if you think anyone deserves a perfect love."

"Enough of your squirming!" Jaron lifted his sword high above his head. "Put that thing down and tell me why! Tell me why you did this!"

The sword came down and I rolled, tossing Elgar to the floor beneath the table and coming to a stop when I bumped into a woman lying prone on the floor. Jaron's sword made a racket as it clanged against the table again and again. The racket stopped with a sudden thunk. I scrambled to my feet to see the tip of his sword stuck in the wood of the table.

"What are you doing?" Jurij appeared at Jaron's side, and he wrapped his arms around the shorter man's torso, ripping him away from his stuck sword. Jaron fought back, grabbing at the table, knocking down a lot of the plates and utensils and souring food that Vena and Elweard must have left when Vena fell ill. Jaron spread his hands out over the table, trying to grip it, but Jurij pulled him to the ground.

I scrambled to pick up Elgar before I jumped back up and took in the scene. Jurij and Jaron rolled as one on the ground with Coll, Luuk, Sindri and Roslyn looking on in horror.

"Get off him!" Roslyn clutched her arm. A makeshift bandage made of cloth was dyed red. I had no idea which wrestling man she was speaking to.

Coll bent down and grabbed Jaron's shoulders when he rolled on top. "You need to calm down!"

Sindri patted Roslyn's hip and joined Coll in peeling Jaron away from Jurij. Jaron looked like a bull in heat, his face flushed and his breath labored. Jurij's false-lord clothing was torn, his hair sticking up in all directions. He stood, staring at Jaron like the man had bit him. Maybe he had.

Jaron took a deep breath and ripped his arms out of Coll's and Sindri's grasp. He huffed but said nothing.

"Darwyn's hurt," said Sindri, his voice cracking. "Pretty bad. We can't find Tayton."

"There are men's clothes out there!" Roslyn burst into tears. She couldn't mean—had men *died*? Again? My heart pounded. "They made such a racket, I had to come and find out what was going on, to see if Sin—if any of you were injured, and I couldn't even walk through the crowd without someone shoving me over and another man trampling me."

Sindri's throat bobbed as he watched Roslyn, and I wondered how they'd gone from acquaintances—former family, I suppose, since they'd married each other's siblings—to a couple in love in such a short time. It wasn't even like a young man finding his goddess. There was something more harrowing, more real about the way the two of them looked at one another.

"What is going on exactly?" The voice came from behind me. The man concerned about his daughters had joined a couple of the others who'd stayed behind. Together, they approached our group. Their faces paled as they looked out the Great Hall doors. "This is worse than the tavern!"

One of the men got ahold of himself pretty quickly. He marched over to Jaron and jabbed him in the chest. "This is because of you! Because you insisted we know these things! What are we supposed to do now that we know? How does that help us? How does that save our women?"

Jaron flicked the man's finger away. "Knowing the truth is always better than living in ignorance. Hang the consequences. Hang your daughters."

The man raised his fist, drew it back and slammed it into Jaron's jaw. Jaron staggered back and cradled his jaw, and everyone else went still.

When Jaron spit, it was the color of blood. "You don't care about how we got to be cursed? Fine. You care about how your daughters got sick? It was her." Jaron's eyes narrowed as he looked at me. "Noll was the cause of both problems."

The man turned on me. "Is this true?"

"Jaron!" Jurij gripped Jaron by the front of his jerkin, nearly hanging the stocky man in the air a few inches. "I told you to leave her out of it."

"Why?" said Jaron, not seeming to mind in the least that Jurij was snarling at him. "She doesn't love you, you know."

"I don't care!" snapped Jurij. "That isn't why! I love her. She's my friend. My dearest friend." He spared me a quick glance in the midst of all this anger. I smiled despite myself. "And I love her sister, too. I don't care if they don't love me anymore. I won't let you do anything to harm either of them."

"Ha!" Jaron turned his head and spit blood again. "You're nothing but a man besotted by goddesses, even with the freedom to choose otherwise." He grabbed Jurij's wrist and their two bangles clanged together. "You don't deserve this." He shook Jurij's too-loose bangle.

Jurij opened his mouth and choked out a gurgle a moment later. I didn't understand what had happened, but I recognized the pain on his face.

"Jurij!" screamed Coll and Luuk as one, and they pushed Jaron back to give Jurij space. Jaron held Jurij's bangle between his fingers. He slid it over his arm, his other hand splotched with... blood.

Elgar slipped from my grip. I watched in horror as Jurij grabbed hold of the handle of a meat knife that stuck out of his abdomen and pulled it out, falling to his knees and then face forward into the ground. His hand moved slightly toward me before he vanished into nothingness.

Chapter Thirty

"JURIJ!" I RAN AROUND THE table to the flattened pile of black clothing, skidding and stumbling to my knees. I patted the clothes with both hands, like he was hiding somewhere beneath them.

"What have you done?" I clenched my teeth and tried to stare at Jaron through the tears. He was nothing but a formless lump above me.

Jaron spoke quietly, but the Great Hall had gone so silent, it was easy to hear him even over the din of the outside fight. "I made myself the lord of the village."

"That's not how it works!" I screamed. "You can't kill the lord and become him."

The ground shook, and I tumbled, falling onto Jurij's clothing. I inhaled Jurij's scent and images of lying together in the fields overwhelmed me. *He can't be dead. He can't be.*

And Elfriede would soon follow. And Ailill—but even if he lived, I could never spend time with him again. Even though they'd granted me my life, the kings and queens would leave me nothing to live for. The shaking of the ground would not cease, and I wanted to melt into the floor and be swallowed up by the movement.

Were the kings no longer distracted? Was this them ripping up petals because I was here, even if I wasn't acting like a leader? Was this them angry because of what Jaron had done? Did they only realize there was something amiss in the village once Jurij showed up naked in their garden—

Jurij was in their garden. He wasn't dead. Not really. He never would be. And there was a chance he could be given life right here again.

As a baby. As a new person.

No. I shot up, not caring that my legs were wobbling. *They'd keep him long enough to talk to him—he was the lord for a time, after all, and he'd be worried about all of us. They'd gone out of their way to comfort that woman a little before they sent her to a new life. He's still there.*

And I will get there. I will save him, Elfriede, and Ailill—everyone. Even if it's the last thing I do.

The quake ceased and I tumbled, but Luuk shot out to catch me. His face was lined with tears. "This is my fault," he said. "You warned me not to make the crowd violent."

"No." I pulled away from Luuk. "No. It's not your fault. They were already agitated. And I'm going to make it right."

"How? Jurij's dead!"

I ignored him and stepped over the broken plates and strewn food to get back to the other side of the table, to put Elgar in my grip once more. The men who'd been at the women's sides rolled the shifted women onto their backs, checking for breathing, their faces panicked. I left them to it and walked past the gawking group gathered around Jurij's clothes to the Great Hall door.

"Where are you going?" sneered Jaron from behind me. "I order you to get back here!"

"You shut your mouth!" said a quaking, deep voice.

I paused just long enough to look over my shoulder, to see Coll gripping Jaron by the jerkin, much as his son had moments before. Coll was even taller and bulkier than his son, so he really did lift Jaron up off the ground. "You killed my son!" screeched Coll. "You were never right, not since you got your freedom! You never understood that we all

238

suffered in our own ways, that it wasn't just you and the others who'd been in the commune!"

"You think I care about that? You think I care about—" Jaron didn't get to finish. Luuk appeared around his father's side and then Jaron's mouth opened and he vanished. Coll was left holding his empty clothing and he tossed them to the floor as the three golden bangles went rolling. Luuk threw down the same knife Jaron had used on Jurij on top of the clothing just as two of the bangles came to a stop at my heel.

I stared at them, then bent down and picked them both up, sliding them over my wrist.

Luuk has killed, I thought as I stood. *A killer made him a killer.* I limped forward, only just aware of the throbbing in my knees—I must have bruised them again in the fall when the ground started shaking—but I kept moving, shuffling forward, dragging Elgar along the ground at my side. *I can undo this. I can even make sure Jaron is reborn somewhere else. Somewhere he won't be so unhappy. I can give Luuk that solace. And I can bring Jurij back.*

I just had to make my way through the throng of specters and men fighting to get there.

η η η

I got shoved a few times, but getting through the rabble was less problematic than I pictured. It was almost like I was invisible, dragging my glowing, violet sword along the ground. While fights happened on one side or the other, the men and specters somehow gave me enough berth.

The closest I got to injury was when a man threw a specter onto a vegetable stand in front of me, breaking the stand and sending pieces of wood flying. I thought the specter was bleeding, but it turned out to be squished tomatoes.

The specter met my eyes and I laughed bitterly. It was Spurn.

"Thank you for encouraging this problem." I shook my wrist with the bangles, letting them glitter in the midday sunlight. "Feel like answering to this candidate for ruler of the village or one of the hundred or so behind me? I need your help getting back to the castle."

Spurn stood, brushing the front of his coat with his hands in vain. The back of him was dyed red with tomatoes. I took that as a sign of his agreeing to follow and moved on, dodging the last of the crowd and avoiding the road that led to the bakery, lest I bump into Siofra or Nissa.

The village was quiet the farther away we got from the heart of the village. I blinked back tears even as my head pounded. I couldn't think about whether or not the specters and villagers would stop fighting. Whether or not there were piles of clothing and more dead villagers in the wake of what had happened. The kings and queens were aware of it now, were aware of my coming, for sure. I couldn't stop. I wouldn't stop.

We ran into no one between the edge of the village and the woods. I laughed as the idea of changing clothes once again danced through my mind as we passed the empty, dark cottage that was my home. I may as well not. I was about to jump into that pond again anyway.

Except that before I could even put a foot off the path, Spurn grabbed my arm. "This way," he said, each word slow and with emphasis. "Through the throne."

I almost forgot I had the bangles on, and that meant he could talk to me. He let go of my arm as I changed direction. "Won't the specters—the other servants there stop me?"

"Gone," replied Spurn, that voice scratchy again. "To the village."

"To fight the villagers." I picked up my feet. "I can see Ailill."

Spurn spun me to face him. "Gone, too."

I felt like he'd reached into my throat and twisted my heart. "Where? Not to the fight?"

"Faded away. Vanished."

My knees buckled. I would have fallen to the ground and banged my knees again, but Spurn was there to catch me.

"Not reborn yet." Spurn tugged to pull me up. "Still at that place."

Ailill's spirit was with the kings and queens, but they'd been no help to him while alive. What could they possibly want with his spirit now?

"All right." I straightened my shoulders and slid Elgar into its sheath at my waist. "All the more reason for me to go."

Spurn followed me silently through the first set of stairs in the castle, past the room where I'd left Elfriede and my mother. I paused, my hand on the door. I didn't have time to comfort Mother just yet, to explain what was going on. "Are they all right?" I asked Spurn instead.

"Still there," replied Spurn. "Woodcarver's wife not eating. Both sick in different ways."

I removed my trembling hand. I kept walking. *Everyone is dead. Everyone is dying. I'll be left alone in this place. Maybe that's what they wanted.*

When we passed the kitchen and arrived in front of the throne room, I faced Spurn. "Will you come with me?"

Spurn gazed at the throne room behind me. "I cannot."

"Haven't the queens been contacting you? They sent you that note, correct?"

"Yes," said Spurn. "It appeared through here." He opened his coat and showed me his inner pocket. The pocket that seemed to have an endless supply of whatever was needed with each servant, except perhaps for the things that were too big to fit in there. "The gold coin, too. And the feeling that it needed to get to you."

The queens *were* behind it. They were cheating at their own game, surely risking the kings' wrath. Had they lied about it all? Had they orchestrated my travel through time, too, or was Ailill right that the queens didn't trust me because I'd done things on my own, things they couldn't affect?

"Is there anything else in there?" My tears should have dried— at least until I'd given up all hope and despite how hopeless things were, I hadn't given up hope yet—but I had to blink them back as I studied the haggard appearance of my red-stained servant. As I pictured Ailill that older age, with me at his side, and how I was likely to never see it. As I pictured that scared boy who'd become this shadow again.

The inner lining of Spurn's jacket softly glowed violet and he stiffened. I wondered how I'd never seen it before or if you couldn't see the color through the outside of the coat.

"Yes." Spurn reached into his pocket. He pulled out a folded parchment and handed it to me.

My hands shook as I unfolded it, recognizing at once the type of paper that filled the book allowing you to watch over the village. I knew looking at the one in the throne room would show me nothing of Jurij and Jaron—nothing of Ailill—if they were all there in that other place. The kings and queens had their own such books in their castle, though, and I wondered if the same rules applied.

Apparently not. The drawing I saw was of Ailill, his wrists bound to a wall with chains. He was slumped over, and I recognized the place where he was: the prison—only I knew for sure I wouldn't find him down the hall from where I was standing. He was in the prison in that place, in one of the mirrored castles of the kings and queens.

The note at the bottom made that all the clearer.

Here his spirit lies for eternity, out of reach of all men.

"The queens?" I asked, sure that the kings wouldn't have imprisoned their own favored spirit, even if they had experimented with Jurij taking his place.

Spurn nodded as his coat pocket glowed violet again. He reached inside and pulled out a small knife, no larger than what one would use to peel vegetables. Along with the knife, there was another parchment, and Spurn handed that and that alone to me.

"Why the knife?" I said, leering at it. I took the paper with cautious fingers.

I kept watching Spurn as I unfolded it, not ready to totally trust he wouldn't stab me the moment I looked away.

Yet I had to see what they wanted me to know. This drawing showed Jurij, with Jaron next to him, in the garden on the bench. The kings and queens were there—at least some of them were; the others may have stood beyond the page's point of view. The note at the bottom of this one was in a different handwriting than the other.

"When I was lord," said Spurn. "I dreamed of you."

You shall be left alone, for all that you have done, read the message.

"Farewell, my lady."

Spurn plunged the knife into his chest.

Chapter Thirty-One

I TRAMPLED OVER SPURN'S WHITE clothes, stained red with tomatoes that reminded me of blood—blood that would have been there, had Spurn been anyone but a specter, a shade of a man that once was. The servants had all vanished with Ailill in the cavern after Jurij stabbed him, but they hadn't vanished when Ailill had this time, nor when Jurij had—if the vanishing was tied to whoever was lord. The kings and queens seemed to have lost all sense of fairness and rules at the moment, ignoring whatever it was they'd decided would be the servants' fate—forcing Spurn to put on a show. I could see the anger on their faces even in the drawing in my hands—the one where they stood around Jurij and Jaron, taunting me to come and save them. To come and face them.

It was hard to push the throne aside without help, but I managed, summoning a strength in my arms from the anger coursing through my entire body.

I didn't even hesitate to step in. I didn't expect to encounter any resistance, any red glow. They wouldn't have taunted me otherwise. They could have simply killed me where I stood.

The edge of the cave glowed violet as I approached the Never Veil, and I stepped through it, hesitating only to touch Elgar's hilt.

No. I won't step in, my sword out and ready. These are creatures of non-violence, who enjoy making others do their violent work for them. I won't give them the satisfaction.

I stepped through.

ŋ ŋ ŋ

I came out through the door to the shared entryway of the kings' and queens' castles, not directly into the garden where they were with Jurij and Jaron, as I'd expected to.

Whether that was by accident or on purpose—or if I'd taken fate into my own hands—I wasn't about to throw the chance away.

Jurij and Jaron are there to tempt me to them, but the queens showed me Ailill for a reason.

I glanced up the stairs to the left—the ones I'd seen the queens descend—and tucked the two parchments into my pocket. No one came out from the garden to stop me, so I made my way up.

There was a black veil at the top of the stairs, and I hesitated for a moment, worried that stepping through would take me somewhere else, but I had no other ideas.

No. You'll make it so you step through to the queens' castle. It doesn't matter what anyone else might have in mind.

I filled my mind with images of Ailill and stepped through. Nothing appeared to have happened. It was just like I'd passed through a curtain with no greater power threaded through it at all.

The hall was empty. Torches lit the way along the wall. I didn't know how long it would take before the kings and queens were after me, so I picked up my skirt and ran.

I came quickly to a halt as I passed an open room. There were three black thrones at the back of a long room that looked almost exactly like Ailill's throne room, but for the fact that there were three seats instead of one. I was already on the floor that mirrored Ailill's castle's third floor, even though I'd just stepped onto the second.

Well, the queens surely have no need for so many bedrooms.

I tried hard to think of what the castle had looked like from the outside, how I thought it was like two of Ailill's castles merged and mirrored into one. I'd missed that there was no third floor.

I suppose this way the throne room and the prison are closer to the ground floor, like they were in tales of kings and queens we used to play to. But they'd never be on the ground floor here, not if that was shared space. Now that I was closer, I wanted to be sure I would indeed find a door to the prison waiting for me beyond the throne room. It was there. I let out a breath caught in my throat and ran toward it.

The door opened so easily in my grasp.

"Ailill!"

There was no answer as I tumbled into the room. No light but the dying flicker of a single torch on the wall. I grabbed it and swung the light toward the first cell. Nothing. I tried the second. Nothing still. *They deceived me.*

My breath hitched as I stood before the third cell. Ailill was there, his hands chained above him as they had been in the drawing. The thought flickered through my mind that he ought to be naked—like this was the time to worry about that—if his spirit had come here, but someone had clothed him in specter garb—the lord's outfit pale as snow.

"Ailill!"

Ailill's slumped-forward head lilted slightly.

I grabbed hold of the prison door, not sure why I assumed I'd find it unlocked. I shook the bars to no avail. "Argh!" I'd come too far for this. I stepped back, drew Elgar out from my sheath and slammed it against the keyhole, like that would make a difference.

It'll make a difference, I told myself, as I slammed the sword against the keyhole again and again, watching the violet glow in the near-darkness. *Because I decide it does.*

Lo and behold, the door swung back. I didn't even bother to marvel at it. I was through the door, Elgar tossed aside, and my hands on Ailill's cheeks as I lifted his head up. "Ailill, can you hear me?"

His eyelids fluttered open. "Noll...?"

I smiled. "I thought we agreed I liked it when you called me Olivière."

The very corners of Ailill's lips twitched. "Too much... to say. Can't speak... Queens' castle... bad for men."

He was speaking in contractions. He was definitely dire.

I stood, reaching for the metal around his wrist. There was a keyhole on each of those, too, and they wouldn't budge. I picked up Elgar and swung it up.

Ailill's head lolled forward a little. "No sword! No... Just you. Just you."

I laughed despite the terribleness of the situation. I expect he worried I might miss. I sheathed Elgar and decided to trust him.

I grabbed one metal bangle in both hands. *Release him*, I thought. *Release him and open. Let him go.*

My hands glowed warm and violet light appeared from my fingers. I jumped back and let out a yelp as the bangle broke open, and Ailill's arm fell down, free.

He tipped his head up slightly and smiled. "See? Just you. Special."

I scrambled back to my knees and did the same for the other bangle, then caught Ailill around the chest as he fell forward.

"The queens' castle makes you weak?" I asked, not sure how a spirit who was neither truly dead nor alive could be weakened by anything. I positioned myself so one of Ailill's arms wrapped around my shoulders.

"All men." Every word caused Ailill strain, like there was a pain somewhere in his abdomen. "Including kings."

I struggled but managed to stand, bringing us both to our feet. "Where can I bring you that you'll be safe?"

Ailill let out a raspy sound that might have been a laugh. "Nowhere. But I will be stronger past veil. Back in entryway."

"Save your strength, then," I said, and we began the slow journey out of the prison and down the long hall.

No one disturbed us, although I feared a king or queen—just a queen, I supposed—would appear from one of the rooms we passed every few paces. I hadn't for certain seen them all on the page they'd sent me, and in any case, they were bound to start looking for me by now. They must have expected me. The page hung heavy in my pocket. Perhaps I could check to be sure. As soon as my eyes passed over Ailill's face, though, I knew I had to get him toward the veil, no matter what awaited me. I would face them eventually regardless.

Ailill's weight seemed to get less heavy as we approached the veil at the end of the hallway. He still leaned on me, but it wasn't like he was hanging off me anymore. His back straightened somewhat. His head lifted higher.

"Let's stop." Ailill leaned against the wall beside the fluttering veil. I wondered where the flow of air came from.

He's still speaking casually. I leaned against the wall beside him, putting myself between him and the veil in case we had visitors. "Are you feeling better, though?"

"Better." He laid his head against the wall. "As soon as we pass through there, I'll be fine."

"Then why stop here?"

"You need to know a few things before we go out there."

I thought of Jurij and Jaron, and the parchment in my pocket. "You do, too."

Ailill rolled his head back and forth. "I'm not dead."

The corner of my lips twitched. "I can see that."

"No, I mean, I didn't die in our village and vanish. Is that what you thought?"

I frowned. "Yes. Well, that's what Spurn told me."

"Who?"

I felt my cheeks flush at the stupid name. "One of the servants. The... first one, actually. It's just a name I gave him."

Ailill's jaw tightened. "I had a feeling they were developing a little too much personality." He hit his head softly against the wall a few times.

"Just the one," I said. "That I noticed anyway." I'd wanted so badly to find Ailill in Scorn, but it was clear now he was nothing but an empty shell of the man.

Ailill leaned his head toward the veil. "It was them. The queens."

"Why?"

"It happened at the end of the life two lives ago... The life before the one you first knew."

"Do you remember that life?"

Ailill clenched his fist together and rapped it against the wall behind him. "Yes. I mean, I can only remember so much of any life, just like you can only remember so much of yours, but there are snippets of memories of all of them. I'm sorry I lied about that."

I smirked. "You're talking in contractions."

Ailill unclenched his fist. "I'm still a bit weak. It helps save my breath perhaps." He rolled his head slightly and glanced at me. "Besides, I'm not lord anymore."

I scoffed. "I refuse to believe a chess game is all it took."

"That and a bangle." Ailill rubbed a hand over his wrist absently.

I opened my mouth to speak but snapped it shut again, holding up a finger. I strained to listen past the veil to the entryway below. I thought I heard movement, but after a few moments of silence, the tension in Ailill's body relaxed and he resumed talking.

"Before we were reborn to the life you first knew, just as were about to step through the Veil, reborn yet again as a young lord... I saw the queens take that shade of me aside." He shook his head. "I don't know how. They must have sufficiently distracted the kings for long enough. He's been working for them ever since—at least he has been since they've been interfering with us over the past few months."

I tried to remember if I recognized Spurn in any of my memories from my time in the castle, but I could hardly tell them apart back then. Besides, kings and queens in another castle were so far beyond my imagination at the moment; I wasn't looking for traitors amidst the stoic servants. "Do you think he willingly helped them? The first you?"

"Who knows? If so, perhaps he thought it the right course of action. Perhaps he was tired of the kings always bringing us back to life... I know a part of me thought that every rebirth. And he'd been with us the longest, seen the most suffering. Shade or not, that must have impacted him."

Ailill let out an exhausted breath and continued. "In any case, earlier, after you left, he guided me to the hole behind the throne room. He practically had to drag me up the stairs. If only the most important rooms weren't on the third floor of the castle."

"I've wondered about that." Although now was hardly the time. "There are two floors here, but still, why the throne room and the prison on the upper floor? Why not on lower floors, and leave the private rooms to the upper ones?"

"The kitchen, too." Ailill nodded toward the row of doors on the wall. "They keep those next to the throne room. In case they feel like dining without the kings. Or on the kings' side, without the queens."

"So they want the important rooms away from the other gender?"

"I suppose," said Ailill. "And since their guests rarely stay long, they had no need for additional bedrooms beyond that which one floor could provide."

"And the castles for the lords and ladies in the villages do?"

Ailill smiled slyly. "Perhaps those leaders are more social than the lord to whom you were accustomed."

"You're speaking formally again."

Ailill's cheeks darkened just slightly. "The villages' castles simply echo the ones here. The most important rooms are high up, out of the reach of enemies. The prison, too."

"Makes it harder for someone to break your enemies out, I suppose."

"Apparently not. Not with an Ailill going around releasing my prisoners."

I leaned one of my feet flat again the wall behind me. "So Spurn led you to the throne room?"

Ailill pursed his lips. "I went through the Never Veil and instead of arriving in the entryway or the kings' throne room, as I usually do, I came out here." He jutted his chin forward. "Through the queens' throne room."

"Better than in some canyon leagues away, I guess."

"Not if you grow weaker the farther you are from this veil."

I stared at the veil, watched it flutter like someone was on the other side, running her hand across it. Maybe someone was. "So I should steer clear of the kings' castle."

Ailill stood at my side. "You should avoid being there alone, in any case."

"I'll remember that—assuming I can ever go back."

He tugged on my arm. "You might be able to pass through the Never Veil behind the center throne in the queens' throne room. That's where the connection is in the kings' room."

"What about you?"

He bit his lip. "I do not think I could make it through. I will try the kings' side."

"Why did they make Spurn their traitorous servant?" I asked after a moment's thought.

"You, I suspect." Ailill took one of my hands in his. "When they turned him into their pawn, they must have known you were coming soon." His eyebrows cinched together. "Actually, you would have already been there, as a young child. I suppose they recognized you somehow."

"Wait, I was... older than you in your last life?" I cocked my head. In a sense, I was older than this Ailill, too, since he was "born" as a young man when I was already eighteen. So that must have been the case before. He was born as a young man already grown and then had lived as the Ailill I knew for what—ten or so years? So had he died an old man before that in the days since I was born? What if I'd met him as an *old man*, what if I'd been expected to fall in love with him when he looked as if he could have been my grandparent? It was maddening to think about.

Ailill laughed. "I don't think you've ever been or ever will be 'older' than me."

"I was when you were a boy."

Ailill paused and laughed again. "So you were." He traced an unseen pattern on the back of my hand. Whoever had dressed him—even if he hadn't vanished and died, someone *had* changed his clothing—hadn't given him a pair of gloves. I was struck by the bareness of his wrist.

"You don't have a golden token anymore," I said. "So why did the queens draw you here?"

"I am certain they wanted to draw you here again."

I raised an eyebrow. "Despite threatening everyone in my village if I ever dared to think of returning?"

"They said that to make the kings think they were working with them, I suspect."

It didn't make sense. Who ordered Spurn to kill himself? The kings? Because they knew what the queens had done? The queens because they were done with him? "You know what? I don't care. I don't care anymore." I watched Ailill's fingers as they moved over my hand, felt the familiar shiver run up my spine at his touch. I put my other hand on top of his. "I'm tired of their game, Ailill. I'm not going back."

The look of panic on Ailill's face was enough to make my confidence waver. "You have to!" he said.

I turned Ailill's hand in mine so we were holding each other again, palm to palm. "No. They have Jurij and Jaron out there, in the garden, right now. They're waiting for me. Suspiciously patiently." I dropped his hand and slid one of the bangles from my own wrist over his. "But I want you to go."

"Absolutely not!" The volume of Ailill's voice made me flinch.

"The queens think you're here. The kings seem to have forgotten about you entirely. If you come with me to the garden—"

"We'll take them by surprise. Perhaps." A faltering smile appeared on Ailill's face. "We go together."

I wanted to say no. I wanted to shove him through a hole in the wall, but there was no way I could send him somewhere he'd be out of the kings' and queens' reach.

"All right." I straightened my shoulders and stood at his side. "Together." We stepped through the veil to the staircase.

Chapter Thirty-Two

MARIGOLD WAITED FOR US AT the bottom of the stairs. Estavan stood as her reflection at the bottom of the kings' staircase.

"We have awaited your arrival," said Marigold. She gestured to Estavan beside her. "The kings did not think it fair that any of us should go see what delayed you in our castle, since they cannot witness it themselves."

Ailill dropped my hand to pat my arm as he took the lead, crossing over in front of me. "Did you know they had locked me up in there?" he asked Estavan.

Estavan studied Marigold, who refused to acknowledge him. "We have been discussing that. We agreed to let Olivière remove you from the queens' castle as soon as we discovered it, since we could not do so."

"You brought Ailill to your castle many a time out of our reach," said Marigold curtly. "You did not find us complaining about it."

Estavan's lips curled into a sneer. "That was different, and you know it."

I gave Marigold a wide berth as I shuffled toward the garden door. I was tired of the petty arguments between these selfish figures. "Are Jaron and Jurij still there?"

Marigold looked like she was holding in a sneeze. "They are." She clasped her hands together in front of her.

"They could not have peace in their new lives until they knew what became of those in their old ones."

They won't have peace in their new lives because I'm sending them back to their old ones. Somehow. Even Jaron. Maybe.

I ran to the garden door and tugged it open.

"Olivière, wait!" Ailill's urgent cry went unheeded.

I blinked twice as my eyes adjusted to the bright sunlight. This land where the kings and queens dwelled was hot and dry and harsh, and it was far brighter than home.

"Noll!" The sound of Jurij's wavering voice was so like his old self. I ignored the standing figures to sit on the bench next to him, wrapping my arms around him. He hugged me back, and it was like all of the terrible things between us, all of the awkward moments, were gone. I pulled back, feeling his face, wondering at the physical form his spirit had in my hands. He had no scar over his eye and cheek now, as if vanishing to this place took all of the hurt from the old life away.

My eyes were drawn to the shifting figure seated behind him and I dropped my hands. "Why did they seat you next to *him?*"

Jaron sat bent over, his elbows atop his legs spread slightly apart, his arms dangling down between his knees. "Hello to you, too, Noll."

"Here are your answers, Jaron." I faced the kings and queens. Marigold and Estavan joined the other four, just as Ailill appeared at my side beside the table. "I hope you were as kind to them as you were to us when you were demanding them."

"I told Jurij I was sorry." Jaron's voice was gruff, with just a hint of the emptiness I remembered from his time in the commune.

"And you accepted his apology?" I asked Jurij.

Jurij rubbed his palms together, his eyes flickering quickly toward the standing figures in front of us before looking down at the ground. "It doesn't really matter now, does it?"

"I disagree." I felt my face go hot as I realized both Jaron and Jurij were naked. I'd just hugged Jurij while he was *naked*. I'd been so glad to see him I hadn't even thought about it. "Ailill, spare your jacket?"

Ailill shrugged out of his white jacket, half a smile poking at his face. "I should really get you one of your own. But then, you would not keep that one, either." He took to the task rather awkwardly, turning away from the kings and queens and then keeping one hand behind his back as he finished. The hand with the bangle.

I grabbed it from him and put it around Jurij's shoulders. I didn't look down. I refused to look too closely at his lap. Jaron could spend eternity in the nude for all I cared.

"Are you finished?" asked Adeyemi. "You have a lot to answer for."

"All right," I said, eyeing Jangmi. "I will be happy to give you all of your answers."

Jangmi stepped in front of Adeyemi, her hands clutched in front of her abdomen. "We agreed," she said to him. "No more discussions with her. We shall decide her fate as a group. She is here. She will stay here until we have decided."

Apparently the queens were still eager to conceal the full extent of their involvement.

"There is far more than that to discuss," said Kin. "Do not think we will let your abduction of Ailill go. You violated the rules."

"You had already selected a new lord for that village by then," Chrysilla remarked dryly. "I see no rules broken."

Jangmi held up a hand. "We shall discuss it all. Let us adjourn to the dining room."

"Very well," said Adeyemi. He nodded toward me. "She must give up her stolen token."

Jangmi held both hands out and I didn't hesitate to slide the bangle off and give it to her this time. I wasn't going to risk their wrath again, and besides, I didn't care if I never went back. I'd stay until I fixed everything.

Ailill moved closer to me, laying his hand without the bangle on my shoulder. No one spoke as the three kings and three queens stepped through the door back to the entryway of the castle. No one spoke for a moment more after the door shut, either. I wrapped my hand around Ailill's wrist with the bangle and smiled up at him.

He turned and slid it off, putting it into my hands.

"Didn't they tell you to give that to them?" Jaron seemed to have woken up from his stupor.

"This is a different one." I stood. "And we'll have to act fast." I ran over to the garden door and started gently probing it. I was afraid of making too much noise, that trying too hard to turn it into a portal would attract the kings' and queens' attention. And the door seemed to be in no mood to turn into the veil.

"Act fast to do what?" Jaron was incredulous. I tried not to look at him much, though. Not just because I was angry at him, but because I had no interest in seeing him nude, no matter how lovely the men of my village were. I didn't like noticing that about someone who'd done so much harm to those I loved.

I gave up on the door and ran to the bush with the purple lilies and caressed the fragrant flowers. I spoke to Ailill, ignoring Jaron. "If breaking one of these blooms causes illness in the village, what can I do to undo it?"

Ailill frowned as he approached. "It is simple to destroy, to cause damage. I do not know how one can repair it. Only the natural rebirth of the flowers can lead to good, I would assume."

Panic seized my throat. We had such little time to get this right. I had little confidence I had any power to do it. My eyes darted over the fountain and I gasped. A glinting flitter of gold sparkled from beneath the still water's surface.

I bent down, dunking my hand under the tepid water, and withdrew my gold coin, holding it up to the light. "They left it *here*! They just left it here... And they left me here with it!"

Ailill put a hand over my fingers clutching the coin, lowering my arm. "I would not trust that. They must have left it here on purpose."

"I don't care. It gives us a second chance." I slid the coin into my pocket, my fingers brushing the parchment I'd nearly forgotten about stuffed in there. I brought both pieces out. *The hole behind the throne. It showed even when the throne covered it. If there's a secret to this garden...* "Ailill, stand here." I maneuvered him in front of the lily-covered bush. I unfolded the piece of paper and saw Jurij and Jaron on the bench, staring forward—probably staring at me, but I was off page. There were no hidden holes on that paper, so I tucked it beneath the other one.

The parchment showing Ailill depicted the exact scene I was looking at. I frowned. The *exact* scene. There was nothing promising.

"What are you doing?" asked Jurij. I pulled his parchment out to keep an eye on where he wandered throughout the garden, too. He stood, looked down, and quickly slid off the single piece of clothing he was wearing, tying it like a loin cloth in front of him with the arms of the jacket behind his waist. I nearly choked and checked to see if Ailill had noticed me. I hadn't witnessed it directly, full color and all, but I could tell from the mischievous look on Ailill's face that he knew what I'd seen on the parchment.

"Looking for something," I said, not turning my head. "Could you walk around the garden?" I looked up. "Both of you?"

Ailill nodded and headed one way, while Jurij stood still, his mouth slightly open. "Like when we saw the hole behind the throne."

"That's the idea. Please. Our time is limited."

He nodded and went the opposite direction of Ailill. I held both parchments out, eager to find anything odd about either of them. I was soon disappointed.

"Nothing?" asked Ailill as he crossed paths with Jurij and the two came to a stop in front of the lily-covered bush.

"Nothing." I sat down between the lily-covered bush and its neighboring one on the lip of the fountain. I let out a sigh of frustration and stared up at half-naked Jurij. "When you came here the first time, where did you appear?"

"You mean on the other side of the Never Veil?" Jurij frowned. "I don't remember actually. It was like I was drowning... And then I came to here—in the garden."

Ailill sat beside me and jutted his chin toward the garden door. "The Never Veil's doorway must have led through the garden door, just like it did when we left last time."

Jurij nodded slowly. "I was wet."

"Wet from the cavern pool," I said, like it was obvious. We sure spent a lot of time wet thanks to that place.

"Or maybe...?" Ailill turned around and ran his hand through the water in the fountain behind us.

"I don't know what you're bothering yourselves for," said Jaron sourly. "These people have the power to do anything to us. There's no hope in fighting them. They said we get to be reborn in other villages, so there's that. As soon as all those women die, we'll have our 'peace of mind' and can get on with things. Them, too. That's good enough."

"No, it's not!" I looked up at Jaron despite myself. "I want to save the people I know. The people I *love*." I was so upset I hardly noticed as Ailill grabbed the parchments from me. "No one else has died yet, since you two came here?"

Jaron eyed the door. "I guess not. Perhaps those kings and queens put a stop to death while they debated. Too many spirits to process at once."

"But that fight with the men and the servants—"

Jurij lifted a finger and went back to the table, picking up a book and bringing it over. He leafed through the pages until he found one and then flipped it over, showing it to me. "That's over. Father and Luuk managed to put an end to it somehow. We've been watching them like little pantomime figures on these pages. I don't know what they're saying, but the men have stopped. They're treating the wounded."

"What about the bangles?" I asked, rubbing the one Ailill had returned to me.

"The servants collected them all," answered Jurij.

"Is that what they were doing?" I sighed and pushed some hair out of my face. "It looked to me like they were in a battle."

Jurij smiled slightly. "A battle with monsters?"

"Who knew then that people could be the monsters," I replied. I gave him a faltering smile back. "That's not true. There's no such thing as a completely heartless monster." My eyes darted to Jaron, who was still slumped over on the bench.

"Olivière, I've found something."

Ailill handed me the paper with the image of his back on it. He leaned forward, almost tipping into the fountain but stretching an arm out toward the stone to steady himself. I was afraid he was going to fall in.

"Look at the parchment," he panted. I did as I was told and saw the paper now showed the fountain as if I were looking down at it and Ailill from the sky.

There was a black hole in the bottom of the fountain, just large enough to fit a person though.

Chapter Thirty-Three

"T**HAT'S IT!"** I WRAPPED MY arms around Ailill's torso and pulled him to an upright position. He tumbled into me as we stood. Our eyes met and I was so happy I could have kissed him—but then I was suddenly overwhelmed with the idea that I'd *almost kissed him.*

I pulled back. *Is that disappointment on his face? He couldn't have known what I'd almost done.* "We can send you back." I turned to face Jurij. It was he I wanted to send back first.

Jurij looked from me to Ailill and back again. "How? I died. It's not the same as wearing a bangle and walking through a veil."

"I'll make it so." I slid the bangle off my wrist and grabbed Jurij's hand, sliding it over his. Jaron's face was incredulous. "I will."

"Noll, how?" Jurij shifted some of my hair behind my ears, a strangely tender gesture in the midst of all of this. "You're not a king or queen."

"I'm the elf queen." I laughed. "Remember?"

The lump at Jurij's throat bobbed. "Noll, I appreciate it, but even if you could send me back—"

"Which I can—"

"Even if you *could*, I don't want to go back. I don't want to go back to a village full of illness, knowing the only people who could do something about it are here, and I left them behind."

I bit my lip and looked back over my shoulder at Ailill. Ailill stepped forward and took the book from Jurij's hands and opened it.

"When someone is reborn into a new village, a new flower blooms." He flipped through the pages. "It's not that that individual life is tied to the individual bloom—there would be hundreds of roses buried beneath the flowers of each bush if so. But the new birth gives an added jolt of magic to the village, and more opportunities for the kings and queens to make an impact on the village." He paused when he got to the very back of the book and frowned, running his finger over the inside of the cover slowly. "I think rebirthing a soul into a village may give Olivière the power she needs to wish the women well again."

"There you go." I stared at Jurij before hugging him, ignoring the strangeness of having my cheek rest against his bare shoulder. It was like what I imagined getting too close to a naked brother might feel like, so I couldn't let us linger for long. "I'm sending you back."

Jaron scoffed from his entirely unhelpful position over at the bench. "They told us we'd be born again as infants when they sent us to new villages. That we wouldn't remember any of this—that we'd been reborn many times before."

"That is when you go to a new village." Ailill still studied the inside cover of the book, his finger and eyes moving down and then back to the top again. "That is why they never send spirits to the same village twice in a row. Not just for fear someone still living there might recognize something of the essence of the spirit in a new child, but because you will grow to remember your past lives. Perhaps not in detail, but well enough." His finger stopped suddenly and his eyes snapped up. "If you take a golden bangle with you, as I did each time I was reborn, you can even stay the same exact age you were when you died, with no loss of memory at all. Or you can choose a younger age. The kings recommended I be reborn at the age at which I became a man, again and again." He shut the book closed. "I agreed because I would be that much closer to my latest demise." His voice softened. "It seemed a small comfort at the time."

A flutter in my stomach told me that Ailill wasn't just being sorrowful at the thought of his past selves, that he had seen something in the book he was keeping from me, something important, but if he chose not to share it just then, then I would have to wait to ask him.

"Jurij, please." I wrapped my fingers around the bangle I'd given him. "Please. I need you back there. I need to trust someone is there, someone who will look after my mother and Elfriede."

"You speak as if you're not planning on coming back."

I placed a finger over his lips. The last thing I needed was an argument from him that he would stay or the promise that he would come back if I didn't show within a certain amount of time. "I will," I lied, not feeling at all bad about it. "But you must give me time, and you must do what you can do for me—and that's agreeing to a rebirth. Give me the flower I need to work with to make the women well again."

Jurij grabbed my hands in his and squeezed them. He looked over his shoulder at Jaron.

"Don't look at me," said Jaron. "You want to risk their wrath, you're welcome to it. Besides, you deserve another chance. I had no right to take your life from you."

Jurij's gaze flickered to Ailill. "Promise me you'll keep her safe."

Ailill slipped an arm around me. "I live for nothing else."

I slipped my own arm around Ailill's waist, knowing it might give Jurij the courage at last to leave me behind. He watched us a moment and nodded. We stepped aside and let him pass through. Jurij lifted one leg and put it into the fountain slowly, testing to make sure he wasn't about to fall into it. He looked back at me. "Can I keep the jacket? Or should I go nude?"

Ailill laughed, and the sound was so strange coming from him. It was genuine, not at all tinged with derision. "Keep it. Please. They let me wear clothing each time I went through."

Jurij's jaw twitched and he put his other leg into the water. He stared down at it. "I can see a bit of red," he said. "Like there's a circle here, but it's red, not violet."

I grabbed Ailill's hand and we approached the fountain together. I reached into my pocket and clutched the coin hard.

Send him home. I closed my eyes. *Send him home, as he once was. As Jurij. Send him home!*

"It's violet!"

I opened my eyes to see Jurij stick one foot forward. He almost fell down but stopped himself. "It just looks like stone, but there is a hole here."

"Hurry," I said, still repeating the line in my head. *Send him home.*

"All right." Jurij hesitated. "Goodbye, Noll. I loved you." He walked forward and then vanished into the ground.

"Quick," Ailill said, and he clutched both my shoulders. He guided me to the lily-covered bush. "Make it happen, Olivière. I know you can."

I leaned in front of the bush and reached in, gently moving the outer layer inside until I saw the white roses. *Send him home.*

Parchment crinkled from somewhere behind me. "He's there!" said Ailill. "The same Jurij, just as we hoped!"

The bush began to glow. A small, violet sphere appeared on a branch, the light rippling like a veil at the slightest touch.

I clasped my hands together over the coin and stared at that forming magic. *Make them well*, I thought. *Undo the sickness in my village. Make them well. Make them well.*

The sound of papers shuffling—Ailill flipping through the book. "The women are stirring! Keep wishing it, Olivière. Keep going!"

Make them well!

The white rose burst into life, scattering the violet light in all directions.

"They're awake!" I got to my feet and spun around, still so unused to hearing casual speech on Ailill's tongue. I wasn't used to the sheer joy that decorated his features, either. "I knew you could do it, Olivière. I knew you had it in you."

I laughed and embraced him, book and all. I don't know how long we stayed that way. I do know that the first thing to disturb us was Jaron's gruff and unpleasant voice.

"Well, now you've doomed us all."

I pulled back, my eyes darting to the garden door, expecting the kings' and queens' arrival, but there was nothing, not yet. They had a lot to discuss, and their perception of time must surely run much more slowly than ours.

I stomped over to Jaron, feeling the weight of the coin in my hand. I don't know when I made the decision, but it came out of my mouth, like it was the only thing to do. "I'm sending you back, too."

Jaron looked at me as if I'd proposed marriage. "Oh, no. No, you're not. You sent the bangle back with Jurij, remember? Doesn't that make it easier for you to send people?"

I jumped as a white shirt flew over my shoulder to Jaron's bare lap. At least now the most embarrassing parts were covered from my sight. Although then I realized that meant Ailill was wearing nothing on his top half.

I didn't realize I could almost faint from embarrassment without even looking at something. I steadied my feet and tossed the coin atop the shirt.

"You'll go back with this."

Jaron stared at me, not even picking up the coin. "You trust me?"

"No. But I trust my friend. The one who existed before he wanted all the answers."

Jaron grabbed the coin and picked up the shirt. He stood, and I looked away as he put his arms through it. He was shorter than Ailill, so I hoped it'd reach beyond his thighs. The next time I dared to look, I saw that it did. He shook his fist. "What if I don't want to go back?"

"Where else would you go?" asked Ailill, slipping in beside me. Just looking out of the corner of my eyes, I caught sight of his bare chest and I had to bite down on my lip hard to stop it from trembling.

Jaron gestured to the bushes all over the garden. "Somewhere I won't remember the things I did."

"We want you to remember," said Ailill stiffly, as if he'd known all along I'd send this terrible man back to our people. "We do not want men to forget their propensity for violence. No more than we want women to forget that men's freedom to love should be equally respected."

I spoke, adding my own reasoning. "Plus, your death made Luuk a murderer. I won't let that be true." Aillil slid an arm around my shoulders, and I found myself leaning into him.

"All right," said Jaron as he brushed past us. "If you're sure."

I nodded and broke away from Ailill, following Jaron to the fountain. He got in quicker than Jurij, more surefooted.

I turned back to face Ailill, my treacherous eyes drinking in his thin but defined chest before landing on his face. "Can I do it without a token of my own?"

Ailill smiled and nodded, and that was all the encouragement I needed.

I clasped my hands together and shut my eyes. *Send him back*, I thought. *Back as he was.* I hesitated. *Perhaps a little nicer.*

Send him back.

When I opened my eyes, he was gone.

Chapter Thirty-Four

ILILL, BARE-CHESTED AND PRACTICALLY shining in the sunlight, walked back to the table and flipped the book open as he sat at the bench. He smoothed the two pieces of parchment torn from it and lay them on the table beside it.

There was still no sign of movement at the garden door. I slid in beside Ailill, resting a hand on his shoulder. His skin felt like fire—in a good way, like comforting, warming, lively fire. It sent pinpricks to my fingers.

Ailill squeezed my hand, shooting the pin pricks from my fingers to my toes.

"Is he back?" I asked.

"I don't know." Ailill began flipping through the pages. There were people I only somewhat recognized and familiar faces—*Alvilda* awake, Siofra and Nissa embracing her—but every page was a good one. There was no worry or violence; only happiness and rest and respite from all that had happened.

Ailill came to a stop on a page that glowed as it wove from the binding, from nothingness into being. As the light faded, it showed Jaron breaking through the surface of the cavern pool and let out a breath. "He is back," he said, speaking slowly. His shoulders relaxed visibly.

I traced my fingers over the length of his back, finding the muscles between his shoulder blades to be as sharp and defined as if they were sculpted out of a large block of wood. Oh, how I missed carving. I wished I'd thought to carve some more after Father's death. I didn't realize I would never again seem to find the time and strength of mind for it.

...I was comparing Ailill to a hunk of wood. They may have both brought me joy, but that might have been the dumbest thing I had ever thought. My cheeks burned.

"You talk less formally when you're happy," I teased, making my fingertips brush his skin even more lightly.

Ailill shivered under my touch. "No, I don't." His face grew flushed. "All right," he admitted. "I suppose I do."

I wrapped my hand around his side and squeezed him into me, ignoring the poke of Elgar's sheath in my side as I did. But I didn't let myself get too distracted. "Okay, we set out to do what I wanted. We saved the women. We saved both Jurij and Jaron." I rested my chin on both hands on the table. "Without any golden tokens, I don't think we can go back. I wanted to send you back—"

"I will not go back. Not without you."

I smiled and let it go. I understood. If he had sent me back but stayed behind... Well, I couldn't bear to think about it.

"How do we stop them?" I asked. "From undoing what I've done?"

Ailill laughed and I turned to see what he was looking at. Elgar was still sheathed to my waist. "They took your golden bangle away," he said. "But since they will not use weapons themselves, they hardly seemed aware of that."

I raised an eyebrow. "You propose we... fight them? With a sword?"

"They will not expect it."

"I suppose not." I ran my fingers over Elgar's hilt. "I... I don't know if I have it in me again. To hurt people with violence."

Ailill slid the book closer to me. Jaron, dripping water, exited the cavern for a moment, but Ailill flipped past that page, past all the pages—Elfriede! Awake and embracing Mother!—until he reached the back.

He was looking at whatever was there before, and I knew even then he wasn't happy with what he found there.

"Do you know what this is?" asked Ailill.

It was a series of names, an almost endless list, written in the smallest possible handwriting. I squinted and looked closer. "I can't really read it. But names?"

Ailill nodded. "The names of everyone who ever lived in our village. It is not a feature the book they gave me shares. I have never been alone with this version of the book long enough to get a clear look."

My eyes widened as I pointed at the page. "Everyone? No wonder it's so small." I peered down again. "Even so, it seems like there should be more."

Ailill ran a finger from one side of the book to the other. "They repeat, and you will find the secondary names of each spirit right there next to the first one. Once a spirit has been reborn in all of the other villages, it returns back to this one."

"Really?" I didn't think anything else could surprise me about how everything worked, but I was wrong. "Does it say who I once was?"

Ailill grinned and tapped a name in the last column at the very bottom. I squinted. It was my own, and there were no other names by it. "Just you. I told you you were special."

"What about you?" I asked.

Ailill laughed and ran his finger over names toward the beginning, in the second column. His name looked strangely empty, but there were a couple of names before it. "Apparently I was reborn in that village two times, before my strange never-ending rebirth as Ailill." He gestured behind him. "But that means I had lives in all of these villages, too."

My eyes wandered up above his name, catching sight of Avery. There were a number of names after hers, and the last one was Alvilda. I gasped. "Your sister was reborn as Alvilda! I thought they were alike."

Ailill coughed and tried to grab the book back from me. "My sister died," he said. "She lived so many lives since, I could hardly consider her current incarnation the same person. In fact, I am surprised there's any similarity at all."

"I'm not." I tugged back on the book, not letting Ailill take it away from me. "The spirit was the same, so how could they not share—" I stopped. The name "Elric" stood out like it was jumping up at me.

"Olivière, I was not sure you should know..."

I let my finger follow the trail of names I didn't recognize from that spirit. Without even seeing the last one, I was sure I was going to find Jaron's name there, but I didn't.

It was Jurij's.

ŋ ŋ ŋ

Getting past the dining room without making a sound was one of the most difficult things I'd ever done. I thought for sure they would hear the pounding of my heart as I did: thunderous, loud and echoing in my ears.

Ailill signaled for me to join him at the end of the entryway. The door to the dining room was open, and instead of seeing the kings and queens debating or eating in there, we found them each playing a game of chess with one from the other team in near silence. Each second it took to pass the room was agony. I was afraid they'd look up and see me, but they didn't.

The fact that the garden door was unlocked—I hadn't tried opening it when I tried to see if I could

271

summon the portal there—made me nervous. Like they were expecting us to walk past.

"*I need a weapon, too,*" said Ailill. "*The kings and queens each keep one hanging over their thrones. As a testament to how things once were.*"

"*A testament to violence?*" I asked incredulously.

Ailill shrugged. "Whatever the reason, I need to get to the kings' throne room to grab one. I can't... go through the queens' again."

I reached for Ailill at the door. He took my hands in his. "Here we part," he whispered. "Take the queens' swords, just in case they decide they want to use them, and meet me back here."

He started climbing the staircase to the kings' castle. I followed. He stopped halfway up the stairs. "What are you doing?" he hissed.

"I'm coming with you," I hissed back.

"You cannot!"

"I must." I steeled myself for the argument. "I will. We're doing this together, right? I won't get separated from you again."

Ailill gestured behind him, glancing down to the entryway. "But the veil will do the same to you that the queens' veil did to me."

"I don't care." I tossed my shoulders back. "I have you. You'll protect me."

Ailill bit his lip and grabbed the railing behind him. "Perhaps we should go to the queens' throne room, then," he said. "I can put up with it and grab one of their swords."

He stopped. The creak of a door widening made us both freeze in place.

"It shall be done," said Adeyemi, some distance below us.

I planted both hands on Ailill's back and shoved him up, pushing him quickly, getting us both past the veil to the kings' castles and out of their sight.

As soon as the veil stopped moving behind me, I felt it at once. I tumbled, shocked that Ailill had managed to put up with this for so long.

Ailill swooped in beside me, catching me before my knees hit the floor again. "We have to go back."

I forced my head up and did my best to send him a reassuring smile. "No. I need your help. We need another sword."

He stood, supporting me with his arms around my waist. I shuffled after him, intent on keeping up a faster pace. I worried that I'd made a mistake, that I slowed him down and had proven a burden to him.

He froze. "May I carry you?"

My first instinct was to say no. My first instinct was to be his equal, to stop him from giving me more than his due, but I'd done my best to support him in the queens' castle. Just because I didn't have the strength to carry him didn't mean I wouldn't have had the option been available to me.

I nodded my assent, even the word "yes" proving to be too much just then. He wrapped my arm around his neck and bent down to place one hand under my knees, the other resting carefully at the small of my back. I shifted Elgar slightly so it would hang from the side away from him.

"See?" I said. "Women can be here. They just need to be friends with a man."

"I hope that by now, we are far more than friends." Ailill bounced me in his arms before taking his next step, closing the distance between us and the throne room at a far brisker pace.

"Jurij killed your mother." The words came harder to me the farther in we went, but at least we weren't headed as far as the kings' prison.

"He did not."

We reached the throne room, which had enough torches to light our way. Ailill hesitated a moment but plunged us inside.

It was like someone was sitting on top of me the moment we crossed the threshold into the room.

"Argh," I said, then, "I'm fine" when Ailill froze in place.

Ailill grit his teeth and kept carrying me forward. "Do you know how many lives that spirit has lived since then? He is not my brother."

I thought of Avery and Alvilda, and how the two reminded me of each other. There was nothing in Jurij that reminded me of Elric. I'd always associated Elric with the more stubborn version of Ailill I knew at the start. There was this way that Elric had looked at me, full of longing, that I'd seen in Jurij, first with Elfriede and then with me... *No. Jurij has so much kindness in him, even when he's doing things that aren't kind.*

We arrived at the dais and Ailill put me down in the left throne. The dark metal felt cold and lifeless beneath my arms, even through the dampness of my skirt. I sunk my head back into it, sure I could never summon the strength to get off the chair again.

Ailill leaned on the center throne and pulled the sword hanging over it down. He placed it on the arm of the throne I was sitting on and did the same for the sword above my head. I stared at the two swords beside me and felt the slightest bit of warmth coming from that direction. I was too tired to be sure, but I thought I saw a glimmer of violet.

Ailill was leaning on the third throne, his hand on the sword hanging over it, when the shadows of figures at the end of the room danced across the torchlight.

"Halt! You traitor!" Adeyemi stormed into the room, followed closely by Estavan and Kin.

Ailill climbed down from the throne, the sword in his hand. "I have done nothing to betray you—"

"On the contrary!" Estavan appeared before me, his hands on my arms before I could even think to fight back. He flung me to the ground in front of the throne, the swords cluttering to the ground along with me. "You put a woman on my throne! A woman!"

Ailill crouched beside me, pulling me closely to him. "Are you all right?" he whispered.

I nodded slightly, the movement sending a hammering echo to my head.

"Where are the two spirits from your village?" asked Kin.

"Why are you asking us?" said Ailill, the slightest hint of a sneer in his voice. So I wasn't the only one he spoke to in that tone.

"The queens took the lily village book," spat Estavan. "I shall assume they are back there."

Kin bent forward and grabbed Ailill's wrists and then mine in turn. "Where are they? Have you been hiding golden tokens from us?"

"Not us," I said, fighting to speak. It was partially a lie, but I didn't care. "Maybe you should ask that of the queens."

Kin's head snapped up and he stared at Adeyemi and Estavan. "They have lied to us. Again."

Adeyemi held a hand up. "We have no proof."

"Proof? We have had enough of that." Estavan scowled and bent down to grab one of the fallen swords. "We have had enough of these games!"

They were talking about the queens lying to them, not Ailill and me. I hoped.

Adeyemi put a hand on Estavan's arm. "Do you know what you risk by picking up that sword?"

Estavan laughed sourly. "There are only three of them."

"And there are only three of us."

Kin picked up the second sword, and Ailill clutched the one he'd taken tighter against him in case they tried to take that, too. Instead of keeping it, Kin held out the sword to Adeyemi with both hands. It made sense. Adeyemi seemed to be a leader, and that sword had come from the center throne.

Adeyemi stared at it. "We give them one chance. One more chance."

"What?" asked Kin.

Adeyemi looked us over. "We tell them what she did. We remind them of what they agreed to, should she upset the games again."

He ran his fingers over the hilt of the blade and took it from Kin, turning it over in the torchlight. "All of the women in the lily village must die."

Chapter Thirty-five

"**N**O!" I FOUND THE STRENGTH to scream that word, no matter how much agony I was in just trying to breathe. "You can't!"

Adeyemi did something I never expected him to do—he crouched down beside Ailill and me. "It is because you have defied us again and again."

"That doesn't matter!" I almost choked on my own breath. "I'm here! Punish *me*. You can't... You can't..."

Ailill embraced me tighter. "Your Majesty. Without women, the men of our village will die out."

Adeyemi stood slowly, dropping the sword to his side. "We have never had a village that was all one gender." He exchanged a look with Kin and Estavan. "Even if no other men can be born without women, perhaps they shall at least know true happiness before they die out."

"No!" I said again. "No. There's more to it than just being able to have children. Men and women... We are a village. We are family. Friends." I rolled my head toward Ailill, not caring about the effort it took. "Lovers."

Ailill touched his forehead to mine before pulling back and facing the kings. "She is right. We are not at war with women, and they are not at war with us. We exist together. Even when women love women and men love men, there is still a need for each other that goes beyond birthing new villagers. We keep the village alive together. We are all just... people."

"*People* you are not." Kin shoved Ailill back to grab the sword that rested on his lap and Ailill's head slammed against the center throne. "You are only experiments. Elves. Our creations." His eyes lingered angrily on my ears, which I knew set me apart from the rest of their spirits. "And we have long been tired of the women of your village being born with ears a mockery of our own."

His words were lost on me. It was all I could do not to scream, but I felt the urge rise in my throat. He had to be alive. He had to be. I didn't see blood. It was just like when Jurij had hit me over the head. He'd wake and soon. Until then, it was up to me.

The three kings towered over us with their swords at their sides. They held so much power over us, over all that we loved, and the weakness I felt in every inch of my body only accentuated the fact. Still, I didn't regret coming here, even knowing I would weaken. I would never part from Ailill again, if I could help it.

Although the movement felt like I was tearing through muscles, I rolled to my knees and pulled Elgar out of its sheath, pointing it toward them. I wanted to stand. I wanted to hold the sword higher, but it was all I could do to keep this position. The blade shook terribly in my fingers.

Kin laughed. "What is this? Did she bring that from the queens' throne room?"

Estavan leaned closer but quickly shrunk back. "Perhaps. I do not think we can get too near it."

Adeyemi waved a hand. "No matter. She has no strength to wield it here. Let her stay there until she collapses from the fatigue coursing through her body. She is no threat to us."

There was a loud scraping from behind me, a sound that echoed in my ears as loud as thunder.

"*I* might be." The deep voice carried loudly across the cavernous throne room.

I slunk back down to the floor. It was all I could do to close my eyes and give in to the exhaustion.

I forced them open again and watched as a man approached from behind the center throne.

Jaron.

I slumped over, still clutching my blade.

ŋ ŋ ŋ

I don't know if I ever expected to open my eyes again. Or if I did, I never expected to see what I saw.

I rolled over. The queens were in the kings' throne room, visibly weakened and each holding a sword. Jangmi did the best job of standing straight—Marigold and Chrysilla both slouched slightly, their swords a heavy weight—but even Jangmi's limbs trembled slightly.

Estavan couldn't stop laughing. "You fools. You fools! You bring your swords here, to our castle? We will not even have to fight you. We simply can lock you in here and leave you to die."

I felt Elgar's weight still in my hands and took a deep breath, slapping one of my palms out against the cold stone floor and pushing, pushing so hard to sit back upright. No one seemed to take notice of me. I searched the room. Ailill was no longer lying against the throne, and I panicked, but his clothes weren't there, either. The throne was moved, a black hole behind it, the edges of a billowing black veil visible through it.

I looked around for Jaron, but there was no sign of him, either. Nor of any empty clothes to signify he had died. *We gave him a golden token. That meant he might have swum out of the cavern pool and walked right into the castle, right through the entryway behind the throne. Right back here. But why? After all we'd done for him.*

"You will not kill Olivière," spat Jangmi, with far more strength than I would have had standing like that.

"You admit you have been helping her, then," said Kin.

"She is a woman," Marigold sneered. "We are allowed to let her be our champion."

"You lost the game!" snapped Estavan. "You agreed she would be dealt with."

"The game means nothing." Chrysilla lowered her sword and then grunted, pulling it back upward. "We shall win the war."

Adeyemi took a few casual steps forward. "If you want to save her, everything is off. The games are over. We shall have war again—we shall have bloodshed."

Jangmi stared at him. "We would rather your blood shed than hers."

Estavan howled and ran forward, his sword drawn. Marigold parried it despite the weakness in her limbs. I'd never seen people actually fight with two swords so deftly. It was different than I imagined in the stories. Faster and with no fumbling. Graceful and not at all awkward.

"Men are clearly the superior gender," roared Kin, and he lifted his sword, diving at Chrysilla, but she flipped over, swinging the sword in a circle, and he missed.

How can she do that? I can barely stand.

"If that were true," said Marigold between panting, "you wouldn't need the advantage of our weakness before you finally attacked."

I stuck Elgar into the thin line between stones on the dais and grabbed hold of the hilt. *If they can stand, so can I.*

"You brought yourselves here. You presented us with this chance." Estavan lunged forward and Marigold barely made it out of his way. She breathed heavily and slammed her elbow hard down on his back, making him cry out. He jumped back, menacing. "If you had not come, we would not have attacked you. Would you have attacked us, even if we had no swords of our own?"

"You had swords of your own," barked Chrysilla. "As soon as we got here, you already had swords in hand."

Jangmi and Adeyemi had yet to actually join the fight. They simply walked around in a circle, staying at opposite sides. Jangmi barely seemed affected, but as I used Elgar to stand on my own two feet, there was a slight wobble in her step.

"That was not us." Kin dodged one of Chrysilla's thrusts and managed to roll her sword in a circle with his, out of his way. "She had them when we got here. And then that lost spirit appeared."

Jaron? Ailill? Had they escaped through the portal? How, if Jaron was the only one with a golden token? I didn't believe Ailill would voluntarily go with Jaron, so he must have still been unconscious.

"What lost spirit?" spat Marigold. "Some other trick to help you do battle with us?"

Estavan scoffed. "No. The second spirit we kept in the garden. That man, Jaron."

Chrysilla panted, her sword lowering to the ground. "He appeared here, in your throne room? You must have invited him then."

"A lie," said Adeyemi, his eyes widening slightly. "Surely you must recognize that. What advantage would we gain from that? He was nothing."

"Perhaps when the other new lord failed you, you thought he would have to do," said Jangmi. "You might be creating a new king-like spirit of your own, to match the queen-like spirit that is Olivière."

Adeyemi paused and lifted his own sword in echo. "So you admit you played a role in her creation?"

Jangmi shook her head. "We did not. But you have always been envious of her. You would not take her existence as a sign that women are clearly superior."

I removed Elgar from the floor and started walking toward the wall, first one foot and then the other. I would get through this long enough to do what I could to stop these mad kings and queens. I sunk into the shadows between lit torches. There were no eyes on me, no eyes on the pawn, even if they seemed to recognize her chances of becoming a queen.

"A lie!" Estavan roared, swinging his sword over his head. "We have known from the start. It is the men who are superior! The women are nothing but charlatans."

Marigold tried lifting her sword. She screamed as she did, as if the sound would give her the strength to block the sword in time.

It didn't.

The sword came down at her neck, and a shower of blood spurt out from it. When Marigold fell to the ground in a heap, the blood soaking her golden tight outfit, I marveled at how she could still live after losing so much blood. Then I realized she wasn't alive. She hadn't vanished, but she wasn't alive either.

People didn't always vanish when they died. Their bodies remained behind and melted into the earth.

"Sister!" screamed Chrysilla, but Jangmi didn't so much as flinch. Her eyes were locked too hard on Adeyemi in front of her.

Kin shot his sword out before Chrysilla could make her way to the fallen Marigold. She brought her own sword up in time, but she groaned with the effort, her perfect hair falling over her face.

Estavan kicked at Marigold's body with his boot, his back to me.

A short distance from me.

I hated violence. The sight of Elric's blood—of the screaming, vanishing men—sickened me, but they would kill all of the women in my village. There was no going back for me. At least let me even the odds again.

Biting my tongue to stop myself from grunting, I tasted blood in my mouth as I lifted Elgar higher, aiming the point right at the bottom of Estavan's back. I hesitated only a moment, and then I struck.

The king gurgled, and Elgar dripped with blood. I yanked the blade out, and Estavan fell, lifeless, on top of Marigold.

Chrysilla's and Kin's swords stopped clashing, and all eyes in the room were on me.

Chapter Thirty-Six

"SHE KILLED ESTAVAN!" KIN'S MOUTH fell open as he lowered his sword. "She killed him!"

Chrysilla, bent slightly forward with exhaustion, glanced at him out of the corner of her eye. Without saying a word—her teeth clenched together—she pointed her sword upward, driving it straight up and under Kin's rib cage.

His open mouth filled with blood and he fell forward, bringing Chrysilla with him to the ground.

I collapsed back against the wall, breathing hard, struggling to keep my feet from sliding in the blood. I fought to keep my eyes open because if this was the end for me, I would see it all. I would go into rebirth—or nothingness, if that's what awaited me—knowing if my loved ones were still in danger.

Chrysilla's arms shot out from under Kin and she roared, trying to shove the fallen king off of her. Her hands were dyed in blood—whether her own or Kin's, I couldn't be sure. Chrysilla made an anguished cry and reached out toward Jangmi. "Sister!"

Jangmi stared down at her. She did nothing as Adeyemi walked over toward the two and drove his sword through Chrysilla's neck.

He turned back to Jangmi and me, flicking his sword and sending droplets of her blood to stain the floor. "I have no brothers left, and now you have no sisters."

Jangmi must have given something away in her face—she had her back to me and I couldn't see it—but Adeyemi's eyes turned instantly to me. "No," he said. "No. She will not be queen! She cannot be queen!"

He didn't cross over to Jangmi right away, instead resuming their slow circling, his path taking him farther away and toward the door. "You are both weakened here," he said. "And you have no help. I let that wandering spirit go in exchange for taking Ailill along with him. You will find no help here."

Jangmi readjusted the sword in her hands. "Ailill? Help us? We have no use for a man. You are mistaken, and you do yourself no favors by sending a man away."

"Wrong," I said, only the second word managing to make it past my lips. I rolled my shoulder into the wall, dragging Elgar with me. "You're... wrong."

Jangmi gave no indication that she'd heard me, so I found the strength to move and ran my sword through her back in the same place I'd pierced Estavan.

Jangmi fell forward, and this time, I let Elgar go with the body as it crashed to the floor. I fell to my knees, already realizing I'd made a mistake. If this was the last bit of strength I had, I should have saved it until I had a chance to attack Adeyemi, should have waited until he'd fallen before turning my attention to the lone queen. But I wasn't sure I'd ever have another chance to end Jangmi's rule, to put a stop to her games of toying with the lives of people she saw as pawns, and I would just have to hope it was enough—that Adeyemi would be satisfied to be the lone ruler.

I was wrong.

"That was foolish, but I suppose I should thank you." Adeyemi strove closer, his sword casually at his side. "Not that I required the assistance."

I said nothing. It was all I could do to stay seated, to face my end head-on. *Ailill...*

Adeyemi raised the sword over his head. "If you think this favor will save the women of your village, you are mistaken. Now there is no one to stop me from ending women in all the villages. Men may perish, but we shall live lives of glory before the end." He brought the sword down.

He fell forward on top of Jangmi, the sword cluttering harmlessly to the ground beside him. He had a blade sticking out of his back.

I could barely lift my head. The white was blinding. "Spurn...?"

"He's gone, remember?" Ailill swooped in beside me to stop me from falling over. "It's far past time for people to lead themselves, to help themselves. I asked all the Ailills to embrace their final end."

I settled comfortably into Ailill's arms and ran my fingertips across one of his cheeks. "Not *all* the Ailills."

"No, not this one. This one will never leave you again." He leaned forward and rested his forehead against mine. "This one should have never left you to begin with."

I found a bit more strength and wrapped a hand around the back of Ailill's head, bringing it forward so his lips would meet mine.

He stopped me, a mere hair's breadth from the kiss. "No."

"No?" My hand fell limply to the floor. My eyes couldn't stay open, but beneath my eyelids, I could feel the tears. "Suppose... I deserve that..."

Ailill snorted and I felt his arms under my legs and behind my back again, felt him lift me up as he stood. "If anything, it is I who deserves your rejection. No. No, we'll do this where we're equal."

I was so close to slumber, his gentle footsteps felt like someone rocking me to sleep.

Strength coursed back through my body, and by the time I felt the soft fluttering of a veil over my face, it was like I was entirely reborn. My eyes jolted open, like I had been slapped awake.

"You're wet," I blurted. He was.

"You're not completely dry, either." Ailill laughed as he carefully descended the stairs with me still in his arms. "I came back through the cavern pool and the garden fountain."

"What happened?" I asked, struggling slightly so he would understand to put me back on my feet. "I passed out, and when I came to, you and Jaron were gone."

Ailill was still. "Do you mind if I still carry you?"

I stopped struggling, my face hot. "What?"

"I know that we are equals here." He nodded his head around us at the entryway. "But I ask that you grant me this boon just once. I like the feeling of you in my arms."

I couldn't look at him. I might have mumbled my acceptance, my hand resting comfortably on his bare chest.

He started walking again. "I was still unconscious when Jaron came back. Otherwise, I never would have let him take me with him."

"But how did you both get back? You only had the one coin between you."

Ailill grimaced as we finished descending the stairs. "According to Jaron, he asked the kings to give him a rebirth, or he would fight them. He told them he would rather die than go back. They certainly considered him no threat, but they promised him they would grant his request if he first brought me back to our village with him one last time. They granted him a bangle so I would have a token to wear as I made my way through."

We reached the garden doorway, which was open, the dying light of twilight streaming in through the garden.

I looked around as we stepped inside. "So where is he?"

"Here," came a voice from behind me. "I've been making a number of trips. Making sure we brought all but one of these."

I pushed harder on Ailill's chest and he lowered my feet to the ground. I smoothed my still-damp skirt and hair nervously, embarrassed at being caught in his arms.

Jaron—with pants on to match Ailill's shirt, I was relieved to see—was seated on the bench in front of the garden table, a shimmering pile of golden bangles behind him. He stood up. "Wish I'd been able to bring you back instead of him. You would have been easier to carry. This fellow's got more heft to him than you'd think, just looking at him."

I glared at Jaron. "You came back."

Jaron shrugged. He was wet, too. "I wondered why you trusted me."

"But you helped us." I looked to Ailill for confirmation. "You helped Ailill cross back through the cavern pool, so he could take the kings by surprise."

"Only because he practically wrung my neck when he woke up in the wrong castle. He promised me you could do what I asked the kings to do for me, so I may as well be on the right side. For once."

I grinned at Ailill and wrapped my arm around his, leaning into his shoulder, not caring that we had an audience.

Jaron clenched his jaw and walked to the table, grabbing the open book and showing it to me. "Your sister is doing well. Your mother, too."

The drawing showed Elfriede dancing, a huge grin on her face. She ran back and forth in front of our cottage, fluttering her arms about with something that might be a shawl catching in the wind, passing by so many recognizable faces: Mother, who had happy tears on her face, and Thea at her side; Roslyn, hand in hand with Sindri;

Darwyn and Tayton sitting against our cottage wall, Tayton's head wrapped in bandages, but a smile on both their faces; Siofra leaning into Alvilda; Nissa nudging sour-faced Luuk and managing to get a small smile to appear on his features; Coll looking on and clapping as Arrow yipped at his heels, Bow panting happily on the ground at his feet. And then Elfriede halted, and I could see the flush on her cheeks even though the page was devoid of color. A man came tumbling into view on the page—a man, I realized, who'd been chasing along after her. Jurij grabbed Elfriede around the waist and lifted her up above him, looking like he wanted to devour her with his gaze.

I guess he figured out his true feelings at last.

Jurij put Elfriede down and leaned forward to kiss her.

Jaron must have seen my face because he pulled the book back and examined it. "Oh. Yeah. Jurij is doing well, too. He was so glad to see Elfriede well again, and she sort of melted into his arms in tears, telling him she never stopped loving him." He scratched his head and shrugged. "I don't know. I only saw part of it. I passed through the castle to get to the other entryway to this place and I met them on their way out. They wouldn't let each other go the whole time."

I guess after enough lifetimes, even a spirit as wicked as Elric's could learn to love.

I eyed Jaron thoughtfully. He wasn't always this way, I was sure of it. He wouldn't always have hurt me, or killed Jurij, or caused the death of my father. "You really want to be reborn in a new village?"

Jaron shut the book closed hard. "I do. You may think I need to live with my pain, but I beg you." He got down on his knees. "I beg you to show me mercy. I did as he asked. I made sure I took all of the bangles here, as many as I could carry each trip, leaving only the one Jurij had on behind."

I looked at Ailill. "You left one with Jurij?"

Ailill smirked and put an arm around me. "He was lord of the village when we left it. They may as well have one leader. A real leader. Someone born in this time. Someone who knows the people well."

I thought about that, and what kind of leader Jurij might make. The lord of the village would lose a lot of his mystery, and if the specters were all gone, he'd need to invite some people to live with him and help him. But Ailill was right—a lot of people knew Jurij. They might trust him more when it came to rebuilding the fragile state of the village—if they could get over the incident at the Great Hall, and if they never learned of his indirect involvement in the fire at the tavern, maybe.

But I couldn't see Jurij doing that, either. Starting his rule with lies or hidden truths. Who knew what the future really held for my village.

"Don't do that," I said to Jaron, who was still kneeling. "Don't bow to me." I threw my shoulders back. "If I can, I'll do it."

A huge smile broke out across Jaron's face. "Thank you!" He got up to move forward, seemed to realize he still had the book in his hand, and quickly dropped it off at the table. Then he grabbed my hand in his. "Thank you."

I felt the warm weight of the coin transfer from his palm to mine.

"All right." I stepped back and lead the men toward the fountain. I ran my fingers lightly over the lily-covered bush and stopped at the next one, covered in yellow blossoms I didn't recognize.

"Daffodils," said Ailill, as if reading my mind.

"I'll send you here." Jaron stepped in front of the yellow-covered bush and I frowned, turning to Ailill. "Will this work if he came here alive, and not as a spirit?"

Ailill saw something greater in my visage than I could ever believe existed, like the beauty of a setting sun over the mountaintops. "Olivière, you can do anything. I'm sure of it."

I bent down on my knees in front of Jaron, clasped my hands together over the coin, and closed my eyes. *Give Jaron rebirth in this village*, I thought. *Give him a new life. Give him happiness.*

There was something there, something I was just about to access, but I was afraid to grab it. "I can't."

"You can." Ailill kneeled down beside me, his hands on my shoulders and his eyes closed. He must have been thinking it, too. *Give Jaron rebirth in this village.*

Set him free.

The warmth shot through my hands and traveled everywhere. I could feel it pulsating up Ailill's arms and back through me, like we were one living being.

I opened my eyes just in time to see the clothing Jaron had been wearing crumple to the ground, to see the violet light burst into life on the daffodil bush.

I laughed. "We did it!" Without even finding the book for that village, I knew. The proof was the golden bangle on my wrist, the coin no longer in my palms. It'd somehow changed into the more traditional token as it spread the power of my wish all throughout my body.

I turned to face Ailill, and I saw that same thing in his eyes that he must have seen in mine. It was more beautiful than flickering fire in irises. It was like the entire sun was reflected in those eyes.

He took both my hands in his and we stood, as one, at once. I was so mesmerized by the sun in his irises, at the fire it seemed to ignite in my body, that it took the glowing golden light from the top of his head for me to tear my own eyes away from his.

I gasped. "There's a crown! On your head! Like the kings wore! Only..." I tilted my head. "It's far lovelier than anything they wore." His crown was made of blossoms of countless different colors, as if a flower from each village's bush had woven together to anoint him their new king.

Ailill laughed and squeezed my hands, bringing me closer to the water fountain. "You have one, too."

I reached up and where I expected to feel nothing, my fingers brushed against soft petals. I bent over to look at my reflection in the water. A crown fit for a queen rested atop the thick black hair I once found so difficult to tame—hair that was far longer now than I remembered. When had it grown so long? Was that part of the magic, too? I felt like it was. That it was a sign that I was no longer just nobody's goddess or nobody's lady—the girl who cut her hair when she wanted to be left alone. I was no longer alone, but I was nobody's pawn. My tresses looked wild even now, but it suited the crown. It suited the woman who looked up at me.

Although Elfriede's wrinkled hand-me-downs certainly didn't.

"So we're the ones who must watch over the villages now." I chuckled as I pulled away and patted my clothes. "We won't have to wear those very tight suits, will we?"

Ailill grinned. "We can wear whatever we please. But perhaps now that my shirt is once again free, I should at least wear *something*." He bent down to pick it up.

"Wait!"

Ailill froze, his hand on the shirt, his eyebrows raised. "Wait to put on my shirt?"

I blushed. "Yes."

"All right." Ailill straightened up. "May I ask why—"

I interrupted him with a kiss.

Acknowledgements

THANK YOU, THANK YOU, THANK you to everyone who has stuck with Noll, Ailill, Jurij, Elfriede and everyone else for three whole books. I hope you're satisfied with their own version of happily ever after, as strange as it might be. I especially appreciate those of you who shared a review and/or who reached out to me to tell me what you thought of the books! You've made this author's day over and over again. You needn't think of Noll's journey as over, although I've finished telling it. Her real life and her true purpose have just begun.

Thank you to the Patchwork Press team and especially Kellie Sheridan for welcoming me to the group for The Never Veil's republication. Thank you to Melissa Giorgio, amazing YA author and long time best friend, for your editorial work on this book and your support every step of the way. Thank you to Bethany Robison for being such an enthusiastic editor and helping me shape this series from the start. Thanks to all of the editors who've helped out along the way. Cover credit goes all to Meet Cute Photography's Rachel Conway Schieffelbein, model Sakinah Caradine, and Makeready Design's Allison Martin. I love these designs!

I appreciate all of the authors I've connected with online, especially through the WIP Marathon and

#WO2016. This crazy world of publishing is less difficult to navigate thanks to your support and advice.

Thank you to all of my family and friends, especially Cameron, Mom, Sara, and Anthony, my homegrown fans.

To my readers—I appreciate every one of you! Special thanks (in no particular order) to Melanie, Karim, Chalyss, Desnica (coiner of The Never Veil power couple name "Ailivière"), Jamilla, Jamie, Ashley, Anniek, Mollie, Annelise, Summer, Isabel, Maggie, Amanda, and the Twinjas. To those I might have missed, please forgive me and I hope you'll continue to keep enjoying my books.

About the Author

AMY MCNULTY IS A FREELANCE writer and editor from Wisconsin with an honors degree in English. She was first published in a national scholarly journal (*The Concord Review*) while in high school and currently writes professionally about everything from business marketing to anime. In her down time, you can find her crafting stories with dastardly villains and antiheroes set in fantastical medieval settings.

Find Amy at amymcnulty.com and on social media as McNultyAmy (Twitter), Amy McNulty, Author (Facebook), McNulty.Amy (Instagram), AuthorAmyMc (Pinterest), AmyMcNulty (Wattpad), and AuthorAmyMcNulty (Tumblr). Sign up for her monthly newsletter to receive news and exclusive information about her current and upcoming projects. Please visit her Goodreads and Amazon author pages and leave a review!

FALL FAR FROM THE TREE EXCERPT

ALMOST AS IF IT KNEW I was watching it, the firefly blinked, fading in and out of existence, swooping up and down and up again, and landed on my stump. I watched it breathlessly for a moment as it danced across two pale, scarred knuckles. It blinked its warm yellow glow over the ragged surface of the skin—light and dark, light and dark. Almost like it was telling me I was meant to have five fingers there, same as on my left hand, same as on all those around me. As if I could ever forget.

Durand stopped skipping through the meadow, his eyes drawn to the little gift from Ytoile that still tickled my skin. The firefly flew off, returning to its brethren who peppered the meadow, awash in the pale moon glow. When it vanished amongst its many sparkling siblings, and I lost track of it at last, I turned back to see Durand still staring at me. My smile began to falter, but I did as Mother Jehanne had told me, and I forced my lips to curl upward again.

"Did you know," I told the small boy, "that fireflies are Ytoile's children on earth?"

Of course, he'd had to have been asleep for the past five or six years not to understand that. He nodded, and sat down on the grass beside me. I felt that stirring of heat inside me, the feeling that made me dread what was sure to come, even if Mother Jehanne had told me time and again not to get so heated at the curiosity of others.

"Why is your hand broken?"

There it was. The question I'd been dreading since he first locked his eyes on the firefly and intruded into my private moment with the stars. The question they all asked once, when the mothers were out of earshot and they thought they could finally speak without reproach.

I shifted my arm to hide the hand under my left elbow. "It's not broken," I said, perhaps a little more bitingly than necessary. I forced the smile back onto my face. "I was born this way. Oh! Isn't the night sky so beautiful?"

Durand bit his lip and continued staring at my stump, as if he could somehow look through the silver cloth of my mother-in-guidance dress, through the skin and bone of my elbow, and see what I'd hidden beneath.

"That hand has led you here, Cateline. That hand that Ytoile blessed you with led you to become one of us." I don't know how old I was, young enough to crawl into Mother Jehanne's lap, old enough to wonder why I was different. It was my earliest memory of her, patting my back and whispering blessings into my ear as twilight ebbed and the sun was dangerously close to rising.

The thought reminded me of Durand's young age. His eyes flit closed and snapped open again. I reached across my lap to touch Durand's knee with my left hand, ignoring the look he gave it, like he were searching for some deformity in that one as well. "Is this your first full night up, Durand?"

The question seemed to do the trick. He grinned, meeting my eyes at last and showing off a gap in his front teeth. "Yeah. Mother Flore said I could try."

I stood and waited for Durand to follow my example. The moonlight reflected off of the silver of my long skirt as I took his hand in mine. "Only the most holy of Stargazers wake at night and sleep during the sunlight." I squeezed his hand. "You're very lucky to be chosen, Durand."

The compliment seemed to snap all thoughts of tiredness out of his drooping eyes. I led him toward the other children, and he let go of my hand, all thoughts of me forgotten as he joined in a game of tag that Ide and Aymon were engaged in.

I watched the children scream and laugh and play for a moment, marveling at the way Ytoile's children sparkled amongst them, Her blessings for the least of us, the cast aside, the unwanted, so evident here in the moonlight. I gazed at the waterfall pouring its sparkling white and blue water into the reservoir, and the two rivers that birthed out from it. One to the forest, the other through the fields. This truly was a blessed place, giving life and protecting life throughout the entire isle. I noticed the small white figure beside the water. I left the other children to their game, slipping beside the child in her white dress and crouching beside her.

"You're not playing, Oriabel?" I searched her face for some sign of tiredness, but if she felt at all lulled to sleep by the false promises of the sun demon, she didn't show it.

"I had a vision." Oriabel pointed to what had so drawn her attention, a pile of white pebbles beside the reservoir, pebbles covered in small black ants. They looked like stars being devoured by darkness. "Yesterday, when I was asleep."

"The sun demon sends visions while you sleep during the daylight," I told her. I thought of my own dreams, those achingly false promises. "He's angry you spend his hours fast asleep."

Oriabel shrugged. "It wasn't like that. It was just a moment with my family. My real family."

I shook my head, thinking of Mother Jehanne's arms wrapped around me, her gentle rocking as she sung me to sleep. "*We* are your real family, Oriabel."

Oriabel's lips puckered like she'd eaten something sour. "It's different for you, isn't it?" Her eyes flickered tellingly to my right arm, but at twelve years, she knew better than to let her gaze linger. "You came here as an infant."

I sighed. It wasn't as if I was the only infant abandoned at the gate of the tower. Oriabel had to know this. But she knew, also, how few survived past those first few months. After all, why else would a parent abandon her baby here if not for the child being sickly? My surviving to live sixteen winters was proof of Ytoile's plan for me. My sickness wasn't in my bones. It was just something that ordinary parents couldn't possibly understand.

"You've been here six years, Oriabel." I sat on the ground and crossed my legs. "I'm surprised you remember your old family at all."

Oriabel tucked a strand of yellow hair behind her ear. "Well, I do."

I reached out to touch her shoulder, doing my best to follow a mother's example. "Ytoile has plans for the least of us." I paused to let the gravity of the statement sink in. "Your parents may have had no use for you, but She wanted you here."

Oriabel snorted. "Every day you sound more and more like a mother, Cateline."

I could tell from her tone that she meant no compliment, but I couldn't stop the smile that spread across my face. I let go of her shoulder, twirling a strand of my wavy red hair in my best attempt to exude the humility expected of me. "Thank you."

Oriabel hugged her knees against her chest, the retort she was about to say quickly lost as her thoughts turned back to visions planted to test her. "I'm not so sure my parents had no use for me."

Most of the kids came to the tower a little later than I did, and they all had these memories of their birth families. Good memories. Hugs and kisses. Laughter and dancing. Stories told around the fireplace on cold winter nights. For some reason, they never spoke of the work they were forced to do from dawn until dusk, how they toiled only in the hours of the sun demon. They never spoke of receiving no education behind the safety of closed doors in the daytime, of having no time to play and frolic through the meadows at night, like they did at the tower.

They didn't speak of that day their parents died, or more likely, their parents decided they'd had enough of feeding them. The days their parents decided the endless hours their children put into harvesting crops and tilling fields would never equal what they could get from hiring an adult, an adult who would take a few gold coins to waste on import food or opium and not eat up precious wheat and vegetables.

I tossed my hair over my shoulder. If I told her the whole truth, she wouldn't believe me. *"Spare the sufferer the harshest truth, if you can."* Mother Jehanne always told me. *"All the sufferer, all the sinner needs to know is that Ytoile has a plan for them."*

"I'm sure your parents wanted to keep you, Oriabel," I lied. "But they probably knew how much happier and healthier you would be under the mothers' instruction."

The look Oriabel gave me as she peeked over the top of her knees was like she was determined to prove that she was actually in abject misery—just to be contrary. "Do you think your parents wanted *you*?"

She hadn't said "wanted to *keep* you," as if it was simply a matter of me not being able to toil during all the hours of the sun demon for a plate of food on the table. Just "*wanted* you."

I stood up, keeping my nose held aloft and refusing to watch the histrionics any longer. "You'll never become a mother if you don't learn compassion," I said coldly.

"*Good.* I have no intention of becoming that kind of mother anyway."

Against my resolve, I spun to face her, a lecture on all the mothers had done for an ungrateful child on the tip of my tongue, when Mother Ermessenda's voice called out across the meadow. "Children, we have finished. You may return to the tower."

By the sound of the sigh Oriabel let forth, you'd have thought she was disappointed that she was a day sleeper, that she'd be free from the rays of the sun demon as she slept. It was clear to me that she would never become a mother, never have any special relationship with the goddess in the night sky.

"Go on, then," I said, pursing my lips. I gently pushed her shoulder. My eyes scanned the meadow for the other children chosen for the night's frolic.

"Cateline!" called Mother Ermessenda, beckoning me over to an area a few yards away. I made my way to her, smiling at the grinning Ide and Aymon as they ran past me into the tower.

"I caught five of Ytoile's children!" shouted Aymon.

"But I caught six!" sneered Ide.

"Liar!"

"How would you know? I let them go!"

I cupped my hand around my mouth to focus my voice in their direction. "Hush, children! Be quiet in the tower! The others are sleeping."

They giggled and disappeared inside just as I reached Mother Ermessenda. She crouched over a sleeping Durand, who lay curled up amongst the stalks of grass like one of the kitchen kittens. Mother Ermessenda scooped him up in her arms. "You let this one fall asleep." It was a statement, but her tone was heavy with accusation and disappointment.

I bit into the inside of my lip, bowing my head. "I'm so sorry, Mother. Oriabel wasn't participating and I was worried—"

Mother Ermessenda grunted, leading the way back into the tower. "Not participating isn't as offensive to Her Holiness as falling asleep after committing to a night awake in Her honor."

I could feel the heat rise to my cheeks, knowing the pale, freckled surface would express my shame and glow deep red. "I'm sorry, Mother."

Mother Ermessenda shifted Durand in her arms, throwing him back over her shoulder. "Who recommended this child was ready for a festivity night?"

"Mother Flore, I believe." I was eager to shift the focus from my own failings.

Mother Ermessenda paused as we reached the entryway to the tower from the inner meadow, and then she clucked her tongue. "Some are always eager to think our children are ready before they truly are." She looked me up and down pointedly, drinking in the silver of my mother-in-guidance dress. I'd received it only two weeks earlier, on a night that ranked among the happiest of my life, in all my many happy, happy nights and even days as a Stargazer.

"Of course." I let my eyes fall, desperate to show remorse. I reached my arms out, offering to take Durand back to his quarters. "I will pray for him as he slumbers."

Mother Ermessenda exhaled sharply. "A mother-in-guidance to pray for a child's soul? I think not. The boy and Mother Flore will have to beg for forgiveness. I don't care if either of them were set to sleep during the hours of the demon. His eternal happiness is at risk."

I swallowed nervously, both for the reprimand to my audacity, and for the idea of poor Durand and Mother Flore spending the next few hours in contrition because I failed to notice the child drifting asleep. "I will beg for my own forgiveness, then," I said, taking a deep breath.

"As should we all, every night, and every day." Mother Ermessenda sniffed. "But you will have to pray with Mother Jehanne. She's asked me to summon you."

I couldn't help the smile that burst onto my face. My gaze locked with Mother Ermessenda's, and I could swear I saw the emeralds of my eyes reflecting off of Mother Ermessenda's dreary blue ones.

Mother Ermessenda's own mouth puckered. "Well, go on then. She's in her chambers. And there's less than an hour left until the end of the night. You wouldn't want to be responsible for Mother Jehanne offending Ytoile as well, would you?"

I made the smile vanish on my lips. "No, of course not." I curtsied and turned to go, not bothering to hide my grin once my back was facing the sour mother's direction. *Mother Jehanne. She summoned me!*

ⅴⅴ

"Come in, child."

I had just raised my fist to knock on the large wooden door leading to Mother Jehanne's chambers, but she knew I was standing on the other side of the door. It was no surprise, really. As I entered, I marveled at her commune with the stillness of the night, how her relationship with Ytoile, her almost entire existence in the blessing of darkness, could allow her to discern even the quietest of movements.

"Good night, Mother Jehanne." I kept my hand over my stump in front of my abdomen, my eyes averted to the large black and silver rug covering the grey cobblestones.

"Good night, Cateline." I could hear Mother Jehanne rocking in the chair she kept at the sole window in her chambers. "The stars were bright tonight."

"Yes." I took a deep breath. Perhaps it was best to get it over with. "I'm so sorry, Mother. I failed one of the younger ones at the night's festivities. He fell asleep before the end."

I dared to look up just a bit and saw Mother Jehanne rocking in her chair, gazing up at the stars without pause. She waved a hand to beckon me nearer. "Come, child, and help me draw the curtain. Dawn is breaking."

I dutifully reached in front of Mother Jehanne and tugged at the dark black material, adorned with silver stars to match her rug. Only the slightest crack of waning moonlight slipped into the room from beneath the thick material, and it took my eyes a moment more to adjust to the near total darkness.

I felt Mother Jehanne grab my hand before I could properly make her out. She cupped it in both her hands, patting the back of it gently. "Do you think me totally devoid of sin, child? Devoid of suffering?"

I thought a moment, chewing on the softness of my cheek. The truth, or the answer she might be seeking? I couldn't tell. "No person is," I said at last, settling for a mixture of the two.

"That's right. And if the holy mother is unworthy of Ytoile's perfection, a mother-in-guidance is bound to make mistakes as well." She squeezed my hand and let it fall. "Fret not over a sleepy child, Cateline. It takes time for a chosen child to adjust to the night. And sometimes a child simply isn't meant to be chosen."

"But I..." It'd been the first time I was asked to watch the younger children alone, without a mother. I'd tried to emulate the mothers who'd watched over us in the past, quietly drinking in the moonlight on the sidelines, only coming to speak with those off by themselves in danger of sleeping. "I wanted so badly to please you."

Mother Jehanne sighed, but it was more of a weary sigh, as if she were burdened by all of the tasks she had to do, and less of a disappointed sound than Mother Ermessenda might have offered me. "It would be impossible for you to displease me, Cateline. Why else do you think I chose you for the mother-in-guidance position? You, and you alone?"

I thought of the other two girls who'd turned sixteen this year, Ava and Malle, who'd left the tower at the same time I'd officially started my training. Sent off to the heart of the duchy, along with the boys our age, sentenced to a life of servitude and day-time existence. For I knew, from what the mothers had told us, what sort of jobs a young orphan woman could hope to find if she wished to stay awake at night. Ytoile may not cherish those who toiled during the hours of the sun as much as she did her Stargazers, but far more offensive to Her were those who used Her holy hours to live a classless life of debauchery.

"I'm sorry, Mother Jehanne." Whatever she might say, the thought of Ava and Malle and the fate that would have awaited me had I joined them only made me more disappointed I'd failed her.

"Enough, child. I'm sure the other mothers are making amends to Ytoile as we speak." It was not Mother Jehanne's duty to attend to the soul of every single child in the tower. No, what we'd shared as I grew up was special. "I summoned you here on another matter entirely. Sit." As my vision grew clearer, I saw her gesture to the stool next to her rocking chair.

We sat in silence for a moment, letting the darkness envelop us. The sliver of light from beneath the curtain was just enough that I could make out Mother Jehanne beside me, her white hair brushing the shimmering silver of her holy mother dress.

"You know that we had some visitors from the city this night."

I nodded, then thought better of it, not sure if she could see me in the dark. "Yes," I said to be certain. For a moment, my chest fluttered. Perhaps I was close to being invited to the festivities with patrons, to stand solemnly in the line of mothers chosen for the task, singing as Mother Jehanne asked Ytoile for blessings for those who would give of themselves to support us.

"We expected two groups. Only one arrived."

I bit my lip. Reality intruded harshly into my dream. "The nomads?" I ventured.

Mother Jehanne cleared her throat. "Most likely." She shifted in her chair, the rustling of the silver fabric sounding a bit like the waterfall. "Thieves and murderers, the lot of them. And desecrating Ytoile's most holy hours with their sinful dancing 'round flames sent from the sun."

I nodded, thinking of the groups of patrons who had been stopped from reaching us before, the number that even now refused to even make the journey.

"We need food, Cateline. And clothing, and books." Mother Jehanne sighed. "I know many of our patrons choose to sleep during the holy hours, even those wealthy enough not to have to support themselves with day labor, but they are beloved by Ytoile nonetheless, for their generosity to Her tower and to the children entrusted to the mothers who love Her."

"Of course." Mother Jehanne would expect my empathy.

Mother Jehanne slammed a fist on her rocking chair armrest. "This cannot stand any longer. Those nomads are the sun demon's children on earth." She took a deep breath. "They must be sent back to where they came from."

I swallowed. To wish a blazing, endless suffering even on a thief, even on a murderer... I could not bear the thought of their pain in fiery torment.

I felt Mother Jehanne's hand on my shoulder. "You will set off for the heart of the duchy, Cateline. Tomorrow, after you sleep. You and one or two of the mothers." She squeezed my shoulder. "Something must be done."

My stomach was a torrent. To be trusted with Mother Jehanne's desperate plea was an honor. To venture forth, before the sun fully set no less, across fields where nomads were known to attack the helpless patrons... I was terrified.

"Of-Of course." It was all I could say. I couldn't bear Mother Jehanne's disappointment.

In the wane light, I took note of Mother Jehanne's weary smile. She patted my shoulder and gestured toward the door. "Bless you, child. Now go. Enjoy your rest. Mother Ermessenda will speak with you in the afternoon."

"Thank you, Mother. May Ytoile bless you." I stood and curtsied, tripping over the stool as I made my exit. I straightened my shoulders and did my best to walk as if I'd never tumbled, exiting quietly on soft footsteps.

Light was breaking, leaking in through open windows and doorways, draping the hallways in shadows. I headed for my chambers, newly chosen for me when I became a mother-in-guidance. They were located at the edge of the dorms for the other mothers, in the room nearest the children's dorms. Someday I'd have a room further in, further away from my past as an orphan.

As I ascended the stairs, I passed a window with its curtains drawn back. I used my arm to shield my eyes from the brightness of the breaking dawn. It'd been a month since I'd seen the light of day properly. A light I'd have to get used to tomorrow. Chosen for more blessed nighttime duties, I slept from dawn until mid-day. I spent the rest of the daylight hours in the safety of rooms with curtains drawn, wondering how much longer it would be until Ytoile won her battle against the demon and would finally bless us with more hours of Her company in the colder months. But even then, I wondered how long I could go without a fire, the cheap imitation of the sun demon. The children never went without one during the winter, but the truly devout mothers, I knew, could sleep and wake without ever relying on a flame's warmth.

Worry about that later. For now, it was the time of the sun demon, the time when his hours were long, and the air burnt with his fiery breath. Amidst the screeching of the cicadas, I heard a woman's lamentation, a scream for absolution, a wracked and heavy sob.

I blinked and shifted my arm a bit up, letting my eyes adjust to the light. I carefully looked up and down the staircase to see if any other mother was watching, scared of being caught paused at a window with its curtains drawn back. But no one was up to rouse the children, and the mothers who did the cooking would have long descended the stairs to start breakfast. They cooked for the children and the day-mothers who sacrificed so much of their time with Ytoile to make sure the children got their education. At least until it was their turn to walk the halls at night.

The window overlooked the meadow and the reservoir. I let my arms fall, my eyes mostly adjusted to the breaking brightness, and felt my heart sink to witness the meadow in the bright light, the green and yellow straw of the grass so repugnant when not bathed in moonlight. Another shriek drew my eyes to the spot where Mother Ermessenda had picked up Durand, a spot awash with daylight, one sure to have hours more of sun scorching its surface. Mother Flore was there, crying and bowing and shrieking. Her silver dress lay discarded beside her, and only a thin shift covered her from waist to torso.

"Scream, child!" she shouted. "Beg for forgiveness!"

Beside her crouched a child, similarly shorn of clothing but for a slip covering his waist. I couldn't make out his face, but I could hear his soft whimpering, the occasional cry of "I'm sorry!" that could in no way match the lamentation of Mother Flore. His dark hair made it clear it was Durand, awoken from his offensive slumber once the sun began to rise. He no doubt had been told he'd have to spend the day in repentance, suffering side by side with the mother who'd had faith in him, the one who'd said he was ready for a night of festivities. The mother who'd thought him ready to know what it was to be among Ytoile's most blessed. *Too soon, perhaps. Even though I was ready at an even younger age.*

I tapped my left thigh with my fingers, searching my mind for any evidence that a mother who'd watched over festivities and failed to keep a child awake had ever joined in the following day's lamentations. There had been from time to time a mother anxious to take her part in the blame and beg of Ytoile's forgiveness. But it wasn't expected of her. She had so many children to watch over, after all. And she wouldn't have been the one who suggested a sleepy child was ready.

I straightened my back and grabbed the hem of my silver skirt, turning to face the top of the stairs. I'd pray for forgiveness in the darkness of my chambers, a venue more likely to reach commune with Ytoile regardless. Perhaps I'd suffer dreams sent by the sun demon as I slumbered, and that would be repentance enough.

I wouldn't think of the pale skin turned red on the fragile child and mother, how the ones out there in the sun would scream and itch and peel away their sins for days or weeks to come.

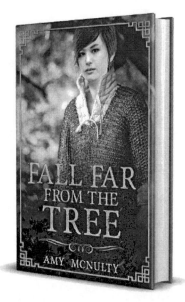

Terror. Callousness. Denial. Rebellion. How the four teenage children of leaders in the duchy and the neighboring empire of Hanaobi choose to adapt to their nefarious parents' whims is a matter of survival.

Rohesia, daughter of the duke, spends her days hunting "outsiders," fugitives who've snuck onto her father's island duchy. That she lives when even children who resemble her are subject to death hardens her heart to tackle the task.

Fastello is the son of the "king" of the raiders who steal from the rich and share with the poor. When aristocrats die in the raids, Fastello questions what his peoples' increasingly wicked methods of survival have cost them.

An orphan raised by a convent of mothers, Cateline can think of no higher aim in life than to serve her religion, even if it means turning a blind eye to the suffering of other orphans under the mothers' care.

Kojiro, new heir to the Hanaobi empire, must avenge his people against the "barbarians" who live in the duchy, terrified the empress, his own mother, might rather see him die than succeed.

When the paths of these four young adults cross, they must rely on one another for survival—but the love of even a malevolent guardian is hard to leave behind.

Add FALL FAR FROM THE TREE to your Goodreads to-read list or order it on Amazon or Barnes & Noble today!

A LOVE FOR THE PAGES
FIRST CHAPTER PREVIEW

I just stepped off the train this morning, and already by the afternoon I'm a soccer mom. Well, the 'game' is track and field, not soccer, and Mom sold the Caravan while I was gone and replaced it with this compact sedan, but it's basically the same thing. I'm sitting here in the car parked with four vans one way and three vans the other, just another woman here to pick up her kid. Okay, my brother isn't 'my kid,' either. I'm a track and field sister, not a soccer mom. The point is, I'm already counting the days until summer is over. Huh. Never thought I'd say that. At least I didn't before college, anyway.

I get a glance every few seconds through the space between two bleachers of one scrawny high schooler after the other stumbling across the track, his arms scrunched against his chest, his mouth open in probably stilted breaths. If pressed to admit it, such a sight used to excite me. Now they all seem like little boys. I unscrew the bottle cap on my lemon tea and take a swig with one hand, rifling through my purse with the other. I find what I'm looking for and slip the well-worn copy of *Pride and Prejudice* onto my lap. I open it one-handed to the page with the most recently bent corner, the book flopping open easily thanks to the wrinkles of the multiple creases peppering the spine. I take another drink, my gaze hitting the corner of my Kindle case sticking out of my purse on the passenger seat. A hundred e-books and counting, and one of my three beat-to-a-pulp favorites are almost always in my hand in those moments between doing something and doing something else. *"Now maybe you can get rid of the books taking up all that space in your room."* Mom beamed as she handed me the graduation gift—it was definitely thoughtful of her. Surprisingly thoughtful. Until Mr. Wonderful opened his mouth and revealed it was less about celebrating my interests and more about being practical, as usual. *"You can't bring a bookshelf to a dorm. You're going to share the space with someone new, and it's rude to bring a bunch of junk that'll just take up space."* Cooper always seemed to forget I was rooming with Deana. Still, he had a point. The books stayed behind mostly. Except for the three books practically starting to disintegrate.

There's a pounding at my window. I jump, sloshing the open tea bottle all over my lap—all over *my book*. I scream and am rewarded with muffled laughter. I slam the bottle into the cup holder and am ready to shoot Owen my most 'you're moronic' look and immediately feel my face flush as I come face-to-face with Sinjin through the driver's side window. I look away quickly, like staring at the steering wheel and ignoring the drops of tea on my lap will make the whole situation disappear. There's more laughter from the other side of the car and more pounding, too. I just keep staring ahead.

"Open up!"

I snap out of it, flicking the unlock button on my side and crossing my arms as Owen opens the back passenger door and tosses his filthy gym bag onto the back seat. I can't bring myself to look to see if Sinjin is still standing there, but even so, I feel this *presence*, like the shivers running down my spine are my own Spidey sense warning me, "He's here. He's here. Don't make a fool of yourself."

Too late for that.

"Yo, earth to Spoon! Guess you killed her, SJ." I hate when Owen calls him that. I hate when Owen calls me Spoon. No one else needs to turn every name on the planet into something new.

My own personal your-ex-boyfriend-okay-you-just-went-to-three-dances-together-and-never-officially-became-an-item-so-is-that-really-an-ex-boyfriend-is-nearby Spidey sense relaxes—and where exactly was that superpower before he pounded on the car window?—and I breathe a sigh of relief. I suddenly remember my wounded (paperback) warrior on my lap and scramble for the Kleenex box on the floor behind the seat, grabbing one tissue after another in painstaking single serve doses, and I look up just in time to see Sinjin bumping his fist against Owen's shoulder, laughing, smiling that chiseled Greek-god smile that lights up his gorgeous dark skin, and I freeze again.

"Hey, how's it going, June?" Sinjin runs a hand through his short black hair and speaks to me casually, as if we see each other regularly, even though we haven't seen each other for months—that little blip over Spring Break while hanging with Margot and Deana hardly counts. His tone gives no indication I'm a laughing stock for falling head over heels at first sight with my best friends' brother. My best friends' *younger* brother. My best friends' he-was-a-freshman-and-I-was-a-junior-the-first-time-I-saw-him-but-how-was-I-to-know-since-he-just-transferred-in younger brother.

I will my hand to finish pulling the fifth tissue out of the box and add it to the crumpled wad forming in my fist. "Great," I lie, mumbling.

Owen finds this hilarious. But Owen finds most things to do with me hilarious. I'm *so* glad to see the last few weeks haven't changed him. As if somehow when I felt like I'd aged a decade as I was cramming like mad for finals and writing half a dozen papers, the world would have also progressed a dozen years and I could look forward to finding a far more mature brother when I got home for more than the occasional weekend visit. No such luck.

Sinjin walks away, and I twist myself back into my seat and dab my book and lap with the tissues. *Okay, good. Bye. Take your Greek-god smile and your smooth, silky, gorgeous jet black hair to some other hapless victim.*

The passenger door opens beside me. "I'm sorry about that." Sinjin pokes his head in. I cringe and do my best to smile. "I didn't mean to scare you. You just didn't notice us beside the car. Here, let me—" He scoops my purse up and lays it on the dashboard, climbing onto the seat. His fingers disappear around his side as he reaches into his pocket, pulling out a small washcloth.

I know what my Spidey sense should tell me. An athlete's hand towel. Probably used for mopping up sweat. About fifteen kinds of oh-my-god-gross. But Sinjin's hand is on my thigh, dabbing the tea stains as casually as if the liquid had spilled on the floor or on the seat. His palm lingers on my thigh—true, there's my pant leg and the washcloth between his skin and mine—but dear lord, his *hand* is on my *thigh* and I just about meld with the upholstery. He reaches his other hand out. "Let me."

I don't know what he wants—I almost hand him my wad of tissues—when he grabs the book from my hand. He raises his eyebrows. "You've got Kleenex on your book." He removes his hand and washcloth from my thigh and dabs at the book with it instead. "I'm so sorry." I don't bother telling him the book has already been soaked a time or two in the bathtub and there's no more damage that little tea spill could really have done to it. I just watch him at work, like a doctor and his patient, treating each wrinkled page with as much care as if it were made of silk.

"Wow." Owen slides into the back seat and shuts the door. "You're about thirty shades of red right now, June. What you're thinking is probably illegal in forty-eight states."

I don't bother asking where he came up with that number. I don't bother pointing out that at nineteen, there's probably some leniency for me to be fantasizing about a seventeen-year-old I used to sort of date. Instead I snort and grip the steering wheel, trying to fluff it off like the ribbing it's meant to be. "If you're guessing I'm thinking about murdering you right now for trying to embarrass me, I'd have to point out that's illegal in all fifty states."

The freeze in my spine lessens a bit as Sinjin shifts backward to exchange a look with Owen. They chuckle. "Finals didn't happen to give you a nervous breakdown, did they, June?" asks Sinjin.

"No, but seeing this place again almost did." I gesture at the bleachers and the two-story-brick-nightmare that is the high school I spent four years at far behind the field and the baseball diamond. I bite my lip as I look over. It's not so nightmare-inducing when I no longer have to spend my days there. At least back then, I didn't have to

317

worry about so much. I didn't have to worry about practically anything. I smile awkwardly at Sinjin. "Thanks," I say reaching my hand out for the book. "That's, uh, good enough. It's nice seeing you."

"Oo, shot down, SJ. Shot down." Owen taps his palms against the back of the passenger seat. "But just as well. This whole sister-slash-best-friend thing has always kind of creeped me out."

I clear my throat. "There was no sister-slash-best-friend *thing*, Owen."

I can't help but notice Sinjin stiffen just a little out of the corner of my eye.

Owen reaches up to pat him on the shoulder. "College boys, SJ. No competing with them. Not when they're just a hallway away."

"There were no *college boys*," I hiss. I turn around to face him, not sure whether to throttle my little brother or just play it cool by not assaulting him despite the ever-present desire to do so. A lecture about how much *work* college actually is—well, for some of us anyway, those of us who just don't have time to date and mess around—is forming on my tongue when my purse starts shaking on the dashboard. I shut my mouth and hope my eyes are enough to convey the world of hurt Owen just escaped. I toss the book atop the dashboard and scramble for the purse, my hand resting on Sinjin's as he reaches at the same moment. We smile at one another like we'd just been caught doing something very wrong and I let go so he can pass me the purse.

"Thanks," I squeak, my voice hardly registering the calm and confidence I meant for it to. I fumble inside and pull out my phone to read the all-important text waiting there: WHR R U 2? DINNER and what's probably a frosty,

318

shivering emoticon but looks more like a blue blob of water. It likely took Mom twice as long to compose that text as it did for her to make dinner.

"It's Mom," I say, shoving the phone back into the purse. I grab *Pride and Prejudice* and shove that inside, too, tea stains or no.

"Let me guess," says Owen. "She sent you to pick me up so she can make a 'Welcome home, June' dinner. And she timed it so we'd start eating about one second after my practice ended."

"Pretty much." I grimace and turn my head just slightly to give Sinjin a smile. "We should get going."

"Sure." Sinjin takes the hint and nods, sliding out the door. "Mamma probably has her own 'Welcome home, twins, make your own dinner' planned." I pinch my lips picturing Margot and Deana coming home to an empty house this afternoon. A gloriously relaxing empty house. Sinjin does this informal salute thing, like he's saying 'hats off to you.' "See ya!"

I grunt something back. Maybe it's the "see ya" I meant to say. Maybe it's some other language. My hands are kind of shaking on the steering wheel.

Owen shuts the door. "Well, are you going to start the car or should I drive?"

"Ha," I say, snapping out of it. I toss my purse back on the seat so recently vacated by the walking reminder of a simpler life, a life where I could have a little crush without feeling like some perv and without worrying I'm wasting my time even expending brain cells on anything but the future and work and research. I shake my head and start the engine, looking behind me to make sure there's no one I'm about to hit with my vehicle. "Mom told me you're not driving until you're forty-three."

Owen crosses his arms and leans back into the seat, squishing his damp blond curls against the headrest. "Mom's just being anal." He shrugs, closing his eyes. "Show me a junior in high school who hasn't snuck out in the middle of the night with his parents' car and a learner's permit, and I'll show you this little horned horse I've been keeping under my bed called a unicorn." He snorts. "That is, an actual human junior. Not Spoon from two years ago, who wouldn't come up for air from a book."

Is it too late to get back on the train to Chicago? I'm sensing I won't be able to make it through the summer without 'accidentally' hitting my brother with a vehicle.

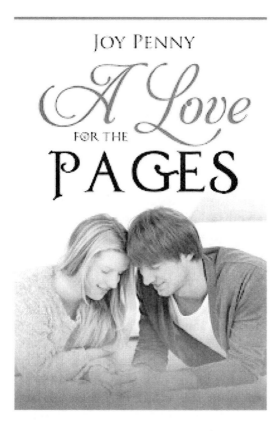

JOY PENNY

A Love
FOR THE
PAGES

Kiss. Marry. Kill. Nineteen-year-old June Eyermann has always known exactly which of her favorite Byronic heroes goes where. She'd kiss moody and possessive Rochester from Jane Eyre and marry prideful but repentant Darcy from Pride and Prejudice, leaving obsessive and spiteful Heathcliff from Wuthering Heights to be chucked off a cliff— but no. She couldn't leave any of her heroes behind. She lives for her favorite fictional worlds.

But June is about to get a serious wake up call when

she returns home for the summer after her college freshman year. Stuck somewhere between feeling like a kid again under her parents' roof and being forced to start acting like an adult with worries about her future career, June looks at the library volunteer position offered to her as a way to keep her sanity for the next few months before she can go back to school.

What June doesn't expect to find at the library is her favorite romantic heroes brought to life—all in the same man. Obstinate, prideful and even a bit rude, Everett Rockford shouldn't exactly be "dating material," even if June's heart rate accelerates whenever she's near him. But after discovering his enigmatic past and witnessing a few fiery moments of tenderness, June can't help but see Rochester, Darcy and even Heathcliff in Everett. If she's going to make it through the summer without becoming a tragic heroine in her own story, she has to separate the man from the ideals of fiction in her head. Because if there's one thing she knows about Byronic love stories, it's that they don't always end happily ever after.

Read *A Love for the Pages*, a NA contemporary sweet romance, by Joy Penny (an Amy McNulty pen name) today! Purchase on Kindle or read for free via Kindle Unlimited. Buy the paperback or audiobook and add it to your Goodreads to-read list today!